FINAL STROKE

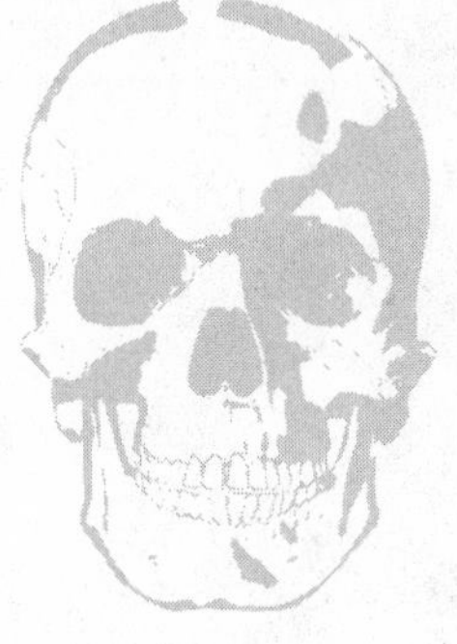

MICHAEL BERES

FINAL STROKE

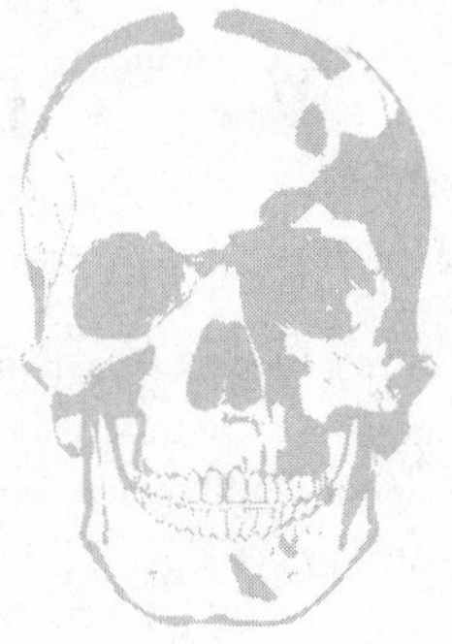

MICHAEL BERES

Medallion Press, Inc.

DEDICATION:

To caregivers and those they care for.

Published 2007 by Medallion Press, Inc.

The MEDALLION PRESS LOGO
is a registered tradmark of Medallion Press, Inc.

Cover Illustration by James Tampa

Printed in the United States of America

Library of Congress Cataloging-in-Publication Data

Beres, Michael.
Final stroke / by Michael Beres.
p. cm.
ISBN-13: 978-1-932815-95-5
I. Title.
PS3602.E7516F56 2007
813'.6--dc22

2007004852

10 9 8 7 6 5 4 3 2 1
First Edition

Previous reviews for THE PRESIDENT'S NEMESIS:

"Beres (GRAND TRAVERSE) goes one step beyond THE MANCHURIAN CANDIDATE in this engrossing thriller, which sometimes seems too obvious but then foils expectations by twisting the reader's mind along with that of the protagonist. Recommended for all popular fiction collections."

—*Library Journal*

"Conspiracy fanatics may enjoy Beres's second novel (after GRAND TRAVERSE), a bizarre political thriller . . . The denouement would be at home in the tabloids."

—*Publishers Weekly*

"A recent article in Publishers Weekly talked about how the current White House does not like that the publisher of this book has used the presidential seal on the cover because there are several bullet holes. I applaud Medallion Press for standing firm on its use of the artwork for this timely work of fiction. The novel is all about conspiracies, presidential assignations, and covert operations. Beres has written a very tense nail-biting thriller that is filled with several well fleshed out characters in tense situations. Beres sums up the discontent voters have for all politicians in this country very well in a few short sentences. THE PRESIDENT'S NEMESIS is a great political thriller."

—*Gary Roen, Midwest Book Review*

"Michael Beres has written a suspenseful novel that delves into paranoia as Stanley Johnson becomes involved in a convoluted plot to assassinate the President. Readers will enjoy Johnson's plunge into madness as people and events beyond his control begin to take over his life. Beres' plotting is brisk and full of twist and turns. Fans of Stephen King and Dean Koontz may want to check out this great beach read."

—*Bob* jabberwockybooksense.com

CHAPTER ONE

"A stroke is a brain hurricane. Everything's still there, but torn up and mixed around in the soup. For example, last time we watched The History Channel at the rehab center, Babe Ruth is standing at the plate taking strikes and the next thing I know my husband is off and running in his wheelchair before Babe hits his homer. It's because the word strike relates to the word stroke, and the fact that the Babe's first name is the same as our last name... When someone you know has a stroke, you look for keys to the past in the strangest places. It's like history rewritten before your eyes... Maybe if world leaders had strokes we'd all be better off because suddenly they'd see things in a new light. In this newer, more childlike world, the name Babe would be as common as, say, the names Smith or Johnson or Carter."

Jan Babe
Stroke Family Support Group
Saint Mel in the Woods Rehabilitation Facility
Chicago, Illinois

In March, damage from the previous hurricane season was still obvious. Recovery was taking longer than expected and memories of that season would linger for a while, which meant at least until the next hurricane season. The March heat, plus the fact that no political campaigns were in progress, acted like a sedative to both tourists and natives. In Dade County the breeze was off the Everglades, the mugginess making folks feel faint and disconnected from their bodies. But on the west coast, in Collier County, the breeze off the Gulf made for a perfect evening. Here on the Gulf Coast it was a different kind of warmth. A sleepy warmth as two white-haired men sat on the porch of a sprawling Naples, Florida, home that, although situated on a rise in the topography, sat low on its prime real estate like a bunker.

The two men watched as the red ball of sun headed down into the Gulf. Optical illusion created a sun grown in size as if it were going into nova and would toast the folks heading out on the fishing pier to get the best view. The folks on the pier stepped gingerly around pelican shit, the pelicans flew back in to feast on fish heads, and the fishermen who had provided the fish heads stared out into the Gulf where their lines glistened like red-hot filaments.

Both Valdez and Hanley were natives who understood south Florida's weather better than any Chicagoan would. Hanley had been a native almost five years since his move from Virginia. Valdez was a born native, having held a post at the Miami office for forty years. Although Valdez was younger than Hanley, both men were obviously past their prime. Valdez wore dress slacks, a short sleeve shirt, and black shoes. Hanley wore shorts, a tank top, and sneakers. Sunglasses hid their eyes.

"Never could see the point in it," said Valdez.

"What?" asked Hanley.

"Fishing. You must not see any point in it either," said Valdez. "Living next to the pier and I've never seen you out there."

"Right," said Hanley, adjusting his dark wraparound sunglasses. "But I'd wager it's more relaxing than what we do."

"That's for sure," said Valdez. "Why are we still in this business at our age?"

"We're in it because we can't get out," said Hanley. "But get back to this Chicago dick named Babe. How did he get that name anyhow?"

"Apparently it comes from a longer Hungarian name," said Valdez. "An ancestor shortened it. A great name when you think about it. I'm told the stroke made him a happy guy. Even though I've never met him, I kind of like him."

"Why is that?"

"Because people who have strokes mix words around in humorous ways and sound like they don't know what they're talking about. They think they're talking about one thing when they're really talking about something else." Valdez laughed.

"It's not funny," said Hanley. "We might be there some day."

"You're right," said Valdez. "Except I heard about this drug on talk radio the other night. They say if you get it right after you have a stroke, your memory loss can be minimized. Apparently hospitals down here are well stocked being that we live in heaven's waiting room."

"I'm glad the hospitals are prepared," said Hanley. "The only problem is the drug they give us when we have a stroke won't be the one they give other people."

"You really think the director put that into effect?"

"A lot of things went into effect after the Patriot Act. But please, get back to Babe. Did you confirm his stroke?"

"We double-checked the medical records," said Valdez. "Our man sat in on rehab sessions. Babe definitely had a stroke."

"Is our contact up there a young man?" asked Hanley.

"Yes, but he knows what he's doing. He's gotten himself into the place as an aide."

"Did he make sure no one else was trying to get to the widow? Because if anyone does, you know what's got to be done."

"I know," said Valdez. "For now we should simply continue watching her. No need to do anything just yet."

"Why do you say, just yet?"

"Because she's becoming more lucid and she's getting visitors."

"Family?" asked Hanley.

"Yes, family. Somebody's probably looking for buried treasure. Our man has ears in her room. So far her words have been meaningless, but that could change."

"Anybody named Lamberti been around?"

"Yes, the nephew. The son's also been there. But the two never visit together. Bad blood in the family, I guess."

"This young man you've got watching her, has he been there since she's been in the place?"

"He has."

"Besides visitors, anything else going on?"

"The usual health care scams," said Valdez. "Rip offs run by the workers. So far, nothing involving the old lady and her family."

"Does our contact think she knows anything about what happened in the past?"

"He can't say. But spouses talk to one another and she spent a lot of years with the old man before he died. Even though she's had a stroke there's bound to be something buried in her head."

"That's been the problem all along," said Hanley. "We can't confirm she's a blank slate."

"Perhaps in this world people with strokes are the lucky ones," said

Valdez.

"You mean because they get a chance to start fresh?"

"Like children," said Valdez. "Except because stroke victims also have trouble comprehending things, their brains stay fresh longer. Instead of being bombarded with media garbage, they have the freedom to ruminate. Instead of being told what to think by pundits, they make up their own minds."

"And," said Hanley, "instead of having their minds occupied by the latest celebrity trial or conspiracy theory, they might also have the freedom to piece things together that we don't want them to piece together."

After the sun disappeared into the Gulf, the crowd gathered at the end of the pier began to make its way back, sidestepping fishermen and pelican shit. A flock of seagulls moved in and two of the gulls fighting over fish guts screamed at one another like belligerent children. Now that the sun had set, the porch on which the two men sat was swathed in darkness.

Valdez took off his sunglasses and put on his regular glasses. "Some day maybe you'll tell me what this whole thing is about?"

"Maybe," said Hanley. "But for now you'll simply have to tell our young aide back there to keep tabs on the widow and be ready to make a move if necessary. However, I do think it's time to assign a backup in case things heat up in a hurry."

After a pause, during which he frowned as he rubbed an aching shoulder, Valdez said, "A backup . . . sure, I'll get on it. By the way, I know this thing goes way back. But at our age, who gives a damn what happens after we're gone? Do you really care what happens after you're gone? Come on, be truthful about it."

Hanley took off his wraparounds and stared at Valdez in the dark.

"Well, do you?" repeated Valdez.

"Yes," said Hanley. "I care very much what happens after I'm gone."

Cars began starting up in the parking lot at the foot of the pier. But because of the stone wall lining the edge of Hanley's property, the men could not see the cars driving off into the hot dusk. After a while Valdez got up slowly, went into the house, used the facilities, then headed out to his own car and the long drive in the dark across the Everglades Parkway.

As Valdez drove he tuned in the satellite radio weather for the central northern states. The Midwest was rainy and cold, especially in Chicago and suburbs where an easterly wind swept off Lake Michigan. Unlike here in south Florida, there had been no sunset in Chicago, no sun visible all day long according to the weather channel.

Valdez could occasionally see a pair of eyes reflected in his headlights. The eyes were behind the safety fence bordering the highway. Sometimes the eyes would disappear as the creature either turned back into the safety of the Everglades, or as it sank back down into the swamp. In a way, thought Valdez, we are all creatures living in a swamp with boundaries beyond which we have no control, beyond which we have no knowledge.

Valdez took off his glasses and rubbed his eyes. Although he'd gotten the glasses less than a year earlier, he had a feeling his prescription had changed yet again. He didn't like this night driving, especially when oncoming vehicles rushed past in a blur. Next time Hanley wanted to see him he'd be sure to arrange their meeting earlier in the day. Driving all this way at night was risky. Sometimes, when he glanced at the rearview mirror and saw nothing but the black night, he had the feeling death was catching up to him. Maybe a one-car accident wouldn't be such a bad way to go compared to having a stroke.

Valdez switched from the weather to a Latin Rhythms music channel. What the hell, too late now to worry about how he'd lived his life. At least he'd made it this far with all his body parts intact. And only one scar after all these years. One knife wound from that crazy bastard Mexican turned terrorist.

As he listened to the music channel, Valdez heard a momentary dropout, probably a plane or a flock of birds or something between him and the satellite, perhaps even another satellite. The momentary blip in the otherwise uninterrupted digital signal reminded him of the old days of amateur radio. All analog back then. First code when he was a boy of sixteen and received his novice license, then voice, first on AM, then SSB. From deep inside his brain the Morse code dots and dashes for the number seventy-three played out. Dah-dah-dit-dit-dit, dit-dit-dit-dah-dah. Seventy-three, the traditional amateur radio end-of-contact signoff, meant good luck.

Valdez had been an amateur radio operator (a ham) when he was recruited by the agency. He and Tom Christensen and George Skinner had all three been hams when they were in training. Upon graduation, Christensen and Skinner had stayed at Langley while Valdez was assigned back to his native Miami. For years he and Christensen and Skinner had communicated on the high frequency bands, a weekly schedule on whatever band was open. But the good old days of ham radio were long gone. Skinner was his current contact at Langley and their only contact was via scrambled landline. Christensen was retired in Arizona and Valdez hadn't spoken with him in years.

Earlier today, back at his apartment on the scrambled line, Skinner had reminisced with Valdez about the old days. He had mentioned Tom Christensen and spoken of the three of them "chewing the rag" with one another and any other ham from any part of the world who could contact them.

"It was so unlike now," Skinner had said earlier that day. "Communication today is viewed as a right. Everyone needs his or her own personal phone. Everyone needs instant communication. It's really too bad when you think about it. Back then it was a nice hobby, and what we could do, talking to the other side of the world, was something only we could do."

The conversation with Skinner, and the mention of Tom Christensen retired somewhere in Arizona, had made Valdez feel his age. It had set him up for this entire day. Aches and pains and having to visit Hanley, who was also retired. The conversation with Hanley about a detective with a stroke and an old widow in a nursing home. And now, after all that, and at his age, he's got to drive back to Miami in the dark.

The rhythm of the music matched the pounding of his tires on the highway expansion joints. It was hypnotic. It was cerebral. He felt at peace with himself. What's done is done. He'd lived the way he wanted and with any luck he'd make it to retirement and his pension bonus and then, like Hanley, build himself a fortress down here designed to withstand hurricanes, and maybe build another place up north for use during hurricane season. He imagined sitting on his own porch watching the sun set into the Gulf each evening. Not a care in the world.

CHAPTER TWO

It had been a winter of strokes, seemed everyone she knew had one. It had been a winter like a stroke, coming on strong in November—surprising everyone, the way cerebrovascular accidents do—and lasting into March. By now there were supposed to be good days here and there—harbingers of spring—but the weather had soured the way words did in her throat when she couldn't get them out. Today, when she looked through the windows of this place, the trees beyond the brown lawns and gray parking lots had looked like skinny soldiers with limbs akimbo marching home from war, marching home in the wet cold month of March.

To Marjorie Gianetti, life could be frustrating. Bad enough when words didn't do what they were supposed to do, what really frosted her was when something was happening and she had no idea what it was.

Like now. Here she is being escorted down the hallway by a young man who obviously knows her quite well, and trees from the woods are marching around in her head like skinny priests in black robes so that no matter how hard she tries, she can't think of the young man's name.

She tried to ask his name, but was aware, even as the question came to the surface, that she shouldn't have done this, because the words that bubbled out, like vile odors from a sewer, were, "Fuck the Pope."

The smile on the young man's face, when she paused within the confines of the walker and glanced up to him, seemed inappropriate. Not because of what she'd said. After all, she was a severe right-brain stroke victim, everyone who ever came to her or washed her or walked beside her in this place knew that. Saying what she said about the Pope made sense to her because these were words from the past, and words from the past had a way of spewing out of her mouth before she could stop them. Not that she'd made a habit of cursing the Pope. No, that wasn't it at all. But because she'd been a devout Catholic, and because the word *fuck* was a curse her late husband—God rest his soul—had used in every other sentence, "Fuck the Pope" had simply popped out. Words erupting from a stroke victim's mouth were sometimes crazy mixes of what had once been there. It was as simple as that.

Although Marjorie Gianetti could not think of her late husband's name at the moment, she did recall one particular time he used the F word. He'd been sitting at the dining room table and that nice black lady who worked for them—if she couldn't remember her husband's name, how could she be expected to remember their maid's name?—had just brought in his favorite dessert—cannoli or something—and he looks at it and smiles and says, "Fuck, that looks good." Even when smiling and happy as a clam he used the F word. It made no sense.

And now, here was something else that made no sense. Here was a smile from this young man accompanying her down the hall, this young man who could never know how it felt to be a stroke victim. A "no-stroker" they sometimes called them in their group therapy sessions on the second floor. But wait. It wasn't simply the young man's smile in reaction to her cursing the Pope that puzzled her. It was the nature of the smile, the underlying meaning of the smile. Goodness gracious, there had to be an underlying meaning because . . .

Because what? She didn't know. She'd already forgotten where this pesky choo-choo train of thought was headed. Mama Mia, now the train of thought became one of the miniature trains her late husband played with Sunday afternoons in the basement. If only thoughts were like those trains she could pluck them off their tracks and hold them in her hands and examine them for clues as to what she was trying to think of or say from one moment to the next. But, although she sometimes tried, she could not grasp her thoughts in her hands and they slipped through her fingers like . . . like when she's in the kitchen helping make dessert on one of those Sunday afternoons and she can smell cigar smoke from the basement and hear the miniature train whistles, one of those Sunday afternoons when she cracks an egg into the palm of her hand to separate yolk from white and the egg white slips through her fingers slowly but relentlessly. That's the way it was with the distant past since her stroke. The moment she thought she had hold of something from the past, it would slip away. Sometimes she heard train whistles and smelled cigar smoke from the basement, other times she heard the sounds of barbells dropped to the floor. But most times she heard and smelled and saw and felt nothing.

Ahead. She continued *ahead* down the hallway, moving her walker *ahead* a few inches at a time, stepping *ahead* until one thigh then the other made contact with the crossbar between the handles. She continued *ahead* trying in vain to think of the young man's name and his relationship to her. The effort to maintain forward movement was getting mixed up with her thoughts. Perhaps a pause would enable her to sort out the jumble in her egg noggin. Walking *ahead* like this, and trying to think of the name of the young man accompanying her, the only word that came to mind was the word *ahead*.

Was the young man wearing a uniform? She'd forgotten since that moment ago when she glanced toward him. If she were in her wheelchair instead of being forced to respond to this damn walker she might be able to close her eyes and concentrate. But walking like this . . .

Suddenly a name drifted into her consciousness, pushed the word *ahead* aside. Mr. Babe. Yes, perhaps the man walking by her side was that nice Mr. Babe, her *paisano* in second floor rehab where they sometimes shared foul language with one another. Mr. Babe holding her right elbow and helping her along. Perhaps they were on their way to the elevators.

No, Mr. Babe was much younger than her. He was here for stroke time rehab, not a permanent resident like her. His room was on the third floor in the main building, so there was no way he'd be down here this time of night.

But wait. Perhaps it was earlier than she thought and she was actually on the second floor. She'd just gotten off the elevator and Mr. Babe was accompanying her. Perhaps she would again try to express a joke they had shared. Marjorie Gianetti and Steve Babe putting their heads together to see if they explode because, like opposite charges in the clouds of their brains, she had a right-brainer and he had a left-brainer and maybe together they could make a no-brainer.

She could almost see the smile on Mr. Babe's face as she tried once again to express the joke they had, a few days earlier, succeeded in telling the speech rehab therapist. Mr. Babe was such a happy man, such an inspiration, even though he denied it. According to him, when he was able to get it out that first time by writing it down, he'd always been a melancholy fellow. The stroke had made him a cheerful son of a bitch, he'd written, and he knew of no reason why he should be cheerful in a place called Hell in the Woods. After writing this down, Mr. Babe had smiled the most beautiful, endearing smile she had ever seen in her life.

Before her stroke, Marjorie had been an incessant talker. In pre-stroke talk, she might have said something like, "That Mr. Babe, when I first met him—I mean when I introduced myself to him his first day here—you wouldn't believe the smile on his face. Some might wonder why I like him. That's only because they don't know him, and think he's laughing at them. He'd have to be a snob to do that, and Mr. Babe is no snob. It would have been easy, at first, to assume he was laughing at my ideas about this place. But he convinced me, even though he can hardly get a word out edgewise, that he never laughs at me, but with me. The first day I met him, I thought I'd cheer him up, and here he was cheering me up."

No, the man escorting her down the hallway could not be Mr. Babe because Mr. Babe would never smile like she'd seen this man smile. And another reason, this man was too young. Although Mr. Babe was definitely younger than her, he could not really be considered a young man. Middle-aged perhaps, but not young, except to the cataracted eyes of some of the near centenarians at the far end of the skilled wing. Besides, Mr. Babe was partially paralyzed on his right side, and this man held her left arm with his right hand.

And of course it couldn't be that speed-walking aide with red hair. Even though some residents said the speed-walker was a bull dyke, that didn't make her a young man. No, not the bull dyke. She'd been fired some time ago when she walked away from Janine in a too-hot whirlpool because she thought Janine had squealed on her for not putting a fresh absorbent pad on Janine's bed. Marjorie had tried her best to convince Janine not to threaten aides because you get more flies with honey, but Janine was a rebel and there was always an aide perfectly willing to make it a little rough next time they transferred you from bed to wheelchair.

Mostly the aides were agreeable, except of course during one of those state inspections when it seemed everyone in her wing had been over-medicated. But who could blame them for conspiring to keep down the whining and moaning that would have started the minute some residents got wind the state inspectors were in from Springfield?

Oh, how she wished the man walking beside her was that nice Mr. Babe, because suddenly she had so many things she'd like to say to him. She probably tried telling some of these things to him in rehab. If she could she'd repeat it all over again. She'd tell him about the over-medication during state inspections and about Janine's turning into a used tea bag in the whirlpool. If she could get the words out, she'd tell Mr. Babe these things because, before he had his stroke, Mr. Babe had been a private detective. Unlike others in this place, who never read mysteries, and didn't know the meaning of the word *conspiracy*, and probably thought things simply "happened" in this world called Hell in the Woods. . . Yes, unlike them, Mr. Babe would understand.

Like a while ago when she and the young man passed poor old Bill's room and she saw the sign on Bill's door that said, "Spending Our Children's Inheritance," with the "Our" crossed out and "My" written in above it. The sign was once a bumper sticker on the motor home Bill and his late wife lived in. Bill peeled the faded bumper sticker off the motor home before he came here, and now it's taped to his door as a reminder to his children that, rather than spending down his cash and moving into a cheaper Medicaid room, he's opted to use his savings for a private room.

This was only part of what she'd tell Mr. Babe. The main thing she'd tell him is that Bill confided to her he knew his children were doing their damnedest to shorten his life in order to inherit his savings before he spent it all at, as he called it, "this hell-hole." According to Bill, his children visited at odd times and even late at night and purposely startled him. That's why he had his television moved next to the door, so he could see when someone came into the room. Bill says his children sometimes called the doctor and made false reports so that suddenly his medication was changed and he'd be out like a light for a couple days. Last time it happened, Bill said they stuffed him full of Dilantin to prevent seizures he never had. "There I was, out like a goddamn light again," said Bill. "On my back with fluid building up in my lungs. They tried to give me pneumonia, but I got wise. Flushed the goddamn Dilantin down the toilet!"

Bill's situation wasn't the only thing she'd tell Mr. Babe. Now that she was at the far end of the wing and was reminded of it, she'd tell Mr. Babe about the scam some aides had going. They'd steal equipment from the wing and report that visitors and family members walked off with it.

Imagine, stealing the basic things that help keep poor old folks half-way comfortable in their so-called golden years, then blaming their kids. But that wasn't all. After stealing the stuff, they had the audacity to sell it back to the place. She knew this because sometimes the very same equipment would end up here in her wing. Like the wheelchairs parked there in the corner. She'd taken it upon herself to make a scratch with her diamond ring in the metal just beneath the armrest every time she used a wheelchair. Then, after a bunch of wheelchairs were reported missing, she inspected the supposedly brand-new replacements and found that one of them had her scratch mark on it. She figured there was a conspiracy amongst some of the aides and that they had a partner on the outside who ran a medical supply company.

Oh, if Mr. Babe were only here she'd rattle on about things. Take the skilled wing. All those expensive beds to keep filled and all the money the Hell in the Woods accountants would stand to lose if any of those beds stayed empty too long. Like one day last September, everyone across the hall from her room is healthy as a horse, the next day they're on their backs in the skilled wing. "Call me a crazy dago," she'd say to Mr. Babe, "but those folks were doing fine until the end of the third calendar quarter. After that they looked over-medicated to me. I hate to say it, *paisan*, but some of the ones I knew personally were in drug overdose, and the only reason was to keep them in costlier beds so the quarterly statement stayed in the black."

Unfortunately, she wouldn't say any of this to Mr. Babe, nor to anyone else, because her stroke would never allow her to talk this way. She wasn't even sure if this was the way she spoke before her stroke. All she knew for sure was that she used to talk a lot. *Mama mia*, she used to talk a lot. And now? Now she could only resign herself to the fact that she would never again be able to express in words the things she could sometimes think in words at odd moments like this. Even though she'd been able to tell Mr. Babe a lot during their sessions at group therapy, she certainly was never able to say things in such clear and concise terms.

She couldn't even talk about simple things, like how quiet it was tonight, being that no jet planes were taking off overhead. For a moment she wondered why there were only certain times jets took off overhead and had the feeling she should know why. In fact she had the feeling someone had recently told her. But that's how it was with this damn stroke. Sometimes it was like waking from a dream. When you wake up you have a vague recollection of having dreamed, perhaps you even know what it is you dreamed about, but the details are lost through the hair net.

Thinking of a hair net reminded her of Mr. Babe again. Mr. Babe telling her recently that he hooked his portable computer up to the Internet in the rehab lab. Mr. Babe telling her she should try it and that it didn't matter if she hits the wrong keys because half the people on the Internet don't know how to spell anyhow.

A hair net was much more real to her than the Internet. She could visualize a hair net. A dark brown hair net made of fine material like her mother used to wear whenever she was in the kitchen. It was one of the few things she recalled vividly, perhaps because it had to do with a net encompassing the head and, therefore, the brain. As if a net could have held in her thoughts during the stroke, at least the larger thoughts. But maybe all she'd ever had were small thoughts, insignificant ones that didn't mean much and that's why so many found their way through the net.

Yet another word came, *dragnet*. And exactly what was that supposed to mean? That's the way it was with words. She could recall the situation—Mr. Babe telling her and Georgiana something about a dragnet in rehab—but she could not recall what he had said about the word in response to Georgiana's prompting.

Georgiana was the prettiest therapist in the rehab center. Even without makeup, and even with her brown hair cut short like a little boy's hair, and even considering that most everyone in the center insisted on calling her George, she was the prettiest. Sometimes Marjorie watched when Mr. Babe helped with the tape recorder and could see the sparkle in his eyes when he looked at Georgiana.

Mr. Babe had gotten to know the tape recorder quite well. And of course he was doing much better with his words than she was. He even made up the term *brain bullet* for their strokes, saying that, for her, the bullet simply plowed through a different place and that just because she spit out nonsense words and swear words more often than she'd like, it didn't mean she was any less intelligent.

Goddamn stroke anyway. Maybe that's why she said, "Fuck the Pope" so often. Who could blame her? None of her visitors seemed to be shocked anymore. Not her son or her nephew. Good thing she wrote her will before the stroke or she probably would have dictated that "Fuck the Pope" be inserted on every other line. Good thing the will was written and sealed a long time ago when she still knew the family secret.

Secret. Why couldn't she remember the family secret? Did it have something to do with family accounts? Or the accounting of her family? Or something buried in the basement? No, there was only her husband and one son, and neither of them had ever buried anything in the basement as far as she knew. Did it have to do with some kind of keys? But if so, why not simply one key? Why so many keys jingling like bells in her husband's pocket? She and her husband in the car stopping at so many places with the keys . . .

Perhaps the family secret had to do with her husband never seeming to be satisfied with what they had. He always wanted more, and had, shortly before his death, when she asked why he was upset, said, "I'm fucking upset on account of these fucking dishonest cops and on account of not having grandchildren at my age!"

Like any man who begins to feel his age, her husband criticized the young men of the day. He gave up cigars and purchased weight lifting equipment. He complained while pumping iron on the mat next to the train table in the basement.

"These young punks got nothin' but time on their hands. Even in the military they got time on their hands because there's no damn war to keep 'em busy. Thank God for Reagan and for what he's doin', but sometimes we could use a war. Without a war to go to, punks got plenty of time to exercise. These days, instead of making something of themselves, they build up muscles, making their arms into telephone poles while their brains turn into mush. And the fuckin' thing of it is the way the military mixes the races. Wops and kikes and spooks and spics pumpin' iron together, drippin' sweat all over one another like a bunch of fairies! Yeah, pumpin' iron while they wait for their fuckin' discharge! Get it? Discharge!"

Marjorie was always disgusted when her husband spoke like this, even if he had good reason to be upset. Of course now, being she was a stroker, she couldn't remember what in the world had upset her husband so much.

They should do something in rehab to help her remember things. She tried to tell this to Mr. Babe the other day. They should do something more so all that knowledge up in their egg noggins wouldn't be buried with them.

Rehab. Perhaps all this walking late at night was a new type of rehab. Perhaps this hurried walk—the young man did seem to be hurrying her now—was the next phase and soon she'd be jogging up and down the hallways of Hell in the Woods in her slippers.

That was odd. Why was she wearing her furry pink slippers instead of her Buster Browns? She never wore her slippers out of her room, not only because they weren't apropos for the hallway, but because of their slippery bottoms on the slippery hallway floors. And now, with this man hurrying her along, her slippers *were* slipping along. Yes, slippers slipping along, slip-slip-slipping along. Just like one of those silly old songs some residents insist on playing on the organ in the activity room.

An organ joke emerged from way back when she was a little girl attending Saint Pius School on the south side. One of the nuns chasing a newly arrived young priest around and around the inside of the church . . . until she catches him by the organ. That was a good one. Maybe she'd tell that one to Mr. Babe. But as soon as she tried to imagine the words she'd say to him, the nun chased the priest out from behind the organ and they ran up to the side altar where baptisms are performed—her son baptized there—and in his frenzy to escape, the priest, who resembles the young man leading her down the hallway, overturns a bottle, and someone screams, "The Ointment!" and the term "fly in the ointment" comes into her noggin and for some reason takes over and all she can think is *There's a fly in the ointment. There's a fly in the ointment!*

They were outside the activity room now, she and the young man standing arm-and-arm like . . . like her father holding her arm at the back of Saint Pius church while Antonio waits at the altar. Antonio, her husband-to-be. Antonio, who was called Tony by everyone but her. Antonio, who, despite his businesses and his associates and what the newspapers said about him, was a good family man. Hadn't he seen to it she'd be comfortable for the rest of her life with a private room at Hell in the Woods? Hadn't he even gone so far as to make certain his heirs for generations to come would be comfortable? Hadn't he once wept because his only son had not wed and did not yet have children?

If only that bitch of a newspaperwoman who wrote the article after Antonio's death could have seen him weep. Perhaps then she wouldn't have called Antonio, "a cigar-smoking mobster from the old school who played with his train layout after Mass on Sundays and ordered his thugs to do his bidding the other six days of the week."

As she stood within her walker recalling Antonio—how he had begun going bald soon after their marriage and never wore a hairpiece—she tried to remember if the young man accompanying her was bald, but could not. Men in Antonio's family went bald early. In the Gianetti family album there were faded photographs of bald young men back in the old country. But then there was lots of thinning hair in this modern world, especially here at Hell in the Woods where even the women have thinning hair. Sometimes she'd look down at the floor and expect to see wads of it like elongated wads of dust beneath a bed, the wads of dust her mother called dust bunnies.

Why could she remember some things and not others? Like now, standing within her walker while the young man pauses, why was she again recalling one of Antonio's tirades from earlier in their marriage? Was it because she worried that the words spoken aloud would awaken Antonio Junior, then just a baby? Was that why she recalled every word?

"It's a fuckin' crazy world, Marge. Nothing's simple like the old days. In the old days they used a little muscle and got what they wanted. Muscle in those days wasn't always the bullet. Some of the boys would have fisticuffs. But today the only muscle they got is a high-powered rifle or a dead guy in the trunk of his car. It's like the damn cold war. Only here, instead of bombs, they got this idea that if a guy pushes too hard, into the trunk he goes with a bullet in his head. . . Hey, maybe if they gave it to Carter the way they gave it to JFK. . . Ah, what the hell. It's a crazy world. A fuckin' crazy world.

"And another thing. They think I'm fuckin' stupid or something? Those Turks and that fuckin' Spilotro think I'm stupid? Those New York hoods playing around with their garbage businesses think I'm stupid? I'm not stupid! They're the ones that're fuckin' stupid! Even the old timers are goin' along. While I stay here in Daley's Mick town runnin' a business more honest than city hall, Accardo's kissin' up to the stars in Palm Springs! And the Greek, he's layin' on the fuckin' beach thinkin' he can call the shots long distance!"

Whenever Marjorie smiled at Antonio calling his business an honest business, or whenever she complained about his foul language, he'd simply wave his hand at her and keep it up, keep it up until there was a moment of silence and she said something about his claim to be a good Catholic and . . . yes, several times she'd said it, "If the Pope could hear you now," and he'd said, "Fuck the Pope!"

Or was it, "Fuck Jimmy Carter," that he said? She recalled him not liking Jimmy Carter. She recalled thinking years later that, if Antonio had lived long enough, he would have really hated Clinton.

Another thing she thought Antonio might have said was, "Fuck Chernobyl." But why would he have said that? How could he have said that? And really, did Antonio actually say any of these things, or was it all simply part of the mix-up, the bowl of mashed potatoes that was her brain since the stroke? Maybe even the word *fuck* came from the mix-up, because *fuck* did seem to be an awfully popular word here at Hell in the Woods. According to Mr. Babe there was a man on the third floor who only said the two words *Jesus fuck*. Nothing else except *Jesus fuck*.

Despite things he'd said about the Pope and Jimmy Carter when he was alive, her Antonio was still a good man. And despite everything the brain bullet had taken from her, no one could take that away from her. She had the definite impression that, behind Antonio's anger with his so-called "business partners," there was a plan. She had the feeling that what Antonio planned, during those last years they had together, would be something wonderful. Perhaps that was the family secret, that Antonio had planned a legacy for which the name Gianetti would be remembered.

Wait. Something was happening. The young man had left her standing in her walker outside the double doors to the activity room. The young man had let go of her arm and stepped away from her. She heard a door open somewhere behind her. Then there was a hissing sound, and a singing. No, that would be silly because who would sing like that? But it was a singing, a singing like in the pipes at home when Antonio was in the shower. Antonio also singing, trying to outdo the singing of the plumbing with his valiant attempt at Verdi.

When the singing stopped and the door behind her closed, the young man was back at her side. No, behind her. She thought he would begin speaking again the way he had when he came to her room to fetch her. She thought he would again begin asking questions that made no sense. Even if she had understood the questions, how could he expect her to answer?

But he did not speak, he did not pump her with questions. Instead, he held her gently by her arms, easing her backward and lifting her arms so that she released her grip on the walker. Then he turned her about. He did not stop the turning so she could face him, so she could look at him, but instead kept turning her. Around and around. In a way it was like dancing, but too fast, so fast she became dizzy. Then she felt him grip her ankles and felt herself flying through the air, the whole world spinning. A rather pleasant sensation until her head hit the floor.

After that was a brief dream. A dream about her husband Antonio and her son Antonio. Both were younger. They were in the garden behind the house, the garden she had always assumed had given her son his love of nature. She watched from within the arbor where it was dark because of the thick vines overhead. In the distance she could hear the sprinkler oscillating back and forth spraying the ferns and tinkling on some of the smaller clay pots along the walkway. It was springtime and Antonio Junior was being thrown into the sunshine by his father. Antonio Junior screaming with delight, Antonio Junior blinded by childish pleasure, Antonio Junior not knowing what would some day be done to his mother, how much pain would be inflicted upon his mother in the name of . . .

In the name of what? Why would he do this to her? Why would anyone do this to her? Was it the keys? My God! Who would take care of the keys!

As the screams of Antonio Junior being thrown into the air by his father died away, Marjorie Gianetti realized that her husband Antonio must have known this would happen. Yes, he must have known it would one day lead to this.

Then the image in the garden faded, and so did Marjorie Gianetti.

CHAPTER THREE

Steve Babe was doing stroke time. It was enough to make a guy laugh his head off. But still, he couldn't help wondering what had caused it. Maybe it was the Hungarian *paprikas*—onion sautéed in bacon drippings, red paprika, sliced beef or cut up chicken with gizzards, dumplings—or the baked goose liver—a milk-soaked two-pounder, goose fat, onion, paprika, salt—or the sour cream pancakes—eggs, flour, milk, sugar, salt, butter, sour cream, extra egg yolks. Or maybe it was his failure to exercise adequately during his first fifty years. Or maybe it was in his genes. Whatever the cause, he was definitely doing stroke time.

Besides the immobility of his right side, the first thing Steve was aware of after his stroke was that he often found himself thinking he wanted to say something but was unable to say it. Case in point—he loved the word *case*. An important word, reminded him of the past. A man with cases. A Sergeant-Joe-Friday-kind-of-guy turning over stones until all the pieces to the puzzle are there on a table in the rehab center. No, not in the rehab center, not rehab puzzles designed to bridge the canyons left when brain cells wash out to sea like in the Mississippi delta. Different kinds of puzzles way back when he was an ex-cop but still had cases. Case in point on this business about not being able to come up with the right words at the right time was what to say to Brenda, the evening nurses' aide, when she told him Marjorie Gianetti had moved upstairs.

He'd wanted to tell Brenda about Marjorie being a fine lady and that he was sorry to hear about her moving upstairs. He wanted to say he wept yesterday when he saw a car being towed in the parking lot and wondered why he could not weep now. He wanted to say he knew damn well what was meant in this place by someone moving upstairs and that it had nothing to do with the floors in the building. He wanted to say he had enough trouble with words and hated the fact that nobody around this place had the guts to use the word *dead*. But most important of all, he wanted to say there was something fishy about Marjorie's death because of something she'd said to him a few days earlier.

"Mr. Babe," she'd said, reaching out from her wheelchair to the arm of his wheelchair and putting her hand on his, "intermediate and skilled hard tile floors are beaners. Bullshit accidents don't happen. Fuck the Pope and Medicaid gets the yolks."

Only after they finished laughing—his habit of smiling at everything like a demented clown having caused the laughter in the first place—did he manage to figure out what she meant. If she could, Marjorie might have said something like, "The reason they have hard tile floors in intermediate and skilled wings is obvious. Residents being incontinent and accidents that might ruin the carpet are bullshit reasons. They have tile floors so if one of us falls there's a better chance it'll be our last, and that saves Medicaid a bundle." He wasn't sure whether the mention of egg yolks had to do with the fragility of the residents, but he knew, by repeated hand signs she had used, that the yolk was the richest part of the egg and her mention of it was an allusion to money.

Marjorie was old enough to be Steve's mother, and she had indeed adopted him on his first day at Hell in the Woods—He and Jan being given a tour of the group therapy rehab center when Marjorie caterpillar-walks out of the elevator, using her heels to pull her wheelchair along. She merges in beside him like a commuter merging into rush hour traffic. She is short with a hump between her shoulders. Despite her age, black strands of hair are mixed in with the gray, the outer strands lifting in the breeze as she accompanies him down the hall that first day. With her hair brushed back Madonna style, she reminds Steve of an Italian mama whose portrait adorns a jar of spaghetti sauce.

Although Marjorie had difficulty getting the words out, she managed, "Gianetti, Marjorie, wife of Antonio. Pleased to meet." She then turned her wheelchair toward Jan and said she was also pleased to meet Jan.

Besides meeting Marjorie for the first time, two other things stuck in Steve's ragtag memory of that morning. The first was the fact that when Jan pushed his wheelchair down halls and into elevators, and finally into his room, he could not see who was pushing him and became frightened that Jan no longer existed. The second was the fact that, when they arrived on the third floor, his name was posted next to his door on an awfully permanent-looking placard, but one which, when more closely examined, proved to be not-so-permanent because, although the name was stenciled into a fake wood-grain card, the card could be easily slid out of its holder when the time came to either leave or, as residents and staff liked to put it, move upstairs.

Marjorie Gianetti was a resident in Saint Mel's nursing home wing.

Although attached to Saint Mel's main building, the nursing home's single-story wing stuck out from the main multi-story structure and, from some vantage points, actually disappeared into the woods. Some at the center claimed Saint Mel's got its nickname, Hell in the Woods, from a clever nursing home resident observing staff members trudge in from the staff parking lot hidden off in the woods behind the nursing home wing. Another theory about the nickname was that the facility was already completed when a rare storm with southeasterly winds blew up and jets from O'Hare Field began taking off directly overhead. Yet another theory referred to incidents in which nursing home residents walked out the loading dock entrance when an errant worker propped open the alarmed door. In each case the walkaway failed to get anywhere because of the chain-link fence surrounding the place. The only opening in the fence was at the main entry road some distance from the nursing home wing on the opposite side of the main building, further fueling nursing home residents' insistence that the name be changed from Saint Mel in the Woods Rehabilitation Facility to, simply, Hell in the Woods.

During Steve's first few minutes in the place, the same nurses' aide who revealed its nickname said Marjorie Gianetti made a point of greeting new stroke victims at the facility whether they were older and moving into the nursing home wing, whether they were younger and moving into the rehab facility, or whether they were in critical condition at any age and moving into the skilled care hospice facility. While accompanying Steve and Jan to his room—speaking exclusively to Jan in a way that made Steve feel he already had at least a foot, if not a leg, arm, and right testicle in the grave—the nurses' aide said Marjorie got the names of incoming stroke victims from the rehab center's updated strokers list and was a self-appointed den mother to incoming stroke victims. According to the nurses' aide, one had to take a lot of what

Marjorie said with a grain of salt and try to ignore her curses concerning the Pope.

Later, after Steve attended several stroker sessions and got to know Marjorie—and especially after she found out he'd been a Chicago cop, then a private investigator—Marjorie began telling him about her suspicions of devious goings-on at Hell in the Woods. She'd say things like, "Mr. Babe, cushy TV floor heads are okay, otherwise, cabbage meals on wheels for me," which actually was a continuation of her hard-tile-floor-Medicaid conspiracy theory that meant something like, "That's why I only walk where it's carpeted. If I take a fall I know this old head of mine will bear the brunt of it. When I'm in the hallways I stay put in my chair so I won't fall and bust my noggin open like a cabbage."

Maybe because he smiled so much, Marjorie told him all kinds of crazy things. Things like over-medication during state inspections and a resident named Janine steeped in the whirlpool like a tea bag. A conspiracy theory about stolen equipment sold back to the place by a medical supply company that acted as a front for the Catholic Church—and they thought the money was all from real estate. Horror stories about skilled-wing patients being eased ever so closer to the grave by the bean counters in the business office.

The wildest conspiracy theory of all was the one Marjorie implied had taken place some time back during a Presidential election. In this one, elderly residents were lined up in the hallway on election day, and the candidate they should vote for down at the polling place in the lobby was printed in ink on the insides of their dry old palms. One of the older aides in rehab overheard Marjorie trying her best to divulge this conspiracy. After waiting patiently for Marjorie to get all the "facts" out, the aide let it be known that, as far as she knew, Hell in the Woods had never had its lobby used for a polling place. Yet after the aide left them alone, Marjorie insisted there was something terribly wrong about the outcome of a Presidential election. He never did find out which election because Marjorie changed the subject, as usual, telling him about her family.

Marjorie spoke often of her husband Antonio, things like his business and his foul language. "Fuck the Pope," he'd say. And so Marjorie said, "Fuck the Pope." And when people heard this they'd smile and Marjorie would smile and, of course, he would out-smile them all. Maybe he even smiled when Marjorie told about her husband being found shot to death in the trunk of his car. Who the hell knew when the exuberant neurons that survived the ransacking of his brain would come out of hiding and do their smiley-face trick?

Or maybe it was all a dream. Steve Babe, the happy son of a bitch on his back in bed—You're on your back. Almost awake. A dream is still there. Two, maybe three things you want to be sure to remember. Sure, you'll remember. But then, the second your feet hit the floor it all begins to fade. You awaken with a vague recollection of having dreamed, but the details are lost through the net around your head, the net that was supposed to keep the details in. According to Marjorie, *that's* what it was like after her stroke.

Marjorie told these things not only to him, but also to Jan—It is evening, down on the first floor, calling on Marjorie at her room, escorting her to the wing's television lounge. The three of them sitting in an alcove at the back of the room while other nursing home residents stare open-mouthed at an episode of Star Trek's newest generation. Marjorie sits between them on a sofa, two wheelchairs parked illegally like Klingon vessels in an aisle between coffee table and side chair so that a male aide named Pete eventually moves the chairs against the wall. Marjorie speaks to both him and Jan but leans more toward him as if his brain will fill in the clipped phrases in the cartoon balloon above her head. When she says, "Choo-choos smoking like El Producto," he can almost hear the toy trains in the basement and smell Antonio Gianetti's cigar and hear the thump of barbells on carpet. After Marjorie says a few more words, he says, "Goodness gracious," and it is as if he has become her, their minds melded by old Spock into one complete mind. Jan joins in laughing with them, three conspirators eyed by the elderly Star Trekkers nearby, the three of them howling with glee, he and Jan hugging Marjorie from opposite sides but also hugging one another in this moment of joy.

Sometimes when Jan visited, she wheeled Steve down to the television lounge on his floor. Not so they could watch television, but because of the windowed alcove overlooking the entrance and the parking lot and the woods that surrounded the place. The alcove reminded Steve of the living room at his and Jan's apartment in Brookfield. Although Jan had since moved into a wheelchair-friendly apartment on the first floor in preparation for his arrival home, the new apartment was directly below the old apartment and shared the same view. Like the windows in this alcove, it looked out at parking lot and woods beyond. The Brookfield Zoo was near the apartment complex hidden beyond a small wooded area. Sometimes on still evenings, when he and Jan had been on their way in from the car, they'd hear one of the elephants, a trumpet being practiced in the distance by someone learning to play. Whenever this happened, Jan would make a comment about the elephant sounding the way he sounded when they made love. And he would say he sounded that way because, before he met her, he used to climb the fence at night and have his way with many of the creatures in the zoo. And then she would say something to the effect that she knew this and his hairiness was part of the reason she married him. And he would tell her a joke from grade school about an elephant meeting up with a naked man and saying, "It's cute, but how do you breathe through that little thing?"

It wasn't all coming back, but bits and pieces were. Except, why these memories? Why recall the sound of an elephant's call and his and Jan's playful comments? Because these were the truly important memories?

Learning. Re-learning. That was something Jan said he would have to do. She had been there from the start. The moment he opened his eyes in the hospital and didn't know who the hell he was or who the hell she was, she had been there. The moment he opened his eyes to this world with its dubious past, she had been there. He was able to remember some of the things Jan told him. Like the elephants in the zoo, or like that morning she was in bed beneath the blankets and he came riding down the hallway and into the bedroom on her bicycle wearing nothing but her riding helmet. That was before they were married, and before they'd become so-called middle-aged citizens.

He'd still been in the hospital when Jan told the story. He remembered her sitting in the chair beside his hospital bed holding his hand. He remembered her eyes and her beautiful hair that had not gone gray but remained the same sandy brown it had been when they met. Although at the time he did not think he could recall the incident in which he rode naked on her bicycle into the bedroom, Jan's words had made the night come alive.

She awoke from a dream in which she'd been riding her bike down a long hill. The road wound through a wood. Cool, calm, always downhill, the rear sprocket on her bike click-click-clicking as she coasted.

She opened her eyes. The room was dark. She reached out.

Gone. He was gone. Yet another one-night stand . . .

But wait, a noise. Was he just leaving? A light on in the hallway, a shadow. A clicking like . . .

Then he appeared, his hand at the light switch as the light came on. He coasted awkwardly into the room. He was naked and smiling, wearing only her bicycle helmet. He coasted around to the far side of the bed, the front wheel jerking back and forth as he struggled to maintain balance. He got off the bike and leaned it against the dresser, his back to her.

When she stopped laughing, she noticed red marks on his back where she had held him during the night, where she had scratched him. Then she saw redder marks on his buttocks. The marks caused by shrapnel when the window glass in his office had been blown in by a tossed bomb.

"You're a detective, Steve. You were a detective ten years ago when I hired you to find out who killed my first husband Frank. When we met, you'd just come off a case that got you in trouble with Miami hoods who came to Chicago and threw a bomb through your office window. Abortion clinics had been bombed and your investigation of a Miami bomb maker, who apparently did work for the mob down there, was not appreciated. Do you remember? After you started the case I was picked up by those men in the van who threatened me. They took off the police guard because that detective named Al Carroll didn't believe me. You stayed with me that night. You'd picked up dinner at Szabo's Hungarian restaurant. We fell in love that night."

Jan told the bicycle story again and again at the hospital, and again and again here at Hell in the Woods. She also told the story of his past without her. His past without her seeming even more removed because the only person he trusted and loved was doing the telling. Jan was the one who told him that before they met he had been dating Tamara, the same Tamara who visited him several times in the hospital and here, the same Tamara with whom he exchanged e-mails as part of his therapy. Jan said that he and Tamara had met while he was a detective on the Chicago Police Department, and that Tamara was still with the Chicago Police Department, a lieutenant in homicide.

Jan told these stories from the past here in the alcove where the windows gave a view of the entrance, parking lot, and the cold rain-soaked woods of March. Here in the television lounge with the large screen television throbbing in the far corner. Here in the television lounge where, just a moment ago, Brenda, one of the evening nurses' aides, told him that she'd just gotten word from the first floor nursing facility that his friend Marjorie Gianetti had moved upstairs, which meant she was dead.

He'd wanted to say something to Brenda about Marjorie. He turned the words over and over in his mind. Those damn backward upside-down inside-out words that were impossible to say. He'd wanted to say there was something not quite right about Marjorie's death because he remembered Marjorie warning him of the danger posed by those polished tile floors in which you could sometimes see your reflection.

He still wanted to say something. He wanted to ask how Marjorie had died. And when he wheeled himself out of the television lounge and into the group of others parked in their wheelchairs at the nurses' station, the Hell in the Woods grapevine provided some answers that made him into Steve Babe, the detective, once again.

Marjorie had fallen in the hallway near the entrance to the first floor nursing home facility activity room. At this time of evening the activity room was empty, and so was the long hallway leading to the room. The only other things down the hallway were the wing's kitchen facilities and the loading dock, which was locked and alarmed in case a resident should try to walk out. Nobody knew why Marjorie had wandered down that hallway so late in the evening. If a staff member hadn't gone down the hall to retrieve something she'd left in the activity room, Marjorie might have lain there all night. She apparently ventured there alone, walking without assistance and without her wheelchair. For some reason Marjorie had ventured out alone, walking, and had slipped on a wet spot in the middle of the hallway where another resident in the nursing facility wing apparently had an "accident" earlier in the day.

The news was delivered by an elderly non-stroke resident from the first floor nicknamed So-long Sue. Sue was in her late eighties and, except for having to get around in a wheelchair, seemed in pretty good shape. Her hair, which should have been completely white, had been curled by the first floor beauty shop to a translucent lavender bushiness, except in back where it was "bed-head" flat as with most first floor women. When So-long Sue spoke, she made moves in her wheelchair much like someone trying to explain a complex matter to a small child. Steve had parked his wheelchair where he could listen to Sue, yet be able to listen in on the reactions of the nurse and aide at the station.

"They call her So-Long Sue because the only way to get rid of her is to say so long and leave," said the nurse.

"She's got a captive audience now," said the aide. "That's why she comes up here when there's gossip to spread."

"What's the gossip today?" asked the nurse.

"One of the elderly ladies fell and hit her head and died before she got to the hospital," said the aide.

The nurse and aide stopped talking to listen to Sue, who was becoming more animated.

"It's scandalous," said Sue. "Two hours and the damn thing's still there. They want us to think one of us made a puddle *that* big. If Marjorie were here instead of moving upstairs, I would have said to her, 'Goodness gracious, Marjorie, if they think one of us girls did it, all they'd have to do is put their ears to the door when we take a pee. Then they'd hear for themselves.' No matter how much they complain about prostate, I bet it was one of the men."

The group of strokers reacted to this by looking to one another and smiling. But Steve did not feel like smiling, and listened intently as Sue continued.

"Can you imagine it? An elderly resident who has also suffered a stroke like you poor people—but at least you young people have time to do something about it—slips in a pee puddle and dies and nobody even bothers to clean it up. They just send for the meat wagon and shovel out the body and everything's back to normal. I can understand them being short on staff, but this is ridiculous. A woman's died and someone should have the decency to clean up the floor. If I were younger and worked as an aide down there I certainly would have done it. That was the way it was in my day. Women taking care of things after someone passes. Women putting things back the way they were.

"Don't they realize doing a day's work in this place is better than old people sit and stretch exercises? Idiotic. You get old and end up a zoo monkey doing monkeyshines for peanuts. And with my dentures, I can't even eat peanuts."

Sue shook her head and sighed. "Too bad about poor Marjorie."

After this final statement, Sue turned quickly and caterpillar-walked toward the elevators at a good clip.

Marcia, the youngest women in the group of strokers waved so long to So-Long Sue, then said, "Now what?"

Paul, another short-timer like Marcia, said, "We stare at our crotches. It's what we do."

After a few chuckles, Marcia turned to Steve. "Steve? Your speech partner?"

Steve nodded sadly as strokers caterpillar-walked past and gave their condolences. A new patient named Phil who had the room across from Steve was last to give Steve his condolences.

Phil turned his wheelchair so that he was facing Steve, leaned forward, and with great effort and apparent sincerity, said, "Jesus fuck."

Steve accepted this with the same nod of thanks he'd given the others and watched sadly as Phil wheeled away. It was the first time in a long time he'd been able to suspend the Pavlovian smile the stroke had given him. As the others in the group headed down the hall, he stayed behind and listened to the nurse and aide.

"Under normal circumstances, talk like that might turn a few heads," said the aide.

"We had to put an ankle bracelet on Phil his first day because he tried to walk out," said the nurse. "Rather than the usual problem coming up with words, that's the only thing Phil ever says. Some residents think he probably used the phrase, "Jesus Fucking Christ" a lot during his lifetime and only two words of it are left."

"No shit," said the aide.

This time of evening there were usually a few procrastinators in the television lounge or wandering the hallway. But tonight, perhaps because of the news of death on the first floor, the hallway in the third floor stroke wing was completely empty.

Steve had on his day clothes, not yet having changed into his pajamas, but figured there was no way he could pass himself off as a handicapped visitor. Security was tight on the first floor at night. But what the hell, he'd take a chance. Yeah, he'd take a little roll down to the first floor and size up the crime scene, or the scene of the accident, which this probably was. And being that it most likely was an accident, there would be nothing at all suspicious about the ambulance whisking Marjorie Gianetti away and things getting back to "normal" so quickly.

No one got on the elevator with him and it did not stop at the second floor. On the first floor, one of two things would happen. The passenger elevators faced the long reception counter in the lobby, and either a guard or one of the staff at the counter would recognize him and he'd be sent back to his room like a child, or the staff and the guards would be busy closing up for the night, waiting for the night shift guards who manned the counter until morning, and no one would notice him. It could go either way, the lady or the lion, but not much of a lady *or* a lion, not much risk at all. Laughable, in fact.

When the elevator door slid open, he quickly wheeled out and around the corner using his good left hand, which he felt was becoming stronger to make up for the atrophy of his right hand. He rolled away from the reception area and, apparently not being noticed by the busy staff behind the counter, headed down the long hall connecting the nursing home wing to the main building.

Although Steve still had trouble recalling things from before his stroke, he was getting better at recalling things from the recent past. He knew that the activity center was a huge room at the far end of the wing. He would have to travel the entire length of the wing. First would be the intermediate nursing home patients, ones like Sue and Marjorie who could still get around. After intermediate he'd have to circle the nurses' station in the center of the wing. Finally he'd have to pass through skilled care where most patients were bedridden. He assumed that at this time of evening, the wing staff would be busy, as they had been on his floor, helping residents who could not get themselves ready for bed.

The hearsay at Hell in the Woods was that the nursing home wing turned into a block-long tomb quite early in the evening. But all was not quiet in the nursing home wing. He'd made it through the automatic double doors and rolled the length of the intermediate section when he heard voices being raised. Apparently a few of the staff were in a room across the hall from the nurses' station. As he approached the sound of the voices, he kept glancing behind him. He figured someone would come up from behind and he'd be sent back upstairs. But, so far, that hadn't happened.

When he got to the doorway from which the voices emerged, he paused, trying to think of a good reason for being here. But mostly, he wondered what had made him come here.

The last time Jan visited, and they'd finished their usual emotional greeting, which sometimes resulted in her closing the door and propping the guest chair against it so they could have a little privacy, she'd spoken again about the case he was on when they met. She had hired him to find out who killed her husband and someone else. Yes, someone he knew. Sam Pike. When Jan questioned him about the case, all he could remember at the time was that it had something to do with kids. He had no idea whose kids or how many kids. He simply remembered that the case had something to do with kids.

Jan was quite excited about this, saying he was getting much better at remembering things. For the few weeks since he'd been at Hell in the Woods, this is how it had gone with Jan. She would prompt him until he recalled some tidbit from the past—or from something she'd said on a previous visit, he wasn't sure which—and she would use this recollection to begin telling him the details of an incident. When he'd recalled that the case involving Jan's husband and Sam Pike had something to do with kids, she told what seemed like a tall tale, but insisted that every word of it was true.

The part of the tale he recalled now was that there were some kids being held on an island and that they were in danger. Young men with automatic weapons guarded the island and it was up to him and Jan to help the kids get away. Apparently those responsible for her husband's and Sam Pike's deaths were holding the kids. The kids were not related to him or to Jan, but someone had to help them. Jan said they took a rowboat out to the island in the dead of night. And something else. Jan said he had his violin with him. Crazy. Jan insisted he used to play the violin, and when she brought it into the hospital shortly after his stroke, he had to admit that, although he could not recall ever having played the violin before, he was able to make sounds on it. But they were terrible sounds, and when Jan said that was how he'd always played, he asked her how she could stand it, and they both laughed like hell.

But there was something more to this island story. Jan said what he did that night showed he was unwilling to let things go, that he was a detective through and through and always would be. Then she said something about him being honorable and that it was in his blood. This, of course, made him laugh. But Jan did not laugh. Instead, she said she would also be a detective, her first case being to help him rediscover his world.

So that was the answer, down here in the nursing home wing because finding out for certain if Marjorie had an accident or not was in his blood.

Voices still came from the room across from the nurses' station. As he inched nearer, he could tell they were women's voices. Although he could not hear complete sentences, he heard one of the women screech out, "Eleven-inch dick! Really! Really he does!" This was followed by laughter and one of them stomping her foot and someone else having a coughing fit.

He decided to take advantage of the moment. Last time he looked he didn't quite measure up, so he knew they weren't talking about him. As he pushed hard on the wheel with his left hand and swung his body to the left to correct the wheelchair's direction, the laughter continued, but the voices seemed closer to the door. He pushed harder, sailing along, a breeze in his face that smelled like soap and bed linen and alcohol and urine. The end of the hallway was coming up fast and he slowed, using left hand on the wheel and left foot on the floor. A shattered image from boyhood flashed by. Memorial Day out in the backyard with the radio propped in the kitchen window . . . Yes, listening to the Indianapolis 500!

He rounded the corner at the end of the hallway just as laughing voices exploded through the doorway across from the nurses' station, shushing one another and going their separate ways. He was out of sight, in the long hallway leading to the activity room.

He parked his wheelchair against the wall to one side and studied the scene. *Scene* was another fine word from the past. The scene of the crime. Yeah, right. Poor Marjorie slips and falls on a wet spot, actually a puddle he could see was still on the floor, and he thinks it's a scene of the crime because he used to be a private dick. Dick, ha. Everything's connected in this damn world. Staff probably left the piddle puddle for the early morning cleaning crew to take care of.

At least on his floor there was an early morning crew, the ones who got out all the noisiest polishers and buffers they could find in janitors' closets and woke everyone up while they made the tile floors into mirrors. Too bad he wasn't a kid in grammar school anymore, because back then he would have sidled up to the girls and had a fine time looking up their skirts.

Thinking of grammar school made him think of Dwayne Matusak. For some reason, since his stroke, he had recalled one particular summer from boyhood in which Dwayne Matusak announced that by end of summer they would have a knockdown drag-out fight and only one of them would come out alive. At the time he actually thought he would die. When he watched Dragnet on television that summer he tried to imagine himself cool and fearless like Sergeant Joe Friday. And now here he was in the hallway of a damn nursing home staring at a puddle of urine thinking about an ancient black and white television series.

Crazy bastard. A stroke was one thing, but at least he wasn't permanent in this place like folks in this wing. Not unless he had another stroke and this one knocked him for a loop. Or maybe in his condition a seizure would do it. He had a seizure a few weeks earlier and, even though the doctor said seizures wouldn't damage his brain, he still wondered.

But what good did it do to think about it? Only thing to do was keep working on it and get the hell out of here. A lot more years left in this old dick. Fifty-three down, or so they told him. Given a week's notice, he could still get it up.

He laughed, then wondered why the hell he was suddenly in such a damn good mood. One minute he's worried about seizures, next minute he's a laughing hyena. Here he is poking into the circumstances of Marjorie's recent death and he gets this idiotic self-satisfying feeling.

The puddle on the floor was not quite a yard across, exactly as Sue had described it less than an hour earlier. But when he leaned forward and studied the edges of the puddle more closely, he could see that it was surrounded by a series of barely discernible rings marking where the puddle had originally extended, but had dried.

Across the hall was one of those janitors' closets he'd been thinking about when he recalled being awakened each morning by the noisy cleaning crew. The closet was straddled on either side by a men's room and a ladies' room so as to line up the plumbing during construction. As he stared across at the door to the janitors' closet with its *Staff Only* sign, he saw where small droplets on the floor had dried. The droplets were in front of the *Staff Only* door and seemed to lead toward the large puddle as if someone had stomped in the main puddle like a kid with brand new galoshes.

The hallway tile was one of those nondescript patterns of flecks on a beige background. Foot squares placed so tightly together it was difficult to see the dividing lines between them. And, because of the apparent randomness of the pattern, it was difficult to find the repetition. Like looking at the photograph of a planet surface. But eventually he did find the pattern, and when he did he saw that each tile had been turned ninety degrees from the previous tile by the installer.

Before the perimeter dried, the puddle had been spread out over roughly a three-foot circle and he could see, because of breaks in the dry line at the edge of the perimeter, that something had disturbed the puddle not long after it was made. When he examined these breaks in the dry line more closely, he could see where thin tires had rolled through the puddle and gone on down the hallway away from the activity room and toward an alarmed door. Although the tire tracks were dry, he could definitely see them.

He rolled down the hallway and studied a floor plan mounted on the wall with arrows showing various emergency escape routes. According to the map, the alarmed door opened to a hallway that bordered the kitchen and eventually led to a loading dock. The spread between the wheels that had made the tracks was too large to be a wheelchair, and each wheel was paired with another that almost, but not quite, paralleled its course. And, since it was way past any mealtime and no food carts would have passed this way late in the evening, he figured the tracks leading away from the puddle must have been made by the gurney that had taken Marjorie away. Made sense that the ambulance would park at the loading dock, back here where residents wouldn't have to watch one of their own being carted away.

Felt good to be doing a little dissecting at the scene, even if it wasn't a crime scene. And Marjorie, who loved mysteries and conspiracy theories, would have been proud. She was probably sitting on cloud nine right now, happy as a clam he was staring down at the tracks of the gurney that took her away. Of course, if he found something . . .

The self-satisfaction he felt a moment earlier turned bitter, then became comic as he imagined himself smiling to death the perpetrator of the so-called "foul play." Or maybe getting out a violin and playing it until the guy pukes his guts out. Or maybe letting word out on the street so Marjorie's husband's old cronies blow into town for a final hit. He could almost see them crawling out of the woodwork of various nursing homes around the country. They'd show up at Hell in the Woods in wheelchairs and walkers. They'd rough up a few aides and nurses. A Keystone Cops scene in which the cronies stagger after the aides and nurses, wielding their canes.

Or maybe it would be different. The guards at the front desk would try to put up a fight, but the crew of cronies, like a wrecking crew come back from the dead, would mow them down with their canes—the canes, of course, having had rapid firing weapons concealed in them James Bond style ever since the cronies went into the homes in case anyone ever sent in a hit on them.

Was this a story he and Marjorie once shared? Or was it really that way? Hoods in nursing homes with loaded canes? Funny. So damn funny.

He backed away from the door to the loading dock, turned and wheeled back to the puddle where the tracks originated. On the side of the puddle nearest the janitors' closet, where the kid in new galoshes had splashed, he saw something else. He wheeled around the puddle. Yes, there was evidence here. Several specks on the doorjamb, hard to see because of the dark color of the doorjamb, but when he reached out and found that the speck he rubbed came off fairly easily, he knew it was blood and not paint. Perhaps there had been more blood, a puddle on the floor near the door and away from the urine puddle, the paramedics wiping up a larger puddle of blood and missing the specks on the doorjamb. But if there was that much blood, why no investigation? Where was the yellow police tape? Where was the cop to protect the evidence? After all her theories about conspiracies, was this how Marjorie would check out? Slipping in a puddle of piss and no one even questions the circumstances or bothers to clean it up?

As he leaned forward in his wheelchair rubbing at another of the reddish-brown specks and examining the stain transferred to his finger, something else bothered him. For a moment he thought he would fall out of the chair, and if that happened, he'd tumble end-over-end, not stopping until . . . until what? He sat up and closed his eyes and tried to think. Yes, something was there. A smell. A smell from earlier while sailing down the hallway, but a smell that was not here. And now, as he sniffed, trying to detect an odor from the puddle on the floor, a memory came to him. A memory from the distant past that made him sit up and close his eyes.

A stairwell. A feeling of being closed in. An unsafe place. The weight of a gun in his hand and he's climbing the stairs and there's the smell of urine. Must be from the time he was a Chicago cop. Even though he hadn't known Jan then, she told him about it, saying she knew a lot of his old cronies and that she would teach it all to him again and he'd be as good as new. But this thing—climbing a dark stairwell with a gun in his hand and the smell of urine all around—

this thing he did not remember Jan telling him. This thing came from someplace else, someplace dark and frightening. And now a phrase emerged. That phrase was simply, *the projects.*

As he sat with his eyes closed recalling the smell of urine from a stairwell climbed long ago, he wondered why, although he had leaned forward in his chair and taken a deep breath, he had not smelled urine here.

Then he heard a sound. Someone else on the stairwell in the project. But when he opened his eyes, he saw the night LPN who everyone called Betty-who-talks-too-much staring at him. Betty was from his floor. She stood on the far side of the puddle with her arms folded. She was smiling and he wondered how long she'd been there. Actually, he wanted to ask her this but, as usual, the words went upside-down and inside-out and he said nothing. Instead of talking he smiled back at Betty who came around the puddle behind his chair and began her one-sided dialogue.

"The desk said I'd find you here, Steve. I'm surprised you'd come down here. I figured a guy like you wouldn't waste a trip to the first floor to visit the nursing home. I figured a guy like you'd be out on the grounds doing wheelies. This place is too old for you. How come you're not glued to your TV watching one of the gumshoe videos your wife brings in?"

When Betty pivoted his wheelchair and began circling the puddle to take him back to his room, Steve wanted to tell her to wait. He wanted to shout it. He wanted to tell her he needed to do something important before he went back to his room. He wanted to tell her there was evidence to be collected before the morning cleaning crew disturbed the crime scene. But, as usual, he was unable to sort the words from the ones spewing from Betty's mouth. So, before she could wheel him away, he gasped and slumped to one side in his chair, sticking out his left foot to put on the brakes.

While Betty was busy putting his foot back up on the footrest so she could wheel him back to his room, she kept rattling on about the time of evening and where he should and shouldn't be.

Damn it, Betty, have a heart! Read my mind, will you?

But of course, Betty could not read his mind. The only person who came close to being able to do that was Jan, and Jan wasn't here.

But someone else was here. Sergeant Joe Friday was here bolstering him for the upcoming fight with Dwayne Matusak. Sergeant Friday, who would have to stoop down to look into a boy's eyes. Sergeant Friday looking knowingly into his eyes. And so, taking a tip from Joe Friday, who often taste-tested questionable substances, he leaned to the side, reached down, and dipped his forefinger into the retreating puddle on the floor. And on the way down the hallway, as the breeze of being rapidly wheeled the length of the nursing home wing cooled him and threatened to dry the evidence he had so astutely collected on Marjorie's behalf, he thought, *Oh shit,* to himself, thought about Joe Friday touching his finger to his tongue in that safer black and white world, thought about germs and bacteria and viruses contained in bodily fluids, thought about who might have pissed here on this floor, figured an octogenarian's piss wouldn't stand up to piss collected from a stairwell corner in the projects, hoped to hell Betty hadn't seen him dip his finger in the puddle or he might end up in the loony wing, and, finally, put his finger to his mouth and took a taste of what, for some reason, he already knew would not be there. Water. Nothing but water.

After backing him into the elevator, Betty was silent. All he could see before him was the closed elevator door and the controls to one side and the floor indicator lights above the door. Perhaps the silence was deliberate, the ride back to the third floor a time during which the psychotic stroke victim was expected to collect his thoughts.

Among the thoughts going up with him in the elevator was a deranged theory that we are all born with pure intelligence and the remainder of our lives is spent destroying it. But as the second floor light above the door blinked out and the third floor light lit and the door slid open, the theory floated out ahead of him like so much vapor. Now, even though he knew it was only water on the floor, all that remained for his effort was self-pity.

Poor Steve Babe, the stroke victim, the fool. Tasting a puddle on the floor to see if it's piss. It's come to this. It's come to this.

CHAPTER FOUR

To celebrate the opening night of her remodeled restaurant, Ilonka Szabo invited regular customers for a lavish feast. It was a dream come true, to invite friends in her adopted country to share in her good fortune.

Unfortunately, her most loyal customer would not be coming and this made her sad. His name was Steve Babe, shortened from the Hungarian *Baberos* at the turn of the century by a great grandfather unaware of jokes the shortened version would generate in the new country. The original name translated as one who is crowned with a laurel wreath as a mark of honor. As Ilonka came from the restaurant kitchen to give a toast she recalled years earlier when Steve told her the details. An immigration official at Ellis Island had confused Baberos with Barabbas, the thief released from crucifixion instead of Jesus. The official had convinced Steve's great grandfather that his descendants would not want to be known as heathens and thieves in their new country.

"A cherished friend is absent tonight," said Ilonka, holding up her glass. "Not long ago he suffered a stroke at the young age of fifty-three. He's at the Saint Mel in the Woods Rehabilitation Facility. He solves mysteries and is quite good at it. Although the stroke occurred at home, he had been working on a case when it happened. A terrible time for a stroke to creep up like a thief in the night. Pray he solves the most important mystery of his life. Pray he recaptures his past and we'll soon have him back with us and be able to share a meal with him."

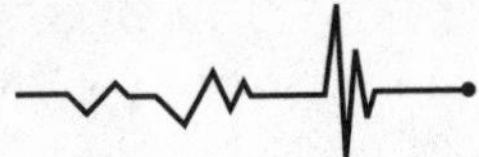

It was unfair to be here. The warmth, the smells, the voices of diners, the smile from Ilonka Szabo, the white tablecloth, the candles, an elegant place setting for two—everything here made it unfair. When the toast was given, Jan saw that Ilonka and several regular patrons glanced toward her table. Jan had the feeling they focused on the seat across from her, the seat where Steve should have been. He would have turned and smiled and said something in Hungarian. She could almost see him there as he joins in the toast with that crazy smile.

Lydia Jacobson turned from Jan to join the toast, smiled. Because of the subdued lighting, Lydia's face was shadowed. When Ilonka finished the toast, Lydia offered another toast. "Here's to Steve."

As Jan sipped the red Hungarian wine, she wondered if a daily dose of red wine throughout Steve's lifetime might have made a difference.

"This place is great," said Lydia.

"It was Steve's favorite," said Jan. "Before they remodeled he used to pick up carryout from here. He probably ate Ilonka's food more often than he should. Americans have the second highest incidence of heart disease and stroke. Can you guess which country is number one?"

"Hungary?" asked Lydia.

"Right," said Jan. "The home of Steve's ancestors is one of many what-ifs. Like, what if he hadn't eaten so much high cholesterol food? Or, what if he'd exercised regularly? Or, what if we'd made love three times a day for the last ten years? I hope to hell he never has another stroke. When he had a seizure a couple weeks back I thought that was it."

Lydia reached across the table and touched Jan's hand. She looked at Jan as if to say, "You can't blame yourself."

Jan and Lydia were close enough so sometimes they did not have to speak. Lydia had been with Jan the night of Steve's stroke. They had been out to dinner, as they were tonight, leaving Steve home doing phone work. Lydia had been with Jan when she found Steve slumped over on the sofa with the phone in his lap. Lydia drove them to the hospital. Lydia was the one who'd heard of the clot-dissolving drug which, if given within three hours of an ischemic stroke, was supposed to lessen its effects. The only problem was they did not know exactly when the stroke had occurred. Jan had tried calling some of the phone numbers Steve had written down on a notepad to narrow down the time, but the latest call she could come up with was to a friend from the Chicago PD and that was nearly two hours before she and Lydia found him. Counting the time to drive to the hospital in an unseasonable November snowstorm, and the time it took to get a doctor to administer the drug, she could not be sure about the magic three-hour window.

So far, Steve seemed to be doing fairly well recalling the recent past, the past after his stroke. But last week, when his mother and retarded sister visited from Cleveland, it was obvious Steve did not remember them. He put on a good act, though, knowing he should show recognition. Faking it was something a lot of recovering stroke victims did.

Despite not recognizing his mother and sister, there was hope. Recently he'd become obsessed by the recall of a boy from grammar school. A boy named Dwayne Matusak who apparently threatened Steve during an entire summer. Dwayne Matusak's name came up more frequently during Jan's visits, and, according to Steve's therapists, during his occupational and speech rehab. Although Jan was able to visit Steve every day, his stringent rehab schedule kept her from seeing him as much as she would have liked. He was in an experimental program consisting of eight to fourteen hours per day of therapy. Steve's doctor said the medication combined with long hours of therapy was Steve's best shot at recovery. Although this might have been more expensive than they could have afforded on their own, the program was experimental and therefore part of the cost was picked up.

Lydia glanced back toward the kitchen door where Ilonka had stood while giving her toast, then turned back to Jan. "I like the name Ilonka."

"It's Helen in Hungarian," said Jan.

"My mom's name was Helen. She named me Lydia because she saw Groucho Marx sing 'Lydia the Tattooed Lady' once."

As Lydia spoke, she touched the scar on her left cheek with her finger and Jan could see the change that always came over Lydia when she spoke of her past and touched her scar. The scar started at the corner of Lydia's mouth and went to her eye. Lydia had long black hair, fair complexion, and a thin face. When the scar had been at its worst, it masked Lydia's beauty and even her personality because, no matter what people said, when they saw a woman with a scar like that, they couldn't help thinking she must have deserved it.

The scar had been made by a knife wielded by a thug who worked for a downtown pimp disappointed by Lydia's repeated refusal to join his harem. It was the pimp's final blow after having gotten her on heroin. Helping Jan get Lydia into drug rehab and in to see a Michigan Avenue plastic surgeon was Steve's doing.

Lydia was special. It was largely because of her that Jan had gotten out of the massage parlor business years earlier. Before the massage parlor business, when they should have been halfway through college, Lydia and Jan were strippers at a club just over the state line in Wisconsin. After the club folded because of all the Chicago and Milwaukee executives building their weekend "farms" in the area, Lydia and Jan ended up on Chicago's north side at a massage parlor frequented by some of those same "farmers."

Later, when the massage parlor business cooled and went underground and got dirtier, Lydia told Jan she was getting the hell out and took Jan with her. Jan got a job as a Loop secretary. Lydia was also supposed to have taken the high road, and insisted she had, but got sucked back into the underbelly of the city by a bastard who said he loved her, and would love her even more if she did certain things for him.

And so here they were, two hardened ex-strippers and massage parlor girls sitting at a small Hungarian restaurant packed with Hungarians drinking wine. As Lydia said when they were out last minute Christmas shopping last year before Steve had his stroke, "You figure in a crowd this size, a few have got to be hiding a past they're not exactly proud of. Someone's got to be ex-hookers and ex-strippers in this crowd of faces, Jan, so it might as well be us."

Lydia spoke as she worked on her goulash.

"We should have my plastic surgeon attach these dumpling guys directly to our waists instead of eating them." Lydia chewed for a moment, then said, "Crazy calling these things guys. Maybe we've all had strokes to one degree or another. You said Steve used to call a thing *him*, or a male nurse *she*, or even *it*. How's that any different than calling a dumpling a guy?"

"Steve's better with pronouns now" said Jan. "Slow as hell, but a lot better than he was back in the hospital. When I first got him the portable computer he was fixated with the idea that the world had changed, not him. Or he'd see news on television about storms and war and earthquakes and look down and shake his head. When he finally started typing on the computer, he wrote, 'It's official, the world has had a stroke.' Back then I wasn't sure if he'd ever talk again."

When Lydia did not respond, Jan continued. "But he is getting better. For a while he was fixated on a mystery man from the past, some guy with dark eyes. One of the therapists said since Steve has dark eyes, maybe he was thinking of himself. They run them through the mill at that place. He's quizzed every day on the names of other patients and people on staff. In one of the hallways on the first floor, they've got an employee bulletin board with mug shots and names. And in vocational rehab they've got another board without names and they make them put names with the faces."

Lydia stopped eating and stared at Jan, a familiar sad smile on her face, a smile that had come to mean, "Go ahead, let it out."

"It's funny, yet not so funny," said Jan. "During the last couple years we'd really been watching our diets, trying to avoid things that would gum up Steve's arteries. We started doing it as soon as we found out his cholesterol was high. I guess we were too late for that one damn clot that went into his speech center and shot the place up.

"But I shouldn't complain because, despite having to speak slowly to him, he seems to understand most of what I say. He likes to cheer me up when I arrive and usually has a funny story to tell. Did I tell you we made a pact to be cheerful as hell for the rest of our lives? Steve said that since the stroke made him a cheerful son of a bitch, he wants me to be one so he won't look foolish in public. I suppose saying cheerful things is a lot better than the first few things he got out. A couple days after the stroke, he wrote down that he'd always wanted to die fast, not like this. It was jumbled up, but I managed to decipher it.

"It's the old emotional roller coaster. When Steve first called Saint Mel's Hell in the Woods, I assumed he'd coined the phrase and thought it was a breakthrough. But the next day I found out everyone who works there, and most of the residents, call it Hell in the Woods. A woman in the business office told me about it. When Steve was moved from the hospital I thought I'd see more of him. But they keep him busy. 'Living the rehab,' they call it. I guess that's part of the reason they call it Hell in the Woods. I've really gotten to know the place, walking the halls when I'm there and can't see him because he's in therapy. In the hospital they were more concerned with the physical, like working on using the walker instead of the wheelchair. But here, although they seem reasonably concerned with his physical abilities, the main focus is on memory and speech."

"Don't stop talking," said Lydia. "You need rehab, too."

"I guess so. But sometimes I feel selfish doing what I'm doing. It's as though I'm trying to remake Steve into what he was, and I'm not sure if that's right. Sometimes I think I'm trying to use the stroke to my advantage by ignoring the lousy life I had before I met him. I've had difficulty telling him about the years as a stripper and about the massage parlors. I can talk to you about this because it's something we share. But to not share this part of my past with Steve now, when he needs everything filled in . . . well, it's like trying to make him love me more than he did. And that's not right. I know I shouldn't go overboard about my past because it's not something we talked about much before his stroke. But I feel that at some point I'm either going to have to spell it out in detail, or I'm going to keep feeling guilty as hell about it.

"About a month after the stroke, Steve said something that really broke my heart. At first I felt angry, then I realized that, because of his difficulty communicating, he was unable to express all the qualifying baggage we sometimes hang on our statements. He could only say it bluntly. He said I should leave him. He said I should find someone else. After I got over the shock, I told him I couldn't. I told him I had a mystery to solve and that I wouldn't stop until I'd solved it. I told him I had to solve the mystery of who my lover was.

"We've made love in his room at Hell in the Woods. We propped a chair against the door a couple of times and made love. It was . . . different. He's like a kid. Goddamn, he's like a kid. Right in the middle of things, he recites a jingle from when he was a boy and asks if I know which is correct. Was it, '*Hi, my name's Buster Brown. I live in a shoe. Here's my dog Tag. Look for him in there, too.*'? or was it, '*Hi, my name's Buster Brown. I live in a shoe. My dog's name is Tag. He lives in there, too.*'?

"When he latches onto something from the past, he can't let go of it. It's like he needs to relive his childhood. Unfortunately he's stuck in this Hell in the Woods place where the average age must be sixty. He's one of the youngest patients on his floor. And at the rehab center on the second floor the average age is even older because a lot of the stroke victims are from the nursing home wing. The other day Steve wrote on his computer that one of the residents from the nursing home says the wing sticks out in the woods as a kind of metaphor for death."

Lydia picked up Jan's glass and handed it to her. "Have a swig."

Jan took a drink of wine and put the glass down. "Sorry, I didn't mean to go on."

"You weren't going on," said Lydia. "But Steve *is* doing much better, isn't he?"

"Sure he is. Of course. And he always puts a positive spin on things."

"Tell me about it."

"Well, he's been told his muscle tone is nearing full-spasticity stage. It's when you try to move one joint, the other joints in the same leg or arm move. But he's using the spasticity to his advantage. He exercises a lot, getting himself ready for when the normal-tone stage arrives. He doesn't need a hand splint anymore, except when he sleeps. The big success was getting rid of the arm trough on the wheelchair to keep his arm from falling. But he still has to wear a right leg brace to keep his knee from buckling. He does fine in the walker now, but he prefers his wheelchair and says he'll miss it.

"In rehab they stress working on both his left and right sides, but Steve had me get him a pair of handgrips and a pair of dumbbells and has been working on strengthening his left hand and arm. He says it's just in case his right arm and leg don't come back fully.

"His occupational therapist is a really nice gal named Gwen. When I spoke with her the other day, she said the way he's mastered the computer and elevators and everything else he can get his hands on, that before you know it he'll be driving."

Lydia had just taken a sip of wine and put the glass down. "I've got a friend up at school named Gwen, Gwen Africa. Great name, huh?"

"Isn't there a black group where everyone changes their last names to Africa?"

"Yeah," said Lydia, "but I don't think she belongs to it. Although she is black. But I interrupted . . ."

"You want to hear more about rehab?"

"Of course. Does Steve use his computer a lot?"

"Yes. Unlike the hospital, where things were more traditional, the rehab center has lots of computers. Steve gets on the Internet, sends messages to other stroke patients in other facilities. He's even sent e-mail to Tamara."

"That cop he used to know?"

"Yes. She visits once in a while. Pretty ironic that an ex-lover of Steve's turns out to be a good friend of mine. Sweet Jesus, I sure can see why he fell for her. She says 'Sweet Jesus' a lot. Here she is a black female homicide cop and she also sings in the church choir.

"But, yes, Steve uses the computer I bought him quite a bit. He's stopped carrying around the electronic thesaurus to help remind him of words. Says he doesn't carry around the thesaurus anymore because it's too much like carrying around part of his brain in a box.

"Even though he was on the melancholy side before his stroke, Steve always had an ironic sense of humor. The other day he took me down to the rehab computer lab. There's this program that's supposed to help stroke victims rebuild vocabulary, and on this program there was this button on the screen you were supposed to click with the mouse in order to show a comparison of two words, I guess if they had any meaning in common. Anyway, the name on the button was misspelled. Instead of saying *Comparison*, it said *Comaprison*. Steve laughed like hell at this, and after he stopped laughing, he managed to get out the irony in this. He said it was funny because if a stroker clicked on the button, they'd go to this *Comaprison*, which he said was a pretty fair description of where strokers do go sometimes."

Jan and Lydia were silent for a moment, then Lydia spoke.

"Last time we talked you said Steve's mind wanders a lot. Does that still happen?"

"Not quite as much. But he still has this thing where he sees something, like on television or out in the parking lot, and it reminds him of something and that reminds him of something else, and so on. And when this happens he says it always seems to end up with something having to do with the environment. Since his stroke he's gotten very concerned with the environment, especially global warming and the problems society is leaving behind for future generations.

"He was looking out his window the other day and could see some people waiting out at the bus stop at the main entrance. He managed to get out that the entrance was far away and there were trees in between, but with the leaves still not out, being that it's only March, he was able to see the people and judged that since they were taking the bus they were poor people. He said people waiting for a bus have no control of what goes on in the world. He said people waiting for buses no longer wear business suits like in old movies on television. He said they're at the mercy of corporations. He said they have no control over the air they breathe or the water they drink. And, although he smiled as always, I could tell this made him sad."

"Did he actually say those things?" asked Lydia.

"No, he wrote it all on his computer. He also wrote that the deteriorating environmental situation in the world was like a long sad song played on a violin."

"Did Steve take up playing the violin again?"

"No. After I brought it to him in the hospital and he played it a couple times, he put it aside and finally told me to take it home. For some reason the stroke left him with the memory that his performance of melancholy Hungarian music was nothing but a series of horrible scratchings." Jan laughed. "Now he claims this was one positive result of his stroke, giving him an objective ear and making him wonder why he had fooled himself all those years."

"Didn't he used to be nicknamed Gypsy?" asked Lydia.

"Yes, but I've never mentioned it to him."

"How come?"

"I don't know. I guess it's one of those things I hope he'll mention on his own."

"Does he still put on a sour face when he says the wrong word?" asked Lydia.

"Sometimes, but I think he realizes he's on the right track even if an inappropriate word comes out now and then. Like the speech therapist says, the idea is to stimulate memory, not to relearn speech."

"You said you were doing rehab. How do you work with him?"

"We go through old magazines together. 'To stimulate the old egg noggin,' as he put it the other day. He says when I bring in magazines it's a lot like bringing in old friends he's forgotten. I'm not sure if he says that for my benefit, but it's what he says. I bring in *Time*, *Atlantic*, *Newsweek*. We go over each one together. When one of the therapists found out, she suggested he make a chronological chart. So now he fills out his chart while we go through the magazines. It's a huge fold-out thing for the last ten years. It's already filled in with tons of notes. Sometimes I quiz him on the notes in the chart.

"You should see the back seat of my car. It's filled with old magazines. I get them at the library. The librarian knew Steve because he did a lot of research there. I used to go with him. We spent a lot of time in the library. It was one of our favorite places. Anyway, one day when I was taking out a few magazines from the shelves, the librarian took me down to the basement and told me I could take all the magazines I wanted because the articles were on the info system and they were going to recycle the paper. Steve was always fond of the library. When I took him out in the parking lot for a walk one time so he could see how full the back seat of my car was, we joked that if I was ever afraid I'd get lost I could throw magazines out the window and leave a trail behind. That was pretty ironic, I guess, because Steve's the one who's lost.

"The reason I use magazines from the last ten years is because those were the ones available in the basement stacks. At least that's what I try to tell myself. How coincidental that Steve and I have been together ten years. But there are things from further back that he finds out for himself while in rehab, or while watching television. For example, when he found out about Jimmy Carter, he seemed really sad. For some reason he identified with Carter's defeat by Reagan. Something about Carter's name being repeated over and over by another patient in rehab. One day, when I got to the facility, I found Steve looking out the window. When I went to the window I saw he was watching a car being hooked up and towed in the parking lot. He had tears in his eyes and he was saying, over and over, 'Poor Jimmy Carter. Poor Jimmy Carter.'

"So here I am back to my original dilemma. Do I try to fill in only the past ten years because these were what I consider the good years? Or do I go back more than ten years to the good old days when Jan Kowalski was a stripper, or when she got boozed up so she could stomach giving massages to bug-eyed hairballs with hard-ons?"

Ilonka Szabo stood at the side of their table. "I hope everything is all right. And I hope Steve will be back soon. Don't feel bad if you do not finish. I understand." Then Ilonka turned to the next table.

"Ilonka has dark eyes like Steve," said Jan. "She reminds me a little of Steve's speech rehab partner. Marjorie's older and Italian, not Hungarian, but there's something about her. Maybe the fact that she's so straightforward. Last time I saw her, Marjorie said some very special things about Steve. It was hard for her to get it out—her speech problems are worse than Steve's—but I understood. She told me that in rehab when she gets upset, Steve holds her and keeps repeating over and over, 'It's okay. You'll be okay.'

"Sometimes Marjorie kids me, saying if she were only younger. And one time she said she trusts Steve more than her family. I guess that's understandable because her husband was in the mob. What other family members she's talking about I'm not sure. Anyway, according to Marjorie, Steve's a real babe. I guess Steve must have heard about Jimmy Carter when he was with her because she told me once she always liked Jimmy Carter, and that Steve has a smile like Carter."

"I remember when you and Steve first met," said Lydia. "When you told me the name I figured we better stop right there. Was it your idea or Steve's to get those vanity plates on your car?"

"My idea."

"Guys still eyeball you on the expressway?"

"Sometimes."

"No, Jan, it's all the time. Remember, I drove here behind you. Had to use my cell phone to call tows for all the rubbernecks' cars that went into the ditch."

Instead of commenting on this, Jan pulled at both sides of her mouth, making a child's scary face.

"You need a weekend away," said Lydia. "I'm taking Friday off to do just that and I think you should join me Thursday night and get the hell out of here for a while."

"Maybe you're right," said Jan. "This afternoon Steve mentioned spring and said I should do more than simply take a night off for dinner. When I asked him what I should do, he said I should go for bike rides. Ten years ago when we met I rode almost every day. I rode to my first husband's business only to find that it was burning and he was inside. And now there's been a fire in Steve's head. He's mentioned the word *case* a lot lately. I think he misses the challenge, but since he can't recall the cases he worked on over the years it bugs the hell out of him.

"The first time I met Steve was when he got on my case. We had a clandestine meeting at O'Hare Airport. Steve was back in town after laying low for a while because of some mob guys from Miami. He sat in the terminal holding up a crumpled newspaper. The word I was supposed to look for was circled in a small headline at the fold of the paper. The word was *Gypsy*.

"We talked about the fire that killed my husband and a friend of Steve's named Sam Pike. Mostly I remember Steve walking away after our meeting that day. I remember it vividly because it symbolizes his stroke. He walked with his shoulders forward as if anticipating an attack from behind, as if his brain knew what was coming ten years down the road. I'll always remember the swagger and momentary hesitation of his cop walk as he disappeared into the crowd. And I'll always remember what he wore. Blue suit, and that tie, that horrible wide green and red tie that looked like a Christmas neck scarf, or a Gypsy scarf.

"Not long ago, when we were alone for a few minutes, I told Marjorie about my first meeting with Steve. When I finished, she kissed my forehead, then she cried like a baby."

Lydia held up her glass. "To all the babes in the woods."

Jan held up her glass, clinked Lydia's glass, and they drank.

CHAPTER FIVE

Tyrone Washington checked his watch, hoping Flat Nose was doing the same. Last fall Flat Nose forgot to turn back his watch for the end of daylight savings time and showed up an hour early and scared the shit out of a resident by putting his ugly face against the small glass window in the door from the loading dock. Ever since then, Tyrone feared Flat Nose would get the time wrong and screw everything up. He checked his watch again and cursed the system, both because it deserved to be cheated, and because it allowed itself to be cheated.

Tyrone was disgusted with the system and knew he had lots of company, especially white folks who seemed to be the main strain around this place. Some said it was a thing called demographics, but he knew it was no such thing. He knew the reason there were more white folks in this place than black was because white folks lived longer. And the longer white folks lived, the more they'd complain about the system while making sure there were plenty of ass wipes like him handy to wipe up after their white asses.

Tyrone knew damn well all the shit started in Washington and was handed down. A congressman farts at the podium and the next thing you know there's another new rule and another new form to fill out. They cut down trees in the boondocks to make paper while turning a river into something that burns, then they ship the paper to Chicago where printing presses three stories tall spit out ten-part forms, then they ship the forms here to Hell in the Woods to be filled out, then, even though they put the data on computers, they ship the forms to Washington so the farting congressman will have a bundle of them before next election to hold up and shake in the air while he complains about government waste like he's the first to discover it.

Tyrone checked his watch again, then stretched his long arms into the air and almost touched the ceiling. Maybe his daddy had been a basketball player. That's what the doc at the retard school said in so many words back when he was a kid with such big hands he could hold onto the basketball with one hand when he was only twelve, even though he couldn't play worth a damn. He overheard the doc saying to another doc, who'd stopped by for a shot of morphine, that his daddy and ma were probably cousins. But the doc said *first* cousins and he knew damn well that wasn't true. Second or third maybe, but not first. Maybe the doc let him overhear on purpose because all it took was to hear that doc saying his daddy and ma were cousins and the next thing he knew he was out of retard school, graduating from high school and getting his first job down at Cook County Hospital where he learned the health care ropes.

Yeah, learned real fast that the health care system was a thing put there to make sure most of the money funneled on up to the docs, and to the drug company executives, and to the supply company executives. Everybody with fists full of forms to make sure all the money was correctly earmarked so the docs and company executives wouldn't stop buying second homes, because in Washington the fart at the podium didn't want to see housing start figures take a nosedive.

After hustling laundry at Cook County Hospital for a couple years, Tyrone moved on to the VA Hospital on the west side where it seemed half the patients suffered from one thing or another having to do with smoking cigarettes since they were PFCs with Betty Grable pinups thumb-tacked to their bunks. His job there was to deliver clean spit-up cups and take away used spitted-up cups. Even though most of the guys at the VA were white, the stuff in those cups made it seem like they were slowly turning black on the inside. One theory he developed while working at the VA was that just before white people die they turn black inside and finally feel how it is to be black, but they also realize it's too late for this realization to do any good and they die hollering and screaming to the Almighty to let them live even if they have to suffer like black folks. He heard plenty of hollering and screaming at the VA and sometimes wondered if part of the purpose of the system was to turn everyone who didn't own at least two condos into niggers.

A while back, when he told Latoya about his theory, she was duly impressed. They'd just done a couple rounds on her living room floor, being that her roommate was out, and while they got dressed she told him just how impressed she was.

"There best be no bruises on me from those big old hands of yours. You hear what I'm sayin'? There any bruises back here? What about there?"

"No, babe, there ain't no bruises. Anyhow, who'd see 'em on you?"

"You sayin' I'm too black for you? That what you sayin'?"

"No, babe, I ain't sayin' that."

At this point he told Latoya it didn't really matter how black a person was, or even how white for that matter, because in the end we all end up turning black inside. He told about the dying VA hospital guys and about his theory that everyone eventually turns into a nigger in the end and finally learns about suffering when it's too late to do anything about it.

"So, what you think, babe?"

"I still think I'm bruised. You're no gang-banger no more, so I figure you got nobody else to beat up on 'cept poor defenseless me."

"I wasn't no gang-banger. I was only a shorty for a while until they sent me to retard school. Ain't that somethin'? Old Uncle Ezra—God rest his soul—convinces Ma to send me to retard school. And the retard school saves me from a life of crime and violence. But come on now, what about what I said about everyone turnin' nigger in the end?"

"Don't you start hintin' about no end games, Tyrone Washington."

"Latoya, I'm serious. You took philosophy at Kennedy-King, so you should know how serious I am. You ain't simply a body, after all. You got a mind, and I got a mind, and I'm not playin' mind games. It's called conversation is what it's fuckin' called."

"All right, honey. I didn't mean it. Maybe you're right. Maybe you've got something. I guess it's kind of like the ashes-to-ashes Bible thing put another way. Seriously? I like it."

After Latoya stood on her toes and laid him a good one on the lips, she said, "But I also like the fact you ain't been down at Johnny-O's wasting your hard-earned money on jail bait."

Yeah, Latoya was a smart chick, and a beautiful chick, especially when she was half-dressed and stood on her tiptoes to plant a kiss on him. Of course, the chicks down at Johnny-O's were somethin' else again, but nowhere near as refined as his Latoya.

Tyrone checked his watch again. When he reached the far end of a hallway, he heard a guy behind in one of the rooms moaning in pain and once more thought about his stint at the VA hospital with the last of the WW-2 vets who lived decades in the past, dreaming of girls back home while they picked up more free cartons of Luckies at the PX. One old fart vet said that during a month-long layover with no assignment, he and a bunch of other guys lay in their bunks all day long sucking unfiltered Luckies and blowing smoke at photos of Betty Grable, eventually turning her skin from the light gray of the black and white photos to the dark golden brown of nicotine and tar. Of course there were younger vets at the VA. Guys from Korea and Vietnam and even a few from the Middle East. But the ones who impressed him most were the WW-2 vets who'd managed to take advantage of the system all those years.

After the VA, Tyrone jumped around from one hospital to another, looking for a place he fit in. Some hospitals were better than others, but in hospitals there were always too many nurses and residents running around. It was like having a hundred bosses. Couldn't even park whatever cart he was pushing and duck into a men's room for a smoke because he quit smoking after his stint at the VA, and after Uncle Ezra died of lung cancer.

Finally, after ten years in the health care system, Tyrone saw the light. What Medicare and Medicaid could do for old folks, it could do for him. After working at Saint Mel's main hospital for a couple months, an ad went up on the employee board saying there were openings for orderlies and aides on the west side at Saint Mel in the Woods Rehabilitation Facility, which everyone called Hell in the Woods. A friend of his named Flat Nose who worked at Hell in the Woods told him it was the opportunity of a lifetime.

Of course now that Tyrone was here, Flat Nose no longer worked here. But he did see Flat Nose quite often. In fact he'd be seeing Flat Nose tonight. Even though Flat Nose was in a new business, he did not try to lure Tyrone away from Hell in the Woods. The reason for not trying to lure Tyrone away was because Flat Nose needed him right where he was.

Tyrone checked his watch. Twenty-eight minutes to go. The reason he checked his watch so often was because timing was important. If he got there too early he'd have to stand around and someone might come wandering down the hall and ask what he's doing there. If he got there too late, one of the late night kitchen workers might make a trip out to a dumpster and see Flat Nose hanging around by the loading dock and ask him what he's doing there.

Yeah, timing was important. He'd get to the hallway outside the nursing home wing activity room on the first floor at the exact time Flat Nose parked in that spot at the loading dock hidden from the kitchen entrance by the dumpster enclosure. He'd disconnect the wire on the door alarm while Flat Nose crept up the side of the loading dock. He'd get through the alarmed door, down the short hall paralleling the kitchen, and open the loading dock door just in time to let Flat Nose in. Then they'd come back into the main hallway and duck into the janitors' closet to make their business transaction. Tonight it was a couple cases of rubber gloves and a couple boxes of individually wrapped Demerols. He'd hidden the stuff at the back of the closet earlier in the day.

Tonight he'd get a couple hundred and Flat Nose would get rubber gloves and Demerols. Of course nothing was that simple. Just like with Medicare and Medicaid there had to be someone on top. In this case the guy on top had a fitting name because the guy on top was named after the Lord.

DeJesus was his name. Christ Health Care Supplies was his game. According to Flat Nose, DeJesus justified his business, which involved selling stolen goods back to various health care facilities in the city, because he, too, was a victim of the country's health care system.

According to Flat Nose, DeJesus' mother—the mother of Christ—would be a nursing home resident if it were not for her son's ability to provide the best in private home care. According to Flat Nose, DeJesus figured Medicare and Medicaid were probably paying about the same for his mother's private health care at home as it would have had to pay if DeJesus had spent down her money and dumped her into Hell in the Woods. So, in a way, it all came out even. The health care system at work. And not only that, Christ Health Care Supplies served nursing homes and rehab centers all over the city without regard to race, religion, or ethnic origin. A bed pad from this place that had been destined to hold the piss of a rich white bitch living in a non-Medicaid private room might end up holding the piss of a wino at Cook County where Tyrone used to work, and vice versa.

Eighteen minutes to go. Time to start heading for the service elevator. By now the old folks on the first floor not dead to the world would be glued to their TVs watching a *Murder She Wrote* rerun. And even if Tyrone did come across a resident in the nursing home wing, she'd be easy to fool since most of them had strokes or Alzheimer's anyhow, especially anyone out wandering around. Just like that lady earlier tonight, out wandering around when she should be in her room minding her own business.

Of course maybe it was unfair to call them all rich white bitches on the first floor. After all, there were some blacks and browns and yellows and even a few men who weren't vets and who'd managed to outlive their life expectancy. Actually Tyrone felt sorry for the folks in the nursing home wing because it seemed all they had to do all the time besides eat and sleep and piss and watch TV was think about death.

Tomorrow or the next day he'd probably get the job of moving the dead lady's stuff out of her room. Whenever he got a job like that he'd see the averted eyes. Sometimes while moving stuff for a resident who had not died but was simply being transferred to skilled or assisted or independent, he felt like hanging a sign on the cart announcing that the person was not dead but simply moving. Maybe then residents and visitors—especially visitors—would smile at him and return his greeting instead of checking out the detail of the floor tile until his cart passed.

No, Tyrone didn't hate the folks in the nursing home wing. The system he hated, but not them. He wasn't like that idiot white dude named Bobby who exchanged morphine and Demerol for look-alikes. He recalled the turmoil in the nursing home wing when Bobby was doing his thing. Talk about screaming and moaning. Sometimes Bobby would even stop in residents' rooms and threaten them if they went on too much about the pain. It got so bad, and Tyrone felt so sorry for the folks, he threatened to have one of the nurses order a couple blood tests and blow Bobby's deal if he didn't stop. Then, when Bobby finally did stop, he wanted into the medical equipment scam. But luckily, Bobby was caught roughing up a patient during a transfer and was fired, one of those quiet-like firings where they sweep it under the rug and hope the old fart who got roughed up won't be able to complain.

Of course sweeping things under the rug is just one of them figures of speech because there aren't any rugs in the nursing home wing on account of the possibility of "accidents."

There were only twelve minutes to go when Tyrone got off the service elevator on the first floor. He'd kill the rest of the time down here. Take a walk over to the skilled wing where nurses and aides bustled amongst the zombies, then into the visitors' lounge at the front of the building where by now the TV would be talking to empty chairs, then he'd head into the nursing home wing where it was bound to be quiet, and finally he'd arrive way off down at the end of the wing with its inactive activity room and its kitchen occupied by the skeleton night cleanup crew and its loading dock where by now the Christ Health Care Supplies van was most likely backing into the spot hidden behind the dumpster enclosure.

In the long run what he was doing was probably a good thing because it helped keep costs high enough so that when the blow-hard congress finally did some cutting, they wouldn't take so damn much away from these poor folks who depended so heavily on the system.

CHAPTER SIX

THE CHICAGO WEATHER FORECASTER USED A PLAY ON WORDS A stroker might use. "This March storm will march in from the coast, leaving snow in the mountains. However, three days from now the storm's march will stall over northern Illinois, resulting in an extensive rain pattern with winds from the southeast and . . ."

"Lordy," said Betty, the night LPN, as she turned down the volume. "In a couple days every jet out of O'Hare will be buzzin' this place. You guys better get a good night sleep while you can 'cause we're in for it now."

As two men in wheelchairs made their way slowly out of the television lounge, Betty continued. "Guess the weather was perfect when they picked the spot to build this place. But that'll all change this weekend. You guys sleep good now, especially you, Mr. Babe."

Even though no residents remained in the television lounge and the two men in wheelchairs were well down the hallway, Betty kept talking while she restacked magazines left askew on an end table. "I hope it was all right to turn down the volume. I'll leave it on in case anyone decides to come back for the Late Show."

As a commercial for Dodge trucks played soundlessly, Betty continued stacking magazines, and talking. "That guy from the first floor isn't even here tonight. Probably sleeping while he can. Yeah, everybody sleeping like babies just the way they should."

When she finished stacking magazines, Betty sat back in one of the chairs, gave off a sigh, and stared at the large screen television. A commercial for Depends had come on and she smiled at this, shaking her head as she stood up and left the television lounge.

Now it was quiet in the third floor television lounge. So quiet, the music that had just started playing in one of the resident's rooms could be heard down the hallway. It was melancholy music consisting of a solo violin wailing sadly in a minor key.

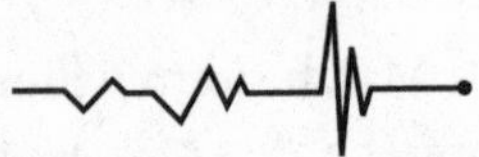

Sometimes, since his stroke, Steve would catch himself feeling an odd attachment to a man in the past. At first he assumed it was his father. Although he did not remember his father, he'd been told his father died when he was a young man. He'd also been told his father had dark brown eyes like his eyes and that the fixation might be his attempt to recapture his own past. Perhaps, in his search for a connection to the past, his mind had played tricks on him. Perhaps that was the reason for being obsessed with an odd array of males like the mysterious man with dark eyes and Dwayne Matusak and Sergeant Joe Friday and Jimmy Carter, and even Sandor Lakatos, the Hungarian violinist. Perhaps his obsession with Lakatos was not a connection with the recent past, but with a distant past, his stroke having cleared the slate sufficiently so eventually he would be condemned to wander farther and farther back in time, farther and farther away from the world to which he belonged.

Initially, Lakatos played alone, his violin weeping. But then the *czardas* began, the rest of the orchestra joining in until the finely tuned melody of earlier turned to chaos.

When the Lakatos tape ended and the cassette player turned itself off, Steve lay in bed staring at the ceiling. He thought of this final piece on the Lakatos tape as a metaphor for his stroke. First would be the single violin, minding its own business. Then would come the speeding up, many violins and clarinets and the cimbalom joining in. Finally the melody would change into the rapid whirl of the *czardas* finale. Within the whirl of music he imagined a weak blood vessel failing. He imagined that single blood vessel as a broken violin string, and he imagined the initial solo a wailing dirge made by violin strings for their brother whom they knew would eventually explode within his cranium. Even though he knew he had an ischemic stroke and not a hemorrhagic stroke, he still visualized blood vessels bursting in his brain.

Although the nightlight in the room was mounted low on the wall between closet door and bathroom door, and although it was aimed at the floor, the shine of the tile floor reflected upward. Some nights the nightlight was out, the high wattage bulbs apparently overheating because of the metal enclosure. When he first arrived at Hell in the Woods, he complained about nights without the nightlight while maintenance took their sweet time getting around to replacing the bulb. Once he even got out his pocket thesaurus and tried to come up with words to suggest to the maintenance man that it might be better if they used twenty-five watt bulbs instead of the hundred-watters he could see on the guy's cart. That was back when he could barely speak and had to use the thesaurus to come up with words. Now that he was off the thesaurus and probably could manage to get out his suggestion, he didn't give a damn. Just like he didn't give a damn about the stupidity of building a rehab center ten miles from one of the world's busiest airports.

The new guy who repeated, "H-A-W-K, Hawk! H-A-W-K, Hawk!" over and over wheeled past. When the guy was finally out of hearing, he heard Phil across the hall say "Jesus fuck," in a low voice.

When Steve turned on his side away from the glare of the night-light, he realized he hadn't taken off his leg brace for the night and hadn't put on his hand splint and almost muttered, "Fuckhead," the way he might have done a couple months back. Stroke victims often resorted to swearing when they became frustrated. His version of this had been to call himself, "Fuckhead." But that was back in the hospital, before he came here and began conversing like a somewhat normal fuckhead thanks in part to Georgiana, who everyone called George despite the fact that she was quite a cute gal.

As he lay in bed he couldn't help thinking about Marjorie Gianetti and her conspiracy theories and the circumstances surrounding her death. That damn puddle on the floor outside the activity room, the overlooked blood specks on the doorjamb near the spot where gurney tracks led toward the door to the loading dock. Why had Marjorie broken her routine and gone down to the activity room without her wheelchair to hold onto? What about the rumor that Marjorie slipped in a puddle made by a resident, when in reality it was only water on the floor? If someone on staff spilled water, wouldn't they have simply wiped it up? Maybe that was it. A staff member spills water, fails to clean it up, starts a rumor about a resident "accident."

A couple weeks earlier at rehab, Marjorie had gotten hung up on the phrase "fly in the ointment," and right now that phrase seemed apt. Of course Marjorie often got hung up on things. When he first met her, she'd said, "Make me whole," over and over. He thought she was referring to her brain, like making her brain whole again. But an aide named Pete who sat in on a rehab session in Georgiana's rehab room one day said it was something Marjorie's husband might have said, being that her husband was in organized crime. "Make me whole is like, pay me in full in the mob world," explained Pete.

Getting hung up had been Marjorie's biggest hurdle when it came to getting out what was on her mind. When she wasn't saying her Buster Brown in a shoe jingle, or a meaningless litany in which she rattled off roads she probably read in a road atlas, she'd repeat phrases over and over. Georgiana would ask her name and Marjorie would say, "Fly in the ointment." The next day she'd answer the same question with another cliché like, "Cat got your tongue?" The next day she'd say, "Keys to the kingdom," or, "It's a wonderful life," or phrases he'd never heard of like, "Max the fly." Other times she'd say, "Poor Jimmy Carter," over and over while in tears.

After a few days of this, Georgiana tried to get into Marjorie's head and apparently discovered the origin of one of the phrases. Using notes and books around the rehab room, Georgiana got Marjorie to concur that "Max the Fly" had been the title of a children's book she'd read to her son. But when Georgiana tried to find out what "Fly in the ointment" meant, Marjorie went off on another tangent, repeating the phrase "black sheep" over and over until she was so upset she broke down in tears and started repeating Jimmy Carter's name again.

Of course who wouldn't be upset in this place? Especially when you can't make yourself understood. Like now. A woman dies and nobody seems to give a damn about the cause. Maybe it has to do with age. The older you get, the less likely folks want to know why you're sick, or why you died. Even if it was an accident, someone should at least be collecting information for a report. Or is the doctor's statement on the death certificate all it takes when someone's in a nursing home?

Maybe having some of Marjorie's husband's old cronies crash out of their nursing homes for one last hit wouldn't be such a bad idea.

The circumstances seemed juvenile, piss on the floor and kids arguing. *He did it! No, I didn't! She did it!* Finally, when he could stand it no longer, Steve reached out to pull his wheelchair close to the bed, put on his robe, and began the struggle to transfer himself on board. Although he could use a walker, and even a cane on his better days, he still got around much faster in his wheelchair.

The hallway lights had been dimmed for the night. Across the hall were the stroboscopic flashes of Phil's television, Phil probably asleep with headphones on. Steve leaned forward in his wheelchair to peek around the opening of his door. The nurse at the station held a clipboard while sorting packets of medication into trays. The appearance of her there, holding a clipboard, combined with the word *station*, triggered a memory of a train station, the nurse becoming a station master, a telephone ringing in another room becoming the sound of a locomotive bell, the flash of Phil's television becoming the flash of crossing signals. In this memory a man bends to shake his hand. For a moment the rooms along his side of the hall become private rooms in passenger cars. But then the phone stopped ringing and the moment was gone.

The nurse was facing in his direction, so he leaned back into his room and waited. After a minute he leaned forward again, and, seeing she had turned the other way, pushed forward, gave the left wheel of his chair a powerful crank to turn himself, and sped down the hallway toward the elevators. Any moment he expected to hear his name called, or perhaps the nurse would simply raise a .357 Magnum she kept behind the counter and let him have it. But neither happened and soon he was in the elevator alcove.

He stayed back from the elevators for a while watching from a grouping of visitor chairs near the windows. A late visitor snuck out from another wing and took an elevator down. Two nurses' aides got off an elevator and went into his wing without seeing him. He noticed a stack of magazines on a table between two chairs. He wheeled over to the table and gave the pile a shove so the titles and dates of the magazines showed. They were old magazines, but not too old, and he realized these were magazines Jan had brought in during the past several weeks, magazines they had gone through in detail. Events described in the magazines had been annotated in the ten-year chart he and Jan were constructing in his room. As he touched the slick surfaces of the magazines he had a horrible feeling that he and Jan were inside the magazines, their past stuck between the slick pages like pressed flowers, their blood staining the paper.

He had to stop thinking like this. Better to keep his part of the bargain. Be cheerful. Tell a joke. Smile. As he stared at the elevators, he wondered if he'd be able to get past the lobby's main desk without being stopped. He managed it earlier that evening, but this time of night there wouldn't be people in and out of elevators to give cover. He was on a mission. Not until he got a good look at that hallway down on the first floor one more time would he be able to sleep.

As he tried to recall the detail of the hallway, he remembered the floor plan he had looked at. It had been mounted to the wall near the door that led to the loading dock. And on the way down there earlier in the evening, he'd seen another floor plan on the first floor near the elevators. Escape plans. How to get out of the building in case of fire.

He wheeled past the elevators toward another wing and sure enough, on the wall next to the stairwell door was a floor plan for the third floor. After studying the plan a few seconds he found what he needed. He spun his chair around, gave the left wheel a shove while throwing his body to the left to keep the chair from going in circles, and went to a short hall next to the last elevator. At the end of the short hall was a door that said Staff Only. He turned his chair sideways to get a grip on the door handle, pushed it down and turned again to push through. On the other side of the door was another short hall, and in the middle of this hall were the wide double doors to the service elevator that would let him off on the first floor out of direct line of sight of the lobby's main desk.

The service elevator was not as fancy as the passenger elevators and the walls were beat up. He went from three to one without stopping, and when the doors slid open he faced a blank wall just like he had on the third floor before the doors closed.

After wheeling out of the elevator, he noticed the first floor hall was longer, with an alarmed emergency exit at the far end. At the near end of the hall was a door to one side he knew would lead to the lobby. Above the door a closed-circuit television camera pointed at him.

He wheeled as fast as he could to the door beneath the camera. Here he could see that the camera had a view of the elevator, the long hallway, and the alarmed emergency exit at the far end. He could only hope the guards at the main desk had not been studying the idiot in the wheelchair with disheveled hair and a crazed grin on his face, because if they had, they'd be standing outside the door waiting for him.

Pulling a door open was a lot harder than pushing through one, and this door was not designed for the wheelchair-bound like the doors in the resident wings. Because his right hand was pretty useless, he had to hook the fingers of his left hand onto the door handle and pull the door open by slowly backing the wheelchair using his left foot. It took a while because every time he managed to pull the door open an inch or two, the door would bump his left foot and he'd have to back up another inch or two.

When he finally got the door open enough so he could wedge the corner of the wheelchair into the opening, he shoved the door aside, expecting to see a couple of smiling security guards. But the guards had remained at their desk. When he peeked around the corner, he could see the tops of their heads above the reception counter. And so, for the second time that night, he turned from the lobby and hurried down the long hallway and through the automatic double doors that led to the nursing home wing.

The hallway in the nursing home wing was lit up as brightly as it had been earlier in the evening. He saw no one at the nurses' station, which was still a good hundred feet down the hall. As he wheeled down the hall he heard snores from doorways. One snore sounded like the distant bark of a dog and this reminded him of Marjorie telling him about dog days and cat days in the wing. One day a week they brought in dogs for residents to fondle, another day they brought in cats. Marjorie had said, "Everybody dogs them, but I don't know about cats," and, after a little back and forth between them with Georgiana egg-nogging them on, he figured out what Marjorie meant. Everybody in the wing liked dogs, but not everybody in the wing liked cats. After Marjorie nodded that this was exactly what she'd meant to say, Georgiana asked Marjorie why some people didn't care for cats. To this, Marjorie had replied, "Sneaky," with a smirk on her face. He recalled it vividly. It was the same smirk she got on her face when she spoke of her conspiracy theories regarding staff members, and even once when she mentioned a nephew of hers, a nephew whom she seemed to be contrasting with her son.

Although he'd never been inside Marjorie's room, she'd pointed it out to him when they were on their way to the activity room for a stroke rehab meeting. Earlier that evening he had not paused at the room, now he did. In rehab, Marjorie once managed to convey that in the nursing home wing they remove the nameplate as soon as someone dies, but they do it surreptitiously.

Thinking of the word *surreptitious* reminded him of the word *detective* and that reminded him of the Chicago Police Department and that reminded him of Tamara who had visited him here and while he was in the hospital.

Crazy bastard. A wife who loves him so much she tells him about an ex-lover, and here he is sneaking around where he obviously can't do any good. Probably end up telling Jan all about his wanderings and maybe even send Tamara an e-mail about it.

Maybe keeping quiet about a resident's death was the right thing to do. Maybe he should go back to his room. According to Marjorie, residents near death were usually transported to the hospital, and the other residents found out the person had died by taking turns hanging around the hallway until someone spied a nurse or aide removing the nameplate. Then they'd pass the word. According to Marjorie, one resident recently died in her sleep. "Him name's gone and she's still in there," Marjorie had said. "Him name's gone and she's still in there," she had repeated, even after Georgiana tried to correct the pronoun.

The word *case* came to mind again, conjuring up something. Not memories, but a feeling, a sense of what has to be done, a sense that things have to be examined, a sense that within him there is a passion to perform this examination. It wasn't so much in his mind. It was in his soul. Perhaps he was Don Quixote. For some reason this idea of him being a Hispanic idealist intrigued him. Yes, a man destined to right wrongs.

He turned on the light in Marjorie's room only after closing the door behind him. The bed was made, a pink spread pulled up over the pillow. He began searching the room before he knew what he was looking for. Her wheelchair was there, backed against the window wall. On the deep windowsill were several framed photographs. The largest photograph was of an older man with a thick nose and bald head. The man wore a dark suit and held an award up before him. "Vietnam Veterans" was printed on the award. The man seemed on the verge of winking and Steve recalled Marjorie mimicking this look when she spoke of her husband Antonio.

Another photograph was of the man—Antonio—and Marjorie together. A studio shot taken decades earlier, Antonio with more hair in this photograph, the faces smooth and flawless as if taken through gauze. Next to this photograph in the foldout frame was another old photo, this one of Marjorie holding a baby while Antonio touches the baby's forehead with his thick finger. The last set of photographs were of Marjorie's son. He could tell it was her son because of the chronological collage.

A toddler in shorts who'd gotten more of his looks from his mother than his father. A little boy with a puppy. An adolescent boy playing the piano. A handsome high school boy holding a National Honor Society ribbon. A fine young man in cap and gown. A young man in shirtsleeves stooped on the ground planting a tree. No photos of him playing baseball or football. No photos of him with his father except the one in which his father touches his forehead with a thick finger while . . . yes, while in the process of either beginning or ending a wink. The father wanting his son to emulate him, but the rest of the photographs implying the son did not do this.

Something Marjorie once said about father and son. Something about the good old days before the son realized who his father was. But also something else, an aside, an indication—"Antonio never able know,"—that at least some good came of her husband's death, that she was glad her husband had died before finding out something. Something.

In the closet Steve recognized many of the dresses Marjorie had worn to rehab. Whereas most nursing home residents wore sweats, Marjorie insisted on dresses. If she was so formal, what made her go down to the hallway outside the activity room in her nightclothes? Along with the rumor that she'd fallen because of someone's "accident," he'd heard she was in nightclothes.

There were several pairs of shoes, but no slippers. He searched the entire closet, inside dresser drawers, and even crawled down from his wheelchair to search beneath the bed, but could find no slippers. They were furry and pink. He'd never seen them but could visualize them because Marjorie had said in rehab that she never wore her furry pink slippers outside her room because they were too informal and too slippery to be trusted in a waxed tile hallway once you let go of the handrail. "Like crossing ice on butter feet," she'd said.

A good metaphor, according to Georgiana. Buttered feet on ice. It had been a happy session, all three of them laughing it up that day. And then something turned off Marjorie's laughter. A word. A single word had turned off Marjorie's laughter like turning off a faucet.

He looked to the photographs on the windowsill. The son. Something about the son not known by the father. A word that had turned off Marjorie's laughter. A word Georgiana had used to describe a happy son-of-a-bitch stroke victim. *Gay.*

Back in the hallway. Rolling silently toward the nurses' station where a nurse faced the other direction staring at a computer screen. Non-glare screen, he hoped. Not like in a movie directed by a fat man who said, "Good evening," in a deep voice before his television show, a movie in which the hero, trying to sneak along a balcony, is seen by the housekeeper in the reflection on the screen.

A nurses' aide arrived—subtle difference in uniform color—and both nurse and aide stared at the computer screen. He rolled closer and lowered his head. The counter at the nurses' station was about four feet high and he rolled to it sveltely like a clever gunman in an old western hiding behind a convenient boulder. The entrance to the station was on the far side and as long as neither nurse nor aide crossed over to this side he'd be safe. They spoke.

"Bill thinks he's being overmedicated again."

"Did you show him the chart?"

"He ignores it. Says the same thing that got Marjorie'll get him."

"And what is that?"

"Says she was overmedicated and didn't know what she was doing. Says she probably slipped in her own pee."

"I doubt it. Marjorie was too straitlaced. Most likely she was walking in her sleep."

"What about the puddle?"

"Someone else from earlier, after last activities. Lasix kicked in too far from the john and nobody noticed to clean it up."

"Beverly's up late telling her joke to the wall again."

"Which joke is it tonight? She has several."

"The one about bananas."

"Haven't heard it."

"She says, 'I might be old, but physically I'm doing just fine. Of course I don't keep green bananas on my windowsill anymore.'"

"Oh yeah, I did hear it."

"You just wanted to hear me repeat it like an idiot."

"Right."

He held his left hand over his mouth. The laugh, from deep down inside, threatened to encircle his neck and choke him. *I don't keep green bananas on my windowsill anymore.* He held his breath, took his hand from his mouth, pushed his chair along the counter. He had to take a chance, get the hell out of there and find a place where he could laugh, where he could breathe.

As he pushed off down the hallway toward the far end of the wing he could only hope the two at the station would not see him. He heard them laughing at something else behind him and this made the pressure to laugh even greater, like that time shortly after he arrived at Hell in the Woods when he stopped in at a chapel service and laughed out loud when Marjorie winked toward him after the priest asked God's forgiveness for everyone's sins.

He pushed the chair faster, jerking his body to the side to keep the chair from turning each time he gave it a shove with his good hand. When the chair almost spun around on him he glanced back and saw that the two in the station had their heads down, apparently studying something one of them held. Finally, where the hall turned toward the activity room and he was no longer in line-of-sight with the station, he let out the stale air of the laugh and took a deep breath. Green bananas. Very funny.

And so, here he was again at the scene of the crime. The phrase "scene of the crime" like yet another joke, making him laugh. Crazy bastard. A woman dies and he laughs like an idiot.

But maybe there was more to it. Maybe when he came closer to being who he'd once been, to doing what he'd once done, his brain got confused in its elation. *The Laughing Detective.* Damn. Jan said there's a story with that title. But the detective he always identified with never laughed. The detective he identified with was Sergeant Joe Friday.

The theme music pounding, *Dum-da-dum-dum* as Joe's badge is magnified to monstrous size on the black and white screen. The television screen on the old Motorola in his parents' living room. Lights off so he can see out the front window in case Dwayne Matusak is there waiting beneath the streetlight.

The puddle still unmopped didn't surprise him. It was around the corner at the end of a hallway where no one important would spot it. Night staff would just as soon wait for the early morning cleaning crew to take care of it with their howling machines meant to wake the dead. Soon the puddle would be gone, along with any other traces. Too bad he didn't have a tape recorder from second floor rehab so he could record his findings. He laughed at this, imagining the unintelligible babble being played back and causing Georgiana to crease her forehead.

The puddle still had what he assumed were dried gurney tracks leading away, but now there were newer tracks that hadn't been there before. When he realized these were the tracks of his own wheelchair catching the edge of the puddle as Betty-who-talks-too-much pushed him away not an hour earlier, he laughed at himself again.

He wheeled around the puddle to the ladies' room, knocking lightly before he entered. The sink was clear, nothing moveable in sight. He wheeled to the men's room and found the same was true there. But in the janitors' closet, after he found the light switch and scanned the closet filled with cleaning equipment and stacked with cardboard boxes, he discovered something interesting. Even if it turned out to be nothing, even if Marjorie's death was an accident, having this bit of potential evidence in his possession would at least make him feel he'd done what he could, that he'd covered all the bases the way Joe Friday would have done.

The water glass sat on a ledge at the back of a deep laundry-tub sink. He knew from the puddle around the glass, and the fact there was a bit of water in the bottom of the glass, that it had been used within the last several hours. He had to push the wheelchair close to the laundry tub in order to reach the glass. He carefully lifted the glass with his good hand, holding it along the top edge, careful not to touch any other part of it. It was one of the water glasses used for residents at meals. Not one of the plastic cups used in resident rooms, real glass, crystal clear, except this one was greasy as if it hadn't made it to the dishwasher in the kitchen since its last use. He eased back into his chair, placing the glass safely between his legs. He thought of tucking it beneath his robe, but he didn't want to wipe anything off the glass. Joe and his partner would have been proud, the partner saying something about delivering the glass to the lab boys.

In a way, all of this was like floating in space. Like one of those moments in life when you say to yourself, "What am I doing here?" One of those moments you could never have predicted even if you had a billion monkey brains working for you. The stroke was one thing, distancing him from reality the way it did, making him question whether Steve Babe had ever existed. But this—inside a janitors' closet where there was a perfectly good mop and bucket on wheels to clean up the puddle outside and still no one had bothered to do it, and him with a water glass held close as if it contained secrets to unraveling what was left in his noggin—this was insane. Any minute they'd bring the strait jacket, and when he mumbled his protests, saying he simply wanted to get the glass in case it had fingerprints on it the way Joe Friday and his partner would, they'd laugh like hell and he'd laugh with them.

He turned his wheelchair toward the open door and shut off the light. When he did this he again recalled the dark living room when he was a boy looking out the window and seeing Dwayne Matusak across the street leaning against the lamppost, daring him to come out. He sat for a moment, trembling with fear dredged up from childhood by his stroke, as he stared out at the harsh lighting in the hallway, at the world outside where everything was clear to everyone else. Perhaps it was the sound of footsteps echoing down the hallway that had triggered the memory of Dwayne Matusak.

A summer in Cleveland long ago. Although he had not recognized his mother and sister when they visited, he recalled the summer in Cleveland, an entire summer consumed with fear of Dwayne Matusak. Visualizing himself as a boy peeking through a partially-open door before he dare go outside made him weepy. His mother visits, weeps and kisses him repeatedly, he finds out his thirty-year-old sister is retarded, and instead of weeping with them and for them, he weeps because of Dwayne Matusak. He weeps because Dwayne Matusak says he hates JFK and all Catholics and because he is Catholic, an adolescent Catholic going to Confession almost every Saturday because he is now old enough to be tormented by impure thoughts, old enough to lust after women the way poor Jimmy Carter once admitted he lusted after women.

Of course it was not Dwayne Matusak walking down the hallway. How could it be? But there was another name. Someone coming to save him where he lay on a lawn near a multistory building. Someone coming in a car, driving a car with a door flying off its hinges as the car skids to a stop. Gunshots. Gunshots!

He did not close the door to the closet all the way, but left an opening of an inch. He leaned forward in his chair and pressed his face to the opening.

The footsteps belonged to one of the male aides dressed in gray slacks and shirt, the wiry black guy not quite tall enough to have played college basketball, but still tall. He'd seen the guy once, maybe twice a day, usually in the late afternoon in his room after therapy and just before the lineup at the dining room for dinner. The guy would come into the room, replace water cup and water pitcher, check tissue and toilet paper supply.

And in rehab. He'd seen the guy in rehab on the second floor, one of many aides the therapists trooped through every day for a week trying to get them to remember their names. After the guy came through, saying good afternoon to everyone and waving his way out, they were asked to come up with something to help them remember his name. What was it Marjorie had said? Something about the guy looking like he was drunk that day. Yes, drunk. But how would Marjorie have said he was drunk? Not directly, because Marjorie never said anything directly. She'd said, "Tied on," and after going back and forth with Georgiana and the other therapist sitting in on the session, they figured out that what Marjorie had meant to say was that the guy looked like he had just tied one on. Tied-one-on. Tie-on. Tie-one. Ty-one. Tyrone.

Although he was thin, Tyrone had the beefy arms and big hands of a kid who might have gone a few rounds. Tyrone's skin was quite dark like kids from deep inside the ghetto when Steve was a kid in Cleveland.

Tyrone checked his watch as he came down the hallway. He stopped and glanced toward the door to the closet. Steve stayed perfectly still, holding the door steadily, being careful not to move it. After a moment, Tyrone continued ahead, veering off to the left instead of heading toward the closet.

Steve slowly opened the door another inch and saw Tyrone standing on his toes in front of the door that led to the loading dock, the door through which they'd wheeled Marjorie. Tyrone had his arms above his head and was using a screwdriver on a small metal box mounted above the door. Judging by the armored cable leading from the box to the ceiling, the box contained the switching mechanism for the door alarm designed to signal the nurses' station or the main desk or both should someone open the door.

After a few seconds Tyrone had the cover off and looked around to be certain he hadn't been seen before putting the cover down on the floor. Then he was at the innards of the device, and Steve could see even from this distance that Tyrone had loosened a wire before replacing the box cover without screwing it into place. After this, Tyrone alternately stared out the small window on the door and checked his watch.

The inside of the janitors' closet seemed hotter than before. Steve could smell the stale buckets and mops, the sharp odors of cleaning fluids. The glass he'd taken from the laundry tub was still in his lap. Now that he could see Tyrone expected a visitor, Steve felt better about his speculations regarding Marjorie's death. After a few minutes, Tyrone opened the loading dock door to let in his visitor. While the door was open, the sounds of blower motors and kitchen equipment echoed in the hallway.

The visitor was much shorter than Tyrone, Hispanic. He wore a White Sox baseball cap with the beak facing forward. The beak of the baseball cap emphasized the flatness of the guy's face. Whereas Tyrone's nose looked as though he might have gone a few rounds as a kid, this guy looked like he'd been used for a punching bag.

Tyrone and the flat-faced man glanced down the hallway that led to the main building, then came into the short hallway. They stood outside the door to the janitors' closet and Steve moved his face back from the door but left it open.

"Watch out for the puddle, man."

"Puddle? What's with maintenance around here? Maybe I'll fuckin' report you guys downtown."

"Wake the hell up, Flat Nose. We're not downtown out here."

"Hey, well, you're still part of Saint Mel's."

"Just don't step in it, you dumb spic."

"Last guy called me that got his nose made like mine, only he didn't know it 'cause he be dead."

Silence for a moment as if there were some truth to the threat.

"Okay, just don't step in it, you dumb fuck."

"That's better."

"Come on, you got my stuff?"

"Yeah, I got your stuff if'n you got my stuff."

"It's in there."

"How many boxes?"

"Only four. We can do it in one trip."

"Here you go, man. You know Jesus loves you for this."

"Yeah, I know. Let's go."

When the door pushed open, Steve backed as far into the corner of the closet behind the door as he could. One wheel stopped against something and the chair turned abruptly. He heard things sliding down the wall and before he could stop it, an avalanche of brooms and mops banged against buckets and onto the floor.

"What the hell you doin' in here?" Tyrone held his arm out toward the door as if to try to stop the guy named Flat Nose from coming in.

But it was too late and Tyrone's hand was held out too high and Flat Nose bobbed and weaved beneath Tyrone's arm and pushed his face close to Steve's face. "Yeah, motha-fuck! What you doin'?"

Tyrone shoved Flat Nose back against the wall and turned on him. "Don't use that language around here, man! We got residents here need all the help they can get and you talk like that?"

"Why's he hidin' in here?"

Tyrone turned toward Steve. "He's not hidin'. You're not hidin', are you? Naw, he's just wandered off from his room and done got himself lost down here in the bowels of this place. Ain't that right, pal? He's like the white old lady on the commercial who's fallen and can't get up, only he's lost and can't find his way out of a closet."

"What's that in his lap?" asked Flat Nose, ducking and weaving in closer, an angry look on his face. "It's a glass. He's got a glass. What you suppose he's got a glass for?"

Tyrone placed a hand on Flat Nose's shoulder. "Calm down, man. He probably wanted a drink of water and got lost tryin' to find the sink in his bathroom. Except I seen you before, man. You're from up on the third floor and got no business down here. You oughta know that. I mean, sure, you're a resident and all, but that don't mean you have the run of the place. Residents especially don't have the run of the place because it could be dangerous. Now you just give me that glass so I can put it away and we'll take you on back to the third floor where you belong. My friend and I were just trying to decide who would get the bucket and mop to clean up after one of your fellow residents, and here you are in here."

Tyrone had been smiling, and seemed quite calm, but Flat Nose was not smiling, and when Tyrone turned and stared for a moment at the angry face of his cohort, he turned back in a different mood. His teeth were clenched, his eyes wide, and before Steve could react, Tyrone reached into Steve's lap, snatched the glass away, and flung it into the sink where it shattered, pieces hitting the walls in the close room and scattering amongst buckets and mops and boxes.

Tyrone shouted into Steve's face. "Don't you realize you scared the shit out of us? How'd you like it if next time I come into your room I sneak up on you like you snuck up on us?"

"Dumb fuck!" said Flat Nose, taking an aggressive stance.

It was insane. From what he overheard he'd obviously caught them in a scam, and now they were acting like schoolyard bullies, their faces contorted as if the uglier they looked the more scared he'd be. It was crazy. Earlier he really had been scared when he recalled that summer Dwayne Matusak had it in for him, but now he wasn't scared at all.

He tried to act scared, but was apparently not doing a very good job of it because both men seemed even angrier, especially Tyrone who obviously wanted to prove to this guy named Flat Nose just how angry he could be. Shit, he was probably smiling a really sarcastic smile, a smile with all the earmarks of someone who would turn them in. He wanted to say something simple to ease the situation, like he was sorry. But the word *earmarks* got overrun by the cauliflower ears the guy named Flat Nose had and instead of apologizing like any normal person so he could make everybody relax, he laughed in their faces.

"Fuckin'-A!" said Flat Nose, grabbing Steve's collar. "I'll use you for a crazy bag!"

"You're a dumb fuck!" said Tyrone, grabbing Steve's right wrist and twisting.

It was a spontaneous reaction. His left hand was his only good hand and before he knew what he was doing he made a fist and punched Flat Nose in the face.

Brooms and mops and buckets bounced off the walls as Flat Nose fell and then slipped trying to get up. Tyrone twisted Steve's left wrist harder and at the same time tried to hold Flat Nose back with his other hand. Flat Nose slipped again on broom and mop handles, fell flat out, sending the brooms and mops and buckets into further disarray. When the buckets and brooms and mops finally stopped flying, Flat Nose sat looking up, a kind of sneer on his face, a look that triggered a reaction in Steve. He'd seen guys look like this before, the calm before the storm, a momentary quiet before the guy shows the true extent of his anger.

"Don't anybody move!" shouted Tyrone, as he seemed to expand to three times his size in the confined closet.

"Flat Nose! Stay down for the count! This ain't the time for it and this ain't what it seems! He's got a brain like a baby!" Then to him, Tyrone shouted, "And you! Mother-fuckin' brain-like-a-baby resident, you go back to your mother-fuckin' room and never do anything like this again! You forget you were ever here or I swear to God I'll kill you!"

Tyrone put his face right up to Steve's face and spoke in a harsh whisper. "And I won't do it like this, twistin' your arm. You're under our control in this place. You know it and I know it. If you say anything to anybody about us bein' here tonight, I'll find out. Then, when you least expect it, some bad food might accidentally come your way, or someone might sneak into your room one night, or maybe there'll be a freak accident when you're sittin' on the crapper. But all of those unfortunate eventualities can be avoided if you simply keep your fuckin' mouth shut! You understand?"

At this point Steve decided not to take any chances because he wasn't sure what would come out if he tried to say yes. So he nodded his head and did his best not to smile. Not smiling was not easy, especially because Tyrone had eased off on his arm and because Flat Nose was back, adding his ugly face to Tyrone's. Even though they really did look like they'd just as soon kill him as spit, the pair of old guys on Smith Brothers Cough Drops came to mind. But Steve managed a serious look by thinking of other threats from the past, threats he'd been told had been made against Jan. He imagined these two roughing up Jan and nodded and nodded and, finally, Tyrone let go of his wrist and the two of them backed off and de-uglied their faces.

For a while longer Tyrone whispered soothing things to Flat Nose about people with strokes and how most of what they said didn't make sense and how no one paid any attention to them anyhow. Then, although he kept glancing back toward Steve with that sneer of potential vengeance on his face, Flat Nose stayed behind straightening the brooms and mops and buckets in the closet as Tyrone pushed Steve out into the hallway. Then Tyrone came around the front of the wheelchair, giving Steve a serious look as he put the foot supports into place.

"Remember, man," he said in a low voice. "Not a word or you won't have to worry no more about your stroke 'cause that motherfucker back there, he's like on a leash, and if that leash breaks . . ."

Steve nodded again, trying his best to put on an equally serious face.

Back down the long hallway, as Tyrone pushed Steve past the nurses' station on the way out of the nursing home wing, he said in a singsong voice, "Look who I found wandering all the way down here from the third floor, ladies. I think they just might have to put an ankle alarm on this one."

From a nearby doorway Steve saw So-long Sue peek out and squint into the brightly lit hall. But there was another Sue. And now the name Sue flew in from somewhere in the past and he panicked. *My God! Someone's killed Sue! Someone's killed Sue!*

Then the overly bright lights in the nursing home wing went even brighter and Steve felt the muscles in his body give a heave and before he blacked-out he saw his legs shoot out in front of him and was aware of sliding down and out of the wheelchair and saw the pretty face of one of the nurses hovering over him and thought to himself, Sue sure is pretty. She sure is. She sure . . . Seizure.

CHAPTER SEVEN

Although the doctor insisted Steve's seizure was minor, Jan couldn't help worrying that when he came around this time, he wouldn't recognize her. Perhaps he would smile at her and hold her hand, and even say her name, but would he really know her? Or would he, as he did when his mother and sister visited from Cleveland, fake it?

It was quiet on the third floor because most residents had gone to second floor rehab. A while ago two newly arrived stroke patients named Linda and Frank had come by to wish Steve luck, then left when they saw he was asleep. Both were right-brain stroke victims with something in common. Instead of having difficulty coming up with the right word, they talked incessantly about nothing at all. Now that they were gone, Jan could not remember what they had said.

Steve's rehab had been canceled for the day so he could rest. Earlier in her vigil a nurse had tried to cheer Jan by joking that stroke victims in this place had seizures to avoid rehab. Jan sat in the chair beside Steve's bed staring alternately at his face and at the three-ring binder on his nightstand that contained the goals diary she'd been keeping for him.

Yesterday afternoon she had been here with more magazines from the back seat of her car, and Steve had made more entries in the ten-year chart. The chart was stored in the closet, leaned into a corner behind hanging clothing. As she glanced toward the closet door, Jan wondered if the notes Steve had made on the rolled-up chart were beginning to fade.

Steve continued sleeping soundly as Jan moved close. She stared at this man who had come into her life a decade earlier at a time when her marriage to a man she hardly knew ended in tragedy. And now she recalled vividly the night she realized she loved him.

She had been kidnapped. She had been riding her ten-speed, and the van had blocked the exit of the bike path from the woods. The men wore rubber masks and dragged her into the van. The men blindfolded her, gagged her, and tied her outstretched in the back of the van. She was to drop the investigation of the fire that destroyed her husband's adult book and video store, the fire that killed her husband and a detective named Sam Pike who turned out to be a friend of Steve's. They said her husband's business was evil and he was an evil man who deserved to die. They kept her in the van that afternoon and into the evening, fondling her as they spoke of God and justice and death.

As she stared down at Steve she could feel the warmth from his face. He was a beautiful man. Of course she'd never told him this. Handsome, yes, but she'd never told him he was beautiful.

His cheeks were rosy, his hair bushy and disheveled like the hair on a stuffed bear. His skin looked perpetually tanned, perhaps because of Gypsy blood from centuries earlier. She reached out and touched his nose. Even though he'd always said it was too large, she liked it. She studied his face. He had a few more lines and his hair had gone more toward gray, but he didn't look much different than he had the night she realized she loved him.

The men in the van had let her go, careful not to leave marks on her. They tied her loosely with her own shoelaces, blindfolded her with a spare inner tube from her bike bag, and left her on a dark road. It was obvious they had tied her loosely so she would escape. It was obvious they left nothing behind that would point to them. Because of lack of evidence and the nature of the business her husband was in, it was obvious the police did not believe her story.

But Steve believed her story. He stayed with her after the police were gone. He questioned her in detail, but also cheered her up by telling stories about himself. One of those stories was of a bomb that had been thrown through the window of his one-man detective agency office.

Despite what had happened to her that afternoon, when Steve animated the circumstances of the explosion in his office, she found herself laughing. He went into detail about how he was sleeping at his desk and how he'd gotten hit by glass through the cutout in the back of his cheap office chair. He told about the ordeal at the hospital during which an emergency room resident picked glass from his buttocks while several nurses and a Catholic priest who happened to be passing by looked on. Then he told about how he once studied for the priesthood.

"My mother's greatest dream was that one day I'd give her Communion."

"And your father?"

"He died after the first tuition payment."

"Are you kidding?"

"No. He died of a heart attack shortly after we received the first bill from the seminary. Of course everyone says it had nothing to do with the tuition. But I've always wondered."

"What brought you to Chicago?"

"A girl."

"Did she jilt you?"

"Sue was killed in a robbery attempt at the drugstore where she worked. We'd been engaged a few months. Obviously I'd abandoned the priesthood by then. I came to Chicago to get away. But the thought that someone could simply walk into a drugstore and shoot a clerk worked on me. I met Sam Pike after I got to Chicago. He was going to the police academy and one day I joined him. After we'd been on the force together for over ten years, Sam Pike went private, then lured me into it, painting a rosy picture of freedom and big bucks.

"Sam Pike saved my life while we were in the force. We were in the projects tracking down armed robbery suspects when shooters opened up from the third floor while a uniformed cop and me were on the lawn on our way in. The uniformed cop was killed. I was saved when Sam rammed the car through the chain-link fence and took hits in the shoulder and arm saving me. I'll never forget how mad Sam was in the hospital when he found out the captain was upset about the damage to the car. Besides the damage caused by the fence and the bullets, Sam had opened the passenger door for me and busted it clean off the hinges while slamming on the brakes to pick me up."

"You're a strange guy," she had said. "First you try to cheer me up, then you depress the hell out of me."

"I want to make sure you still want to go through with the investigation. Telling you about my past is my way of saying nothing is certain and no one can guarantee success."

"I want to go through with it. I'm tired of being pushed around."

Steve had stood and held out his hand. "I wanted to be sure."

When he shook her hand that night ten years earlier he held it longer than necessary, smiling and looking sad at the same time. Even though she had known him only one day, she knew then that she loved him and wanted to spend the rest of her life with him.

An aide came into the room and she sat up straight. A bed table had been brought in because the doctor said Steve would probably take his breakfast in bed, and the aide replaced the water glass and pitcher. The aide paused, glancing down at Steve then smiling at her. He was a tall black man she'd seen before. As he paused she noticed his large hand almost wrapped completely around the water pitcher.

"He'll be all right, ma'am. Don't you worry about a thing. I've seen this before. Sometimes when they come out of it they don't make much sense. It's like they been dreamin' and they're still in the dream. But eventually they come out of it and go back to therapy and everything's fine."

When the aide turned to leave, she said, "Thank you," and watched as he paused to smile back at her before disappearing into the hall.

When she turned back to Steve, his eyes were open. She bent close and kissed him.

"Shave," he said.

This simple word made her want to hug him and weep, but she controlled herself. "Yes, you do need a shave."

"He gone?"

"Who?"

He motioned with his head toward the door.

"That aide?"

He nodded, pulled his good hand from beneath the cover and held his finger to his lips. "Later. Tell me aide later." Then he held her hand, closed his eyes, and rested.

By that afternoon, with lunch in him, Steve seemed physically recovered from the seizure. While he took a prescribed walk in the hallway, Jan stood at the nurses' station talking to the LPN on duty about Marjorie Gianetti and the circumstances surrounding her death. The reason Jan did this was because after lunch Steve kept repeating Marjorie's name along with the phrase, "Fly in the ointment," and the phrase, "Investigate now." When he said these things, he held Jan's hand the way he always did when they spoke seriously.

After Steve's stroke, Jan had discovered that, along with shakes of his head, she could tell a lot about his reactions to questions, or exactly how he felt about something, by holding his good hand. The world of words had become a secondary world for Steve, with time needed to interpret what he was trying to say. The subtle squeezes and movements of his hand filled in the blanks, especially at a time like this when he was excited. Coming out of the sleep following the seizure had left him more excited than she'd seen him in a long time. She wanted Steve to concentrate on physical recovery as suggested by the head physical therapist, but Steve wanted desperately to communicate something and was having a hell of a time doing it. And, significantly, he was not smiling the way he usually did.

Jan tried to convince Steve they already had a very important mystery to solve, and that it would be better to let the system handle Marjorie's death. But he was persistent, squeezing her hand harder than usual. Perhaps because of his agitation, the words came out in a jumble. And when she alluded again to them having a more important mystery to solve, he squeezed her hand very hard and shouted at her.

"What goddamn mystery?"

And she shouted back.

"You, Steve! Remember? We were trying to find out who the hell you were! Or have you given up on that?"

The result of this outburst, one of the rare ones they'd had, was a long embrace, a bunch of sobs, looking into one another's eyes for a while, and an unspoken agreement to resume their patience and resolution in trying to communicate around the roadblock set up by the stroke.

And so, as Steve did a slow march up and down the hallway regaining his strength by using his walker, as prescribed by the head physical therapist, Jan spoke on his behalf. Jan knew the reason he kept up the pace in his walker instead of joining in was because he might interrupt with an inappropriate word or phrase and keep the questions from being answered as they were asked. But he did manage to hear part of the conversation, nodding toward them each time he passed while Jan questioned the LPN about Marjorie Gianetti's death.

She was told the night LPN named Betty had found Steve down on the first floor staring at the puddle that had caused Marjorie to slip and fall. Jan knew something about Marjorie's death was bothering Steve. But more importantly, she knew he wanted her to find out everything she could about the circumstances of the death. She smiled and nodded to Steve when he passed to let him know she understood the assignment and would do the best she could.

According to the LPN—a thick-bodied woman who wore no makeup and, whenever Jan dealt with her, seemed all-business—Marjorie's death had been an unfortunate accident that resulted from the fact there weren't enough staff to watch each and every nursing wing resident when a thought from out of the blue hits them and they go off on a tangent.

Apparently, Marjorie had walked out of her room and down the hall to the end of the nursing home wing near the kitchen and activity room in the evening when all of the staff were helping other nursing home residents get ready for bed. Apparently, she slipped and fell when she rounded a corner and stepped into a puddle that had been made by another resident earlier in the day, the puddle not having been discovered so it could be cleaned up. Apparently, Marjorie had not been her usual self because she normally dressed whenever she left her room and always took her wheelchair. Even if she wanted to walk she took her wheelchair and walked behind it. Because of these circumstances, the staff concluded that Marjorie might have had a dream combined with an ischemic spell or even a mini-stroke.

"I sometimes work in the nursing wing to fill in for summer vacations," said the LPN, "and I've seen how stroke can affect the elderly. I've seen people who I didn't think could get around without assistance jump up and start running. It's like when you hear about someone lifting a car to save another's life. I've still got the remains of a bruise here on my arm where one of them squeezed me. I'm sure they don't do these things on purpose, but it does happen. In a way, that's why I'm happier on this floor. Younger people who've had strokes seem to have better control of themselves."

Steve passed when the LPN said this and she smiled toward him, but Steve did not smile.

"What kind of injury did Mrs. Gianetti sustain?" asked Jan.

"They say she hit her head quite hard and apparently had a hemorrhage. She died in the ambulance on the way to the hospital. The paramedics left in a hurry and cleaned up where she bled, but I guess because nobody else was around down there that time of night, and because someone was always at the nurses' station to make sure nobody else went down there, the puddle was still there when your husband decided to investigate. For all I know the puddle stayed there for the morning cleaning crew. I don't hold it against your husband that he went down there. I know he was a detective and it's common for stroke victims to act out things they used to do."

"Did someone initiate an actual investigation?" asked Jan.

"I don't think so," said the LPN. "We have to file a special report if the patient dies here, but she died in the ambulance in transit, so it's up to the hospital to take care of the death certificate, if that's what you mean."

"No, that's not what I meant. I guess what bothers me, and what seems to be bothering my husband, is that there are some loose ends here."

The LPN opened her eyes wide. "Loose ends?"

"Yes," said Jan. "For example, if the paramedics took time to wipe up the blood, as you said, wouldn't that indicate they weren't in a big hurry to leave and that maybe she was already dead?"

The LPN shook her head. "I don't know. Maybe there wasn't any blood, or maybe someone on staff wiped up the blood after the ambulance left."

"But if someone other than paramedics wiped up the blood, why wouldn't they take time to mop up the puddle?"

Steve slowed his walk as he passed the counter, giving Jan a smile and a nod when she turned to him, apparently pleased with what he heard. It was a turning point, the first smile since his seizure. Then he continued his walk at a faster pace, the rubber feet on the walker beginning to squeak on the tile floor.

The LPN made a smirky half smile. "Well, perhaps you'd have to know something about health care procedure to answer that. Perhaps it had something to do with paramedics always being more careful around blood because of the obvious risk of exposure. Perhaps part of their procedure is to remove any blood from the scene of an accident."

"What if it wasn't an accident? I'm sure when paramedics treat someone who's been shot they leave the blood there for evidence. Who exactly would have the authority to determine if something like this really was an accident? I know there wasn't a weapon, but things happen and if I were related to Mrs. Gianetti I'd want to know *exactly* what happened. That's all I'm saying."

Jan tried an engaging smile, but it was obvious by the LPN's face that she felt threatened.

"That's what I get for trying to be nice," said the LPN, looking down and shuffling papers behind the counter. "If you want to talk to someone about this any more, you'll have to contact the business office."

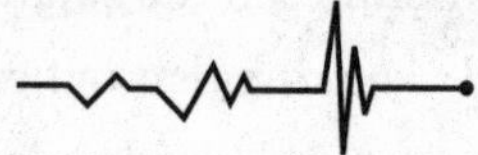

Later that afternoon, Jan and Steve sat in their usual alcove in the third floor television lounge with windows facing the parking lot and woods. It was early, most of the others in the wing still down in rehab. Steve had brought the chart from his room on which they sometimes transferred information gleaned from whichever handful of magazines Jan brought in from the back seat of her car that day. But they did not unroll the chart on the coffee table or open any of the magazines yet, because it was obvious Steve wanted to know about Jan's trip to the business office. She had promised to go to the main business office, which was downtown at the main hospital, then fill him in if he promised to take an afternoon nap like the doctor suggested.

Steve sat to her right on the sofa that faced the windows and held her right hand with his left hand. He sat forward and watched her face as she spoke.

"It was the typical bureaucratic nightmare. I had to tell my tale to four people before someone finally sent me to the legal office, and then the legal guy made an appointment for the two of us to go talk to the head hospital administrator. Basically, they said that in a hospital, or in one of its branch facilities, it was reasonable for staff to assume the malady that brought the patient there might be considered the cause of death when the circumstances fit. They said many patients, and especially stroke victims, act differently than they normally act because of physical or emotional stress. They said it would be impossible to launch an investigation every time someone died in a hospital and would only take away resources from others. They also said they could not stop nursing home residents from walking off unassisted if that's what they wanted and that falls were more common in the nursing home wing for that reason.

"When I asked under what circumstances they would launch an investigation, they said, for example, if Marjorie had fallen and anything that could'd have been used for a weapon had been found, then they would have investigated. They said the only thing that was found near the body was her walker, and they did not consider that a weapon."

Steve squeezed her hand. "Walker?"

"Yes. They said they found her walker nearby. I asked if it had been upright or lying down and they said they didn't know but they could ask the staff member who found her."

Steve squeezed again. "Fast walker?"

"Right, I thought of that. From what the LPN said earlier, it sounded like Marjorie was doing the hundred-yard-dash down the hall and I wondered how fast she could be going and how hard she could have fallen if she was using a walker."

"Find out?"

"I did. When I brought it up, the administrator had someone call the nurses' aide who found Marjorie. She was on duty and they had her drive over to the hospital while they made a big deal about treating me to coffee. The girl who found Marjorie was scared, probably her first job, and I felt sorry for her. But we all went ahead and questioned her and determined the walker had been found some distance from where Marjorie fell. She said the walker was at the corner where the hallway turns, and it looked like Marjorie might have left it there and went off down the short hall without it. She said she called for help right away and tried to revive Marjorie until help came. She said she had a pulse, but that it was weak. Then, when the paramedics arrived and took over, she said she didn't know what else to do and took the walker back to the nurses' station so no one would come around the corner and trip over it.

"She seemed to be telling the truth, Steve. If there's anything fishy about this, I don't think she had anything to do with it. She just found Marjorie and determined she wasn't dead and called for help."

Steve smiled and squeezed her hand twice. Two squeezes was his positive signal. Sometimes it meant yes, sometimes thanks, or sometimes it meant he was glad she was there.

Steve had brought his water cup from his room and he picked it up and handed it to her. There was no water in it and she knew he hadn't had a drink from it so she asked him about it.

"Yes, I see it's empty. You thirsty? You want me to fill it?"

"No."

"So it has something to do with what you want to tell me?"

"Yes, Marjorie."

"This cup has something to do with Marjorie's accident?"

He stared at her for a moment and she could see the look of mild frustration he always got when he wanted to say something but could not. She put the cup down on the end table on her side of the sofa and held his hand. "Go ahead, I'll try to figure it out."

With a look of concentration on his face, he squeezed her hand and stared past her at the cup on the table. Finally he said, "Cups in the water. No, water in cups. The place . . . very good if you know what it is."

When she did not answer, he let go of her hand, reached across her to pick up the cup, grunted as he pulled himself up into the walker that stood before him, and made his way to the window. Then he pretended to drink from the cup and tapped on the window glass with his fingertip.

"Had one, but broke," he said.

"You had a cup. No, you had a glass, but it broke?"

He nodded, then came back to the sofa and sat down. He handed the cup back to her and held her hand again. "Downstairs. Me. The broken thing. Water. Floor."

"You mean the urine that Marjorie slipped in?"

Steve shook his head, spoke slowly and deliberately. "Water. I know. Tried it."

When she did not respond, he displayed one of his overly exasperated looks. "Listen. One word at time."

"Okay," she said. "One word at a time like you do in rehab."

"Good."

After a pause he began, spacing the words, sometimes by several seconds. "Water. Floor. Not pee. Glass. Sink. Shit."

"Take your time. I won't interrupt."

"Okay. Glass. No . . . sink, then glass, then water, then floor, then me, then . . . yes, then fingerprints . . . then crash."

"You mean the puddle on the floor wasn't urine? You mean it was water?"

Steve nodded and gave the come-ahead signal like playing charades.

Jan went through several iterations of this until she got it right.

"Okay, one more time. The puddle on the floor was water, so it had to come from somewhere. There was a sink nearby and you found a glass with some water in it. You were going to bring the glass back and get someone to fingerprint it, but the glass broke."

Steve hugged her and laughed.

Jan knew better than to ask qualifying questions like, how did he know it wasn't urine, because that would simply throw him off track and they'd have to start over. Instead, she repeated the scenario about the water and the sink and the broken glass and simply led Steve on, trying to get him to add information, bit by bit, piece by piece, the way they did when she visited and tried to get him to recall a magazine article they had gone over on a previous visit.

After an hour or so of letting Steve go on with his single word concepts, and Jan filling in the gaps to make sentences, this is what she had: When he heard Marjorie had been found dead, Steve remembered things she recently said to him in rehab. One day, while they were watching *Wheel of Fortune* and playing along, Marjorie said her family had big money, enough to keep her there forever, but for whatever reason, this upset Marjorie and she said something to the effect that a bunch of keys would be needed sometime in the future. Another thing that upset Marjorie was that she suspected staff members of stealing equipment, and maybe even drugs. Another thing that upset her was her claim that her son was different from other boys. This didn't bother her so much, but she knew it would have bothered her dead husband, and that bothered her. Although she never came out and said it, Steve figured her son must be gay. Marjorie had often spoken of the fact that her husband had been a mobster, but never in detail, and not in a serious vein, not until recently. Another thing Steve got across to Jan was Marjorie saying in rehab that her husband loved Ronald Reagan and hated Jimmy Carter, and that something had been said before the election, something about waiting until the votes are in. All of this on its own didn't seem to mean much, but taken together, and having a gut feeling about Marjorie's accident the way Steve did, he'd decided to investigate and now felt he'd proven, if only to himself, that perhaps Marjorie's fall was not an accident. Things had happened in the past that upset her and he had a feeling these things had something to do with her death.

Jan had written this all down, and Steve, reading it, smiled with pride. But then he frowned.

"A fly in the ointment," he said.

"Right," she said. "It sounds like there could be one or two."

"Something else . . . other things."

"There are other things that are fishy, but you can't remember them right now?"

Steve nodded. "No . . . funeral." He pointed to Jan then to himself. "Us? Her funeral?"

"Right," she said. "I'll find out about it and we can go."

Steve smiled. Then he said, "Last time . . . seizure . . . thought stroke. This time I know . . . just seizure."

They hugged and went back to his room where they closed the door and kissed. After the kiss, while Jan straightened her hair, Steve managed to push the chair from beside the bed to the door and prop the backrest beneath the door handle. Then he leered at her, trying to make it look as obscene as he could.

She went to him and put her arm around his waist to help him walk back to bed. "Do you think we should so soon after a seizure?"

"What the hell," he said, holding the back of her head with his good hand as they walked slowly toward the bed. "What the hell."

"What the hell has become our own private shorthand. It stands for all the clichés. Life is short, we're not getting any younger, and if we don't do it now we might kick ourselves later."

Steve held her with his left arm and swung his right arm around behind her. She could feel his right hand caress her buttocks weakly.

"Physical therapy," he said. "Physical therapy."

CHAPTER EIGHT

FOR A CHANGE OF SCENERY, VALDEZ TOOK OLD ROUTE 41 ACROSS to Naples instead of the Everglades Parkway. When he left Miami, after the morning call from Skinner, the sun had been in his face, forcing him to lower his visor and squint ahead into the haze of the horizon. He'd used eye drops before he left Miami, and because of the air conditioner in his face during the drive, used them again when he parked in the shade of the visitor breezeway at the side of Hanley's palm-lined drive. Although it was not quite noon, the heat felt like a flame-thrower when he stepped out of his car. Yes, like he was a young man again in simpler times before all this global warming and terrorist crap. A young man new to the agency sent out to use flame-throwers on a cannabis crop planted out on the Keys by a bunch of Cuban immigrants.

He recalled that back then—decades before cell phones and the Internet—he had told his friends Skinner and Christensen about the flame-throwers during one of their regularly scheduled evening contacts on whatever amateur radio band was open at the time. They had probably used the forty or eighty meter band because he recalled heavy static during their conversation. Skinner and Christensen joking that they could hear the crackling of the fire. Anyone new to Miami's agency office in those days was sent out on these ATF and FBI-style assignments in order to maintain the office's clandestine stature. All those years working out of the same office. All those years piled up so he and his wife could some day retire in comfort. All those years working and waiting, and then cancer comes along.

During the short walk in the overwhelming heat to Hanley's front door, Valdez felt as if the years trudging behind him were about to overtake him.

Hanley answered the door. "You're just in time for lunch."

"I'm too old for this," said Valdez, stepping through a wall of cool air.

"Too old for lunch?" asked Hanley.

"Not that. I mean the heat, and the drive."

"But this time you won't have to drive home in the dark," said Hanley.

Valdez followed Hanley through the cool house to the breakfast room that overlooked the lanai and the pool on the north side of the house. The table was set for two with a frosty pitcher of iced tea in the center. Valdez was glad to see they would not be having lunch out in the heat. Maria, Hanley's Cuban housekeeper, brought salads from the kitchen.

"Good morning, Mr. Valdez. How was your drive?"

"Good morning, Maria. Except for the sun, the drive was fine. I'd forgotten the reason I used to come for dinner. Now I'll have to drive back into the setting sun."

"Clouds are predicted this afternoon," said Hanley. "So perhaps you'll be spared the sun in your face . . . Thank you, Maria. Give us a few minutes to finish our salads."

Hanley and Valdez waited until Maria went back into the kitchen and closed the door behind her before they began speaking.

Hanley got right down to business. "Please tell me what's new with Mr. Babe."

"We checked again," said Valdez. "He definitely had a stroke. At first we thought he might have been a plant to find out what Mrs. Gianetti knows. But now we don't have to worry about Mrs. Gianetti."

"What do you mean?" asked Hanley.

"She's dead."

Hanley poured glasses of iced tea and they began eating their salads, glancing out toward the view of the coast to the north through the lanai windows. The sun shining down through the haze made the coast disappear several estates up from Hanley's estate. Valdez thought this was appropriate, climate change and pollution erasing the Naples estates in the distance, estates most likely owned by executives of some of the biggest polluters.

Hanley finished chewing a mouthful and put his fork down. "What's the game?"

"Game?" asked Valdez.

"The details," said Hanley. "We're both old enough as it is. You know how I despise dragging out the fact-gathering."

Valdez put down his fork. "Sorry, I wasn't sure if you knew."

"You're my source," said Hanley. "That's also part of getting older, and being retired."

"Mrs. Gianetti slipped and fell at the facility. It's been reported as an accident, but we're checking into it. Apparently, so is Babe. Or at least his wife is. She's questioned the staff about the old lady's death."

"Is there any indication that Mrs. Gianetti's extended family might have been involved?"

"We checked the bugs on Chicago mob phones," said Valdez. "No chatter there."

"How can you be sure?" asked Hanley.

"I thought you knew," said Valdez. "We've had access to the frequencies and codes for their cells phones for quite some time. The Chicago mob isn't as sophisticated as it used to be. Low level hoods let things out for a price."

"Any indication she might have revealed something before she died?" asked Hanley.

"That's always a possibility," said Valdez. "She might have said something to visitors, to someone on the staff, or even to Babe, since the two of them attended rehab together. As I said last time, our man has been watching and listening, but he can't be around all the time."

"I thought you were going to get a backup," said Hanley.

"I have assigned a backup," said Valdez, smiling as he leaned back in his chair to reach into a side pocket. He pulled out several folded sheets of paper and handed them across the table to Hanley. "She's new from Langley, but sharp. She was able to get hold of a notebook kept by the detective's wife, Mrs. Babe. She made a copy of the contents and got the notebook back to Mrs. Babe without her knowledge."

Hanley took a pair of reading glasses from his shirt pocket and put them on. After studying the sheets of paper for several seconds, he stared at Valdez above the reading glasses. "Your office has had more time to study this than me. What do you think it means?"

"Apparently the detective thinks Marjorie Gianetti might have been murdered."

"Do you think there's anything to it?"

"Could be," said Valdez. "There are a few entries referring to some kind of Gianetti family secret. And I assume that being who her husband was . . ."

"Yes," said Hanley, studying the sheets again. "If I were you I'd be especially interested in the nephew . . . Lamberti. He's the type who could make trouble."

"What kind of trouble could he make?" asked Valdez.

Hanley put aside the sheets of paper, put his reading glasses away, and resumed eating his salad, chewing two mouthfuls before continuing. "Lamberti's a typical hood. His father was tied in with the Teamsters, probably helped rip off the unions and maybe even get rid of Hoffa. This Lamberti is the same. He'll go after the money and I'm concerned that in doing so he'll dig up more than he should. On the inside they call him Max the Fly."

"Why do they call him that?"

"Because like his father he has a tendency to buzz around looking for ways to make money off old mob ventures."

Valdez also resumed eating and finished a mouthful before commenting. "I still don't understand why our predecessors left Gianetti senior with all that money."

"It's too late to try to understand the actions of our predecessors," said Hanley.

Valdez smiled. "I'm old, and I'm curious. The original plan, what was it for?"

Hanley smiled. "It goes way back."

"Illinois politics or national?"

"National," said Hanley. "Heads could roll if it ever got out."

Valdez glanced toward the view of the hazy coast. "Does it have anything to do with the fix we're all in now?"

"What fix is that?" asked Hanley.

"All this global warming crap. All these so-called weather-related incidents."

Hanley took a sip of iced tea before answering. "In a way. But then, in our world everything affects everything. You know that."

"This isn't like that other incident from the nineties, the environmentalists disappearing. Or is it? I wondered because of Gianetti Junior being an environmentalist."

"No," said Hanley. "It's not like that at all. But I'll let you in on one thing. Keeping this one under wraps is more critical than keeping that episode under wraps. In fact, I would say this is the most critical matter we've come upon during our stroke watch."

"I noticed," said Valdez, "there are references in Mrs. Babe's notes to President Reagan and President Carter. Apparently Mrs. Gianetti said her husband was fond of Reagan but not so fond of Carter. Would I be right to suppose it has something to do with one or the other?"

Hanley smiled as he swallowed a mouthful, then said, "One, or the other . . . or both."

"Well," said Valdez, "I guess during my stay on this old earth I'll never know everything that's happened. And I take back what I said before. I'm old, but I'm not that curious. You know what frightens me most?"

"What's that?" asked Hanley.

"What frightens me is that some day I'll have a stroke or get Alzheimer's and they'll send in a younger guy from the Miami office so he can watch me drool and shit my pants."

Both men laughed and continued eating. Maria came from the kitchen with sandwiches and a fruit bowl. They waited for Maria to leave before speaking again.

Hanley turned back to Valdez. "Since my wife passed away I've grown very fond of that woman."

"I know what you mean," said Valdez. "At my age, and with my wife also gone, I've begun admiring many women. Actually, any woman over eighteen and under sixty will do."

They laughed again, and resumed eating their sandwiches and

fruit.

"Tell me," said Hanley, "is the young woman from Langley good looking?"

"I wouldn't throw her out of bed," said Valdez.

"Do you think she'll be able to spot trouble early enough to nip it in the bud?"

"She'll do fine," said Valdez. "In her last report she insists being able to shadow Mrs. Babe without her knowledge. She says only another woman could do what she's been doing. Her reports are very detailed. As a side note, you'll be happy to know that Mrs. Babe and her husband have not allowed the stroke to interfere with their sex life."

"That's good news," said Hanley. "Perhaps an indication there's still hope for us." He glanced toward the kitchen door through which Maria had disappeared. "However, if Mr. Babe is well enough to perform in bed, I wonder how well he's able to practice his old profession?"

"A fair question," said Valdez. "A question that's at the top of the list for both our contacts."

Valdez left soon after lunch for his drive back to Miami, telling Hanley this might give him time for female companionship later that evening if he played his cards right. He took the Everglades Parkway back rather than the so-called scenic route he'd taken to Naples that morning. The sun was still high during the drive. A much more pleasant way to travel. He had aimed the air-conditioning vents toward the passenger side so the dry air would not irritate his eyes. He had tuned to the Latin Rhythms music channel, its beat pounding away relentlessly like the rapid heartbeat of a younger man during sex. If the weather was lousy in Chicago he didn't want to know. All he wanted to know was that nothing Mrs. Gianetti knew from her husband would come around and bite someone more powerful than him in the ass. As long as that didn't happen, and as long as real estate prices didn't outdistance the savings he'd managed to put away by attending to these special projects for Skinner, he'd live to be an old fart in his Naples estate and maybe get himself a Maria to wile away his time on this old earth.

CHAPTER NINE

Tyrone was watching this guy by the name of Steve Babe and his babe very closely. He needed to make sure they didn't do something stupid like go to the cops. Of course he couldn't watch Babe's babe all the time, only while she was here visiting. But he figured if the guy happened to mumble something, and if she happened to take it upon herself to tell someone else, the first thing that would happen would be the asshole from security showing up, then security from the main hospital, then maybe the cops. So far none of that had happened, and Tyrone figured as long as Babe was scared and stayed scared, and as long as his babe understood he was scared, it didn't matter if he said something to her about the janitors' closet, because she'd keep her mouth shut to protect him. Tyrone had seen the two of them over in the lounge playing grabass, and this afternoon, when he tried the door to Babe's room, it was jammed shut from the inside. So, they were already scared, or they wanted privacy for extracurricular therapy. Either way it meant she'd be careful not to put him in danger.

Another reason Tyrone wasn't too worried about Babe saying

anything to his babe about what happened in the janitors' closet was because he'd already tested the waters. This afternoon, when Mrs. Babe was leaving the floor, he "accidentally" bumped into her with his laundry cart, nearly knocking her down. Then he ran around the front of the cart and did a step-and-fetch-it apology and asked if she was all right and said he remembered seeing her earlier and that he hoped her husband was better after his seizure. Someone from Hollywood should have been there to see it. That's how good he was. Even the new Hispanic chic who someone said was doing research for the main office seemed impressed.

Anyway, Tyrone was certain Babe hadn't said a word about what happened in the janitors' closet because all the time he talked to Mrs. Babe, he watched her. It was easy to read a woman's reaction when it had to do with her man. There was no reaction, no indication Babe had said anything to her about the big old black dude in the janitors' closet and his flat-nosed shit-for-brains partner with a short fuse.

Besides watching Babe and checking out his wife, Tyrone had also tuned in to the Hell in the Woods grapevine for any information on the old Gianetti lady who smashed her head on the floor outside the janitors' closet where they found Babe. Apparently Babe had hung around with the old lady in rehab, and word was Babe was down on the first floor that night because he found out where she'd died and was checking it out. One sticky thing Tyrone lifted from the grapevine was that a Gianetti family representative had been hanging around asking questions. He'd checked a little further and found out it was an ambulance chaser who wanted a list of the old lady's acquaintances and had talked to that new aide named Pete, to the Hispanic chic from the main office, and also to the speech therapist they call George.

George, crazy name for a cute burr-headed white chick speech therapist. But not as cute as that other speech therapist named Bianca who wouldn't have anything to do with him. Yeah, Bianca was one chick Tyrone would like to do some tail-twitching therapy with.

Except for the part about Bianca, Tyrone told all this to Flat Nose the next day and assumed Flat Nose would calm down. Especially when he was informed everything was cool and there weren't any punches being telegraphed in their direction. But Flat Nose had told DeJesus what happened during the exchange for rubber gloves and Demerols, and DeJesus apparently took his own name in vain and got Flat Nose all worked up like a manager sending him out for round one.

"I don't know why you want to do this," said Tyrone, as they got into his DeVille in the parking lot after his shift.

"Because I got to prove to DeJesus we got control of the situation."

"How's following her home gonna prove anything?"

"Easy, man. I tell DeJesus we know where she lives so he knows that if this Babe guy starts to say anything, we can put the heat on. It's a good thing he had a stroke. That way if we have to shut him up, everyone'll figure he's touched in the head and there'll be no harm done once we get his wife to get him to shut the fuck up."

"I still say we're wastin' time," said Tyrone. "I already put the heat on him in that closet, and again on the way back to his room. He had a seizure, for Christ's sake. Did you tell DeJesus about that?"

"Yeah."

"So what did he say?"

"He said his ma has seizures all the time and that don't mean a damn thing. He also said if we fuck up his business and he can't take care of his ma no more, he won't bother breakin' our jaws with his big old fists. He'll send out hits on us."

"Naw. He said that?"

"Yeah, man," said Flat Nose, his voice higher in pitch so he sounded like a little kid. "We was in his office and he picks up this basketball he keeps on his desk just to show how he can palm it and he says if his business goes down and he gets sent up for this, he can order hits from prison. He says there's a boss bigger than him who's in on the take but lets DeJesus run his own show. That's how it is with these big shots on top, they keep their noses clean. Another thing DeJesus said is that this big boss has plenty of trigger men."

"You're jivin' me."

Flat Nose held his hand up to the light coming through the window, crossing his fingers. "See this? DeJesus says he and the big boss are like this because they was in the 82nd Airborne together at Fort Bragg. A couple of mean motherfuckers. You try an' hurt one of 'em, the other'll get you." Flat Nose lowered his hand from in front of the window. "He told me they killed a guy crossed them at the base. An' to top that, because they're still pissed at him, they let things cool a while, then invite the dead guy's cherry out . . . The two of 'em, imagine it . . . And when they're done with her, they send her to meet her old beau. And of course nobody at the base gives a shit because the guy and his cherry were minorities like us."

"Flat Nose, you're full of shit."

"I ain't full of shit. If DeJesus wants you dead, he'll take care you get that way. Besides, he's got hands bigger than yours."

"Hands don't mean nothin'. Just because a guy's got big hands doesn't mean he's a killer. This whole thing's a jive."

"I ain't jivin'. I can give you his exact words and that says I ain't jivin'."

"So, give 'em to me."

"Okay," said Flat Nose, pumping himself up bigger in the seat. "He says, 'Flat Nose my man'—he's called me his man ever since he backed me in the fight game—he says, 'You know this ain't no spaghetti-head organization I'm running. You know I ain't no greaseball

Italian or Greek. We're cut from the same cloth,' he says. 'You and me got the same ancestors. You and me take care of our own. And, being we're cut from the same cloth, you know if anyone fucks over my ma, they'll get fucked over or I'll die trying. If I go up, I got plenty of friends who owe me, especially my buddy from Bragg.' After he says that, he reminds me about the bankrolling he done for me. I owe him, man. I know him, and he means it."

"I don't know," said Tyrone. "First you say he'll order hits on us if his business gets closed down, then you say he'll order hits on us if his business gets closed down, *and* if he goes down for it, then you say he'll only order hits on us if we fuck over his ma. Which is it? And who's he gonna send out on the hit? Saint Michael the archangel?"

Flat Nose turned toward Tyrone, lowering himself in the seat and bending forward slightly as if to present less of a punching target. Because of the glare from parking lot lights coming in the side window, his face was in shadows. "Real funny, man. How the hell do I know exactly *how* he said it? I didn't have a goddamn tape recorder going. All I know is he's not happy and telling him we found out where Babe's wife lives will be a good thing to tell him next time I see him."

"I still don't understand why you and DeJesus got your balls in an uproar. Everybody knows the health care system is fucked and most folks try their best to screw the system when they get a chance."

"You still don't get it," said Flat Nose, shaking his head slowly. "DeJesus ain't afraid of the short stint he'd pull for his health care business. He's worried that if he gets caught, his ma'll end up in one of these places. His business is the only way he can afford to take care of her. It's a mother-son thing we're dealin' with. You fuck him, you've fucked his ma."

"Well," said Tyrone, "that part I can understand."

"About time you understood somethin'," said Flat Nose, turning to look out the windshield. "It's cold in here. Start the engine and put on the goddamn heat. Why'd you buy a damn old Caddy anyhow? You should've gotten a Beamer like me."

"It's a classic car. I had an uncle who always had a Deville and I swore when I had the dough I'd have one. Besides, I've seen old guys and dying guys and I can tell you it wouldn't have mattered in the end if they drove a damn BMW when they were younger."

"Your trouble," said Flat Nose, still staring out the windshield, "is that you're fuckin' livin' in the fuckin' past."

Tyrone could tell Flat Nose was in one of his moods. When Flat Nose got this way, the best thing to do was shut up and hope the slow burn sizzling inside that rattled brain went out. They did not speak again until Tyrone saw Babe's wife coming out from under the lighted portico at the front entrance. When Tyrone pointed her out, Flat Nose's mood changed.

"You mean that's her? You mean that chicky in those tight jeans?"

"Yeah, that's her."

"I'll tell you one thing," said Flat Nose. "I sure ain't no woman hater like DeJesus and his buddy. Even if she's not a member of my particular minority, that's eatin' stuff."

"She's old enough to be your mother."

Flat Nose leaned forward, the shit-eatin' grin on his face lit up by the glare of an overhead light. "What is she, forty?"

"How the hell do I know?" said Tyrone.

When Tyrone put his car in gear and turned down the aisle Babe's wife had walked into, Flat Nose slapped the dashboard and Tyrone had a vision of the air bag going off and flattening Flat Nose against the seatback.

"Take it easy, dumb fuck!"

"Okay, okay, I'll take it easy. But look at that tight ass. I really like a more mature woman who's not afraid to wear tight jeans to show off her tight ass. And look, man. She's getting into an Audi. She's got a beautiful ass, she's all broken in and probably gets as slippery as an eel, and she drives a kick-ass red Audi Quattro. I'm in four-wheel-drive love."

"Put it back in your pants, Flat Nose."

"What's the matter? Afraid Henry'll poke a hole in your air bag?"

"That's exactly what I'm afraid of."

Tyrone followed the Audi at a distance. They got on the Eisenhower Expressway for a couple miles, then got off and headed south, ending up in Brookfield. When they passed a sign for Brookfield Zoo, Flat Nose said, "I knew it. She's an animal. Fuck, man, I wish I was a leather seat in an Audi right now. I hope her husband does spout off because I sure would like to spread those thighs and threaten her with old Henry."

"Shut the fuck up already, Flat Nose!"

"All right, all right."

"She's parking. Write down the address of the apartment building."

"Hey, wait a minute," said Flat Nose, turning toward Tyrone.

"What?"

"You said address."

"So?"

"Why didn't you just get Babe's address down at the business office?"

"Shit. How the hell do I know?"

Flat Nose began laughing. "This is really funny, man. I could've been down at my chick's place stretching leather, and instead, we come out here like a couple wetbacks who never heard of a phone book."

"Yeah," said Tyrone, "but I'll tell you what's really funny."

Flat Nose laughed some more. "Yeah, tell me one, man. I bet it'll be one of those really witty jokes you hear from college cats. Shit, he works at the place and could've gotten the address easy and here we is like we're *both* a couple of dumb-ass niggers."

The laughter was one thing, but that word *nigger* . . . Before he could stop himself, Tyrone reached out, grabbed Flat Nose by a fistful of shirt and shoved him forward so hard the shoulder belt engaged. Then he dragged Flat Nose out from behind the taut shoulder belt and pulled his face close.

"Don't ever laugh at me!" hissed Tyrone, spitting the words into Flat Nose's face. "I said I'd tell you what's funny! I said I'd tell you what's funny, and when I do, then you can laugh! What's funny is that you could ever find a woman, no matter her fuckin' race, color, or creed, who would let herself be diddled by a piece of shit like you!"

After Tyrone let go of Flat Nose, he could hear Flat Nose breathing steadily as they watched Mrs. Babe walk up to her apartment building. At first Tyrone thought maybe he'd scared Flat Nose. If this were true, he'd be in control. He'd take care of things if he had to, but he'd also be sure to take care of himself first. Maybe he'd even put down Flat Nose and DeJesus and DeJesus' mother if he had to.

But Flat Nose's breathing neither slowed nor quickened, and when Tyrone glanced toward him he could see that Flat Nose was staring out the windshield, his face in profile against the glare from a nearby streetlight. The flat-nosed face was pushed forward aggressively as if staring down an opponent during the referee's instructions. And below the face, fists took turns doing slow nervous warm-up punches into open palms.

Tyrone wondered if he'd pushed it too far. Flat Nose's fuse was lit, and this time he wondered if he'd be able to put it out.

Shit. Only way to deal with the little bastard was to joke with him. Shit! Why the hell did he have to deal with this stuff?

And so, as Mrs. Babe disappeared inside the apartment building,

Tyrone got ready to joke with the crazy bastard sitting next to him, but also resolved that next time he'd take care of things himself, prove to DeJesus, and even to Flat Nose if it came to that, he could be tougher and smarter than both of them put together.

CHAPTER TEN

As Steve waited for Jan to pick him up the morning of Marjorie Gianetti's funeral, he couldn't help thinking of the words *impaired* and *crippled* and *disabled.* After putting on his trousers over the brace, he sat on the edge of the bed and used his handgrip exercisers. Instead of alternately squeezing one grip with each hand like he was supposed to in order to get his bum right hand to respond, he paired the grips in his left hand and squeezed the two of them repeatedly and angrily. As he did this he thought of the black dude from the janitors' closet and imagined he had the guy down on the floor of the closet and that his left hand was around the guy's neck. But trying to take out his frustration this way didn't work because the guy resembled Percy, one of the physical therapists here at Hell in the Woods.

He put aside the handgrips, finished dressing, wheeled himself to the alcove of the television lounge down the hall from his room, parked his wheelchair at the window, and looked up at the sky. It was sunny after days of overcast. The weatherman on the television at the far end of the lounge was saying something about enjoying the weather while you can because there was a cold front on the way that would bring a couple days of cold rain. The winds would be from the southeast during the rains and he knew that meant planes from O'Hare would be taking off directly over Hell in the Woods, giving yet another reason for the place to deserve its nickname. But at least for today, until the cold front came closer, there would be some sun and poor Marjorie wouldn't be slipping in any puddles on the way to the funeral.

He hadn't mentioned his suspicions concerning Marjorie's death to anyone except Jan, partially because he wasn't one-hundred percent sure, and partially because if he did try to say something to anyone but Jan, they'd figure half of what he said was simply lingering verbal apraxia from his stroke. They wouldn't be completely wrong. Jan was the only one who understood him. Even Georgiana in speech rehab wouldn't understand what he was trying to get at because Georgiana's job was to help him communicate on a basic level. Jan was the only one who knew him and could ask the right questions. When he and Jan were alone seemed the only time he could really communicate. In public, like at a funeral, he best keep his mouth shut.

Because it was bright outside he couldn't see his reflection in the window. He hoped he wasn't smiling. Sometimes, since he'd become such a cheerful son-of-a-bitch, he'd catch himself smiling or even laughing at the oddest times and he hoped to hell he wouldn't do it today. He recalled reading a piece by Mark Twain recently in the Hell in the Woods library, a piece about etiquette at a funeral, Twain saying something about not stepping on your neighbor's toe at an inopportune time during the eulogy. Now he knew he was smiling, he just knew it. So maybe it would be best to let Jan do the talking and trail along behind like . . . Yes, like his sister Renee trailed along behind his mother when they visited.

Although he had no idea who the two women were when they first came into his room, he now knew his mother lived in Cleveland with his retarded thirty-year-old sister. Crazy. A guy loses his memory and people come into his room and want him to believe his name is Babe and he used to be a cop, that he became a cop because his girlfriend was killed during a robbery years earlier, that he once studied for the priesthood, and that most recently he'd been a private detective who once had a bomb thrown through his window by the mob. Who in his right mind would believe it? If it wasn't for Jan, he wouldn't have believed it. But Jan had a way of bringing it all back. And now, after weeks of fishing around in his noggin with Jan's help, he actually thought he could remember some of it.

Like recalling that summer Dwayne Matusak was after him and he watched Joe Friday on Dragnet and tried to make himself cool and collected like Joe when it came to dealing with Dwayne. Now, as he thought about Joe Friday, he could see the 714 badge blown up to screen size at the start of the show and in walks the woman who visited the other day. In walks his mother and says he can't watch the show tonight because they have to go to a wake. Can't remember whose wake, but now he remembers being there. Not much about it, just that at one point, after the priest finishes reciting a bunch of prayers and touches the body like he's saying a personal goodbye, a woman in one of the cushier front seats runs up and leaps into the coffin so that it takes both the priest and the funeral director to get her out. It was one of those childhood memories you can't forget. And now he remembered it!

He'd be sure to tell Jan about the woman leaping into the coffin. But he'd wait until after Marjorie's funeral. Better to wait until the appropriate time to tell some things. That's what he'd been telling himself when it came to the episode in the janitors' closet. Better not to tell Jan about it right now because she'd only worry about him.

And, because of his inability to explain the subtleties, she might jump to conclusions and think he thinks the bastards in the closet killed Marjorie. And if she thought that she might do something that would put her in danger.

The guys in the closet might have killed Marjorie, but even if they did, there was more to this than a couple of scumbags caught in the act by an old lady. There was simply more to this. He knew so because lately there'd been other things going on. Like that new aide named Pete with his out-of-style long sideburns who happened to pop into speech rehab one time too often. It was a gut feeling he had, something from his past. He wasn't sure what it was, but he knew Pete was there not only to help folks out, but also to get information and to give it to someone else, someone on the outside.

According to one of Steve's therapists in rehab, the stroke had caused him to have trouble keeping his mind focused. He'd see something and this would remind him of something totally unrelated, and that would remind him of something else, and so on. Case in point—down in the parking lot below the window, he sees an old car drive in and park. It belongs to one of the housekeeping staff, a woman he's seen changing bed linen. The car is maroon, but the maroon is faded. This reminds him of the heat from the sun, and that reminds him of someone being burned on the beach, but the burning doesn't show up until that evening when the burned person is going to bed and rubs against recently-laundered sheets. This reminds him of sheets hanging on a line in a stiff breeze. That reminds him of the wind off a car passing by quickly as he stands at a curb. A faded maroon Chrysler Corporation car passing by quickly as he stands at the curb somewhere in the past. In this vague memory from the past, if that's what it is, he's not the only one standing at the curb. There are men in business suits on either side of him. Men who should know better than to manufacture a car that will fade so easily, or men who should know better than to pollute the air so heavily when they made the steel for the car, men who pollute the air and get a President to call what they do the Clear Skies Initiative, men who should know better than to stand by while the ozone layer is depleted . . .

Yes, that's the way it was in the stroke world. Things popping into his mind at key moments and making him forget his original train of thought. He was thinking about Marjorie's death and the incident in the janitors' closet and the new aide named Pete who seemed to be nosing around in rehab a little too much. No, he couldn't tell Jan about the closet just yet. Outside the window, down in the parking lot, the sun glinted off the finish of another car, this one shiny and bright red. Jan's Audi had turned into the entrance of the parking lot. Jan arriving to take him to Marjorie's funeral. And then there was another car. But this car parked farther back in the woods where all the employees parked. A Hispanic woman he'd seen talking to nurses on his floor hurried toward the building.

Was the woman following Jan? Of course she was following Jan, you crazy bastard. Both Jan and the woman who worked at the damn place wanted into the building. So why wouldn't they both be headed toward the nearest entrance?

Steve spun his wheelchair around and headed back to his room for his jacket.

The casket had been selected by Marjorie Gianetti's son. It was finished in West Indian mahogany. A subtle but intricate motif of grape leaves and bunches of grapes was carved into the fishtail just below the lid panel and on the lugs to which the pallbearer handles were mounted. The handles themselves were gold-plated.

The mattress, lid overlay, pillow, and interior panel were done in antique cotton linen. The embroidery on the interior panel depicted a peaceful garden scene that seemed three-dimensional. Within the garden, surrounded by hedges made up of elaborate loops of various green threads, were several small trees and an arbored bench. The bench, within the shadows of the arbor, was empty. A winding path led to the interior of the arbor, apparently inviting the departed, who would have to look at the inside of the lid for a long time, to come inside and sit down for a much-deserved rest.

The cloth that had been draped over the open casket to keep dust from settling on Marjorie's face had been removed, but the overhead pinkish flesh-tone recessed lights had not yet been turned on. Several flower arrangements late in arriving were being set up by two funeral home workers. The legs of the many easels holding the arrangements crisscrossed at the front of the parlor as if the flower arrangements were the bodies of a flock of birds and the legs of the easels were the legs of the birds.

"I never seen so many flowers," said the younger of the two funeral home workers.

"That's because you haven't worked here as long as me," said the older worker. "I was here when old man Gianetti had his funeral. There were twice as many flowers then. We had to borrow Slone's flower car 'cause ours didn't have enough room."

"How long ago was that?"

"Must be over twenty years. Man, time sure flies. Things were different back then. I remember they had the casket closed because of all the bullets in his head. I saw the body downstairs. His head looked like a spaghetti strainer. The irony of it was everyone knew the guy who put all those holes in his head was probably at the funeral."

"Yeah, I heard about it. I think I was in grade school at the time."

"Don't rub it in."

"It was something about drugs, wasn't it? Maybe South Americans got him."

"I doubt it. With these people everything's a family affair. And I don't mean family like sons and daughters. Even though she probably had nothing to do with what her husband did for a living, they'll come to her funeral because of her connection to him."

"Yeah, I was watchin' last night at the wake. You could tell who was important by the number of soldiers lined up behind him. Especially that Lamberti guy."

"He's the old lady's nephew. I've seen him here with the boss lots of times over the years when a vet's gone down. Of course those times he didn't have such a big entourage. I guess he had to be backed up last night because there were so many others in his line of business here. Couldn't afford to take any chances."

"Is it true he always pays for the flag and banner when it's a vet?"

"I guess so. He also pays for the plots."

"I thought vets got free ones."

"Yeah, because Lamberti paid the cemetery for the whole damn grove. At Resurrection, the cheap grove out by the highway is covered by contributions, but at Chapel Grove, the vets get laid to rest in prime plots up on the hill in the oak grove."

"In his own way, Lamberti must be a good guy."

"I wouldn't want to cross the guy. I don't even feel comfortable talking about him."

"You see that one crony of his?"

"Which one?"

"That younger guy. His name's Dino. I know him from high school. His old man got out of the rackets, but Dino jumped back into it even though the old man tried like hell to keep him out. One thing I remember about Dino was that he never liked girls too much, if you know what I mean. We all thought he'd end up doin' what we're doin'."

"In the funeral business?"

"No, arranging flowers. When I saw Dino here last night, it made me wonder about Max Lamberti's relationship to the guy and whether there's a Mrs. Lamberti. Made me wonder whether Lamberti is like the old lady's son but puts on a good show of bein' a tough guy."

"I don't think so, but that's none of our business."

"I hope her son doesn't have too many of his friends here during the funeral."

"Why?"

"It'll be uncomfortable seeing these guys huggin' one another the way they did last night. For a while there I wondered whether they were just using the occasion as an excuse to dry-hump one another in public."

"I don't think you should be talkin' like that in here."

"Nobody'll hear. The doors are still locked and the boss is in with those black folks."

"It doesn't matter. I just don't think you should talk about people who come here to pay their respects."

"What's wrong? You think the place is bugged?"

"No, I don't think the place is bugged. But I do think there are things that shouldn't be said unless you're at home behind locked doors."

"Well, there sure are a lot of fuckin' flowers."

"Yes, there sure are."

For a moment Steve imagined he and Jan were riding in a horse-drawn Gypsy caravan and in the back of the caravan someone was trying desperately to play a violin and having a difficult time because of the rough ride. It was a strange feeling, like he was back there instead of up here in the front seat next to Jan. He wanted to tell this to Jan. He also wanted to tell her she looked great in her black dress and gold hoop earrings glittering in the sun. But then the car changed direction and Jan's keys, swinging back and forth where they hung from the steering column, drew his attention.

Something about keys. Marjorie saying something about the keys to the kingdom while speaking about her family. When Marjorie spoke of the keys she became confused, not the usual confusion, but a melancholy confusion, a turning inward. Yes, there was something about keys. She had said it more than once. And now he recalled other phrases Marjorie had gotten hung up on during her melancholy periods. She'd say, "Dead issue," and wave her hand as if to say she did not want to talk anymore about it. Or she'd say, "Dead seed." Or she'd say, "Carter smarter," whatever that meant. Sometimes she'd even repeat the name "Chernobyl" again and again. One time, after saying these things, she got hung up on the two phrases, "Fly in the ointment" and "Max the fly." That was in speech therapy the time Georgiana managed to get from Marjorie that "Max the fly" was the title of a children's book she'd read to her son when he was little, and "Fly in the ointment" referred to the son of her dead sister, the nephew she considered one of the "Black sheep" in her family.

Steve looked away from the keys hanging from the ignition and looked out at the road. Roads. Something about roads. Yes, Marjorie had this litany she'd go through. Georgiana had figured it out one day in rehab. Georgiana had gotten out a road atlas and figured out that a bunch of letters and numbers Marjorie recited actually consisted of the names of road routes in the road atlas.

Steve felt confused by this. A bunch of road routes. What good was that? He looked for something in the car on which to focus his attention. He stared at the cell phone in its holder between the seats. Then he turned toward Jan.

"Black dress," he said.

"You like it?" asked Jan.

"No . . . Yes."

"Okay, you like it, but that's not what you meant to say."

"Right. Black something other. Animal."

"Black bird?"

"No. Four shoes."

"Oh, four feet. Black cat?"

He felt the frustration bubbling up inside. At least that's the way one of his first speech therapists described the frustration of not being able to come up with a word. He had to force the frustration back down and take his time because Jan was helping, and with her help the word would eventually surface and be there plain as day, right side out and right side up, and he'd be unable to figure out how he could have gotten it twisted around.

"No, not black cat."

"Something you'd find on a farm?"

"Yes."

"Something you can eat?"

"Yes."

"It wouldn't be a black cow, would it?"

"No."

"Stop me when I hit it."

He held her shoulder with his left hand.

"Pig. Goat. Chicken . . . No, you said four legs. Calf. Horse . . . No, I guess not. Lamb . . ."

He squeezed her shoulder.

"Black lamb?"

"Again."

"Sheep? Black sheep?"

He laughed. "Got it."

"Okay," said Jan. "Let me speculate. We're driving to a funeral and you're thinking about black sheep. At a funeral families come together and the term black sheep is used to refer to a family member. Is that it?"

He laughed again. "Wow."

Jan smiled a great big smile. "Thank you for the compliment."

"You're welcome."

She reached over and touched his thigh. "Take your time. I know it'll be hard trying to get anything across to me at the funeral with all the people and distractions. I'll keep my eyes open and remember about black sheep. Maybe we'll see one. Keep it all in your head. Then you and I can talk about it afterward when we're alone."

Steve leaned close, put his arm around her, and stared at her gorgeous profile while she drove.

Steve saw the hood at the funeral home as Jan pushed his wheelchair back from the front where they had viewed Marjorie's body and given their condolences to several men and women who stood at the front. At one point he thought of a wedding reception line and imagined telling this to Marjorie in rehab and further imagined Marjorie leaping out of the casket and saying she's the bride and everyone has to kiss her, especially this guy in the wheelchair. If she could have done this, it would have been like Marjorie to do it because she enjoyed a good laugh. As he bit his lip to keep from laughing, he saw the hood.

He saw the hood again in church and wondered if the hood would get up and say something when the priest finished his eulogy and asked if anyone else wanted to say something. But the hood did not get up. Two men in their thirties or forties got up and spoke briefly. One, a slight man with very short thinning hair, mentioned "Mom," and said, "She always knew kindness and understanding, not only to me, but also to those who sometimes did not deserve it. She loved nature. She always said the right thing, even after her stroke, if one simply took time to listen. I . . . I'll always love her." The other man was larger, had thick black hair and mustache, mentioned "Aunt Marge," and said, "She was the best aunt a kid could have. I'll miss her a lot because of so many things she did for me that I can't even count." The frail-looking son wept and had difficulty finishing his statement. The burly-looking nephew took out a handkerchief with a flourish and wiped at his eyes at the conclusion of his statement.

He saw the hood again at the cemetery. The hood was one of a group of men there without the accompaniment of women or children, a group of men who seemed to answer to the burly nephew who had spoken in church. Steve could tell by the way they whispered to one another, and the way they stood at overly-dignified attention, and the way they scanned the crowd and formed a barrier around the nephew, that they were there to protect the nephew and perhaps watch those who attended the funeral and report back later.

The reason Steve recognized the hood was because he had a recollection of having had this man's face very close to his, and of him holding his semi-automatic nicknamed Attila pointed at this man. Suddenly he was immersed in detail and the memory became vivid . . .

The smell of celery. A warehouse with trucks backed in. Stacks of ventilated wooden crates and cardboard boxes. Fresh vegetables. He's there to ask questions the way Joe Friday would ask questions. He asks a kid hauling crates of lettuce on a two-wheeler about someone. Suddenly the guy he's looking for appears and lets go with a head of lettuce from behind a waist-high stack of crates. He chases the guy around crates, through the warehouse, and up to a backroom door that slams in his face. When he tries the door it is locked.

A clattering behind him. He turns. The kid has dropped his two-wheeler, spilling crates of lettuce across the floor. The kid grabs him from behind. A tough kid, bone and muscle, arm around his neck. He tries to spin away but the kid hangs on.

"Dino?" a voice shouts through the locked door.

"Go, Pa!" shouts the kid.

He elbows the kid hard in the gut, feels breath and spit on his neck.

"Dino?"

He spins and drops, grabbing an ankle, pushing on the knee, tipping the wiry kid off balance. He has Attila out before the kid can bounce back.

"Pa!" shouts the kid. "A gun!"

"Wait!" shouts Steve. "Don't bring no goddamn gun out here! I only pulled it to calm your boy!"

He sees several workers looking in from the dock. A couple of the men are old, looking like hit men making ready to come out of retirement. But no one moves toward him when he raises his semi-automatic so they can see it.

"Look, Rickie!" shouts Steve toward the closed door. "I'm not a hit man or a cop. I'm a private investigator just doin' my fuckin' job! So why not come out or let me in there and we'll talk and I'll get the hell out of here? And tell your kid not to move! I hate guns, I really do."

No one moves.

"Rickie, if I was from the mob would I have walked the fuck in here?"

The door opens wide and Rickie comes out, his hands clearly visible, and the door shuts tight behind him. Rickie gives in like he's done it before, knowing the right moves to show someone whose finger is on a trigger.

Rickie tells his son to go out front and wait, to get rid of the gawkers. Steve puts his gun away and they sit on cool lettuce crates to talk.

The memory from the loading dock at a vegetable market came to Steve while the priest mumbled prayers and sprinkled holy water over the casket, and while the hood stared at him. The hood was the kid, Dino. He pulled Jan close and whispered to her.

"Rickie's son, Dino."

"Okay," she whispered back. "I'll remember. The guy staring at you?"

"Yes."

As he stared back at the hood, Steve recalled how hard it had been in the beginning, right after his stroke, to say a simple word like *yes* or *no* after Jan asked him a question and stared at him, waiting patiently. Yes, one thing he had learned from all this was patience. Finally, after several more seconds of staring at one another, the hood looked away.

The priest asked for a moment of silent prayer. During this silence, just above the drone of distant traffic, a dog began barking in a nearby neighborhood. The barking dog caused Steve to again recall the piece Mark Twain had written concerning funeral etiquette. The piece had gone on about not criticizing the person, ". . . in whose honor the entertainment is given," and it had warned against comments about the "equipment" and gave recommendations for displays of sorrow depending on how closely related the guest was. The last recommendation had been, "Do not bring your dog."

Laughter bubbled up, threatening to strangle him. The only way he could keep from laughing was to cough repeatedly as if he were choking. Jan stooped beside his wheelchair, held an open handkerchief to his mouth and patted his back firmly. It probably looked like she was trying to help him breathe or trying to console him, or both. But he had a feeling she knew the commotion was an effort to contain laughter, laughter that Jan and Marjorie, but no one else present, would understand.

After the laughter and tears were wiped away and Steve was able to compose himself with Jan's help, mourners began filing back to their cars.

Marjorie's son thanked mourners as they were leaving. To Jan and Steve he introduced himself as Antonio Junior, saying that's what his mother called him, but everyone else called him Tony.

"I'm glad Mom had friends at Saint Mel's," he said as he shook Steve's left hand—a delicate handshake, good eye contact, good diction. "The last time I visited she said you were her best friend there. But don't worry. I know you're not old enough to have been in the nursing home wing. She said you were from upstairs."

Jan answered for him. "Steve still has trouble getting out exactly the right words, especially at times like this. But I know how much he admired your mother. I remember Steve's first day at Saint Mel's. Your mom was right there at his side, giving the rookie patient, and the rookie patient's wife, lots of encouragement. We'll both miss her."

Tony Junior shook Jan's hand. "Thank you, Mrs. Babe." Then he smiled, first to Jan, then to Steve. "By the way, I really love your last name. When Mom first told it to me, I wasn't sure if she was getting it right until she went on about how you'd told her about it being a shortened form of a Hungarian name. Thanks again."

Marjorie's nephew, backed up by his entourage, also thanked mourners as they were leaving. To Jan and Steve he introduced himself as Maximo Lamberti, saying that's what the tax collector called him, but that everyone else calls him Max.

"Glad you could come," Max said as he reached past an extended left hand and grabbed Steve's right hand from his lap and shook it—a rough handshake, not looking at Steve, but leering at Jan. "Last time I was there, Aunt Marge said you tell good jokes. Not enough good jokes in this world. She's probably upstairs laughing like hell at all us jokers runnin' around down here."

Max dropped Steve's limp and burning right hand back into his lap and grabbed Jan's hand, holding onto it rather than shaking it. After repeating his name to her, Max said, "It's good to meet such a healthy woman as you, Mrs. Babe. So far the weather's cooperated." He winked. "Probably 'cause I slipped a big envelope in the donation box at church."

While he spoke, Max stared at Jan. And as he stared, Steve recalled Jan telling him about another rough-talking guy, about some other guy long ago who stared at her as if he owned her. It was not something Jan had recently told him, but something from before his stroke. A guy who got her a job somewhere, then wanted something for his efforts. The words *somewhere* and *something* lay there in his head as if on a blank sheet of paper.

When Max finally let go of Jan's hand and moved on to the next set of mourners in line, Steve looked behind Max and could see the young hood named Dino staring at him between the big shoulders of two older hoods.

While he and Jan waited in the car for the exchanges of thanks and condolences to conclude so the single file of cars on the one-lane cemetery road could leave, Steve noticed a man in a wheelchair who had been hidden behind Max's entourage. The man was big, a brutish guy completely bald except for curls of hair around his ears. The guy was dressed in a black suit coat on top, but was covered with a plaid blanket from his waist down. The blanket reached down a little below the wheelchair seat and the footplate extenders had been removed. There were no feet to put on footplates, and no legs visible beneath the blanket. The guy's arms were so huge, the sleeves of the suit coat were stretched.

While the socializing continued, the legless man in the wheelchair turned and wheeled himself across the lawn toward the cars parked at the head of the procession. When he passed Jan's Audi, the guy glanced over, smiling. His face was disfigured by a diagonal scar that gave him a disjointed look like a Picasso painting. It was obvious as the guy passed by and looked back toward them that he was staring at Jan.

"Howdy, handsome," whispered Jan, covering her mouth with her hand.

"Don't make me laugh," Steve managed to get out.

"Sorry."

One of the hoods who had been behind Max followed the legless man and when they got to one of the limos in line, opened the back door. Instead of helping the legless man do his transfer to the back seat of the limo, the hood stood back and watched as the legless man's hands grabbed door and doorframe and his massive arms vaulted his bulk inside. The hood pulled the chair back slightly, apparently to put it in the trunk of the limo, but the legless man had hold of it. After a brief tug of war, the legless man folded the chair and pulled it inside with him all in one motion.

Steve no longer felt like laughing. The strength of the brute without legs made him feel weak and helpless. Jan, as she often did, sensed his feelings, reaching over and gently rubbing the back of his neck. When she did this he closed his eyes and, as he had done before when alone with Jan in the car, imagined he had not had a stroke and was in the driver's seat and Jan was rubbing his neck as he drove.

When he heard cars in the procession begin starting up, Steve felt an automatic urge to reach out with his right hand toward the ignition, and his hand did move some, knocking against the door handle.

He opened his eyes when Jan took her hand from the back of his neck. Reaching out to start the Audi, Jan smiled a sad smile as if she knew what he'd been thinking.

CHAPTER ELEVEN

Steve wanted to go somewhere to talk. "Not Hell," he said. "Make me whole somewhere." And so, because she knew Steve needed a place with as little distraction as possible, Jan drove them to Ilonka Szabo's restaurant. When Jan told Ilonka they'd come for a quiet lunch, Ilonka wiped her hands in her apron, kissed Steve on his cheek, said something in Hungarian as she wheeled Steve to a table, told Jan there was no need to order and that she would bring something light, and left them alone to talk.

Jan knew Steve wanted to go over who he'd seen at the funeral. "Make me whole," he had said, and she knew this was a phrase he'd gotten from Marjorie. A mob phrase from Marjorie's late husband. At the funeral Steve had told her to remember, "Dino, Rickie's son," and when she reminded him of this, things began falling into place and she worked with him to get it out.

The restaurant provided a perfect environment for communication. The recording of Hungarian violins was turned low. The few other patrons there for late lunch were finished and soon left. When

Jan asked Ilonka if she minded that they sit and talk for a while, Ilonka was more than cooperative, saying she'd be closing until dinner time, but they should stay as long as they wished and that she would be in the kitchen preparing the dinner menu. It took time to get it all out, but the atmosphere seemed to instill a greater patience in Steve. In Ilonka's restaurant, empty except for them, he was able to keep his thoughts from wandering and he told it with relatively little prompting from Jan.

He told her that the man he had pointed out at the funeral was the son of Rickie Deveno, who quit the mob years earlier and changed his name to Rickie Justice. Jan recalled the names, and when Steve began describing the incident at the produce market, she remembered him having told her about it. The incident at the market in which Steve confronted the son named Dino had taken place years earlier, when Dino was a teenager working at the market. And today, this kid from the past named Dino was at the funeral and seemed to have gone back to the life his father had abandoned.

Marjorie had spoken of the Chicago mob in rehab, not in detail, but enough. Marjorie's husband had been a kingpin in the mob, and now Steve felt that Marjorie's nephew played the role of mob kingpin quite well, and the kid named Dino was obviously one of the nephew's thugs. Mixed in with the description of Marjorie's husband having been in the mob was something about him having been good to Vietnam veterans. From other things Marjorie had revealed in rehab, it seemed her husband inherited an old hatred of the Kennedys from his mob predecessors and, in later years, became interested in politics himself. Something about "getting out the votes" and "getting rid of Carter," so perhaps he worked for the Reagan campaign.

When Steve mentioned the nephew named Max, Jan recalled him vividly. "Maximo Lamberti, but everyone calls me Max," he had said.

The way Max looked at her as he held her hand reminded Jan of thugs she'd known in the past. Maybe he was high up in the local mob, but once a thug always a thug.

In contrast, Marjorie's son Antonio, whom they'd also been introduced to, did not seem to be allied with Max and his thugs. During the service, Antonio held his hand in front of his face at one point and appeared to speak harshly to his cousin Max. Although Jan had not heard what was said, she felt Antonio had been upset that Max brought his entourage to the funeral.

Antonio was shorter and much thinner than Max, and was going a little bald. Now that she thought about Antonio's baldness, she was certain, because of the contrast, Max had worn a hairpiece. Not only was Max's hair too thick, but the hairline at his forehead was too far forward on this six foot tall man who probably weighed in at well over two hundred.

When Jan recalled Steve telling her earlier he thought Marjorie's son Antonio might be gay, she had to admit that at the funeral she'd seen a gentle man, a more fragile man. Especially when she contrasted him to his cousin Max.

While Steve tried to recall everything Marjorie had ever conveyed to him about her family, he indicated there were certain phrases Marjorie had used. She had said, "Dead issue" and "Dead seed" and "Family secret" and "Carter smarter" and "Keys to the kingdom" and "Fly in the ointment" and even some kind of litany of road routes. Finally, after wracking his brain for some time, Steve said, "Max the fly." Yes, Max was the fly in the ointment, the black sheep. She waited before asking a question, and when he was silent for a while she asked Steve what the reference to Carter meant. He said it must have something to do with the son. Something about the father hating Carter and the son not hating Carter.

But what did any of this have to do with Marjorie's death? Just because some members of her family were in the mob or were associated with the mob, and just because Marjorie might have objected to family members being in the mob, and just because father and son might have had differing political views, why would Steve feel this had anything to do with Marjorie's death? When Jan asked why he felt this way, Steve shook his head and said, "Maybe . . . maybe not. Something long time ago . . . something dug up. One key . . . many keys. Who knows?"

For a moment, after succeeding in getting out all he had gotten out, Jan felt Steve was withdrawing. That shake of his head and the lowering of his voice seemed to say, "In my condition I can't do anything about it anyway, so maybe I should let it go."

Steve stared at her silently from across the table, the glow of the candle on the table reflecting in his eyes making him seem distant and vulnerable. Not his old melancholy self like before the stroke, something different. He looked like he needed more than rehab at Hell in the Woods, or going through old magazines trying to reconstruct the past. That's when Jan decided to tell him about the investigating she'd done.

"Ever since you brought up the fact that you had a funny feeling about Marjorie's accident, it's been bothering me. We both wondered why no one bothered to clean up the puddle in the hallway that night. I began to wonder if someone felt they should leave it there for a while as proof she *did* slip and fall, that is *was* an accident. I also began to wonder about Marjorie dying en route to the hospital. Why would the paramedics take time to wipe up the blood if Marjorie was still alive and might be saved?

"So, yesterday and the day before, I did a little checking. I spoke to that nurses' aide who found Marjorie, the one who took Marjorie's walker back to the nurses' station. When I first met her in the hospital administrator's office, I could tell she was reluctant to say anything that might get her in trouble. So this time I met her for lunch, treated her to lunch to be exact. We spoke about other things at first, to make her feel comfortable. Then I brought up Marjorie's fall, telling her that whatever she said I'd keep between the two of us. Well, maybe the three of us.

"Anyway, I found out she's pretty sure Marjorie was dead when she found her. And the reason the paramedics reported the death took place in the ambulance was that she knew one of the paramedics and he suggested they do it that way to avoid unnecessary paperwork as well as any problems she might have with her superiors because of her being new on the job.

"After that I got in touch with the ambulance service and spoke with the two paramedics. They were pretty touchy about the whole thing, but I had a feeling they'd be that way if anyone came asking about time of death of one of their patients. They wouldn't admit to anything except that sometimes determining the actual moment of death is tricky, especially in an emergency. When I asked about wiping up the blood, they said one of them had time to quickly wipe it up while the other was wheeling Marjorie out and that it did not delay their departure."

Jan could see this had aroused Steve's interest. He reached across the table and squeezed her hand. He smiled a big old smile like the one he always gave her when she came to visit. Then he said, "You fishy kid."

He laughed at this, apparently realizing how silly it sounded, then said, very slowly, "Went fishing . . . but something else. You did it . . . back to square one."

"So," she said, "you think I did good on my fishing expedition?"

"Yes."

"Think I eliminated the possibility of a conspiracy at Hell in the Woods?"

"Could be."

"Should I check some more?"

"No." He'd said it a little loudly, and repeated it more softly, squeezing her hand. "No."

"You said something earlier about Marjorie indicating there was something in the past that might be the key."

"Keys," said Steve. "More than one."

Then Steve squeezed her hand again and frowned. "No more. Us."

"Us?"

"Yes."

"You want to talk about us?"

"Take care."

"We should take care of ourselves instead of fishing around?"

Steve smiled. "Yes. You rest. Go with Lydia. Me back to rehab."

On the way to the funeral she had told Steve that Lydia was driving to Wisconsin for a long weekend to visit friends from college. "You mean you remember me saying Lydia is going on a trip?"

Steve smiled. "Yes."

"And you want me to go?"

"Go. Vacation. Getaway."

She stood, went around the table and hugged him. "The hell with going away now, especially after the magic you did in your head today, pulling out details the way you have."

"You should go," he said, looking up at her.

Before they left the restaurant they said goodbye to Ilonka who gave them a box of strudel to take with. "New low fat recipe," said Ilonka, smiling and wiping her hands in her apron.

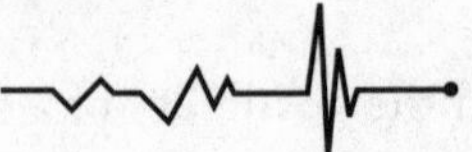

When Jan arrived home that night she changed then went into the kitchen. She put ice in a glass, a shot of Johnnie Walker, water. Maybe Steve was right. Maybe it would be good to get away for a long weekend with Lydia, especially the way Steve insisted before she left him.

In the living room she went to the stereo cabinet and rummaged through a shelf full of CDs and old cassette tapes. Several tapes Steve had added to her collection when they married. She selected one of Steve's tapes and put it into the cassette deck. When she sat down on the sofa and the music began, she felt a melancholy wave of nostalgia for this music of ancestors she and Steve shared, both of them having had grandparents who lived in Hungary. But this was not the real reason for her nostalgia. The real reason was because the tape she selected was the same one Steve had played for her ten years earlier just after they met.

She remembered he had gone out to his car to get the tape when, while asking questions related to her husband's murder, he found out she was half Hungarian. She stood and took her drink to the window and looked out into the parking lot.

When she'd gone to the window ten years earlier in the previous apartment on the second floor and looked down into the parking lot, there had been an unmarked police car parked there, the police left to guard her because of her brief but terrifying kidnapping earlier that day. When Steve went out to his car to get the tape, he waved to the cops in their car on his way down the sidewalk, then ran back to the apartment like a little kid, his prize in his hand, his coat tails flapping like a bird too young to fly.

It was violin music. A music she remembered from long ago.

Something her grandfather played for her on his small record player at the nursing home before he died. She had been in high school then, already dressing pretty outrageously—jeans with holes, tee shirt with no bra—and she remembered that her grandfather seemed the only person in her family with whom she could communicate.

"My grandfather had records like this," she had said.

Steve had smiled, his smile more melancholy then. "It's Sandor Lakatos, the famous Gypsy violinist. He learned the violin from his father, and his father from *his* father. Five generations of Hungarian Gypsy violinists."

The solo violin began slowly, almost weeping, exactly the way it had been on her grandfather's record player back in the nursing home. Although the tune increased in momentum, it maintained a haunting feeling as each note faded in and out. In a way, the music was like a stroke, starting slowly, then going faster and faster, approaching a climax using the mystery of its minor keys.

She recalled Steve standing on the other side of the coffee table playing an imaginary violin, swaying from side to side as he stared at her with those dark eyes that seemed larger at a distance.

The music sped up, other instruments joining in. Steve kept playing the imaginary violin, smiling at her, then laughing when the music became so fast he could hardly keep up. When the song ended they both laughed and, following Steve's lead, Jan drank down the wine she had poured for them.

The next song was very slow, at first seeming sad, but there was a contradictory pleasure to the anguish, the music soothing like watching a sad movie and enjoying the sadness.

Again, Steve played along, swaying as he bowed his make-believe violin, alternately staring at her and closing his eyes. Perhaps he'd been thinking about the tragic death of his fiancée in Cleveland as the music played. His first love struck down in pointless violence. Perhaps she'd been thinking that she would become like him, melancholy for the rest of her life.

They drank the wine down between songs, put the glasses on the table, and danced. Steve held her tightly and they danced slowly, his arms strong, his legs pressing against hers, his breath at her ear. When the music sped up they continued holding one another as they danced faster and faster and the music grew louder and louder.

"The *czardas*!" said Steve.

"I know! I remember my grandfather dancing it with me at a wedding!"

"How old were you?"

"Very small! He bent over!"

They danced around the living room, into the dining room. When the *czardas* ended, another slow song played and Jan led, waltzing them slowly, very slowly, down the hall to her bedroom.

They fell onto the bed in the dark, side by side, Steve's arm across her breasts. After a moment Jan stood and turned on the light. Steve looked up at her, sat up. The music from the living room sad as hell and Steve's eyes sad as hell and her sad as hell she hadn't met him twenty years earlier.

When the music ended and the tape deck clicked off, Jan put down her glass of scotch. She had wished the scotch into red wine served ten years earlier. For a few minutes, while the music played, Steve had been there. She had been able to recall the evening vividly because it was the first time they had made love. She wondered if the same evening was somewhere in Steve's brain. That evening trying its best to fight its way through dead and injured brain cells to make itself known once again in sad minor keys. Could those have been the keys Steve referred to when he mentioned Marjorie's past? Perhaps

Marjorie's death reminded him of his mortality. Memories from the past locked away, and if only one could find the keys before . . .

As she stared at her empty glass, Jan recalled what Steve had said about the glass he'd found near Marjorie's body. Something about a sink in a janitors' closet and him thinking maybe the puddle on the floor had been made by someone using the glass to spill water there. He'd wanted to have her give the glass to someone to get fingerprints off it, but somehow the glass had broken. Now, as she recalled Steve telling her this, she wondered if the disappointment he expressed was because of a glass that had broken, or because of his realization that the story of the glass might have been concocted in his head.

She thought of Lydia again, and the long weekend coming up. It was late, Lydia had said she was going to leave Thursday night and was probably already gone. Obviously she had delayed calling because she did not want to go, but wanted Steve to think she'd gone. She recalled Steve saying, "You fishy kid," and wondered if the "fish" in what he said was an indication he'd been thinking about what she was thinking right now. A fishing expedition.

A name came to mind, someone Steve had used for fishing expeditions. So easy to go on a fishing expedition when she and Steve knew a guy like Phil Hogan who had his fingers in so many things and had a reputation at the Chicago PD for being unable to keep his mouth shut, especially when he was drinking, and, according to some, he was always drinking.

She recalled that, before his stroke, after a phone conversation with Tamara, Steve had said something about Phil Hogan maybe being on the take, something about wondering whether Phil should be trusted. But Phil seemed friendly enough, especially lately. Could be a good sign. Could be Phil was having some luck getting off the booze, not drunk all the time and that's why he'd been calling more often asking how Steve was doing.

Jan wondered if maybe she should call Tamara and ask her what she thinks, both about the fishing expedition and about whether Phil was someone to be trusted. But if she called Tamara, it wouldn't be a fishing expedition. What would happen is that Tamara would want to arrange to speak with Steve and her together. Then, if there was something worth fishing for, Tamara would insist on opening an official investigation. And, for some reason, it seemed that was something Steve did not want to happen right now. If she was going fishing, it had to be on her own. Chances are she'd find nothing, but at least she'd feel good knowing she'd done it. At least she would have tried. Steve seemed genuinely pleased with her questioning of the nurses' aide, and she'd done that on her own. No involvement on Steve's part, no big waves, only small ones.

She reached for the phone and punched in a number.

"Yeah."

"Phil?"

"Jan, that you? Hey."

"Yeah, Phil, it's me."

"Hey, honey, how's good ol' Steve doing?" Once Phil relaxed his guard she could tell from his voice that he'd been drinking as usual.

"He gets a little better each day. But it's gradual and I find myself wanting him back exactly the way he was, yet knowing it may never happen."

"Yeah, I been thinking 'bout you guys a lot. Everyone downtown who ever worked with Steve asks about him. Even his old boss from cop days."

"Donovan?"

"Yeah, Donovan the schnause."

"Phil, Steve asked me to tell you about this other guy named Phil who's got a room across from his at Saint Mel's. He asked me to do it when I was listing names of friends one day and your name came up. He said to tell you what this other guy named Phil says all the time."

"Oh yeah? Did this guy have a stroke like Steve?"

"Yes, he did. But a little more serious."

"Okay, I'll bite. What does this Phil say?"

"Apparently he's only able to say two words, always the same two words. I've heard him and sometimes it's kind of funny. I guess that's why Steve wanted me to tell you. He likes to tell people things that make them laugh."

"Okay, Jan, honey. Make me laugh."

"Jesus fuck."

"What?"

"Jesus fuck. That's all the guy ever says. If you say hello to him, he says, Jesus fuck. If you ask how he's doing, he says, Jesus fuck."

"I guess that could be pretty funny, depending on the circumstances," said Hogan, beginning to sound more sober, as if he knew this couldn't possibly be the reason she called.

"Anyway," said Jan, "I promised Steve I'd call you sometime and tell you that. And one other thing as long as you're on the line."

"What's that?"

"Suppose someone at a nursing home was found dead and happened to be related to a guy named Max Lamberti. And suppose someone else at that nursing home thought maybe some water was spilled on the floor to make it appear that this older relative had slipped, but she really hadn't slipped. And suppose further the glass that had been used to spill some water around was available to fingerprint."

When he did not answer immediately, Jan wondered if she'd said too much.

"You there, Phil?"

"Yeah, I'm here."

"So, what do you think?"

"I don't mean to be rude, Jan, honey, but I don't know what you're talking about. Is this something Steve wanted you to ask me?"

"No. It was someone else at the nursing home attached to the place where Steve's a resident. This woman I've gotten to know there told me this crazy story, and when I told her I knew a cop or two, she asked me if I'd ask around about it."

"This woman gave you that name . . . What was it?"

"Max Lamberti? Yes, she gave me the name."

"The name rings a bell, Jan. Of course I don't personally know the guy, but with a name like that in a city like this . . ."

"The mob?"

"Could be, Jan, but it would only be a guess on my part. If you like I'll check around and give you a call if I find anything."

"Thanks, Phil. I really appreciate it."

"Sure, Jan, sure. And say howdy to Steve next time you see him."

After Jan hung up she retrieved her glass and went into the kitchen. She rinsed the glass in the sink and put it on the counter. As she stood at the kitchen sink staring down into the drain where the disposal waited to tear apart flesh or anything else that would fit down there, she remembered the cesspool in hell joke Steve said he shared in rehab. Standing in a cesspool up to their chins, all the people in hell who'd chosen the door behind which there'd been no screams of pain are whispering, "Don't make waves," to one another.

So maybe it was time for her to make a few waves. Or maybe she'd already made some, because she knew damn well Phil Hogan must have known exactly who Max Lamberti was. Phil Hogan had been one of Steve's main sources at Chicago Police Headquarters. And during the last ten years, Jan understood enough about Steve's cases to know

Phil Hogan made it his business to know all the hoods in the city.

As she got ready for bed, she made plans for the next day and hoped she was doing the right thing. What the hell. Maybe she *could* do something to find out if there was a possibility Marjorie had been murdered. And if so, the unearthing of a case for the two of them to work on would most likely do more for Steve's recovery than all the magazines in the world.

After turning out the bedroom light, she realized she'd left the light on in the living room. On her way down the hall to turn out the light, she saw movement at the kitchen window and paused in the hallway. After a few seconds, and having seen nothing, she mumbled, "Right, probably a monkey escaped from the zoo was swinging in the tree branch. Or better yet, maybe there's this thing called wind that moves the branches from time to time and causes shadows from the parking lot." Then she realized the reason the movement had caused her to stop was because she was still used to the kitchen window on the second floor where it was above the small tree near the entrance.

In the living room, after turning out the light, she parted the drapes to look out at the parking lot and saw a man standing beneath the light in the center of the lot. The man was short and his clothes were baggy. Although the light was above and behind him, she could see he wore a baseball cap. And by the way he moved, punching the air like a shadowboxer, she saw the cap was on backward. Funny thing about this was that even though it was obvious the cap was backward, there didn't seem to be much of a profile on the man, or at least much of a nose.

As she watched the man shadowboxing in the parking lot, she couldn't help wondering if the movement she'd seen at the kitchen window might not have been a tree branch. Lifting the drape a little more and glancing toward the tree outside the kitchen window, she detected no movement at all, no wind.

After shadowboxing for several seconds, the man in the parking lot went directly beneath the light and used the light pole to do stretches against. He was wearing baggy sweats and white athletic shoes. She couldn't tell much else about the man except that his nose was very small, or flat. Yes, flat like a boxer.

After a few more seconds of stretching, the man jogged in place, then began running and soon disappeared into the darkness where the parking lot bordered the road that paralleled the fence surrounding the Brookfield Zoo grounds.

Jan reached for the phone in the dark, picked it up, and punched at the lit numbers. Although she knew Lydia would not be there, she decided to leave a message saying she had decided not to join her for the long weekend.

When Jan finished with the message, she couldn't recall exactly what she had said and how she had said it. She walked down the hall but did not go into the bedroom. Instead she continued to the end of the hall and stood outside the door to the spare bedroom. Although is was dark, she knew that inside the room was the cabinet where Steve kept his gun and ammunition, and she also knew that just a few steps behind her, in the bathroom medicine cabinet, inside a band-aide box, was the key to the gun cabinet. But she did not retrieve the key to unlock the gun cabinet, and instead went to her and Steve's room.

As she lay on her back in the dark planning what she would do the next day, she decided that going fishing did not require a gun, and that in order to be successful during her fishing expedition, and also to help Steve rediscover who he'd been, she should be careful not to allow paranoia to stand in the way of objectivity. Before she closed her eyes to try to sleep she saw a light flash onto the bedroom curtain and heard a car start up and drive away.

CHAPTER TWELVE

HELL IN THE WOODS REHAB WAS A SEVEN-DAY-A-WEEK GRIND. The end of each week was especially hectic because of staff shortages and shift changes, causing Friday sessions to be grouped rather than one-on-one. Younger stroke victims complained when the skeleton Friday staff insisted on playing taped Wheel of Fortune shows, but eventually they went along. Bernie and Louise, a couple of new strokers, sat with their mouths hanging open. And Phil, as usual, only worked his mouth occasionally, saying, "Jesus fuck," as Vanna put up a couple of letters.

Steve was usually pretty good at Wheel of Fortune, but today he wasn't doing well at all. Words came to mind, but these had nothing to do with the puzzle currently on the screen.

When a contestant yelled out an R, he thought of Rickie Deveno who had changed his name to Justice years ago and had a son named Dino. When a contestant yelled out an N, he thought of the word *nephew* and the name Max Lamberti. When a contestant bought an A, he thought of Antonio Gianetti junior and Antonio Gianetti senior.

When an M was yelled, he thought of the mob and wondered if the same organization that had once been headed by Antonio senior still existed or if there was a new organization, and if all or part of that organization was now headed by Max. Then, when a T was yelled, the Gianetti family and their connections were drowned out by the cheering Wheel of Fortune audience and all Steve could think of was the name Tyrone Washington.

Tyrone Washington, he'd seen the name beneath the photograph on the employee board in vocational rehab. Tyrone Washington, the guy in the janitors' closet with the flat-nosed accomplice itching for a fight. Although Steve could not concentrate on Wheel of Fortune today, mulling over hunches in his mind felt good, even if he couldn't put it together.

When Wheel of Fortune ended, he was sidetracked. The blond recreational therapist everyone called Charming Charmaine went from stroker to stroker, charming them as usual. At dinner a few days earlier, all the strokers agreed that the men in the group purposely rolled their eyes and sat with their tongues hanging out so Charmaine would spend more time with them. Sometimes Charmaine would move in close, touching a guy's back, putting her head close to his so he could smell the musky perfume that went well with her gorgeous face and body. When Charmaine snuck up on Steve that morning and bent in close, and her head and his head were side by side, and he turned to see her big blue eyes right there, he recalled that Marjorie also had blue eyes. Marjorie parking her wheelchair next to his and leaning in close and saying they should put her brain and his brain together and make a no-brainer. The recollection made him laugh, and his laughter made Charmaine giggle.

After Charming Charmaine finished her rounds, the cute speech therapist named Bianca gave her speech about the staff putting the pressure on for their own good. Steve had heard this speech aimed at new strokers in the group many times and began to tune out. Even when Bianca launched into her musical "Name Game" exercise in which those in the group were quizzed about one another's names, he tuned out.

He needed to get back to his hunches. Marjorie stumbling, yes, but stumbling upon someone who didn't want to be stumbled upon? Like maybe a punch-drunk flat-nosed guy? Or maybe Marjorie stumbled upon something else, and then someone worried that speech therapy might pop something out of Marjorie's head one day, causing the shit to hit the fan down at the administration office.

Maybe when he gets back to his room he should type all these crazy hunches into his PC. Then, when he reads them the next day after they've had time to cool, he can see if his hunches make sense, or they are simply a product of a stroke zapping a brain that's a cesspool of old hunches. And if anything coming out of his noggin does make sense, then what? Call Tamara? E-mail her? It wouldn't be the first time he'd e-mailed her. But in the past it was always day-in-and-day-out stuff, part of therapy in the computer lab. Maybe, instead of doing the usual word drills on the therapy software, he could get on the Internet and send e-mail after e-mail, dumping all the crazy hunches from his head until . . . until Tamara loses patience and Steve Babe becomes known at Chicago PD as the crank-head down at Hell in the Woods?

When the "Name Game" ended and the strokers wheeled down the hall for coffee, they passed floor-to-ceiling windows that looked out on the courtyard. Some frowned up toward the cloudy skies and rain slanting down and spattering the windows. Although Steve noticed the change in weather, he stared at the floor, wheeling himself slowly behind the others. The word *case* was there again, its meaning and importance having escalated. If this was a case that needed investigating, how could he do it? Now that he was able to use the phone, maybe he should call Tamara because there was no way to get across so much detail on e-mail. By the time she read her mailbox and responded to one question—probably with a question of her own—the circumstances of the case could have changed completely. So maybe he should call Tamara. Not tell her about the case on the phone, his speech wasn't good enough for that. But he could ask her to visit, and when she did, he'd be prepared with his notes and maybe be able to show her in writing what was on his mind. First he'd tell her he didn't think Marjorie's death was an accident. Then he'd tell her he had . . . what were they called? Leads. Yes, he had leads pointing in two directions. One direction, perhaps the most obvious, was toward the staff guy named Tyrone Washington who was clearly ripping off supplies or maybe drugs at Hell in the Woods. The other direction, not as obvious but a whole lot more interesting, was Marjorie Gianetti's family. This direction would be hard to explain because a lot of it was intuition, things picked up when Marjorie was alive, things she'd said in speech rehab.

But calling Tamara seemed a great idea only if he were alone in the world. Calling Tamara would be selfish. Not because Jan had told him he and Tamara had once been lovers. No, the selfish part would be him, a damn stroker, going after a case as if no one else mattered. He wasn't alone in the world, and he couldn't do that to Jan.

As he rolled slowly behind the others to the central rehab lunchroom for coffee, he felt extremely melancholy. He was supposed to be a happy son-of-a-bitch, but this feeling that, after finally finding out who he'd been and what he'd done, he'd have to give it up . . . well, that depressed the hell out of him.

During physical rehab that morning, Percy put a restraint mitt on Steve's good left hand to encourage him to do more with his right hand. Exercises like picking up balls and putting them into baskets. But instead of using the balls, Steve grabbed one of the grips and began squeezing it as best he could. He worked hard on strengthening his right arm and hand, squeezing the grip clumsily until Percy came by.

"Take it easy, Steve. I told you you're going to pull something if you keep up like that."

When he went back to his regular routine, Percy smiled and patted his shoulder. "That's better. The idea is to work on the entire routine so you'll rebuild those neural pathways. Number and quality, not brute strength. You'll need finesse to drive a car in a few weeks. Keep your mind on that."

When Percy said this, Steve thought again of driving a Gypsy caravan with some idiot in back trying in vain to play a violin. Yes, an idiot like him, thinking too much about a past that's lost to him instead of thinking of the here and now.

At speech rehab, in one of the small speech rehab rooms, Georgiana asked Steve to set up the tape recorder while she went to the computer lab with Hiram, the local computer expert.

"Set up a blank tape, Steve. We'll be working with a new arrival named Harold. He just checked in today and you can help with the exercise."

"Hope that ain't my daddy," said Hiram, standing in the doorway with several colorful computer software cartons under each arm.

"What?" asked Georgiana.

"My daddy's name was Harold," said Hiram. "Hope he didn't dig himself out of Martin Luther King Cemetery and have himself a stroke. Otherwise you'll have to find someone else to load all this new software."

Instead of answering, Georgiana rolled her eyes toward Steve, then went off to the computer lab with Hiram.

Harold was not Hiram's daddy, definitely not recently exhumed from Martin Luther King Cemetery on the south side. Harold was not only white, but much too young to have been Hiram's daddy. Steve figured Harold must have been a weightlifter before his stroke because he had monstrous muscles in his upper body. The aide named Pete delivered Harold to the rehab room and hung around for a while, slouching down in Georgiana's chair. Pete fiddled with his long sideburns and stared alternately at Harold and at Steve.

"How's it goin'?" asked Pete.

"It's goin'," said Steve.

There was something about the way Pete fiddled with his sideburns that Steve couldn't put his finger on. He should remember what it is, but all he could think of was reaching out and, because he'd thought the words, actually putting his finger on one of Pete's sideburns. He didn't do it, but something from the past made him want to do it. Instead, he found himself rubbing his chin with his left hand. Then he recalled it. Yes, having a new beard and rubbing it simply because it's new. Or fiddling with the beard the way Pete fiddled with his sideburns as if the sideburns are new and need getting used to.

Pete didn't get up from the chair when Georgiana returned from the computer lab until Georgiana asked him whether he had work to do somewhere else in the facility. Reluctantly, Pete unfolded himself from the chair, gave a heavy sigh, and left.

After taking her seat, Georgiana announced that Harold had the rare privilege of being the youngest stroke victim to ever have been enrolled at Hell in the Woods. Harold was twenty-seven, his stroke an apparent result of overdoing steroids when he was a teenager.

Harold's age shocked Steve, making him forget his own dilemma for the moment. He concentrated on giving Georgiana a hand. When

Harold was unable to pronounce a word correctly after finally managing to get it out, not only would Georgiana ask Steve to play it back, but she also asked Steve to say the word. Steve knew this was part of the program. Set up a little competition, put a little pressure on poor Harold who had obviously put a little too much pressure on his circulatory system during his young life. He and Marjorie had seen this done before, had even done it to one another during their sessions.

Harold would try to say, "Hand," but it came out more like, "Aggehnd." Then Georgiana would play it back and have Steve say it.

As speech therapy for Harold went on, Steve returned to his earlier ruminations because repeating words and operating the tape recorder had become routine. He thought about his case again, and about the possibility that pursuing it in any way might bring danger to Jan either from Tyrone or, worse, from a "family" member who didn't care for anyone nosing into their business. Jan had wanted to check around, and if he kept bringing this thing up, he knew she'd eventually do something that might backfire. She'd already questioned the nurses' aide who found Marjorie, and the paramedics.

Why the hell couldn't he keep his mouth shut? Why the hell did he have to tell Jan about Dino Justice and things Marjorie mentioned about some idiotic fly in the ointment and her nephew, Max the fly? Probably better that Jan was gone for a long weekend because who knows what else he'd say to make her want to help him? When it came right down to it, he wasn't sure if he'd still be alive if it wasn't for Jan's help in the first place, and then to use her like this . . .

As he sat there alternately pushing the Record, Rewind, and Play buttons on the recorder, he noticed someone standing at the doorway to the small room. At first he assumed it was Pete again, or maybe Hiram returned from the computer lab. But when he looked up, he saw Tyrone Washington looking in at him, a strange smile on his face.

And just at that moment, Georgiana spoke up, saying Steve's name and asking him to demonstrate a word for Harold. And so, without taking his eyes off Tyrone, he said it.

After he said the word, Georgiana seemed on the verge of laughter. "Steve, I don't think that's the word I had in mind. It's been quite a while since I've heard you use it."

When he turned from the doorway and looked at Georgiana and Harold, both were trying to suppress grins. He looked down at the recorder, saw that the red Record button was depressed and rewound the tape. When he pushed Play, he heard his own voice say, "Fuckhead."

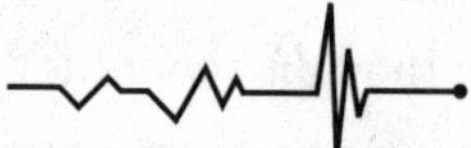

Fuckhead? Shit, if he ever got caught saying something like that, Tyrone knew he'd get the pink slip. And if he got the pink slip, he'd lose his connections. And if he lost his connections, he wasn't sure what he'd do.

Fuckhead? A paycheck was one thing, but if he got canned out of this place he'd lose the extra dough he got from Christ Health Care Supplies by way of Flat Nose. And now he'd bought the DeVille from the classic car shop, so he needed that extra dough more than ever.

Goddamn system. White bastard calls him a fuckhead, then white bitch with her dumb-ass name like a man's name laughs at him. Good thing that fox speech therapist Bianca wasn't around to overhear him being called a fuckhead. No way he could ever hope to get into her pants if she heard him being called a fuckhead and being laughed at.

Maybe right now was the time to teach this Babe guy a lesson. Maybe tonight he'd come back and pay the bastard a visit. Shit, this was getting complicated. Coming back to this place on his own free time. Just what the hell did Babe and that old lady talk about all those times they were in that little room with that Georgiana bitch and her damn tape recorder? Sure, it was good not having the nosy old lady around anymore, but why the hell did she have to leave this Babe guy behind with his dumb-ass name?

Maybe, instead of waiting until tonight, he should deliver a couple cases of toilet paper to the storage room behind the nurses' station on the third floor and snoop around Babe's room. Hardly anyone on the floor this time of day. Unless that bitch wife of his is there with all her damn magazines so the two of them can sit down later tonight and point to pictures instead of watching TV and keeping their mouths shut like normal asshole resident families. Yeah, the bastard pointing out pictures that would probably make his skin crawl. Pictures of glasses, or maybe a water spigot with water coming out, or maybe even an advertisement for janitor closet shit like brooms and mops, or maybe something about door alarms or some damn thing. Shit, why hadn't he thought of that before? Just because the bastard couldn't talk so good, didn't mean he couldn't point to those damn pictures.

As Tyrone got on the service elevator to go down for the cases of toilet paper so he'd have an excuse to be up on the third floor, he wondered if he might really have to do it. He wondered if he'd have to sneak into the guy's room late at night and . . . and what? Twist his good arm behind his back and whisper sweet nothings?

He could say, "Listen to me, motherfucker. And don't go looking for your call button 'cause I already got it."

He'd have to research it. Watch him for a couple days to make sure he really was a right-brainer, which meant his left arm would be the good arm. He could say, "Don't holler or nothin' 'cause it won't do no good. If you holler I'll break it. I seen stuff you wrote down in your room. If you don't stop poking that big nose where it don't belong . . ."

No. It'd be better to take another approach.

He could say, "Don't you understand everybody screws the system in this place? Even you screw it with your damn insurance forms. So how about we reach a little understanding?"

The guy would nod then. And he'd finish by saying, "That's better. Now I really shouldn't do this, but I'm gonna tell you a couple things that'll help you understand the situation a little better. See, it ain't just me. There's bigger cats out there that'll cut your balls off and throw you down the elevator shaft if they find out you're trying to put them out of business. These bigger cats, they're not health care workers like me. They don't give a shit about health. Not your health, and especially not the health of that nice lady comes to visit who drives a nice red Audi. You get my drift?"

Another nod.

"Good. You should get my drift better this time than last time. Maybe the seizure made you forget, maybe it didn't. Anyway, messing around with this business is like messing with God himself. You'll get burned and so will your wife. You're messing with big fish here, man. I mean big fish. You still listening?"

Nod.

Back on the first floor, Tyrone went down the hall toward the storage room to get the cases of toilet paper. But he stopped off at the men's room to think. He wished he was out with Latoya right now instead of in this place. If he ever told Latoya about all this, she'd probably tell him to get lost. That's how straight she was. Even when he got the DeVille and made up some shit about a loan, she saw right through him.

If there was any more trouble from this guy Babe, he guessed there was only one way out of it. As he flushed the toilet, he vowed that if this went any further, if Babe kept up his interest in the closet and in Tyrone's business, maybe it would be best to let Flat Nose or even

DeJesus handle it. Of course DeJesus wouldn't handle it himself. No, DeJesus would have a flunky do the dirty work, a short-fuse flunky like Flat Nose.

Shit, he was probably lucky Flat Nose hadn't killed him after the squabble in the car outside Mrs. Babe's apartment. Must have been a lucky night all around, him feeling his oats at the exact same time Flat Nose was side-tracked sniffin' beaver. But one thing Flat Nose had was a good memory. Ever since that night Flat Nose obviously had something on his mind, one of those things that won't let go until he blows his fuse and levels someone. He'd seen Flat Nose like this before, like he's got a plan and won't be satisfied until he carries it out. Worst of all was the possibility that Flat Nose and DeJesus might have something going down they haven't told him about. If that was true, and if they were looking to put him out of the picture, he'd better damn well do something to save himself.

When Tyrone left the men's room, he continued walking toward the storage room where the toilet paper was kept. Besides needing some on the third floor, he'd have to bring some back where he'd just been because he used the last of it.

CHAPTER THIRTEEN

Although it had been only a few days since their last meeting, Hanley insisted they meet again. Only this time, instead of having to drive across the state to Naples, Hanley arranged to fly into Miami. They agreed to meet at the airport in the bar outside the security area. Valdez was on time and saw by the flight monitor that Hanley's flight would be late. While he waited, Valdez had a glass of red wine. For several years, since hearing reports of the benefits of red wine, Valdez had made a habit of sipping a red wine at some point during his day. Usually, because of other commitments, he had to wait until evening. But today, because he did not have to drive to Naples to meet with Hanley, he decided to take advantage of the situation. He'd even turned off his phone. No need to stay in contact with anyone except Skinner, and Skinner never called him on his cell phone. By the time Hanley arrived, Valdez felt quite relaxed.

Hanley dropped his small carry-on bag onto one of the extra chairs at the table and, seeing Valdez's wine glass, asked, "What are you having?"

"A California Merlot."

"Perhaps I'll have one," said Hanley, raising his hand to get the bartender's attention.

Valdez turned, pointing to his empty glass, to himself, and also to Hanley. A few seconds later they clinked glasses like old friends and sipped their wine.

Except for Hanley's white sneakers, both wore casual business attire, slacks and button shirts. To airline passengers rushing past the bar, they probably looked like a pair of typical Miami old goats after an early morning round of golf.

"Did you bring your clubs?" asked Valdez, smiling.

"Golf clubs?"

"Yes."

"You know I don't golf."

Valdez took another sip of wine. "No fishing and no golfing make Hanley a dull boy."

"Right," said Hanley. "How many of those have you had?"

"This is only my second," said Valdez.

"If you're driving you'd better make it your last."

"I wasn't sure how long you'd be. Besides, you know what they say about red wine."

"What do they say?" asked Hanley.

"Helps keep the arteries clear. Less chance of a stroke."

"If anyone's listening in we must sound like a couple of old farts."

Both men smiled and chuckled.

"Seriously," said Valdez. "I took the afternoon off. And since I knew you'd be here eventually I thought I'd let you drive. I assume you'll want to stay at the condo tonight."

"Right," said Hanley. "I think it best I stay in town until this thing in Chicago is resolved. Have you heard any more news from the rehab facility about our friend with a stroke?"

"I have," said Valdez. "Contact number one now thinks the stroke patient is aware of more than he is letting on. He and his wife attended the funeral and met with members of the family. Their meeting might have had a purpose beyond simply extending condolences."

"In what way?"

"Our second contact thinks the detective must have communicated information to his wife. She called an acquaintance in the Chicago Police Department and made implications. Apparently both the family and the local scam artists have become possible suspects."

"That's interesting," said Hanley, taking a gulp of wine before continuing. "You know what will happen if either the husband or the wife pursues this."

"The nephew?" asked Valdez.

"Right," said Hanley. "Max the Fly will buzz around until something blows up in someone's face. You know we can't let that happen."

"I know," said Valdez. "What do you suggest?"

"I'll stay in town," said Hanley. "Tell the office to have a plane to Chicago ready."

"You're going to Chicago?"

"Not only me," said Hanley. "Both of us. If the elderly lady repeated things to another stroke victim that we're not aware of, we have no choice. And who better to pay a visit to a rehabilitation facility than two old farts? If we do go, by the way, get yourself a pair of sneakers or at least lighter-colored shoes. We'll need to be in character. And even though I don't golf, perhaps we'll take along a couple sets of clubs."

"We're taking clubs to Chicago?" asked Valdez. "The weather's lousy there."

"We've been on a golf excursion and we're heading home to see how our wives are doing at their rehab. Wear a golf jacket with deep inside pockets. I've got a golf cap to wear. Old guys always wear caps, so maybe you could come up with one."

"Deep inside pockets," repeated Valdez. "Well, I guess if someone has to go it might as well be us. We'll fit right in."

"By the way," said Hanley. "What's the name of our number two out there?"

Valdez smiled. "You old goat. It's Maria and you know it."

Hanley downed his wine and stood. "We'd better get going. We can speak in more detail at the condo and I'd like to have time for a workout at the health club and get a good night's sleep in case we have to fly out tomorrow."

The two men walked down the long hallway toward the parking lot. Their gaits were noticeably slower and somewhat bowlegged compared to the younger people passing them in both directions. The only two older than the pair was an elderly couple being transported by a skycap in a beeping electric cart. At the conveyor walkway, both men paused, the younger of the two taking the carryon while the other rubbed his arthritic hands together. On the walkway they stood one behind the other as men, women, and children rushed past them.

CHAPTER FOURTEEN

ALTHOUGH IT WAS EARLY IN THE DAY, THE WEATHER OUTSIDE made it seem like night. The two day shift guards at the Saint Mel in the Woods Rehabilitation Facility main lobby desk amused themselves watching smokers try to suck down a few drags without getting soaked as wind-blown rain slanted beneath the portico at the entrance. Technically, smoking was allowed only around the corner from the entrance in an unprotected area with benches and a sand bucket for butts, but the wind from the southeast caused smokers to try to find whatever protection they could, a course of action that amounted to pacing along the western edge of the portico.

"Think one of us should go out there and tell them they're supposed to be around the corner out in the rain?"

"Wouldn't do any good. They always insist they're on their way in or out. That's why they keep pacing. They've lost their regular smoking spot and they've got to keep moving."

After a man in an overcoat stepped around the corner to smash out his butt, he ran back inside, taking off his coat and shaking it out in the vestibule.

"Won't see many smokers this day. Look at him, like a hound dog come out of the pond."

The next smoker to venture out was in a wheelchair, a man in a leather jacket and a red baseball cap. The man had gotten off the elevator, circled the front counter and was now sitting outside beneath the portico puffing away.

"Think he's a patient or a visitor?"

"Could be a rehab outpatient. I've seen him before."

"If he is, he's new. Not here long enough to know he can go up to the fourth floor and use the private balcony."

"What private balcony? I didn't know there was a balcony up there."

"Nurses and aides smoke out there, and sometimes use their cell phone minutes out there. As a courtesy, they usually allow smokers in wheelchairs, too. Of course they lock up the balcony when the inspectors are here."

"Look now. He ain't just smokin', he's got a cell phone."

"Yeah, maybe he went outside to use it instead of in the building."

"We gonna roust him for smoking under the portico when he comes back inside?"

"What do you think? Is it worth it? Or should we let it pass?"

"Maybe the guy's got no car to smoke in. Maybe he took the bus here like a lot of us poor folks has to."

"I see your point."

"Another thing in the guy's favor, he's using his cell phone outside even though usage isn't as serious here as back at the hospital. Not as much equipment that can get messed up."

"Okay, so we don't roust him."

"Would you say the same if he was black?"

"Come on, don't get on me."

"Okay. Didn't mean nothin' by it."

"Here he comes back. Soaked from the lap down."

"Yeah, wind blowing under the portico. Notice how his phone is tucked away so we don't have to say anything that'll complicate his life or our lives."

"Is it a lot quieter working this place than back at the hospital?"

"Hell yes. Back there you don't know what might come through those doors."

Both guards glanced back as the man in the leather jacket and red baseball cap headed for the bank of elevators. Directly in front of the elevators, mounted in a frame on a high chrome stand, was the sign announcing that cellular phones were not to be used beyond this point. When the man wheeled his chair past the sign and into an elevator and the door slid closed, the two guards turned back to look outside, waiting for the next smoker.

"It's usually like a graveyard here at night. Sometimes I can hear the old folks snoring out in the nursing wing. 'Course in this weather with the flight paths at O'Hare switched around . . ."

"When you goin' on nights anyway?"

"I feel like I'm on nights now from the look of that sky out there."

"Come on, for real."

"In three weeks I go on for two."

As the two guards stared out at the rain slanting beneath the portico, a rumbling gathered overhead. In a lounge to one side of the lobby, visitors, unfamiliar with the fact that strong southeasterly winds changed the takeoff patterns at O'Hare, stared up at the ceiling in disbelief.

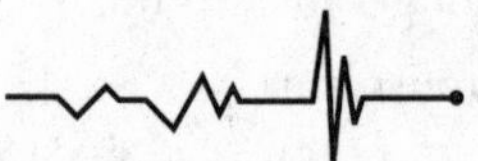

The sharp cold of the morning rain surprised her. Although there had been no wind at all the previous night as she peeked out the front window of the apartment at the man shadowboxing in the parking lot, that had apparently been the calm before the storm.

A couple weeks earlier, weather reporters had been hyping the early spring weather, one even implying that the warm weather of late February and early March might be a positive effect of global warming. But now, strong wind slanted the rain as if it were snow, biting when it smacked her face. As she ran from the apartment entrance to her car she imagined a reporter using this cold snap to discredit global warming. If she were with Steve and a reporter used the cold snap to do this, she knew it would make him sad. He'd stop smiling, look down, shake his head, and she'd know what he was thinking. He'd be thinking that the entire world and everyone in it had had a stroke.

On the roads, drivers who had also been bitten by the cold and wet were angry, honking and cutting one another off even though it was Friday morning and folks should be looking forward to the weekend. At a stoplight, when a car refused to move ahead so the honking car behind could squeeze through for a right turn on red, the Hispanic woman being honked at held up her middle finger for the Oriental man behind to see and the man reacted to this by angrily holding up his middle finger. Perhaps because the weather made outdoor activities impossible, traffic was heavy, folks out banking or grocery shopping or getting the dog groomed, or simply letting off steam on the last day of a hectic work week.

To Jan, the world seemed an especially cold and violent place that morning, a place in which no one would give a damn if an old woman in a nursing home was shoved through death's door prematurely, a cynical place where disability is equated with death. That some might even wish early death to the disabled in order to ease the health care burden on the economy depressed her. But when she parked her car and ran into the library, it was warm and bright and the head librarian greeted her and she recalled the times she'd been here with Steve. Suddenly she felt much better about the world and got down to work.

It didn't take long on the computerized newspaper and periodical search systems to find references to the Gianetti family. The first was a series of articles published after Antonio Gianetti's death in May of 1986. Gianetti's life fit the mold of a mobster. The organization he allegedly headed (there was always that word *allegedly* in the references) had been into gambling, loan sharking, construction and trucking scams, prostitution. According to the articles he'd been one of the last old-time Chicago hoods. Even his death—found shot in the head in the trunk of his Lincoln—followed the pattern.

A columnist in the Chicago Sun-Times wrote a semi-humorous piece shortly after the killing indicating that there hadn't been this kind of gangland execution in a long time in Chicago and perhaps the city fathers could capitalize on it by having some kind of lakefront festival. It would be a celebration of the old days with its "olde-time" lessons. The serious part of the article speculated that someone outside Chicago might have fingered Gianetti for giving organized crime a bad name, perhaps having the hit man, or men, flown in and out. The article further speculated that a national or international organization might have felt Gianetti was getting too wholesome of late, being he hadn't been in the news in a long time and seemed to enjoy the privacy of his family life. The article also hinted the killing might have had something to do with Illinois or Chicago politics, but gave no specifics.

When Jan searched for other things that might have been going on in 1986, she found the Chernobyl disaster had taken place shortly before Gianetti's murder. The Chernobyl disaster occurred in late April, but because news was slow coming out of the old Soviet Union the news peaked in early May, Chernobyl taking over the front pages while reports of Gianetti's murder were buried inside. Chernobyl, 1986. Yes, that was probably the reason the word *Chernobyl* was part of Marjorie's vocabulary. Her husband murdered when Chernobyl was in the news.

Jan spent over an hour going through all the articles she could find on Antonio Gianetti. The result was more of the same. Gianetti had been suspected of heading an "old-fashioned Chicago-style" organization for almost three decades, had been charged with numerous crimes but never prosecuted, and apparently leaned toward so-called "clean" businesses like gambling and construction and the wholesale produce business, only occasionally venturing into prostitution. The two things that stood out after reading all the articles were that Gianetti had maintained a low profile in the years prior to his death, and had also managed, during his entire career, to keep any mention or coverage of his family out of the media. In all the articles, not once was his residence, or even whether he lived in the city or suburbs, mentioned. One article written after his death alluded to this, saying maybe Gianetti had been more powerful than anyone imagined, and implying that, over the years, he was able to get to newspaper editors as well as television and radio station managers in order to maintain his privacy. Apparently he'd been a big Reagan supporter and worked behind the scenes to make sure, as one article put it, "There'd be no more Kennedy or Carter style Democrats put into office." There was no mention in any of the archived articles from the eighties and nineties of Marjorie or Antonio Junior.

Looking further back into the seventies and even the sixties, Jan found a cross-reference mentioning Gianetti in a *Newsweek* article about waning support for then President Nixon. Gianetti was one of several "so-called self-proclaimed patriots" quoted in the article.

"Yeah, I like Nixon," Gianetti was quoted. "I got a nephew come back from Vietnam with his arms blown off but I still support the guy (Nixon). Someone's got to stop the Commies." The article went on to say that Gianetti apparently put his money where his mouth was, using his influence to get jobs for Vietnam veterans in Chicago's busy produce market district where it was rumored the Chicago mob controlled a lot of what went on.

When Jan sidetracked into the Chicago produce market topic in her search on the computerized system, she came across Steve's name. Her first thought at seeing his name on the computer screen was of his stroke because, in a way, the world seemed a much smaller place now, the world shrinking because of the media and mass communication the way it suddenly shrinks for a stroke victim.

The article mentioning Steve concerned a suspect in a then recently-exposed scam in which trucks entering the South Water Market Street produce market were expected to pay a "parking fee." During police questioning of the suspect, whose name was Rickie Deveno, there was an implication that a Chicago private detective might have been hired to enforce some of the fees, and Deveno had named Steve Babe. But the article went on to say that, after Babe was brought in, and after several truck drivers were questioned, it was found that Babe was not involved and Deveno had apparently pulled Steve's name out of the air to protect his relatives who were actually the ones providing the muscle in the scam.

Back on the Gianetti track on the computerized system, Jan read an article from a Chicago magazine praising Gianetti for his support of the handicapped, especially Vietnam veterans. The article, published in 1988, said that before his death, Gianetti was a big supporter of handicapped veterans, and after Gianetti's death in 1986, his nephew, one Maximo Lamberti worked to continue that legacy. According to the article, Lamberti, who did his stint in the military in the eighties, had no less than seven handicapped employees, three of them Vietnam veterans, working for him at his produce company.

When she finished with the Gianetti references in the archives, Jan looked up Max Lamberti. It seemed Max's father before him, then Max, had been involved in some kind of peripheral organization, but not much was known about it. There was a photograph of Max as a much younger man in his military uniform posing with his father. The caption said the photograph was taken during Max Lamberti's first leave after boot camp and that soon he'd be headed for Fort Bragg and the 82nd Airborne Division. In the photograph, Max held his service cap at his side and, because the boot camp haircut had grown out some, Jan could see that Max had already lost a lot of his hair back then. She recalled Max at the funeral, leering at her while holding onto her hand unnecessarily. Now she was certain Max wore a hairpiece because the mane of hair that plunged down onto his forehead was much too thick for a transplant.

The only connection she found between Antonio Gianetti Senior and his nephew Max was a hint that Max worked for the Gianetti organization when he first got into organized crime after his military discharge, and that he probably learned the ropes there before stepping into his father's shoes after his father died. None of the articles implied Max took over Gianetti's old organization after Gianetti's death. In fact, one of the articles went out of its way to show that the old organization seemed to die with the senior Gianetti.

One thing that did stand out, after reading about uncle and nephew, was that Max, the nephew, had apparently been involved in the business of bringing drugs into Chicago. In contrast, her earlier reading about Gianetti indicated he had a great disdain for drug trafficking. This difference made Jan think of Steve's references to a "fly in the ointment" and "Max the fly" and she wondered if Max's peripheral organization trafficked exclusively in drugs, and if that's what made him a "black sheep" in the larger family.

Jan moved from the archive computer to one of the Internet computers where she searched out more recent references to the Gianetti family. In these articles the name Antonio had been dropped in favor of Tony. There she found several articles about Tony Junior and even a couple articles written by him. As she read the articles about global warming and other environmental issues, Jan recalled Marjorie saying something about her son being a lover of nature. One of the articles, bylined Tony Gianetti, with no mention of him being a junior, was from *Sierra Magazine*. The article was from 2004, itemizing what he considered President Bush's environmental failures and giving reasons why Bush should not be re-elected President.

As Jan sat at the computer reading outspoken environmental and political articles by Tony Junior, the librarian came over. Her name was Bonnie and she had a soft look and sallow complexion that made it seem she never went outside the library into the sunlight. Of course Bonnie wouldn't have been able to go out into the sunlight this day because the rain was still slanting sideways against the large windows in the reference area.

Bonnie's hair was long and straight, tied behind her head. She wore a maroon sweater over a white blouse and gray wool skirt. It looked like one of only a few outfits Jan had ever seen Bonnie wear. She remembered Steve once saying maybe when the three or four skirts got threadbare they could buy some new ones for Bonnie. Though this may have seemed cruel at the time, it was not. Steve had been perfectly serious, the statement not a joke at all, but an indication of his concern for Bonnie.

Bonnie had once had problems with a library patron from whom she accepted an invitation for a date. Following the date, which turned out to be a date rape, the man had stalked Bonnie. She was working evenings at the time and the stalker kept showing up at the library before closing time. He would wait inside, watching Bonnie close up behind the front desk, then he would go outside to wait for her in the parking lot. She told Steve about this one evening when she could stand it no longer. Jan did not know what Steve said to the man, all she knew was that Steve approached the man in the library that evening, sat beside him, opened a book and pretended to read while he spoke softly to the man. The result of this one-sided conversation was that the man left, saying goodnight to those at the counter, including Bonnie, and never returned.

Bonnie pulled out the chair next to Jan. "Mind if I sit?"

"Not at all."

"You looked busy," said Bonnie. "But I didn't want you to leave before I had a chance to ask about Steve. How's he doing?"

"Not bad. They're working him pretty hard, running him through the mill at Saint Mel's."

"I've heard good things about their program," said Bonnie. "Is he still getting a lot of physical therapy like at the hospital?"

"Quite a bit. At first it bothered him, having to be shown how to do simple things, but he got used to it. At the rehab center the physical and occupational therapy is more advanced—using the phone, computers, and they've even mentioned the possibility of driving soon. But they mainly work on verbal and written communication skills."

"How's the aphasia?" asked Bonnie.

"Better," said Jan. "It turns out the damage to Steve's left brain caused mostly expressive aphasia rather than receptive aphasia. That means he's pretty good at understanding what you're saying, but has trouble responding. The way he describes it, sometimes the words are there, floating right in front of him, but they're upside-down or inside-out. And at other times, when he finally comes up with the word that matches the concept and he's ready to say it, it's like grasping at straws. The word is there, but when he goes to grab it, it slips away. But he is getting much better typing things. I was just reading something about global warming and it reminded me of what he typed the other day. He said when he came out of the stroke and started trying to follow news on television about global warming, it was as though the world had had a stroke."

Bonnie reached out and put her hand on Jan's for a moment before pulling it back. "It must be very frustrating for Steve and for you. He was always one who knew how to say just the right thing. I should know."

"It is frustrating sometimes," said Jan. "He's been referring to the stroke as a brain bullet. I guess the description is about right. After the stroke some circuits are shot, some aren't. It's pretty random."

"What about the medication you told me about last time?"

"The Citicoline?"

"Yes," said Bonnie, "that was it. The article I read said they have high hopes for Citicoline helping the injured brain repair itself by somehow internally bypassing or fixing damaged circuits."

Jan looked toward the window at the droplets running into one another on the glass, then cascading down in a stream. "Steve's doctors say the Citicoline did some good, but that it can't bring the brain all the way back. There's also the timing. Citicoline is supposed to be started within twenty-four hours of the stroke, and within the first few hours for maximum effect. They gave it to him right after they gave him the clot-dissolving drug. But there's still some question as to whether we got him to the hospital and got the Citicoline in him within the window for . . . for maximum effect."

"We don't have to talk about it if you don't want to," said Bonnie.

Jan turned from the window and looked back at Bonnie, saw the sad face, reached out and touched her hand. "It's okay, Bonnie. He's doing better. In speech therapy he runs the tape recorder and demonstrates word pronunciation to newcomers. It's just that I'm always there, and from one day to the next it probably seems as if nothing's changed, when in fact he's making steady progress. We've kept a goals diary for Steve since he first went into the hospital like they suggested, and I suppose if I looked back in it once in a while, I'd see how much he's progressed."

After she and Bonnie exchanged goodbyes, Bonnie came back. "I almost forgot. You looked so busy on the computer. Is there anything I can help you find?"

"I think I've about exhausted it, Bonnie. I've been looking for information on Chicago organized crime figures. It has to do with something Steve . . . well, it has to do with Steve."

"Do you have names?" asked Bonnie.

After she gave Bonnie the names Gianetti and Lamberti and told about what she'd found so far, Bonnie led Jan to a small file behind the checkout desk. After a while Bonnie wrote something down on a card, then had Jan follow her to the audio-visual department. There she searched through educational videos until she came out with one. She had a smile on her face.

"It's a four-part PBS program on organized crime. Part three is an hour-long segment on Chicago, past and present. It was aired a few years ago, but maybe you can find something."

The excitement of the search. Jan began to feel it when Bonnie handed her the tape and took her to a viewing room. The feeling grew even stronger at the beginning of the hour-long Chicago segment when the introduction showed flashes of Chicago crime figures, including a photograph of Antonio Gianetti right in there with those of Capone and Spilotro and Accardo. And the feeling reached it's peak when she got to the part of the video covering not only Antonio Gianetti Senior, but also his nephew, Maximo Lamberti.

Although there were only stills of Gianetti, apparently because Gianetti Senior valued his privacy and did not give interviews, there was a brief interview with nephew Max.

In the video, Max was a few years younger than the man she met at Marjorie's funeral, but older than the boot camp graduate she'd seen photographed with his father. He had not yet grown a mustache, but he'd already donned the thick black hairpiece. He stared at the camera as he spoke, leaning closer to it. As she watched the interview, it became obvious to Jan that Max was not one to shy away from the limelight the way his uncle had.

"Tell me," said the interviewer, "was your uncle part of the organization or wasn't he?"

"My Uncle Tony?"

"Yes."

"My Uncle Tony was a good man. He might have been part of some kind of organization, I don't know."

"By organization, I mean organized crime in Chicago."

"Jesus, you mean the mob?"

"Okay, the mob. Specifically, the Chicago mob. However, before the interview you asked me not to use the word."

"That's right," said Max, staring at the camera. "I don't like the word *mob.* But if you're going to ask questions and you expect me to answer, I've got to call a spade a spade."

Max looked to the side, smiled and reached out, shoving at someone off camera. "Hey, don't take it so serious. . . Okay, you want to know if my Uncle Tony was in the mob. Sure he was. But things were different back then. Truck drivers were in the mob and grocery store owners were in the mob and politicians—especially politicians—were in the mob."

"I see your point," said the interviewer. "But what about more recent times? What about just prior to his death? Tony Gianetti died in 1986. Was he still in the mob in the 1980s?"

Max smiled and nodded at the camera. "That's a very good question. But I'm sorry to say there's no way to know the answer. I was in the military in the eighties serving my country, so I couldn't exactly keep track of what was going on back here in Chicago. As far as my Uncle Tony was concerned, he was a very private man. He never did interviews or any of this. He never wanted publicity. And in his later years, he was even private from his own family. He was a good man, giving to charities, especially the Vietnam vets. But he never wanted a medal for it."

"I understand you've taken over where your uncle left off, hiring veterans and supporting their causes."

"Something bad about that?"

"No."

"Sure, just because there wasn't a war when I served, doesn't mean I don't love my country. I've hired U.S. vets from all services and all conflicts to work for me. And not only vets, but other handicapped people. I got one guy who got his legs chopped off in a combine accident. He's just standing there one day out in the field in Kansas and the combine . . . see, it's dark out and the driver can't see him and . . . what's the matter?"

"Nothing. I just wondered if we could stick to the topic."

"Okay, if you insist."

"I understand the Vietnam Veterans of America recently presented you with an award."

"Yeah, that's true, but I don't like to brag about it."

"Are you a member of the mob, Max?"

Max's face went sour, but the smile quickly returned. "That word, *mob*, it's one of those funny words that can be okay sometimes, but not okay at other times. This is one of those times when I don't care for it."

Because of the edit on the tape, Jan wasn't sure if the interview had ended there or not, but by the look on Max's face she figured it had.

The interview with Max was near the end of the Chicago segment, and the conclusion showed a video clip that encapsulated everything she had read about while on the computer search system earlier. The clip showed Max on a motor yacht cruising out of Burnham Harbor. He sat at the stern in the sun with several younger men gathered about him. The Chicago skyline was behind Max and it was obvious the shot had been taken through a telephoto lens. It appeared Max was lecturing, driving his right fist into his left palm for emphasis. The voiceover during the clip asked, "Are these young men recruits for tomorrow's Chicago mob?" What made the clip important to Jan was that she recognized one of the men as Dino, a much younger Dino, but definitely the one Steve pointed out at the funeral. And now she recalled the way Steve said, "Dino, Rickie's son," and how this had reminded him of a past incident involving Rickie Justice, Dino's father, who had changed his name from Deveno back when she first met Steve.

After giving the video back to Bonnie and thanking her, Jan returned to the computer and looked up Dino Justice and Rickie Justice. She found nothing under those names, but when she looked up Deveno, she not only found the article about the produce market scam in which Steve had been mentioned, but she also found another reference to Rickie Deveno.

This article, written in 1992, concerned a huge drug bust that took place in 1980. Deveno was mentioned as one of several mobsters who disappeared or dropped out of organized crime in the Chicago area in the years following the drug bust. The article implied that perhaps some of those who disappeared were in reality living on tropical islands. The article said that during the drug bust in 1980 on Chicago's south side, cocaine and heroin having a street value of 280 million dollars had been confiscated. Drawing on other evidence, the writer of the article showed the drugs were in transit and were most likely just about to be turned over to a buyer or buyers when the raid took place. The writer wondered what had happened to the money that must have been gathered for such a huge deal.

Suddenly, as Jan sat at the reference room computer rereading the article, she thought of something Steve had told her several years earlier. He had been on a case involving the missing wife of a cop he once worked with. At one point, when evidence seemed to point to foul play, and when the cop insisted he knew nothing about a certain piece of evidence, Steve had mentioned the 1980 drug bust and told Jan about a theory that had made the rounds.

According to Steve, several Chicago Police detectives had been murdered or had so-called "accidents" during the eighties. What many insiders wondered was whether the money gathered for the drug deal had actually been there at the scene when the bust came down. And if it had been there, who had provided it and how had it disappeared? The theory that had made the rounds was that the money came from the east coast organization and a group consisting of cops and hoods had agreed to hold the money back, lie low, and split it later. The under-the-table agreement was that the deal to lie low and keep quiet would go sour and Chicago mob figures would end up with most of the cash, leaving the crooked cops with the rest. The internal turmoil had supposedly resulted in an increase in the number of deaths among

Chicago detectives.

Pure speculation, Steve had admitted at the time, but the thing that came to her now, the really important thing Steve had said, was that the rise in deaths among Chicago detectives seemed to have lasted only a few years. Perhaps, he'd said, this was due to a general increase in violence against authorities in the eighties. Or, he speculated, perhaps it really did have something to do with the 1980 drug bust. Maybe the money was there, then a few years later, it just wasn't there anymore. Or maybe those who had an interest in the money were gone, one way or another, and it ended up in the hands of someone who outlasted the others.

Jan read the article about the 1980 drug bust again. The writer of the article speculated that at the time, in order to purchase drugs with a street value of 280 million, one could assume that at least 140 million would have been needed. Then the writer speculated about what this 140 million would be worth today, twelve years later in 1992 when the article was written. At a conservative six percent per year, the money would have grown to almost 282 million, or over a quarter billion dollars in 1992!

On a whim, Jan searched for organized crime involvement in health care and was surprised to find an entry. It was a short article about a health care brokerage, supposedly having mob connections in New York, that put pressure on companies to accept deals with certain insurance firms and not with others. One sidelight of the operation was that, in brokering deals, mob figures and their families and friends were sometimes illegally put on the insurance rolls of companies that got their coverage through the brokerage.

Jan got up from the computer and went for a walk to the drinking fountain. After a long drink, she returned to the reference room, but instead of sitting back down at the computer, she sat at one of the tables and buried her head in her hands.

Was she looking too hard? What did health care brokers in New York have to do with anything? And, for that matter, so what if Max Lamberti flaunted the fact he was in the mob? Steve had often said, when one *wants* to find something, it's much easier to discover evidence pointing in that direction. Was she finding connections simply because she wanted to find them? Did the fact that Gianetti was murdered in 1986 and the apparent fact that killings of Chicago Police detectives dropped off around the same time have anything to do with one another? Did Steve's statement back then that maybe the money was in one guy's hands mean more than she had thought at the time? Or was all of this just a convenient way to get Steve back into the work he loved, and therefore back to the man he'd been?

Prior to his stroke, Steve had involved her more and more in his cases. She enjoyed this involvement because it was part of him, because she loved him. And now here he was with a stroke. But the stroke—the aftermath of it—was part of him and she'd just have to love that too!

Perhaps it was okay to speculate, to make a few waves, as Steve would say. And if Steve were here now, if he were the one sitting in the library, what would he do? What would he think? Before his stroke she often came to the library with him. It was one of his favorite places. He always said that here he could speculate to his heart's content.

If Steve were here now he'd probably say something he once said when referring to another case he was on, a case involving the disappearance of a large sum of money. Nowhere near 140 million, but she recalled that a couple hundred thousand had disappeared from a savings account on which parents had put the names of their children. When the parents died suddenly and the account was found to be empty, two of the children hired Steve to see if he could find the money. While working on this case, Steve had told Jan, "When big bucks are in question, people change. They're like blindfolded kids with baseball bats in their hands all trying to see who can hit . . . what's that paper mache thing with candy and goodies they hang from the ceiling?"

"*Piñata,*" she had answered.

"I couldn't think of the word," he'd said. "It's like blindfolded kids trying to hit the *piñata*."

Steve was right, nothing like a library to help a person speculate, and nothing like a pile of money to further that speculation. Here, with her head in her hands on a library table, a son and a nephew and a few cohorts could easily have gotten together and determined that an old lady, who is perhaps sitting on the *piñata,* should go ahead and die, since she's close to death anyhow. But Steve had also reminded her many times that, although it was easy to speculate in a library, one had to constantly remind oneself there are separate sections for fact and fiction.

Of course, sometimes it didn't hurt to use speculation to make waves. That had also been one of Steve's tenets. She'd already made some waves telling Phil Hogan about the fingerprints on the glass that didn't exist. So, where else could she make waves? She didn't know where Tony Gianetti Junior or Max Lamberti lived; she knew their addresses weren't in the phone book or on the Web because she'd looked. Of course there was one place that should have an address. She'd been there just the other day, and today she wouldn't look out of place if she went there because this morning she'd chosen to wear dark blue slacks and a blouse and a dark blue raincoat instead of the jeans she might have worn.

It was still raining when she left the library. After throwing her purse and notebook onto the passenger seat and folding the umbrella inside before it blew away, she was about to slam the door when she noticed that the car parked two spots away was running. Ordinarily she wouldn't have noticed this, but the car was a BMW with squat fat tires mounted so they stuck out beyond the fenders. This wouldn't have mattered so much except she was certain the car had arrived at the library when she arrived. She'd seen it behind her while waiting for a car to pull out of a space. And now, since there was an empty space between her car and the BMW, she could see that the driver wore a baseball cap and was short and had a flat-nosed face.

CHAPTER FIFTEEN

Despite heavy rain Jan could see him behind her. The wide stance of the BMW with its fat tires sticking out the sides was a giveaway. On the Stevenson Expressway, the BMW's tires flung rainwater up into the air creating rooster tails at the sides of the car.

Was it possible she had already stumbled onto something? Was the case going too fast? She recalled Steve once saying that the gathering of evidence can draw you in, or worse, can sweep ahead of you and cast you aside. You need to be careful, he'd warned, that you don't become part of the circumstances of the case before you even know what's going on. Had she pursued this avenue of investigation partially because she simply didn't like the looks of a guy who held her hand a bit too long at yesterday's funeral? Steve had also said it was best to maintain control at the start of an investigation. Was she in control now?

What if Marjorie really did have an accident, and what if the flat-nosed guy in the BMW behind her was on staff at Saint Mel's and felt he was responsible for the accident? Perhaps that's why he was following her, to make sure she didn't get him in trouble. And here she is chasing down hoods and racketeers because they deserve to be guilty of something, don't they? But there was still the drug money. Was it really a connection? Or had she simply been waiting in the wings for an excuse to regress into a condition the stroke victim family counselor had warned her about weeks ago?

Sometimes, the counselor had said, a family member tries too hard. She thinks she is helping the loved one when in reality she is simply becoming active and agitated in order to get away from the situation and, therefore, from him. Sometimes running errands and speaking with staff can indicate a natural need to escape. The counselor said it was normal to have these feelings, but to accept them and to deal with them. Had she failed? Was she off on a wild goose chase because, like a child, she thought when she returned Steve would be all better?

Damn bitch, she should forget about all this. She should have either stayed with Steve or been honest with him and gone off for the long weekend with Lydia. But what about the guy behind her? Was he really the guy she'd seen shadowboxing last night in the parking lot? Now that she'd exited the expressway and made several turns it was obvious he was following her. Although she felt strangely guilty, somewhat frightened, and angry at the same time, she continued driving a zigzag route across the west side of the city. At one point she thought another car was following her, a car driven by a Hispanic woman. Could this be the same Hispanic woman she'd seen earlier that morning giving the finger to another driver?

Crazy. Now she *was* getting paranoid. First it's the guy in the BMW, next it's a Hispanic woman she saw once at a stoplight. How could she possibly recognize a driver she'd seen hours earlier in her rearview mirror through rain-streaked car windows? Finally, after a few more blocks of zigzagging, it appeared no one was following her.

When she arrived at the funeral home, Jan could tell by the numerous cars in the parking lot there was a funeral this morning. Arriving cars were being lined up nose to tail the way they had been lined up when she and Steve came here to Marjorie's funeral. The only difference was that it had been clear and sunny and calm, and today it was stormy. Although she did not see any squad cars at the moment, she knew there would be one or two later during the procession to the cemetery. If she stuck around and joined the funeral after doing what she'd come here to do, she'd be able to get the attention of a cop if the flat-nosed bastard was still following.

And so, she got in line, watched as a funeral home worker hanging onto a battle-weary umbrella came toward her car, opened the window slightly to accept the funeral sticker, applied the sticker to the inside of her windshield as instructed, then got out and ran inside as if she knew the deceased. On the way in from her car a gust of wind turned her umbrella inside out, but she managed to pull it back into shape as she ran for the canopied entrance. Once inside the vestibule shaking out her umbrella, she wondered if she had made a terrible mistake.

The funeral service had not yet begun and at least a hundred mourners stood crowded together in the lobby, with more inside the chapel. She might as well have worn jeans, or perhaps a bikini, because everyone in the lobby, and apparently, as word spread, everyone inside the chapel except the corpse, was aware she'd arrived. Not that any of the mourners knew her. All they knew was that a white woman with a soaked rat's nest of sandy brown hair had arrived and all of them were black.

Steve would have loved this. And when she told him about it, he'd probably have a good laugh. There were a few smiles, especially from a group of older women stationed near the door. One of the women nodded to her in greeting.

When she glanced back outside, she saw that her car was already hemmed in, two cars having been parked behind her by the funeral home worker, a white man—how tricky—in his fifties. If she worked at the funeral home—something she considered faking—she certainly would not have parked in line with the mourners. The group of older women near the entrance, who had a clear view out the window when she arrived, obviously noticed where she had parked. She tried to see if the BMW, with its wide-set wheels, was in the parking lot, but more black people were running toward the entrance and this blocked her view.

All right, idiot white lady, she told herself. Deal with it. These are people who've just lost someone, the way you almost lost Steve.

And so she returned nods and smiles politely, was about to drift off to the side of the lobby toward the restrooms and the offices—her original destination—when it became obvious by the aisle made for her and the subtle turning of bodies toward the chapel, and the fact the group who came in behind her was waiting, that she was expected to go inside and pay her respects.

The deceased was a man. About sixty or so. Appropriately, the mortician had fashioned a coy smile on the man's face. She stood before the casket a few seconds, then turned and said she was sorry to the few people standing near the front, nodded yes when asked if she worked with Ralph, then headed quickly for the back of the room where another white mourner stood.

And now Steve would have more laughs. This guy, the only other Caucasian in the place besides her and one of the two funeral directors who had started arranging the service, apparently thought this coincidence was an excuse to put the make on her. His name was Dutch, he said. He was at least as old as the deceased and said he'd worked in the sewer for the Chicago Sanitary District with Ralph for twenty-five years and that he was glad to meet her and wondered if she would mind if he sat with her at the luncheon. But the service saved her from answering.

A minister began prayers and she knew that soon the two funeral directors would take over and have everyone file past the casket, then out into the lobby and to their cars. She seized the moment, during which all heads were bowed, sliding along the back wall, being careful not to knock over flower arrangements. Once out in the lobby, she headed in the direction of the restrooms. But at the last second, with a glance back to make sure those at the double doors were not watching, she ducked to the side and turned the knob on the door labeled *Office.*

The office was windowless and dark. She found the wall switch and turned on the light as soon as she closed the door behind her. It did not take long to find what she was looking for. Three large four-drawer filing cabinets were arranged alphabetically and she located a file marked Gianetti in the bottom drawer of the first cabinet. The address for Tony Gianetti Junior was on a copy of a statement. She took her notebook out of her purse, copied down the address, noticed that the casket alone was seventy-five thousand, and put the file back. Then, as she was about to open the door to leave, the knob turned from the outside and the door opened in on her.

It was the guy from outside who had been parking cars. She flattened herself against the wall behind the door, but he had not opened the door fully and now closed it quietly behind him, leaving her exposed. His back was to her as he rummaged on a shelf on the far wall. When he turned she prepared to be caught. She'd say she wanted to arrange a funeral, make something up about her father, pull out her handkerchief. But he did not see her because his eyes were closed as he put a pint of whiskey to his lips and took a deep swallow. After this he turned back to the shelf, replaced the bottle to its hiding spot, wiped his mouth with the back of his hand, sprayed his mouth with mouth spray he took from his inside pocket, shut off the light before opening the door, and left the office.

After sneaking out of the office she spent quite a while in the ladies' room. To her astonishment, while sitting in a stall, she overheard two young women not only mention her, but also the flat-nosed man who'd followed her.

"Uncle Ralph's widow lady shure-nuff has some thinkin' to do."

"Why's that, girl?'

"Not, 'Why's that, girl?' 'cause I'm talkin' about the white bitch went up front like she owned the place, that's all."

"She didn't come in like she owned the place. Everyone who visits goes up front. How old you think she is?"

"I don't know, like they say, it's hard to tell the ages of white folks."

"Mama said she probably worked down at the District in the office."

"That's my point exactly. What's Uncle Ralph doin' spendin' time in the office when he's supposed to be either out in the truck or down in the sewer? What I'm sayin' is maybe Uncle Ralph had a certain part of him that was a mite younger than the rest of him."

Both young women laughed at this, then continued.

"Did you see that Puerto Rican or whatever he was?"

"Yeah, a lightweight like my old boyfriend Daniel, except it looked like this guy went down for the count."

"Well, he sure looked nervous, especially when Derrick and Sean gave him the eyeball."

"So that's why he run out and took off in his pimpmobile Beamer. You asked Derrick and Sean to protect your honor 'cause he was sayin' he come to look for his favorite lady by the name of Tiffany."

Laughter, then scuffling sounds, then a purse hit the floor and was retrieved, then more laughter until the door opened and an older woman mumbled something and the two said, "Yes, ma'am," and left the ladies' room.

The door to the ladies' room opened and closed several more times, but there were no more conversations. As she waited, she could hear the muted sounds of voices in the lobby. When it sounded like most of the mourners had gone outside, she left the ladies' room, walked quickly through the lobby and to her car, not bothering with the umbrella. On her way between cars, a window came down and Ralph's white coworker said, "Don't forget. See you at lunch."

While driving in the funeral procession south along Harlem Avenue, she saw the BMW in her side mirror. It came up fast in the left lane passing the procession until it neared her car, then it slowed. But the procession went through red lights and, even though the BMW made it through one light, there was a squad car straddling the next intersection and the BMW was forced to stop while the procession continued on its way. She ducked out of the funeral procession shortly after this, cut over two blocks and headed back north. As she drove she wondered how long Ralph's white coworker would search for her at the luncheon. But most of all she wondered where she would sleep tonight, because she knew she would not go back to the apartment.

Tamara. Perhaps she'd visit Tamara, tell her about her day and admit she'd made a fool of herself. But first she had one more stop.

On the Tri-state Tollway, heading north in the rain, she reached over with her right hand and pulled the funeral sticker off the inside of her windshield. She tried balling it up and throwing it on the floor but the sticky side was out and she couldn't let go of it. The sensation of her fingers held in place by the balled-up sticker reminded her of Steve, how his right hand had been weakened by the stroke. Finally she managed to attach the sticker to the carpeting on the side of the transmission hump.

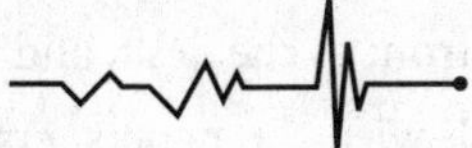

The Gianetti residence was in Highland Park, one block from Lake Michigan in a very exclusive neighborhood. A large house on a wooded lot with a circular drive. An Asian maid asked her name and what business she had with Mr. Gianetti. Jan said she knew his recently deceased mother and needed to speak with him about something.

The vestibule resembled a garden. Ferns grew in numerous clay pots lining the walls, and the doorway to the interior of the house was preceded by an arbor covered with vines that grew from more clay pots. The vines were so thick they blocked much of the light, making it dark within the arbor. After a few minutes the maid came back and took her through the darkness and fragrance of the arbor to a long hallway with many closed doors.

One of the doors was open. What might have once served as a formal library because of the built-in shelves, was now a working office. There was nothing showy here, simply a large cluttered office with plain office furniture, the built-in shelves crammed with books, some boxes overflowing with folders. She could see by some of the book titles and by some magazines lying around that much of the material had to do with environmental topics. The terms "Global Warming" and "Climate Change" and "Green House Gases" were prominent. The little wall space that did not contain shelves was covered with wildlife posters and calendars. When she walked in and the maid left her there, she thought she was alone. But then she heard some taps on a keyboard and Tony Gianetti Junior wearing a Sierra Club sweatshirt and jeans stood up from behind a large flat-screen computer monitor that was surrounded by stacks of books on the desk.

Tony Junior absentmindedly brushed at his short thinning hair with his hand and came around the desk. He bent to remove a pile of papers from the chair in front of the desk, and while going back around the other side of the desk with the papers, crammed them into a spot above some books on a shelf behind him. When he turned back to her he motioned her to sit down. Back at his desk, he moved his chair to the side of the computer monitor and stacks of books so he could face her. Above his head was a poster showing a bald eagle in flight.

Tony Junior looked thinner than he had at the funeral, delicate. Although he was going bald, the sweatshirt made him look like a kid. After staring at her a moment with a cautious look, he seemed to relax, and even smiled a little, apparently because she was smiling.

"We met at my mother's funeral, Mrs. Babe."

"My name is Jan. Some people feel uncomfortable using our last name, at least that's what my husband says."

"Yes, I met him, too. He was the one who knew my mother at Saint Mel's."

"That's right. Both suffered strokes and spent a lot of time in rehab together."

"And?"

"Yes, I guess you'd wonder why I'd come here."

"I guess I would."

"I guess I should get right to the point."

"I guess you should."

"You see, Mr. Gianetti . . ."

"Tony. Although my mother insisted calling me Antonio, everyone else calls me Tony."

"Yes. You see, Tony, your mother and my husband spent a lot of time together in rehab."

"You said that."

"Okay, sorry. The point in rehab, at least when they were working with a speech therapist, was to communicate. And to get right to the point, your mother said some things to my husband that seem to make him think there might be a possibility her accident might not have really been an accident at all."

"Really?" he said, but she noticed no particular reaction, no surprise, no resentment of her having said this, nothing.

"Yes," she said. "I realize it may seem impertinent of me to be here, but I do everything I can to help my husband get back to normal. And if you could possibly shed some light on any of these things he's concerned about, I'd greatly appreciate it."

"Okay." He leaned forward, folding his hands on the desk. "So let's get right to the point. Exactly what things did my mother say that concern your husband?"

How to do this in a way that might cause a reaction she'd be able to notice? Steve used to tell her he did it sometimes by asking more than one question. First question to make the person comfortable, then another question out of the blue to see if there's a reaction.

"Well," she said. "Steve mentioned that sometimes your mother would say things about the staff at the nursing home, how some of them might be doing things they shouldn't do. I wondered if your mother ever said anything to you about it. And also, sometimes she'd say things to Steve about there being a fly in the ointment, which I assume is a reference to one or more staff members who might not be as honest as we'd like them to be. And then there was something having to do with the key to making a lot of money, or maybe the keys to getting a lot of money, something like that. I'm sure you, of all people, realize it's not easy to communicate details like this with someone who's had a stroke."

While she spoke, Jan watched Tony Gianetti very closely. At first, judging by the puzzled look on his face, she thought there would be no reaction. But then it had come. Steve had taught her well. When she said the word *key*, there had been a very subtle recognition, the kind one sees when someone suddenly recalls something they were going to say.

After this mild sign of recognition from Tony Gianetti, she had seen a more significant reaction to the plural, *keys*. When she said *keys*, he involuntarily unfolded his delicate hands and held one in the other as if he were holding someone else's hand. She could also tell by a stiffness in his jaw that he had to work to refrain from showing a reaction on his face. Yes, he had to work hard to maintain his simple look of puzzlement.

When Tony Gianetti did not answer, Jan continued, knowing that sometimes this could draw out even more reaction. "I know all of this sounds ridiculous, but it's something I promised I'd do for my husband. I told him I'd ask you if any of this meant anything."

"I see," he said finally. "Was there anything else you were supposed to ask me?"

This was the confirmation she needed. Instead of referring to one of her questions in detail, he asked for more. She might be wrong. After all, only Steve and Lydia had told her she was good at reading people. But it certainly seemed to her that Tony Gianetti was now trying to find out how much Steve knew.

"I guess there was something else." She glanced down for a moment to show discomfort, but looked right back to catch his reaction. "I guess your mother spoke about quite personal things with Steve. He told me she said something about you having a secret from your father, something he never knew about, but something she knew about. This is very uncomfortable for me, but I promised Steve."

Tony Gianetti stared at her for a moment, then stood up and took a small magazine from the bookcase behind him. He dropped the magazine on his desk and sat back down. It was not a glossy magazine with an illustrated cover like most of the others she saw scattered around. This magazine had a matte cover with the table of contents printed on the front. The title of the magazine was, *Pride and Perseverance.* The subtitle was, *Gay Rights in the New Century.*

"Although environmental research and writing is my main interest, I do have other interests. I came out of the closet after my father died. Perhaps you've heard of The Organization for Pride and Perseverance. This is our journal. I'm the editor. Unfortunately, I don't understand how this has anything to do with someone's unfounded suspicions that my mother's death might not have been an accident."

It was over. He was indignant now. She lowered her head contritely, but as she did so, looked at the things on his desk besides books and magazines. Not much except double-spaced articles with editorial marks on them, and a couple of letters to Tony Gianetti, one of which was on Sierra Club letterhead. But there was something else. An envelope addressed to him, but not at an address. The reason the envelope drew her attention was because it was made of expensive linen. The envelope was simply addressed "Tony" and the return address pre-printed in fancy gold script. The return address looked like a legal firm. A downtown Michigan Avenue address. Melton, Iwanski, and Brown.

"I'm sorry," she said finally. "I should have minded my own business. It's just that my husband used to be a detective before his stroke and I guess I was hoping . . ."

The phone rang, but Tony didn't answer and it stopped ringing after three rings.

"Look," he said, "my mother just died. If there were secrets in my family, they weren't between the two of us. She knew I was gay before my father died, and I think I see what happened here. The big secret was that my father didn't know I was gay. Or if he did, he never revealed he knew. Does that answer your questions?"

"Yes, it does. I guess your mother might have said certain things about your father that confused my husband."

"What things?"

She tried to look flustered. "I'm sorry. Really I am. It's just that my husband's stroke has made him want to repeat things other people say and I guess he and your mother talked quite a bit about . . . about what your father did when he was alive."

He smiled and nodded. "I guess I can understand that." Then he leaned back in his chair and stared toward his computer monitor as if he were looking out a window. "My father found peace in his later years. I think he found a way to put the earlier part of his life behind him. He loved his family very much. Perhaps you expected me to say negative things about him, but I won't. He may have done things I'm not proud of, but no one's perfect. When I knew him he was a peaceful man. He even admitted to me he'd done some things in his life he regretted. But he also said he wanted life for me to be different."

He turned from the computer monitor and looked at her again. "He told me he wanted to give our family name new meaning so future generations of Gianetti's would be proud. During the last years of his life he tried to make an honest go of it. He even lost money in some crazy schemes reminiscent of Ralph Kramden on the old *Honeymooners* show. Near the end of his life my mother was becoming the head of the household."

Tony Gianetti's mention of the name Ralph threw off her concentration for a moment. She'd been trying to formulate a response to this when the name made her think of poor old Ralph in the casket at the funeral home who was probably six feet under by now with folks gossiping about him at the funeral luncheon as the white guy named Dutch went from table to table looking for her.

"As for my mother being paranoid about the staff at Saint Mel's," continued Tony . . .

The maid came in and interrupted him.

"What's up?" he said to the maid.

"A phone call," said the maid. "He said it couldn't wait. He called in on the other line."

"Who is it?"

"Mr. Brown."

"Okay." To Jan he said, "It'll only take a second."

He turned to a side table hidden by his books and computer monitor. He lowered his voice, but Jan leaned forward slightly and could hear his side of the conversation.

"Buster?"

"Right, crazy times."

"Okay, like I said."

"Yep, Orland."

"Sure, the one at Route 45 and 6. It's one-hundred fifty-ninth down there."

"We'll find out where to go from there."

"Don't worry, we won't have to book flights."

"That's what he wanted everyone to assume."

"Right, hour and a half."

"I'll make it."

"I've told you time and again, just because it's a hybrid, it's not slow."

"I'm always careful, and I've got rain tires. See you there."

As Tony spoke, Jan recalled Marjorie's funeral and how different he seemed from Max. Two completely different men with completely different goals. Not a pair one would expect to launch a devious plan together. She wondered if she should mention Max, perhaps say something about Marjorie's use of "Max the fly" when referring to the "fly in the ointment."

After Tony hung up he swiveled his chair back to face Jan. "So, where were we?"

"You were saying your mother was sometimes paranoid about things at Saint Mel's."

"Right. She used to tell me stories about aides who steal things and sell them back. And perhaps some do. Perhaps she saw something, or someone else saw something and told her about it. If that were true, and if your husband had some hard evidence . . . well, I guess it wouldn't be hard for someone to get away with things at Saint Mel's they couldn't possibly get away with in the outside world. What I'm saying, Mrs. Babe—Jan—is maybe I'd like to pursue this. Not jump in with both feet, because both of us know we don't have anything definite. Unless, that is, you're holding something back."

"No," said Jan. "Not at all. It's just like I told you. My husband has these feelings about things your mother said and I'm following up on it."

He leaned back in his chair. "I've got to leave for a meeting, but I'd like to follow up on this. Where do you suggest we go from here?"

"I guess I should go back and tell Steve what you've told me and see if he has anything else to say."

"I guess that's the best plan."

The way Tony sat there, waiting, she was certain he wanted to see if she would say anything else. Like he was the one probing for information instead of her. She decided to bring something up out of the blue.

"One more thing your mother used to say that my husband recalls. She used to mention Jimmy Carter a lot."

Tony studied her for a moment before answering. It seemed he had been about to stand. He said he had to leave for a meeting, but now he sat back and stared at her.

"My mother mentioning Jimmy Carter is both interesting and understandable. Back in the 1980s, when I was a teenager, my father was a big Reagan supporter. This support often came out in tirades against Jimmy Carter and what a lousy President he'd been. He used to refer to the 1970s energy crisis and to Carter's 1977 energy policy speech. You might not remember it. Carter talked about not being selfish and about providing a decent world for our children and grandchildren. He talked about our being the most wasteful nation on earth and how we needed to sacrifice for the good of the planet. He talked about oil companies profiteering. In my humble opinion, Jimmy Carter's biggest problem was that he was two or three decades ahead of his time.

"Yes, your husband might have gotten the impression through my mother that my father hated Carter. However, in later years, when I began publishing environmental articles, my father changed. He even told me once that Jimmy Carter had gotten a bum rap. He said our family—he was referring at the time to the organized crime family from the past—our family had been just like any political family. He said political families don't care about the environment, and that their main interest is business as usual."

Tony paused, pointed to a small poster on the wall. It consisted of the letters "BAU" in a circle with a diagonal line through it.

"A few months before his death my father took me aside. I'd done some articles on the environment in the school paper. He told me something he did not want my mother to hear. He said that during the Carter years an environmentalist and political writer disappeared under mysterious circumstances. At school I'd chosen this same profession as a career goal. My father told me he admired what I'd chosen to do but that he wanted me to be careful. He said when I turned eighteen he wanted me to carry a gun. He said he would give me one."

Tony turned back and stared at her. "So you see, there's always more than meets the eye. Even when you're talking about a mob boss there's always more than meets the eye. Do you know when my father was killed?"

"Somewhere in the mid-eighties?"

"He was killed days after the Chernobyl disaster. There's been speculation that whoever killed him chose that date because it would diminish news coverage given to the murder. It's an old mob trick. Kill one of your own when everyone is busy thinking of other things."

"So you think it was someone in another organization who killed your father?"

"That's the prevailing theory. But it could have been anyone." He turned, pointed to the "BAU" poster. "Especially someone with a very tough business as usual attitude. In a way, I think that day my father took me aside he knew the end was near for him. Perhaps he even knew his killers."

Tony seemed to come out of a trance. He stood, held out his hand. "But that's enough for now. Sometimes I go on and I'm sorry if I did."

She stood and held out her hand.

As Tony shook her hand, he said, "Again, regarding these notions my mother had about aides stealing things at the facility, what we agreed to do is for you to go back and tell your husband what I've told you and see if he has anything else to say. Please disregard that last part of our conversation about my father. And by the way, thanks to both of you for coming to the funeral. I appreciate it."

She continued holding onto his hand, recalling for a moment how she held Steve's hand while they spoke in order to help the conversation along. "Well, there is one more thing I should tell you. This is very difficult, but it seems your mother was unhappy for some reason about your cousin Max."

Tony pulled his hand away and stared at her, looking upset with her for the first time. "Did Max send you?"

"What?"

"I said, did Max send you?"

"Why would he send me?"

He continued staring at her, but appeared to regain his composure. "Sorry, it's just that my mother never cared much for Max, but always kept it to herself. It wasn't like her to say anything negative about him. And if you ever spoke with Max, outside of yesterday at the funeral, you'd know he and my father were not on good terms. Max's business is his own business. He was always fond of my mother, perhaps because he lost his own mother when he was a boy. And she was always good at covering up what she really felt about him. He visited her from time to time at Saint Mel's. But now that she's gone, I doubt if I'll see much of Max. I guess you gathered we don't exactly share the same interests in life."

Tony smiled again. "You certainly caught me at a weak moment. I've revealed more about my family than I should. Now I've got to leave for my appointment."

CHAPTER SIXTEEN

WHILE JAN HEADED SOUTH ON THE TRI-STATE TOLLWAY IN A driving rain, traffic slowed to a bumper-to-bumper pace. Inching along in traffic gave her time to think. Not only did she wonder why Tony assumed his mother had bad-mouthed Max, she'd also been thinking about Tony's big house and his hybrid car. On the way out to her Audi, even though it was raining, she made a point of looking further up the driveway. She'd seen a red Toyota Prius, and on the Prius was a bumper sticker, the same "BAU" with a line through it.

She thought about Tony's environmental activities and his gay rights organization. Ironically, a lot of his activities these days were probably funded by his father's organized crime ventures from the seventies and eighties. She wondered if Tony's father was rolling over in his grave or if he was happy with his son's life. She thought about whether it would be wise to try to talk to Max Lamberti. Then, while wondering about how to find Max Lamberti and while looking at road signs, she visualized a map of the Chicago area and recalled looking at a map with Steve not long ago when they were trying to solve the riddle of what Marjorie could possibly mean by the U.S. routes litany she had recited in rehab. Steve said the therapist had gotten out a map and been unable to figure out what it could mean. Then she remembered that when she and Steve got out a map, she had written the riddle down in her notebook.

Why hadn't she put it together earlier? She'd gotten ahead of herself, thinking about Max Lamberti instead of working with what she already had. If Steve were here he wouldn't try to see Max because that would tip his hand. No, Steve would go with what he's got. And she had almost let it slip through her fingers until she thought of Steve looking for details, always details, and trying to connect those details in a systematic, logical way.

The first detail was the Buster Brown jingle Marjorie recited from time to time. Steve told her Marjorie had two slightly different versions. In speech therapy the therapist named Georgiana had asked around in rehab trying to see if anyone knew which was the correct version.

"Hi, my name's Buster Brown. I live in a shoe. Here's my dog Tag. Look for him in there, too." Or was it, *"My dog's name is Tag. He lives in there, too?"*

It didn't matter how the jingle went. What mattered was the man on the phone with Tony Gianetti. Tony had called him Buster, and the maid had definitely referred to Mr. Brown.

The next detail was Marjorie's litany of U.S. routes. While traffic was stopped, Jan got out her notebook and found the litany.

"*U.S. 6 and 45, U.S. 30 and 50, U.S. 20 and 41, U.S. 14 and 94, U.S. 14 and 45, U.S. 20 and 83, U.S. 30 and 34, U.S. 7 and 30, U.S. 30 and 45,*" and it repeated over again starting with U.S. 6 and 45.

So there it was, staring her in the face and she almost missed it. On the phone Tony had said, "Route 45 and 6," and right now he must be driving in his Prius to meet someone named Buster Brown at that first intersection listed on the litany of routes. It was too much for coincidence. Steve was right. There was something here. Something.

When the crawling traffic merged to the left lane and finally cleared the scene of a multi-car accident, Jan stayed in the left lane behind a limo and took the Audi up to seventy. Tony had said his Prius had rain tires. Months earlier, before his stroke, Steve had put rain tires on his old Honda and wanted to put them on her Audi, saying rain tires would go well with the four-wheel-drive. As she passed through the spray from a line of trucks, the Audi skittered slightly because she never did get a chance to purchase rain tires. While correcting the slight skid, she had a quick memory of the strong smell of rubber in a tire shop. Steve, days before his stroke, standing in the brightly lit store running his finger down the deep center groove of a rain tire on display, the deep center groove branching off to side grooves resembling arteries providing lifeblood to brain cells so they can think their crazy thoughts.

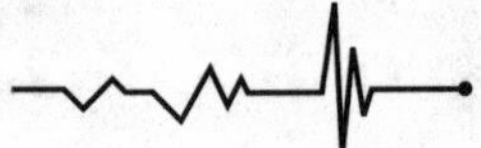

The intersection of U.S. Route 6 and U.S. Route 45, Orland Park, Illinois, was about twenty-five miles southwest of downtown Chicago. Jan had been to Orland Park several times, most recently with Lydia Christmas shopping last December at Orland Park Shopping Mall. It had been a few weeks after Steve's November stroke and she hadn't wanted to go, but Lydia had insisted. She remembered buying the new computer for Steve. She and Lydia had driven south of the Orland Park Mall to a Best Buy. She remembered the Best Buy had been in another shopping center at the intersection of Route 6 and Route 45. All she could recall about the intersection was that it was busy and there were various shopping centers with huge parking lots and numerous stores and restaurants and maybe a gas station or two on the corners.

A haystack, she thought. I'm driving to a haystack to look for a Prius I saw briefly in a downpour. And who's to say that wasn't the maid's Prius and Tony has a few more in his multiple-car garage? But she drove on, exited the tollway and cut over on Interstate 55 to U.S. 45 south.

The rain had let up some, but traffic, as she approached Orland Park from the north, was heavy. Typical Friday afternoon shopping center traffic. Tony Gianetti had said he'd be to the intersection in an hour and a half. She wasn't sure exactly when she left his house, but she was certain the hour and a half must be up by now.

As she wound in and out of the slow traffic she got in behind a motor home that was going fifty-five instead of the forty-five limit. The motor home reminded her of another drive to a vague location to find something not yet defined.

She and Steve had gone to Montana because they had gotten a lead that the cult her husband had once belonged to, and the cult leader who turned out to be responsible for his death, had settled on an island in the middle of a large lake there. Then, when the lead turned out to be a trap and they were almost killed, they went into hiding, posing as an elderly couple traveling in a motor home. They had even gone so far as to put on gray wigs.

She recalled how, during the four hundred mile non-stop drive across North Dakota, they talked about cults and missing kids and raids on abortion clinics. She recalled how it all seemed so unbelievable, even more unbelievable than Marjorie Gianetti being murdered, until the missing ingredient was added. And the missing ingredient had been money. Ten years earlier, when they were posing as an elderly couple in a motor home, a cult leader with money and connections had gone underground. At first it sounded like a scandal sheet story. But add the fact that years of fundraising by the cult and its thousands of followers allowed the leader to take millions of dollars underground with him, and believability no longer seemed an issue. And now, driving south to an intersection in Orland Park, was it possible a quarter billion dollars from a botched drug deal was at stake?

As she followed the motor home, she saw through its large rear window that a woman was making her way down the center aisle. The woman stood in profile, swaying with the motion of the motor home. An elderly woman, perhaps making coffee. Or was it a young woman dressed as an elderly woman? Who could be sure because that's the way she and Steve had traveled from Montana to Minnesota on that wild trip so long ago. She had made coffee in the motor home after she put on the cruise control and Steve slid in behind the wheel and took his turn driving. She recalled that Steve had brought his violin along on the ride and, before making the coffee, she stood in the center aisle in back trying to play Steve's violin, but was barely able to get out a couple of screeches.

"Ah," Steve had said, "a melody from my homeland. An old folk song entitled, *My Foot Rests beneath the Wheel.*"

"Very funny," she had said, putting the violin and bow back in the case. "Gangsters used to carry machine guns in violin cases."

"I know," said Steve.

She remembered turning on the counter light and firing up the motor home's generator. She remembered putting two cups of water in the microwave and returning to the cab with steaming cups of instant coffee. She remembered placing the cups in the holders on the console. She remembered bending and kissing Steve on his ear.

"I wish this thing had an autopilot," he'd said.

"So do I," she said, as she sat on the floor between the seats and leaned her head against his hip.

Beneath the vast console of the motor home, the engine throbbed endlessly, and on the console the ripples in the cups of coffee had looked like bull's-eyes in the greenish glow of the dash lights.

She remembered all of this, and felt tears come to her eyes when the thought struck her that Steve might not remember any of it.

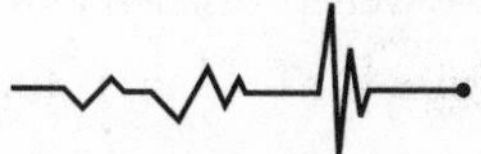

The intersection was a traffic jam with multiple stoplights for shopping center parking lot entrances. She turned into one of these and slowly made her way through the parking lot for Best Buy and other smaller stores. All she could think of to look for was a red Prius. Any red Prius.

After meandering in the Best Buy parking lot, she worked her way back to the stoplight and crossed over to the shopping center in which a Target store was central. She spotted a small red car, but when she got closer she saw that it was a Ford. After this shopping center, she turned out onto Route 6 and waited at the intersection to get across to a large restaurant at the opposite corner. She drove around the back of the restaurant, thinking there was a chance Tony Gianetti and Buster Brown might have planned to meet for a business lunch. But there was no Prius and she crossed back over to the other corner where there was a bank behind a gas station.

Suddenly, there it was. In the bank parking lot, partially hidden by a dividing wall between the bank and gas station, was a red Prius with a "BAU" bumper sticker. When she negotiated the left turn at the intersection and got into the bank parking lot via the crowded side entrance road, she saw what she needed.

The license plate on the Prius was PP2000, which made sense since the name of the gay rights journal Tony Gianetti had shown her was *Pride and Perseverance, Gay Rights in the New Century.* And parked next to the Prius was a Mercedes with license plate BBROWN.

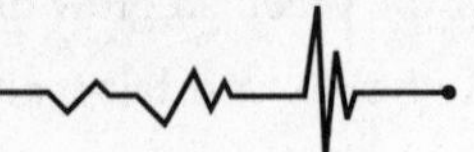

Jan sat in the corner of the well-furnished bank lobby, hiding behind a large foldout bank brochure she held up before her. Within the bank brochure she held a Chicago area map she brought in from the glove compartment. While she waited, she began marking the intersections from Marjorie's U.S. Routes litany written down in her notebook. The sofa on which she sat was soft and deep and she knew that, with all the other people in the bank filling out deposit and withdrawal slips and waiting in line, she would more than likely be overlooked back here even if Tony Gianetti looked directly at her.

She'd entered the bank carefully, watching for Tony. She covered her cautious entry by pretending to search for something in her purse, while at the same time scanning the bank lobby. Now, because she had not seen him, she sat waiting, and working on her map. Either Tony and this guy named Buster Brown, who was probably his attorney, were somewhere in the bank, or they had met a third party and driven elsewhere. If that were true . . . but it wasn't, because suddenly they appeared through an opening to her right. They were behind a waist-high door in the counter that had to be buzzed open. She realized they had been back in the alcove containing the vault holding the safe deposit boxes.

Although Buster Brown's hair was dark brown, Jan thought it looked dyed and figured he was older than Tony, probably upper forties, her age. Tony wore a sport coat over his Sierra Club sweatshirt while Buster wore a suit. Both men carried briefcases and umbrellas.

If they had come to retrieve something from a safe deposit box, it was in one or both of their briefcases.

Because they faced the counter she could watch them carefully. Buster said something to Tony and Tony reached into his pocket and showed Buster a key. This made Buster smile and nod. When a teller approached the counter where they stood and handed Tony another key, Jan noticed that he put this key in his right jacket pocket, whereas the key he had just shown Buster was in his left jacket pocket. Tony and Buster thanked the teller, then headed for the door.

Jan imagined herself asking the teller what Tony and Buster had been doing in the safe deposit box vault and had to laugh. Not because such a move would be pointless, but because it was this kind of thinking Steve had always said to never overlook. "Think the obvious and even the absurd and often you'll come up with things floating just below the surface," he'd said. Well, if there was anything she could uncover here, without getting arrested, she could do it later. For now, she knew what Steve would do is follow Tony to see where he went next.

They left together in Tony's Prius, leaving the BBROWN Mercedes behind. As she drove out of the parking lot, careful to keep at least one car between them, but close enough so she wouldn't get caught by a stoplight, she thought how appropriate the jingle seemed.

Hi, my name's Buster Brown. I live in a shoe. Here's my dog Tag. Look for him in there, too.

As she followed the Prius, she was aware they were heading in the direction of the next intersection from the litany.

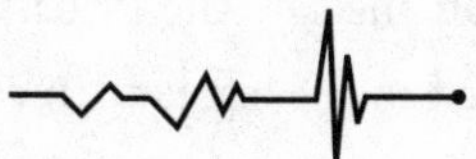

South on U.S. Route 45 out of Orland Park, the highway becomes divided before it intersects Interstate 80. The speed limit is fifty-five, but traffic often travels faster near the interstate as if the sixty-five-mile-per-hour speed limit of the interstate were a living organism able to spread onto this U.S. Route. As if speed has fingers reaching out to grasp motorists fearful of being rear-ended. As if Tony Gianetti and Buster Brown might be aware they are being followed and want to lose her. That's what she thought about when the huge red semi passed her.

She was doing over sixty when the truck barreled past. The spray of grimy water lifted from the pavement by numerous groaning tires blinded her. She turned her windshield wipers on high speed, but it made little difference. The air horn on the truck sounded long and loud, frightening a slower car out of the left lane. She cursed aloud at the driver of the truck, recalling a recent accident in which a brake part had dislodged from a truck and caused the death of a family. Didn't the trucker realize she was working on an important case? What was so important to this trucker that he had to drive like this?

When the truck moved far enough ahead so she could again see, three cars were between her and the Prius. The Prius was barely visible, riding alongside the truck within the spray from its tires. The Prius shot ahead for a moment, Tony apparently speeding out of the blinding spray. Then the truck's brake lights came on while it blasted its air horn and another frightened driver escaped into the right lane and dropped back.

The truck was on fire with speed, a tidal wave of steel and rubber, the driver in his perch above traffic able to see while everyone else is blinded. On a rise ahead she saw the Prius just beyond the truck in the right lane. She moved to the left lane to catch up, passed cars that had slowed, intimidated by the actions of the truck driver. When she moved back to the right lane, the truck and the Prius were side by side about a hundred yards ahead.

Then it happened. A guardrail that narrowed the shoulder where the road bridged a creek helped it happen. The guardrail was there and the Prius could not get over it when the truck suddenly moved over, whipping like a snake striking. The center of the trailer straddled the Prius for an instant as it disappeared beneath the trailer.

She thought the Prius might be low enough to come out the other side. But it was not low enough. Sparks spewed from beneath the truck as it crossed back over to the center lane. It was insane, like children racing cars and trucks willy-nilly across a floor. The truck's rear wheels locked up, smoke billowed, the Prius turned sideways, and the rear wheels of the trailer rolled over the Prius causing the trailer to bounce high into the air as if it had been rolled at high speed on kitchen tile and had suddenly hit the edge of the living room carpet. The effect was complete when the Prius rolled like toy into the weedy flooded median beyond the bridge.

She slammed on her brakes and pulled off onto the left shoulder. Bystanders, who had moments earlier been in their cars, materialized from the mist. The truck was some distance ahead, stopped on the left shoulder. The driver, a large man wearing a baseball cap, jumped down from the truck and started to run back, then stopped and covered his face with his hands. Those running to the wreck in the median from both sides of the highway were men and boys. A nurse would come running soon, she thought, picturing the nurses at Hell in the Woods. But no nurses were in sight unless . . .

Yes! Unless one of the men who arrived at the scene first was a nurse, or a doctor.

It seemed a group of men had taken charge already, two of them bent low reaching into the crushed and steaming wreckage, while three more did their best to hold the curious back. She expected the Prius to burst into flame, and some spectators kept their distance as if it might, but it did not burst into flame. As she watched the scene, Jan lowered her window slightly despite the rain. She wished she could do more, but did what she thought best. It was an automatic reaction. While the men reached into the wreckage and others surrounded them and eventually blocked her view, she realized she had already retrieved the phone from its mount on the center console between the front seats. She dialed 911 and gave the location of the accident in a remarkably calm voice to the operator.

CHAPTER SEVENTEEN

Steve's physical therapist was not a fuckhead. Percy was gentle and understanding no matter how much the victim complained. Steve did not complain at all that day because the stretching exercises and range-of-motion exercises and resistance exercises felt good. He knew part of the reason they felt good was because, instead of trying to think about the past as he sometimes did while exercising, he thought about something that had happened quite recently. He thought about the janitors' closet, and in so doing, mentally included a bigger and rougher black guy than Percy in on whatever exercise he was doing. When Percy had him stretch one of the giant rubber bands, Tyrone's neck would be there and he'd be stretching it until poor Tyrone thought it would break. When Percy had him do range-of-motion twists, he made a fist and would give Tyrone a good clout on each turn. Any time he got hold of the handgrips and squeezed the hell out of them with his good left hand, he imagined he had hold of Tyrone's throat. Pretty childish stuff, he thought, after thanking Percy and heading to the elevator.

In his room, Steve stared into the paper cup Betty-who-talks-too-much had just placed on the bedside table. Tegretol, Coumadin, Heparin, Amitriptyline. "That Amitriptyline's the antidepressant," said Betty. "It'll turn up the corners of your little old mouth even more than it usually is, Mr. Babe. It surely will. I'd stay and talk more, but I've got to run."

After taking his lunchtime medication he rolled out into the hall, took the elevator back down to the second floor and headed for the cafeteria. In the hallway on the way to the cafeteria, Linda and Frank, the two right-brainers who talked incessantly, were arguing. Frank kept referring to rehab as childish, saying they treated them like "goddamn little shit kids." Linda answered by saying it felt good to be babied sometimes. Of course what they really said wasn't that simple. There were all matter of adjectives and adverbs tossed in at random in their strange conversational brew, and he'd heard this argument before, so he moved on.

A little farther down the hall he saw the new nurses' aide. He couldn't think of her name, but she had red hair and was in her early twenties and cute as hell. For a moment he recalled the redheaded aide down on the first floor Marjorie claimed was fired for being rough on residents. Marjorie had said the aide was a bull dyke. Well, this new one was certainly not a bull dyke. He elbowed Phil, his across-the-hall neighbor, as he rolled to a stop outside the cafeteria, pointing to the new redhead and saying, "Cute kid."

Phil nodded appreciatively and whispered, "Jesus fuck."

The floor-to-ceiling windows in the cafeteria were streaked with rain. Instead of letting in sunshine, the windows brought in the gloom and cold. Thick rain clouds made it dark enough to force drivers to switch on their headlights. He could see the line of headlights in the distance on the main road through the naked trees bordering the entrance road.

As Steve ate he looked forward to hearing Jan's voice. They'd be practicing using the phone again in occupational therapy today and he'd take a moment to call his own number so he could hear Jan's cheery voice on their voice mail. Since finding out he called their voice mail during therapy, Jan had changed her greeting quite often, keeping it general, yet between the lines he was able to sense the cheeriness in the message was not for the person from the long-distance company or credit card company, but just for him. One thing he had never told Jan was that he sometimes called their voice mail service number and keyed in the access code to bring up the maintenance program that would allow him to change the personal greeting. Of course he never changed Jan's greeting. All he wanted to do was listen to it. And, in the middle of the night, if he called their number, he would have awakened Jan. So, instead, he sometimes called the voice mail service number for a shot in the arm in the middle of the night.

During the free time after lunch, he took the elevator back to the third floor. In his room he freshened up in the bathroom, then went to his phone. He called home, and when there was no answer after four rings, Jan came on. "Hi, you've reached the Babe residence. All of us Babes and our security guards must be cleaning our weapons or on the phone right now. Leave a message and one of us will call you back. *B*-ye."

The "*B*-ye" was for him. He could hear it in the way Jan had started the word on a high pitch and ended it on a low pitch. After hearing her voice, he considered calling Jan's cell number, but she usually left the phone in the car instead of carrying it with her. Besides, he didn't know whether they'd taken Jan's or Lydia's car to Wisconsin.

He hung up and called the voice mail service number and keyed the access code to get to the mailbox. There were four messages: One hang up, another from a woman at the billing department here at Hell in the Woods, the third from Phil Hogan.

"Jan, this is Phil. Give me a call. I might have something."

Have something? Phil Hogan? He pictured Phil. Always in the same lousy suit, a wrinkled shirt, his tie askew, his face red from too much booze.

What the hell was going on? If a cop was checking into something for Jan, it had to be about Marjorie's death. But why would Jan ask a loser like Phil for help? And why now when she's not even around? Damn it Jan! I told you not to mess with this!

The fourth message was from Lydia Jacobson.

"Hi, Jan, having a great time. Guess who I met up with? Remember that girl in the Black Power group who changed her name to Gwen Africa? Well, she kept the name all these years and we've been hanging around together and she's a riot. She teaches here and has this bitch of an apartment. Anyway, I'll get off before my time runs out. Gwen says she remembers you and wants to visit us down there. Sorry you couldn't come. Say hi to Steve. See ya."

"Sorry you couldn't come?" he said aloud. "Jesus fuck, Jan!"

He called Jan's cell and got a busy signal, which meant she was using the phone. When he called back thirty seconds later, he got the canned message saying the cell phone customer was unavailable or had traveled beyond the service area. He'd told Jan to leave the phone on when she wasn't with him. He'd also told her to sign up for all the other services like messaging and call waiting. When was that? Not too long ago. Wait, a new cell phone. She'd gotten a new cell phone and said she hadn't bothered setting everything up on it. But he'd gotten a busy signal earlier which meant she'd just been on the phone, and if she was just on the phone . . .

Maybe if he kept calling back. But when he called back less than a minute later, he still got the unavailable message, and kept getting it again and again each time he called. He must have tried calling Jan twenty or thirty times. While he punched the numbers and listened to the message again and again, he felt as if he'd just recently had the stroke and was going through a strange repetitive therapeutic exercise. He knew he probably wouldn't get through, but he kept calling anyhow.

As had happened in the past during stressful times in rehab, he recalled how Jan had, from the beginning, immersed herself into the bizarre mystery of who he was, or who he had been. And now he wondered if, because of his arrogance—thinking he's still a damn detective and knows something's fishy about Marjorie's death when he probably doesn't know shit—he had gotten Jan into trouble. He'd made her do it. He'd been a selfish bastard, wanting even more attention than he was already getting. He cursed himself out loud. "Bastard! Selfish bastard!"

While he continued cursing himself, he looked around his room for something that might help the situation. His computer was on the small desk near the window. He knew that inside the single desk drawer was the plug-in modem and the telephone cord. He wheeled to the desk, opened the drawer and began frantically unraveling the cord while at the same time backing the wheelchair toward the baseboard plug where the phone on the bedside table was plugged in. He'd plug into the world, get on the Internet and . . .

And what? Send an e-mail to the state police to look for Jan's Audi? Sure, they'd do that. They probably dropped everything whenever they got an e-mail from an idiot on the Internet.

"Crazy bastard," he said, as he sat with the tangled telephone cord in his lap.

There must be someone he could e-mail. Get his message down exactly the way he wants it so the situation is crystal clear. But that would take time, and if Jan were in trouble, which she probably wasn't . . .

No. Not e-mail. No other choice. No other choice but to open his mouth and let some words come out and hope for the best. There was only one person who would listen and, perhaps, do something. Only one person outside this place, besides Jan, who wouldn't hang up on the creep on the other end of the line who sounded drunk or demented because he couldn't get his words right.

He put the tangle of wire aside, sat back in his wheelchair and took several deep breaths with his eyes closed. When he felt he was calm enough, under control enough to use everything he'd learned in rehab, he opened the bedside table drawer and took out the sheet of phone numbers he kept there. Then he picked up the phone and called Central Division Homicide, Chicago Police Headquarters.

"Homicide."

Breathe in, concentrate, talk. "Detective Harris."

"Which Harris? Sergeant Bob or Lieutenant T?"

"Lieutenant T."

"You can dial direct to 6466, but I'll put you through."

A pause, then, "Lieutenant Harris."

Her voice was so smooth it threw him for a moment. He pictured her face, her skin dark and smooth like her voice.

"Hello?"

Breathe in, concentrate, talk. "Tamara. Steve."

"Hey, Steve. How you doin'? Jan called the other day and said you had a seizure. Everything okay there?"

He could hear the concern in her voice. Breathe in, concentrate . . .

"Take your time, Steve. Didn't mean to sound rushed. I'll bite my lip and shut up so you can talk." She paused for a while, then said, "I'll only interrupt once in a while, like I just did. I'll try to keep my mouth shut like when I visit. You want to say 'repeat' or something like that to cue me like we did last time I visited?"

"Yes."

"Okay. I'm here with my lips zipped."

Thank God for Tamara. But don't bother thanking her. Concentrate on what's got to come out.

"I love you, Tam. Shit. Okay, take it easy."

Breathe in, concentrate, speak slowly. "It's Jan. Something fucked up. I mean, maybe gone, maybe trouble, I don't know. Should be with Lydia, university reunion. Not there." He paused a moment, then said, "Repeat?"

"Okay, Steve. I've written it down. I'll talk it back to you slow so you can think about it. I guess what you're saying is Jan's missing. Or at least you don't know where she is. She was supposed to be with Lydia at a reunion. I assume that's Jan's friend Lydia Jacobson?"

"Yes."

"Okay, Steve, but just because she's supposed to be with Lydia but isn't, you can't know she's in trouble."

Silence, his turn to speak. But what to say? "I . . . I do."

"How do you know?"

"Fuck! I do!"

"Okay, all right. Just had to make sure . . . you know, with drug side effects and all. You don't need to comment on that last comment. I'm just being straight with you. I know that's what you want. So if you need to try this out on me, let's get back to what you know, and what I know. I'm aware that Jan and Lydia met a long time ago when they were at the University of Wisconsin in Madison. The reunion Jan's supposed to be at must be there. It that right?"

"Right. More. Gwen Africa."

"Was that a name? Did you say Gwen Africa?"

"Right. Teacher. Call. Talk to Lydia. Where the hell's Jan?" He was about to say more, but lost his train of thought and said, "Repeat?" instead.

"Okay, take it easy, it's no big deal. You want me to call a teacher at the University of Wisconsin named Gwen Africa. You figure she'll know how to get in touch with Lydia. Then when I talk to Lydia, if I can find her, I'll ask if she has any idea where Jan could be. Is that about right?"

"Hooray. I mean, right. Also . . ."

The word *also* made him stumble as if the four letters of the word were two feet tall and he was walking down a path in the dark and there they were banging against his shins. But he concentrated, forcing the two-foot-tall letters back down the side path in his brain from which they'd emerged, and tried to go on.

"Jan spoke Phil Hogan," he said. "Not sure what. You see? Repeat that?"

"Uh, okay. You also want me to talk to Phil Hogan over at the Eighth District because Jan spoke with him about something?"

"Right. Checking for Jan. Don't know what."

"Okay, Steve, I guess I can try to do this." Tamara hesitated, then said, "You know it's probably nothing and we'll laugh about it tomorrow. I guess the bottom line is you think Phil was checking into something for Jan and you want me to feel him out in a way that might help figure out where she is and what's going on. Is that it?"

"Absolutely."

"And of course you can't tell me exactly what this is about, is that right?"

"Right."

"Huh, just like old times."

Steve waited in his room for Tamara to call back. While he waited, he called Jan's cell number several more times but kept getting the unavailable message. Finally, he fired up his computer, accessed the notepad and typed some.

When Nadine, an elderly volunteer aide from the rehab center, came in to see why he hadn't returned for the afternoon session, he turned the computer to her so she could read it.

Nadine read the note aloud. "Tell Georgiana I can't come rest of day, doing rehab here. Important phone business."

Nadine turned the computer back toward him. "All right, Mr. Babe. I'm no truant officer, but don't blame me if they send me back. Have a nice day."

When Nadine left, Steve wheeled himself to his window. He placed the computer on the windowsill, handy in case he thought of something he should note. He reached out with his good left hand and touched the window glass. It was cold and the glass fogged where he touched it. His window faced the woods where he could see the flash of headlights as cars and trucks rushed to and fro on the wet roads outside the fence beyond the woods. Although it was only one-thirty in the afternoon, the overcast sky made it as dark as evening. He much preferred the view from the television lounge that overlooked the entrance and parking lot to this view of the woods. But maybe that was only because there he would often watch for Jan's red Audi in the evenings when she was due to visit.

Although it seemed like an eternity, Tamara called back an hour and a half later at three.

"You were right about Lydia being with Gwen Africa, Steve. She said Jan left a message begging off going with her for the long weekend on Thursday night. She said Jan didn't say anything special was going on, but she felt Jan had not wanted to leave you alone the entire weekend. It's probably nothing. Maybe she went shopping and she'll be there any minute with a surprise or something and then you'll have to explain to her why you're so strung out."

"No. I know something. I really do. Tell me, Phil Hogan."

"All right, all right. So long as you promise you'll take it easy and not jump to conclusions. Agreed?"

"Fine."

"Lord, I don't know why I'm telling you anything. You're supposed to be there to get better, not on the phone stirring up trouble where there probably isn't any trouble."

"Tam!"

"Okay, but don't try to make connections where there aren't any. I spoke with Phil, and also with a contact of mine who works at the Eighth District. Phil acted like he didn't know what I was talking about, which isn't unusual for him. He kept asking why I'd call him about Jan and I said I was calling everyone I could think of. He sounded phony the way he usually does, like something's up and he's under pressure. My contact says everyone's been watching Phil lately. Says Phil's been out of the office a lot, but not on business. Says Phil's pattern has changed. Instead of disappearing from the office for a few hours and coming back tipsy, Phil puts in a full day on the street, then comes back sober and worried and apparently has his booze hidden there because he stays in the office late and gets drunk before he heads home. Of course it doesn't sound good. Between you and me, sounds like someone's pressuring him. But that's between you and me, Steve. And it probably doesn't have a damn thing to do with Jan."

"Thanks, Tam."

"You aren't thinking of doing anything, are you?"

"Yeah."

"Like what?"

"Not sure."

"Well, look. If for some reason you don't hear from Jan pretty soon, which I'm sure you will, you know what's next. I know you wouldn't want me to do it yet, but if too much time goes by and I don't hear otherwise from you, you know I'll want to put out a missing person on Jan. And then maybe I'll just come on down there and we can have a face-to-face."

He waited, knowing Tamara wanted him to be careful, and also knowing some time would have to go by before she could take any official action to find Jan.

"Steve?"

"Yeah?"

"Stay by your phone and I'll transfer mine to follow me if I go anywhere. I'll try to do some more checking on Phil. Sound like a plan?"

It took a while longer, but he got through to Tamara that Jan's cell phone indicated it was unavailable. He asked if she could try it every so often. Tamara agreed and they hung up.

Although he had an urge to go out to the television lounge, he stayed in his room, trying Jan's cell number. Not that he wanted to watch television, but he did feel a need to simply look out into the parking lot. Somehow, he felt that if he looked out into the parking lot he'd see the red Audi driving in, the fog lights on because of the weather. Jan would get out, pop up her red umbrella that matched the color of the Audi, and head for the building. But he knew this was only a dream and the risk of leaving his phone wouldn't be worth it.

Because he couldn't help thinking any minute Jan would arrive to tell him what she'd been up to, he wheeled into the hall just outside his room where he'd still be able to hear the phone. From this vantage point he could look down the hall toward the elevators each time he heard the bell. As he sat there he realized he was twisting to one side because of a pain in his right side. Not good to have pain this time of day, especially after Percy had worked him over in rehab this morning. Probably stress. And as he twisted to one side while staring down the hall toward the elevators, the pain was, in a way, reassuring.

After a while he turned to look the other way down the hall toward the television lounge. He figured the lounge would be empty because everyone on the floor except him was still down in rehab. But the big-screen television was on, he could see it reflected in one of the rain-soaked windows. And there was someone watching. A man in a wheelchair. Although the man was not facing him, he had definitely been looking this way and had turned as soon as Steve spun his wheelchair around.

Steve moved his wheelchair forward a little and could see the man was not one of the aides who had plopped down in a vacant wheelchair for a break the way they sometimes did. He could also see the man was not a resident from his floor. The man was not dressed in so-called street clothes like a resident would wear for a day of rehab, but real street clothes for this kind of weather. Brown leather jacket and a red baseball cap, the cap not on his head, but held by its beak, the cap wagging back and forth slowly on the arm of the wheelchair in which the man sat.

The man was in profile and kept glancing away from the television to look down the hall toward Steve. Normally he wouldn't have thought anything of it, but he'd noticed that the first time the man glanced his way, there was a pause. And now, when the man glanced his way again, he seemed to be trying to make it look a little too casual. He'd stretch or yawn or drop his cap and pick it up from the floor so he could start wagging it back and forth again.

A situation from the past loomed up, a crazy situation in which he'd been hired to watch a guy who, it turned out, had been hired to watch him. He could picture the situation. A sunny day, hot weather, each of them sitting in their cars watching one another, a situation in which both he and the man he was watching tried to make it seem they weren't watching one another. He recalled that, despite his parking spot in the shade of a tree, it had been stifling in the car, no breeze coming in the windows. Just like here in the hallway at Hell in the Woods. No breeze, no fresh air.

The longer Steve sat in the hallway, the more he was convinced the guy in the wheelchair in the television lounge was watching someone or something. And even though the guy was not an aide or a patient from this floor, Steve was sure he'd seen the guy before. Earlier that morning when they were all on their way to rehab, he'd seen the guy hanging around the desk outside the rehab center.

The guy was probably in his twenties. Thick, shiny black hair. His face had smooth features, but there was a definite beard shadow, even at this distance.

Footsteps from behind. When he spun around, Nadine wagged her finger at him. "George says for me to come back here and see what you're up to, Mr. Babe. She says she needs help with the tape recorder and would you kindly reconsider coming down to rehab."

He wheeled about, catching a glimpse of the man looking his way, then rolled into his room, motioning for Nadine to follow. He retrieved the computer from the windowsill and began pecking at the keyboard with the index finger of his left hand while Nadine watched over his shoulder.

He typed, "Got to stay. Tell Georgiana waiting for important phone call."

"Well, my goodness," said Nadine. "If you'd said that before . . . now I'll have to go all the way back down there."

He typed, "Sorry." But when Nadine turned to go he reached out with his left hand and tugged at her sleeve.

"What now?"

He typed, "Down in the television lounge."

"What about it? You want to go there? I thought you were waiting for an important call."

He shook his head and pointed to the screen of the computer, then struggled to type his question. Nadine tried to leave a couple of times, saying she was busy, but he pulled her closer and she finally stayed long enough so he could type his question in a way she could understand. After a few tries, he typed, "The man in the lounge. Leather jacket. Who is he?"

"That's funny, you're the second one who's asked me about him today. His name is Mr. O'Connor. He's a short-timer from the first floor. I spoke with him earlier this morning. He's in for physical rehab on his leg. Comes up here during breaks for some peace and quiet. I guess things are a mite hectic down on one."

He typed, "Why leather jacket?"

Nadine laughed. "I asked him about that, too. He says he's getting out soon and wants to be ready to go. Says he drives a motorcycle. I told him this sure isn't the weather for it. Says he hurt his leg falling down on his motorcycle but that he'll keep right on riding it. Some people never learn."

He typed, "Who else asked?"

Nadine had a puzzled look.

He typed, "Who else asked about O'Connor?"

"Oh, it was that aide named Pete. You know, the one with the sideburns. Funny thing, Pete's been asking all kinds of questions lately. Putting in the hours, too. Guess he was trying to impress somebody down at the office. I think he was overworked. That's probably why he had that accident in the stairwell today." Nadine paused, staring at him. "Didn't you hear about it?"

Steve shook his head.

"Oh, yes. Poor Pete fell down the stairs with a load of files or something. They say he was too impatient to wait for the elevator. He ended up downtown at the hospital. They say he has a concussion."

After Nadine was gone, Steve pictured the aide named Pete. The guy with out-of-style long sideburns. Yes, Pete scratching at his sideburns like they were brand new sideburns. The same guy who visited rehab a little too often, making it obvious to Steve he was after something. The same guy who spoke with him about Marjorie's husband having been in the mob. Of course it could all be his imagination, but if not, if Pete had been sent in by someone to nose around and see what he could find out, and if that same Pete was in the hospital because of an "accident" . . .

Steve decided there was nothing he could do regarding Pete now. What he had to do now was find out about Jan. And, damn it, in order to do that he'd have to sit here and wait like . . . like an invalid.

But maybe there was something he could do while he passed the time waiting for the phone to ring. Maybe he could perform a little test on Mr. O'Connor. After all, Mr. O'Connor was not in the hospital like poor old Pete. Mr. O'Connor was right here.

Steve turned his wheelchair toward the door and rolled out into the hallway to make sure O'Connor was still there. Then he backed his chair into his room. After trying Jan's cell number again, without luck, he waited several minutes. He could hear the television in the lounge, but not enough to tell what was going on. So he got the remote from his bedside table and turned on his television with the sound off. He switched channels until he found the action that fit the sounds filtering down the hallway.

It was a B thriller on a classic movie channel. A scantily clad woman had just screamed at a severed head that had spoken to her, and the host, Svengoli, came on. Steve waited for the commercials to end and positioned himself at the door. When the movie came back on and showed the scantily clad woman running in terror as the head thing skittered after her on the guts protruding from its neck, Steve wheeled suddenly out into the hall.

Leather-jacketed Mr. O'Connor apparently didn't like watching scantily clad actresses fleeing from severed heads on the large screen television in the lounge, because instead of watching the television, O'Connor had turned his wheelchair and sat facing the hall, staring directly at Steve.

CHAPTER EIGHTEEN

The Prius had landed right side up, but its roof was collapsed, with only rounded indentations made by the seat backs when the car had been compressed by the weight of the truck. Blood spattered out onto the battered hood and rear deck said it all. The car was no longer a Prius, and the men she knew as Tony Gianetti and Buster Brown were no longer men. Although she had not meant to look for ghoulish details, she saw pieces of what had earlier been these men glistening in the brown weeds. Pinkish lumps of flesh and bone, no longer human beings, but mere components scattered like exploded seedpods.

Besides struggling to keep from getting sick, there didn't seem to be anything else she could do. She had called 911, then gotten out and gone closer to the wreckage. It was strangely quiet and she heard pessimistic mumblings from nearby onlookers. Someone praised Japanese engineering for having designed the Prius so its gas tank was protected during the crash and did not rupture. Though she stood alone, she felt an odd kinship with the other onlookers. Each group, and several lone observers like her, maintained yards of distance from the next group or loner, as if to leave space for death's spirit to make its way through. Some stood in the shadowy gloom like death observing death. Some stood on the unevenness of the embankment like bent statues in a quasi darkness. Although it was afternoon, the thick clouds made it dark enough to see drizzle falling through headlight beams. The cold drizzle touched her face and neck as she and the others watched the men who had gotten to the wreckage first. The men knelt in the mud, apparently trying to determine if either of the occupants was alive. Then someone tapped her shoulder and mumbled something.

A man in a hooded sweatshirt stood at her side and she could feel a rush of adrenaline as she took a step back. Although the man had spoken to her, he stared at the wreckage and she could not see his face. When she turned toward the man, the hand that had tapped her shoulder was pushing deep inside a pocket in his sweatpants. A shiver ran through her as she recalled the flat-nosed man she had seen outside the apartment in the parking lot. But that man had worn a baseball cap. Yes, worn backward when he ran, then forward when he was following her in his BMW. Not a hooded sweatshirt. She breathed easier when the man turned toward her and she saw his pointy nose and his beard.

The skin around the man's eyes appeared sallow in the gray light. When his mouth opened, parting his full beard, she could smell his stale breath. He pulled his hand from his pocket and held it toward her, looking down in an odd way as if he had done something for her and expected a tip. "Lady, your phone."

"What?"

"Your phone. It's an emergency."

She looked down at her side where the man was staring and realized she had brought the phone with her. After using it she had unplugged the cigarette lighter plug and now the cord hung down, the plug dragging in the weeds.

"I . . . I already called 911. I just brought it out here in case."

"No, lady. For this other guy back there. Says he knows the driver. Wants to call someone." The man held his hand closer, almost touching her. "Please, lady."

She handed the phone to the man. "Of course. Certainly." Then, to be helpful, "It doesn't need to be plugged in. I just left the wire on . . ."

She turned to watch as the man gathered the charging wire up with his other hand and took the phone to a group gathered near a van. The man handed the phone inside the van, then nodded back to her.

It began raining harder and she could feel cold droplets running down her scalp and between her collar and neck. If she went to the van to see who was there who knew Tony Gianetti, she'd be asked about being here. She'd be standing in the rain and whoever was inside would stare at her while she tried to explain. She'd have to make something up because the truth would be absurd. Whoever was in the van must have recognized the Prius. Perhaps the vanity plate and bumper sticker were visible from behind, but she could not tell from this angle. She imagined standing at the side of the van staring in at weeping effeminate men from Tony Gianetti's gay rights organization. Suddenly the world took on a backward aspect, one of those moments in which the impending chaos of civilization becomes real. She took a step toward the van, then stopped, shivering from the wet cold and imagining herself being able to do nothing more than add to the anguish of whoever was in the van.

She shook off the chills and went back to her car for her umbrella, noticing that the man who had borrowed her phone was watching, apparently so he could find her when whoever was using the phone was finished. As she stood outside her car beneath her umbrella, she could see that others had also gone back to their cars for coats and hats and umbrellas.

The men attending to the wrecked car seemed the most prepared of anyone, and she heard two bystanders agree they were glad the three men had arrived first. The three men at the wreck wore black knit caps, and she noticed all three had on leather jackets, and jeans, and good boots. One of the bystanders said the men told the others to stay back, that because the car was a hybrid they had to be careful of the high voltage of the batteries.

Beyond the wreckage Jan saw a Hispanic woman talking on a cell phone. Could this be the same woman she'd seen earlier on her way to the funeral home? Right, how could she possibly tell in the dark with the emergency lights flashing on the woman's face, the woman standing at a distance on the far side of the wreckage, the woman standing in the rain without an umbrella or raincoat and . . .

The man who had taken her phone returned, ducking his head beneath her umbrella and startling her. "The guy in the van says thanks, lady. He was really cryin'."

She took the phone from the man. "Yes, I suppose if he knew the driver . . . did he say whether there was anyone else in the car?"

"He didn't say nothin' like that." The man motioned back toward the van. "You know how people are in situations like this. He was concerned he was using up your battery."

The man pointed to her cell phone. "He used to sell those things, so he knows a lot about them. Wouldn't you know, here he is out where he needs one and he left his charger in his own car so his batteries went dead. That's why I came out here to borrow yours."

When she held up the phone as if she were going to use it, the man touched it gently to get her attention. "I wouldn't use it right away until you plug it in for a while. My friend says he could see your batteries were low so he kept his conversation short. He says cold weather like this kills these batteries fairly quickly. He also says you're not supposed to keep it plugged into your car all the time and that you should use your home charger. I guess he figured you keep it plugged into your car all the time because of the charging wire hanging from it. I guess these things don't get their full charge unless you use the home charger once in a while. So you see? That's pretty much all he seemed to care about was the condition of your phone. It's just like him. One of his best friends dies and here he is worried about batteries. Anyway, my friend says you should definitely plug it in for a while before you even think of using it. He says if you let the batteries run that low you'll lose your memory and everything."

"Well," said Jan, "I hope your friend is all right. I was just wondering if he knew about anyone else in the car because . . . well, because if he lost another friend . . ."

The man stepped around in front of her. "Who's to say no one survived the crash? I've seen people survive worse. You know what I mean? Anyway, you want to talk to my friend yourself? I'm sure he wouldn't mind. That's the kind of guy he is. Always thinking of others."

"No, that's all right. I just thought if he could recognize a car that's been smashed so badly, he might know more."

The man turned toward the wreckage, but as he turned he seemed to move in even closer. Droplets of rain dripped from his beard and steam rose from his breath. "Yeah, that's right, but see, he didn't recognize the car. What he recognized was the license."

The man moved even closer beneath the umbrella, held his hand up before her face and pointed behind the wreckage. He spoke more quietly as if to keep others from hearing. "We came in that way and you can read the license plate from back there. P-P two-thousand. That's what my friend recognized."

The man's stale breath filled the space beneath the umbrella and she could feel his arm press against her arm. She stepped back slightly and when she did he turned and stared at her. He'd been excited about sharing the moment, but now she saw something else in his face. Something deep down beneath the dark eyes and sallow skin and black beard. She had a momentary feeling they both knew she wanted nothing to do with him, that she might even be frightened of him. This feeling was telegraphed between them in an instant, too late to say or do anything, impossible to say or do something that would not be misconstrued. In the years before she met Steve, the life she'd led had put her in this awkward situation many times before, terminating conversations with men she did not know.

As the man continued standing near her, several squad cars and three ambulances and two fire trucks arrived in rapid succession. When paramedics took over from the three men in leather jackets at the wreckage, the men did not stick around as she thought they would, but seemed to disappear as quickly as they had appeared.

There was no hope of either Tony Gianetti or Buster Brown being alive. She could tell this by the wave of a hand from one of the paramedics after the Jaws of Life had been applied to one side of the crushed roof. Although she had never really forgotten what had gone on earlier in the day, it wasn't until a policeman took two briefcases out of the wreckage and carried them to his squad car that it hit her. Something in those briefcases might be very important to her. Something so close, yet so far away.

She felt relieved when another policeman approached her and the man standing at her side. "Go back to your vehicles, folks. The southbound lanes are open and we'd like to get everyone moving. If you move on I'm sure others will follow." The policeman motioned them along. "I appreciate your help, folks. Thank you. Have a pleasant evening, if that's possible."

Saying nothing, she went back to her car, started the engine, locked the doors, and plugged in her phone. Bright headlights lit up the inside of her car from behind. When she looked in her mirror she could see that the van carrying the man who had borrowed her phone had pulled up very close. When it sounded its horn she put her car in gear and started off. The man who stood at her side had disappeared quickly after the policeman approached and was apparently doing what he had been told, moving on.

"All right, all right," she muttered, as the van followed her closely back onto the road.

She considered staying at the scene because she witnessed the crash. Maybe she should have given her name and address to the policeman in case they wanted to contact her.

As she continued slowly away from the scene, very slowly because of the crowd of gawkers that had grown to perhaps a hundred, she saw the driver of the semi sitting on the ground at the side of his cab. Two policemen stood over the driver looking down, apparently questioning him. And stooped down on the ground, consoling the driver, was one of the men who had been at the wreckage before the emergency vehicles arrived. Black knit cap, leather jacket, boots.

As she drove away, she could see in her mirror that, besides her and the van, several others were leaving. The road south was empty, but on the other side of the median, traffic was stopped dead in the northbound lanes and lined up as far as she could see.

Tony Gianetti was dead, and so was her whole stupid investigation. She wondered if she should tell Steve about any of it, or just let the whole thing drop. But of course she knew she would tell him eventually. Part of the reason she had come out here was because she was part of him and he was part of her. She couldn't keep anything from him, especially when he needed her so much. She could almost see him trying to put on a show of anger that she should do such a thing, but smiling, always smiling. He'd ask for details and it would be good therapy. He'd struggle to ask questions, and now that she had left the scene of the accident, she realized one of the questions he would ask would be whether or not she felt the death of Tony Gianetti and Buster Brown was just a bit too much of a coincidence to be an accident.

And then of course there was the weird guy who had borrowed her phone. Why, if his friend knew Tony Gianetti Junior, was the van leaving the scene? What about the flat-nosed man who had obviously followed her? When she told Steve about him she was certain he'd not think the accident was a coincidence. But if it wasn't a coincidence . . .

No, it had been an accident clear and simple. She had witnessed it. Others had witnessed it. Someone familiar with Tony Gianetti's gay rights organization had recognized the license plate. Someone who knew Tony Gianetti had used her phone to call someone else and by now perhaps friends and associates from all over the Chicago area were calling one another to deliver news of the fatal accident. Yes, it was an accident. Although the truck driver had driven recklessly, it was still an accident.

The lights from traffic following her were blinding. When she looked in her mirror she could see the shape of the van, and realized the van with the weird guy inside was following her. The van's brights were on and she tried to imagine the conversation in the van, the weird guy describing his conversation with her.

She glanced down at her phone in its holder and . . .

Wait! If the friend of Tony Gianetti Junior called someone, the number would still be stored on her phone. Later, when she had a chance, she could call the number. But maybe it would be better to wait until she was back with Steve. Maybe bouncing everything that happened off him would be best.

As she drove away from the scene, she glanced in her mirror at the frenetic flashes of emergency vehicle lights multiplied a thousand-fold by droplets of rain on the rear window. The van finally dropped back a little but its brights were still on, making it difficult to concentrate on the dark road ahead.

Although she knew it would be pointless to go back to the accident scene, and that she'd be viewed as a crackpot if she did, she decided she just might go to the police. Maybe that would be better than dragging Steve into it. And if she saw the flat-nosed man following her again, she'd definitely go to the police. Yes, maybe she'd call Tamara and get her advice on what agency to call when an accident just doesn't seem like an accident. She was tempted to use her cell phone to call Tamara, but decided it would be best to let the phone charge and maybe go see Tamara in person as she had planned earlier. Better to explain face to face to her husband's ex-lover the circumstances surrounding her bungled investigation. The irony of having Tamara as one of her most trusted friends added to the confusion of the night.

She headed south until the northbound backup ended where police were diverting the traffic east on a crossroad. Because there was no reason to continue south into farm country, and because she didn't want to turn east into the traffic jam of the detour, she turned west.

After turning off the main highway she picked up her phone and flipped it open. When it did not light up she assumed the man who had used it had turned it off. She held it closer to her face so she could find the On button. She would have found the On button and powered the phone on but bright lights from behind blinded her again and she put the phone down.

At first she assumed the headlights turning west onto the two-lane behind her belonged to others trying to go back north and avoid the detour traffic jam heading east. But why follow her if they had been heading south on Route 45 prior to the accident? And why drive with their damn brights on?

On both sides of the road were embryonic housing developments with names referring to hills and lakes she could not see. A few models were completed, but the rest of the land was flat and weed-covered except where it had been torn up to put in utilities. At the entrance to one housing development where the road swerved she could see that two cars and a van were behind her, their headlights glaring in her rearview mirror. They had not turned into the development as she had hoped, and now the land on both sides reverted to farm fields.

Suddenly, the pavement ahead ended, the road west becoming gravel, and the road south paved. There was no road going north so she turned south. The two cars and the van also turned south and now she wished she had gone straight ahead. Of course, if she had done that, and if they had followed her on the gravel road . . .

Who could blame her for being paranoid? In a single day she'd been followed by a guy who looks like a boxer, then the car she's following is suddenly destroyed. Maybe she should have stayed at the scene, or gone south on 45 until she got to a main road, or voiced her concerns to the policeman back at the accident. Steve always said it was good to ask questions because the process of doing so—even if the answer was, of course it was an accident—often led one to other questions that might not seem so ridiculous.

No more housing developments. Driving south was nothing but farmland, the groupings of farm buildings spaced at least a quarter mile apart. Despite the fact it was still mid-afternoon, she could see lights on in one of the farmhouses she passed, but the next farmhouse was boarded up. She had assumed the two cars and the van following her knew a short cut. But now, as they came closer, she knew this was not the case. And to make things even worse, it was getting darker and had begun to rain very hard.

Then it happened. Her outside left mirror exploded in white light as one of the cars pulled out to pass. The car's headlights flashed up into the cold rain ahead as the car bounced repeatedly after hitting a series of chuckholes on the left side of the road. She was going nearly fifty, it was raining like hell, and this idiot in a huge behemoth of a car was passing on a road that was awash with rain and wasn't even a full two lanes wide!

As the large car caught up she could hear the splash of water from its front tire drumming the rear fender of the Audi. Then, when the car got alongside and the splash from its front tire pummeled the windshield so that she could not see, she braked hard so the idiot would get by more quickly. But the driver of the car also braked and, before she could react, the large car veered to the right and hit her front fender and door. The sounds of metal tearing and tires rubbing created an insane rhythm. She thought the car would bounce off, but it stayed with her, steering into her. She tried to turn left but it was useless against the mass of the large car. She was being pushed off the road.

Gravel banging beneath the Audi. Dead weeds laid flat by winter snows brushing loudly at the bottom of the Audi. She floored the accelerator and the Audi's four-wheel-drive carried it up the slight incline of the shoulder and back onto the road ahead of the large car. It was a Lincoln or Ford. It was keeping up. When it touched her rear bumper she screamed, floored the Audi again and raced ahead. In her mirror she could see the large car that had hit her was being followed closely by the van and the other car.

It was insane. Minutes earlier she had been in the midst of a crowd, had even talked to a policeman, had even talked to the 911 operator, and now she was being chased, the two cars and the van using up the entire road, getting out of one another's spray. Who were they? A gang of idiots who had seen her at the accident scene? All kinds of characters there like the one who asked for her phone so someone in a van could borrow it. Was the van behind her really the same van? On this dark afternoon colors blended into one another so that the light blue van at the accident scene could be this van that appeared gray in her rearview mirror. How many men were there? Would they rape her, then kill her? And if they did kill her, what would Steve do?

"Goddamn you bastards!" she screamed.

The road went through a series of curves ahead and she took the Audi through the curves as fast as she could. When the road straightened she had gained several hundred feet on them. She steered to the center of the road, reached for her phone, made sure the road was straight, then flipped open the phone, found the On button in the glare of headlights, held the On button in. But the phone did not light up.

"Come on, phone! Come on!"

When the phone still did not light up she pressed 911. Nothing. She tried pressing the On button again and again, made sure the charger plug was all the way in. The green light on the charger plug was lit but still the phone would not light up.

The three pair of headlights slithering back and forth like reptiles dimmed and brightened because of the bumpy road and the spray from her car. They were getting closer. She was going eighty-five, the Audi hydroplaning when it hit puddles, and they were getting closer!

Even though the phone had not lit up, she kept pushing the On button and putting the phone to her ear. Nothing.

She recalled Steve telling her to go to Wisconsin with Lydia, recalled the insistent look on his face as he struggled to tell her that she needed a vacation, that she needed to get away.

She kept glancing side to side, hoping she'd see someone at a farmhouse staring out at these idiots speeding down the road. Someone, anyone, who would call the police. Or maybe there would be a policeman at a side road. So far, all of the side roads had been gravel, the rain dotting them with puddles. And the lead car was following too closely for her to brake and turn into a farm driveway. By the time she saw a driveway loom up out of the rain and gloom, it was too late to brake. Even if she did manage to turn into a driveway, what then?

As she drove she began sounding the Audi's horn. If she could attract someone's attention, wake someone up in the farmhouses she passed . . . but they wouldn't be in bed. Although it was dark, it was afternoon. By the time she passed the farmhouses, people inside would shrug and go about their business. And if a farmer were out in the barnyard, he'd probably do the same. Unless . . .

There was another curve ahead and she sped through it, almost losing control, but managing to hold on and stay ahead of the two cars and the van. Back on straight road she reached between the front seats and into the back seat. She grabbed handful after handful of magazines, magazines she had been carrying around for weeks, magazines she took into Hell in the Woods a few at a time to go over with Steve. She would do something. Anything. Maybe a page from a magazine would flatten itself on a windshield and cause one of them to go off the road. Maybe magazines flying out the window would anger a farmer enough to call the police. Maybe she was nuts, but she had to do something.

And so, as she took the Audi up to ninety, steering it toward the centerline of the narrow road to keep the wheels out of the puddles, she pushed the button to lower the passenger window and, with her right hand, began flinging handful after handful of magazines out the far window.

It worked! Or at least it caused the car behind the van to pull to the side and stop. Now there were only two following. She kept throwing magazines out, reaching into the back seat to get more. But when the road came to a T and she had to slow down, she saw the third car was catching up to the others.

She turned left at the T, hoping this would take her back east to Route 45. She assumed the direction was east, but because of the curves she had gone through she wasn't sure.

This road was bumpier than the road she'd turned off of. The Audi's steering wheel, normally firm and steady, became a live snake. She could see, by the way their headlights bounced and the way they steered side to side, that the three behind her were also having trouble with the road. The van had slowed down and now the following car passed it. Then the van slowed more and soon after she passed a gravel road to the left, the van turned down that road. In her mirror she could see its lights as it seemed to drive across the rain-soaked fields.

The road got even bumpier and went through a series of curves bordered by a wooded area. The two following had dropped back. Soon she would be back on Route 45. Soon she would be able to speed back north to where the police diverted traffic around the accident scene. She had stopped throwing magazines out the window and she could feel the wind and rain coming in the passenger window. She was about to raise the window when she saw it.

A sign ahead, double black arrows pointing left and right on a yellow background. Another sign, "Pavement Ends," loomed up from behind a lone tree at the side of the road. Not knowing what else to do, and thinking in the back of her mind that this would be good evidence to leave behind after she is raped and killed, she began throwing magazines out again, flinging them as fast as she could across the seat and out the passenger window. And as she did, she screamed Steve's name. Then she began crying, especially when she saw the van. It had taken another road and was approaching the T from the left in order to cut her off.

She turned right at the T, just ahead of the van. Left had been gravel, but she had no choice, and now the Audi fishtailed, bogged down, and finally bottomed out in mud that splashed ahead of the tires and came up over the hood so the windshield wipers seemed to be clearing the windshield of black blood. She tried to accelerate, spinning all four tires, but she was stuck in a deep puddle and it was no use.

As the van pulled around her to the left on higher ground, its tires splashed mud onto her driver's window. The Audi's engine roared as she tried in vain to escape. Finally, she let off the gas, raised the passenger window, made sure the doors were locked, and pressed her hand down on the Audi's horn.

A few seconds later there was a loud banging on the driver's window that caused her to let go of the horn and look up.

A man used a gloved hand to wipe away mud from the outside of her window. He wore a knit cap. No beard, no hooded sweatshirt, not the man who had borrowed her phone, but his face looked familiar. Soon he'd explain it all. There would be a logical reason for this. They'd help her with her car and explain everything because, after all, she'd seen this face before. Somewhere. He'd been in a suit and tie. He'd been . . .

My God! It was the man Steve had pointed out at Marjorie Gianetti's funeral, the hood named Dino. He was not smiling and now she saw that the thing he had tapped on the window with was a gun!

"Open up!" he shouted.

She picked up the phone and held it up to the window. "I . . . I already called the police!"

Now he did smile. He put the gun away in one pocket, then reached into another pocket and took something out. He held a roll of tape close to the window so she could see it.

She held the phone closer to the window. "I called state police and sheriff's police, and a bunch of local cops! They know! They're on their way!" She turned to look back down the road as if she believed what she was saying, as if saying it would make it true.

But the hood named Dino simply smiled and pulled a long piece of black tape from the roll he held and ripped the piece off the roll and stuck it diagonally across her window.

"I'm afraid you'll have to call your phone company, Mrs. Babe!" he shouted. "They'll have to credit you for all the calls you made to the police!"

He pulled off another long piece of tape and applied that to her window on top of the other piece of tape, making an X.

"Isn't it wonderful what a handy thing tape is, Mrs. Babe! Some of my friends find duct tape handier, but I find it a bit brutal for my tastes! Now, black tape, this is really handy! With black tape, you can do all sorts of things! You can tape something so it's waterproof, or you can even tape electrical contacts on plugs and on battery packs so the electricity won't flow!"

He pulled off more tape and put a horizontal piece across the X he'd made on the window.

"Or, you can use black tape to tape a safety glass window so that when you break it, it won't make so much of a mess! But wait! I guess the duct tape would be faster for this!"

Shadows around her car in the gathering darkness. Rain beating on the roof of the car as they gathered and as both black tape and duct tape began to completely cover the driver's side window. She could see men through the windshield now. Two wore knit caps and leather jackets. And one of the men was the one who had borrowed her phone. She recognized his hooded sweatshirt and the sallow skin of his face framed by the black beard. She was about to scream when she saw a man approach from the front of the car with something long and shiny raised into the air. She had not even gotten the scream out when the driver's side window exploded into the car and the taped safety glass fell in onto her shoulder.

Then the doors opened, her seat belt was taken off, and she was in the rain with them. At least five of them, faces averted, hung low in the rain as they shoved her about. Her arm felt as if it had been pulled from its socket, her head throbbed where it struck the roof of the car when they dragged her out. She was pushed against the back of the van, her hands taped behind her. Hands all over her, too many to resist. Heavy breathing as she tried to drop to the ground, but the hands held her up. One hand from behind, wrapped around her and at her crotch, copping a feel while other hands put more tape on her wrists.

Then, her face held sideways against the cold wet steel of the van, she felt one of them move close, hot breath at her ear.

"Where do we go next?" said the low voice.

She thought the voice was meant for someone else, one of them wondering where to take her, or where to go with this. But the voice repeated more loudly into her ear, "I said, where do we go next?"

She was pulled sideways, her face sliding along the cold metal of the van's rear doors. When her face reached the corner of the van she heard a buzzing sound, and when she opened her eyes she saw a platform had emerged from the side of the van like a huge tongue and that someone in a wheelchair was emerging from the van onto the elevated platform.

"I wouldn't recommend it, Legless," said one of the men holding her, his voice firm but calm as if giving a parental warning. "You'll get those skinny wheels stuck in the mud and end up on your stumps."

As the legless figure in the wheelchair sat on the platform, apparently considering what had just been said, the only sound besides the in and out of her breath was the gurgling of exhaust from the Audi as it sat idling in the deep puddle.

CHAPTER NINETEEN

THE SKY TO THE WEST WAS BRILLIANT ORANGE ABOVE THE Everglades. Not that he could see the Everglades from where he was. What he could see, from his apartment on the fifteenth floor, was mostly city, being that his building was near the ocean. At dusk, on a clear night like this, the orange sky and city lighting combined to create one hell of a view. It was almost enough to make a man forget about the past and imagine that his wife, her health intact—his wife of thirty years who had originally wanted an ocean view but acquiesced to his desire for a sunset view, his wife five years dead this past winter—awaits his return inside so she can be at his side.

Valdez was out on the patio of his downtown Miami apartment when the phone rang. The wine that afternoon at the airport had made him hungry. He had grilled his dinner, a chicken breast and some vegetables, and had just put it on a platter. He shut off the grill and carried his dinner inside. As he put the platter down on the island he could tell, because of the light on the phone, that it was the secure line, which meant a call routed through the Miami office communication center. He went around the island, sat on a barstool, and, while staring at his steaming platter, picked up the phone and heard George Skinner's familiar voice.

"Valdez?"

"Yes, it's me."

"Sorry I'm calling so late."

"That's all right."

"When we were young men we might have contacted one another over the air waves on an evening like this."

"Yes, times have certainly changed. No more Morse Code, no more worrying about the atmospheric skip."

"Have you eaten yet?"

"I'm just starting."

"Well, go ahead and finish. But after you're done, Hanley will be calling from the condo. It seems things have come to a head in Chicago. I'll give Hanley the details, but I wanted you to know so you'll be prepared to do whatever needs to be done."

"So you've been contacting both of us all along?"

"Yes, but Hanley's unaware of our relationship. As far as he's concerned, I'm *his* contact at Langley. More importantly, my old friend, I called you first. You and I and Tom Christensen were old ham buddies together. After that we inherited certain obligations. You understand."

"Yes."

"Anyway, go ahead and finish eating so you'll be ready when Hanley calls. And Valdez?"

"Yes."

"You know what this means, don't you?"

"I know."

"It's for the sake of future generations."

"I agree."

"All right. You'll both be wearing golf jackets with deep pockets, so be careful."

"I will."

"Then seventy-threes, my old friend, and take care."

"I'll do that."

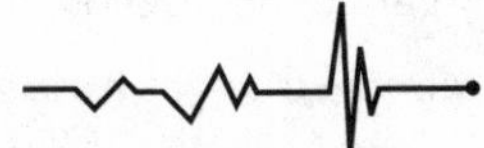

At the condo, Hanley had Valdez wait in the living room while he finished dressing. Against the far wall, Valdez could see the two golf bags that had been sent over by the main office. Valdez stared down at his shoes. White sneakers, the only pair he owned. He felt odd wearing white sneakers as soon as he left his apartment, especially when he exited the elevator and headed through the lobby. He also felt odd wearing the "I'd rather be Golfing" cap he picked up on his way to the condo. The odd feeling that he'd stick out in a crowd didn't leave even when he got back into his car after buying the cap and no one else could see him. The only time he'd worn the sneakers was the rare occasions when he went to the pool. The sneakers were part of his past, purchased when his wife was still alive. They'd gone to the Keys for their twenty-fifth wedding anniversary. It seemed so long ago. His wife rubbing aloe on his sunburn in the hotel room. If only she could be here again. If only she'd been able to share in this so-called retirement that was just around the corner.

Hanley glanced at his watch as he came out of the bedroom with his carryon bag. "We've got time," he said. "They've got to file the flight plan and there's no need to get there too early. I like your cap."

Hanley was also wearing a golf cap, but his had a golf club logo on it and Valdez wished he had purchased a different cap.

Hanley placed his carryon bag on the floor next to the golf bags and joined Valdez on the sofa. "Thank God we'll be able to sleep on the plane. It's been a long day for both of us."

"I guess we should thank God for something," said Valdez, turning to stare at Hanley. "And now, what is this all about?"

"The situation in Chicago has deteriorated," said Hanley. "That's why our friend at Langley called me directly. Our number one contact at the rehab facility has managed to get himself taken to the hospital, apparently having been confronted by one of Lamberti's men. And the other contact . . ." Hanley smiled. "Maria. Well, she seems to have lost track of Mrs. Babe."

"They're sending two old men to Chicago because a couple of rookies couldn't cut it?"

"Not exactly," said Hanley. "We're going to Chicago because Mrs. Babe may have stumbled onto something from the Gianetti past, and because Lamberti and his men are loose cannons. In the process of going after the money, they've managed, in a single day, to kill the son and his attorney, beat up one of our contacts, and throw the other contact off the track. We can't allow this to go forward because of the possible ramifications."

Valdez looked down at his sneakers. "And what exactly are those ramifications?"

"I thought I made it pretty clear in one of our earlier conversations."

"Not exactly," said Valdez, turning to Hanley. "All you said was that it was political and had to do with two past Presidents, Reagan and Carter. That wasn't much to go on."

Hanley smiled. "Yes, I guess, since we both have to go, it's time to make it clearer."

Valdez looked at his watch. "You want to talk here or on the plane? I'm not a very fast driver."

Hanley looked at his watch. "All right, on the plane. It has to do with politics and political talk always has a way of becoming long-winded."

Hanley and Valdez stood slowly and went to the door. Valdez was already wearing his golf jacket and watched as Hanley put his on. Golf jackets, thought Valdez, which meant jackets with deep pockets. Too bad it had to come to this.

When the two men hoisted their golf bags onto their shoulders, they both grimaced and looked at one another.

"Damn arthritis," said Hanley.

"Damn arthritis," repeated Valdez.

CHAPTER TWENTY

IMMEDIATELY AFTER THE STROKE, LYING ON HIS BACK IN THE hospital, Steve had felt as if a great weight pressed down on him. He had not been able to move and, more importantly, had not been able to think. The weight affected him not only physically, but mentally as well. The weight had a life of its own, because when a flicker of memory showed itself in the distant darkness, the weight redistributed itself to make certain the memory remained just that, a flicker.

Immediately after the stroke, lying on his back in the hospital, the first thing he'd seen when he opened his eyes were the eyes of a woman. He knew she was a woman and wondered how he knew this when he didn't seem to know anything else. Yes, the first thing he'd been aware of after the stroke was that the eyes belonged to a woman and that he was a man. But there was more. Despite the weight holding back the flickers, he gathered the woman was fond of him, and this made him fond of her. Then, because she must have known him before the stroke, he presumed they had been together and shared many things flickering in the darkness.

Immediately after the stroke, lying on his back in the hospital, words had been elusive. But even though words were elusive, concepts began coming back. The first concept was that of love. He knew the woman at his bedside loved him, and he loved her. As if love between them existed in his blood rather than in the cells of his tormented brain. Another concept that made its way to the surface was motivation. He wanted to poke holes in the cloak that had descended over him. He wanted to search for flickers from the past and bring them closer so he could examine them. In order to be able to initiate this search, he realized early on that he must live and not let the stroke take him down.

She stayed with him during those early days. She was the one who had given him the test to see if he'd had a stroke—Have the person try to smile, raise both arms, speak a simple sentence. She was the one who looked into his eyes and stroked his head where another thing called a stroke had assailed him. She explained things, like the same word—stroke—standing for her act of caressing his head, and also standing for what had happened inside his head. This and many other things he had tried to comprehend. His initial comprehension of the world seemed to take a long time, but he'd gotten through it because of a thing she called desire, a desire he knew had been spawned from the underlying emotion of . . . love.

Initially, her love for him was apparent when she was with him, then became apparent when she was not there. At first he wondered if he were being taught how to love. But he soon realized her love unearthed tunnels into the past in which he could explore, tunnels in which he could search, tunnels like blood vessels through which nutrients destined for brain cells traveled.

The concept of time came alive because of her. It was measured by the intervals of her presence and absence. One morning, shortly after the stroke, when he was able to take food by mouth and she was there early to feed him, he'd been able to relate this to her by removing her watch from her wrist, hiding it in his fist, then revealing it and pointing to her. It was strange during those first days following the stroke. Although he could not remember his wife's name, he knew he loved her and he knew this thing on her wrist measured time. What made it even stranger was that this business of knowing some things and not others drifted in and out of focus so it was difficult to put it all together into one single frame of reference.

His first spoken word after the stroke had been her name. He said it in the middle of the night when she was not there. He'd been visualizing her and the name had floated in like a leaf falling from a tree. When he heard himself say her name aloud that first time, he believed that saying her name would make her appear. The lights would come on in the room and she would be there, her face hovering above him the way it had when he first came awake after the stroke.

"Jan."

It was a wonderful name. The movement of tongue against palate while the lower lip juts out slightly and the mouth opens rapidly to allow trapped air to escape for the J, felt sensual. When he succeeded in saying her name the next day while she was there, she wept. He wanted to tell her it was all right, that there was no reason to weep. But the conglomeration of words necessary to express this concept played hide-and-seek in his head and, instead of trying to say she should be happy, he held her and kissed her and drew her atop him.

"Jan." He said her name now as he sat in his room wondering where the hell she could be. He repeated her name as he squeezed and released the grip exerciser with his good left hand. He repeated her name as he curled the dumbbell again and again with his good left arm.

It was his fault. She had not gone with Lydia to the reunion because he had opened his big mouth, changing everything. The consequences and seriousness of the stroke were in the past, yet they were not in the past. The seriousness of the situation had crept up on him. But what could he do? How could a stroker, paranoid because he's being watched from down the hall, do anything?

While he waited for Tamara to call back again, he exercised physically and mentally. He tried to recall something, anything that would give him a clue to where Jan might have gone. He'd hoped the physical exercise would make it easier to keep his thoughts focused. But it was no use. Interspersed with thoughts of Jan he recalled the man at the end of the hall, and this made him think of Dwayne Matusak.

A bad summer. The constant threat hanging over him. A knock-down drag-out fight from which only one would come out alive. At least that's how he remembered it. Perhaps growing up in a rough neighborhood was why he'd looked to Sergeant Joe Friday for help. Joe Friday, with the 714 badge and the definitive "dum-da-dum-dum" refrain signaling that in the end good wins out over evil. Joe Friday staring knowingly into his boyhood eyes. (Did Joe Friday have dark eyes? He wasn't sure.) And at the end of the show, with badge 714 blown up to screen size, in walks the stroke, shooting up his brain despite return fire from Joe's thirty-eight from behind the medulla oblongata.

As he continued exercising he could hear the sound of the television down the hall. Something about it not being too early to get your boat order in for the upcoming boating season. He closed his eyes and could see, inside his head, a lone water skier being dragged about. He imagined beings from another world looking down on the planet and assuming this was how these creatures called humans punished those who had committed petty crimes. The channel changed and now the sound was a news report from a war-torn part of the world. As a result of this, the beings from another world would assume this was how more serious crimes were punished. The criminals were made to put on uniforms and fight one another. Fighting one another in order to see who can squander more of the planet's resources. Crazy. A planet that's had a stroke. But is the stroke ischemic or hemorrhagic? It was hard to tell.

Finally, when the volume of the television down the hall was lowered, he heard footsteps and the squeak of wheelchair tires on the tile outside his open door. When he opened his eyes and looked up he expected to see the man from the end of the hall in his leather jacket, his baseball cap wagging in his hand, but what he saw was Phil and Frank and Joe wheeling past.

The room had darkened while he exercised and his train of thought had wandered far afield. He turned on his lamp, looked at his watch, and realized the other strokers were coming back from the rehab center to get ready for dinner. How much time had gone by since he realized Jan was missing? And, for that matter, was she really missing? When Phil wheeled up to his door and motioned for him to get ready for dinner, the phone rang. He motioned Phil away, heard a muttered, "Jesus fuck," and answered, "Jan?"

"It's me, Steve," said Tamara. "You heard from Jan?"

"Tam. No."

"Okay. Slow, like before. Stop me, or let me know if you want me to repeat anything."

"Right."

"I filed a missing person report on Jan."

"You filed? Why?"

"I filed it because of some things I've found out. Listen for a while and don't try to talk. After checking on Phil Hogan at the Eighth District, my contact wanted to know what I knew about Phil's recent activities. I said I knew nothing. Then he told me he talked to his chief and asked if I could put a tail on Phil. So we did, and Phil wasn't out of the office a half hour before he made contact with a prominent member of the organized crime brotherhood that's officially not supposed to exist in Chicago anymore. I don't know if you remember Max Lamberti, but the organized crime unit's been after him for years. He's related to the Gianetti family, Tony Gianetti's nephew. Supposedly he took over some of the operation after Gianetti's murder back in eighty-six. Anyway, it wasn't long after this that I heard about a fatal traffic accident in Orland Park this afternoon. Gianetti's son was killed and I think it's becoming too much for coincidence. His full name is Antonio Gianetti Junior. His attorney was killed with him. William Brown, known as Buster Brown downtown."

Tamara paused to let this sink in, but Steve's mind was working too fast to respond.

"So," said Tamara, "I called in a missing person report on Jan. There's probably nothing to it. Most likely she's at a shopping mall or stuck in traffic, her phone switched off or broken. Even so, I decided not to take any chances. Jan contacted Phil Hogan, Phil seems to have something going on with Lamberti, and now Lamberti's cousin and his attorney are dead. It's being reported as an accident, but I talked to the Orland Park chief and he says the accident is under investigation and they might at least file a manslaughter charge.

"So it's like this, Steve. On the remote chance Jan's ruffled some feathers, I thought it best to reel her in. If there's nothing to all this, which there probably isn't, you can help me explain it to her later."

Steve held onto the phone tightly with both hands, closed his eyes, worked his jaw, trembled, but was unable to say anything. He wanted to suggest logical steps, to say things that would start an investigation in the right direction. The names Max Lamberti and Marjorie Gianetti and Antonio Gianetti Junior and Rickie Deveno and Rickie

Justice and Dino Justice floated in his brain, but he could not say them. He wanted to tell Tamara about Marjorie and how this all started. He wanted to tell Tamara he should have known better than getting Jan involved in something like this. And now Jan grabbing onto this thing because she wanted to create a case for him. A new case for Steve Babe, the failed detective who most likely brought on his own stroke and deserved whatever he got. He's so selfish he drags Jan into a goddamn fantasy so once again he can be who he used to be.

Details swam in his head, and the details became enmeshed with the words, everything coming to mind at once. Even the stupid jokes shared in rehab. He tried to concentrate, to say one solitary important thing that might help, but all that came out was a whimper.

"I'm sorry, Steve. You want me to call someone there? You need some help?"

Yes, he needed help. *Jan! My God, Jan!*

"Steve? You need help? I can come there if you need me. You want me to come there?"

He looked to the window where gray sky was turning into the blackness of night. A jet rumbled overhead, vibrating the window glass. The lights had gone on in the parking lot and they were reflected in raindrops on the outside of the glass. The raindrops flickered as the jet passed overhead, thousands of coded messages from the signal bridges of thousands of ships lost at sea. Signals he could not comprehend. Tamara was waiting for an answer to her question. Did he want her to come there? Would it do Jan any good, wherever she was in that darkness, if Tamara came to his room at Hell in the Woods? Finally, he took a deep breath and said, "No."

Before he changed out of his grays and went home for the night, Tyrone took the elevator up to the third floor to check on the bastard. He picked this time because he knew it was just before dinner and it would be busy up there.

After shooting the breeze a while at the nurses' station, complaining about the weather and jets from O'Hare taking off overhead, he made like he was doing a last errand before going off shift and headed down the hall to the bastard's room. If the guy was with his wife he'd try to listen in, see what they were talking about. And if they were talking about that old lady who happened to kill herself near the closet where he did business with Flat Nose, well then, maybe he'd just have to come back tonight. Give him the old bigger-cats-out-there-that'll-cut-your-balls-off-and-throw-you-down-the-elevator-shaft bullshit. And if that didn't work, maybe he'd say something about this other guy who's been watching his wife and knows where she lives.

Part of the reason for checking up on the bastard was because of Flat Nose. Not that Flat Nose said he had anything planned, but it was the way Flat Nose was acting. All that staring-down shit had gotten on his nerves. He'd even begun to wonder whether DeJesus and Flat Nose had separate agendas. To Tyrone, the stare-down shit from Flat Nose was like the distancing a gang-banger might have done before he pounced in the old days. If he checked on the bastard himself and satisfied DeJesus, maybe he'd get DeJesus and Flat Nose off his back. Yeah, time to steal the show, stop acting like a shorty who doesn't know shit.

The bastard was alone in his room, sitting in his wheelchair between the bed and the window. He was staring out the window, but the phone from his bedside table was in his lap and he seemed to be shaking all over like someone had already gotten to him.

Tyrone slipped into the room, figuring he'd pretend to check the heating register below the window. He walked slowly across the room, and when he saw the guy glance up at him, he gave him a smile to throw him off guard.

The guy turned slowly toward Tyrone, smiling back. This guy always smiled, even when he was shaking. The bastard even smiled when he'd called him a fuckhead earlier in the day. Yeah, calling him fuckhead and making off like it's the stroke did it. But now, for some reason, the smile looked different. Tyrone thought he'd seen a smile like this before, back when he was a shorty and that cat DeAndre used to threaten kids in the block if they refused to join. Smiling, yet not smiling. Yeah, smiling, but behind the smile was a guy showing you he was thinking about what he'll do to you if you don't play the game.

The smiling guy rolled his chair toward Tyrone. The telephone in the guy's lap was still connected to the wall by its cord, and as the guy rolled toward Tyrone the phone slipped off and clattered on the floor. But the guy didn't seem to notice this and Tyrone saw that the guy wasn't shaking the way he had when he'd first come in.

Then the guy was all over him. He sprung from the chair like a jump-shot artist and caught Tyrone off guard and now they were on the floor. The guy growled and had Tyrone by the throat. And although Tyrone was able to throw him off, one side of his neck throbbed where the guy's good hand had been.

"Crazy bastard!" screamed Tyrone, sitting up.

But no sooner had Tyrone sat up and the bastard was on him again, slithering toward him with one side doing all the work the way he'd seen it in physical rehab. The guy got Tyrone's shirt front with his good hand and banged Tyrone's head on the floor.

This was enough, thought Tyrone. He rolled away, stood up, and kicked the bastard in the gut, making him spit and sputter. After kicking him once more for good measure, he bent over and grabbed him by the shirt collar.

"We'll meet again, motherfucker! Only next time I'll bring a friend! Between the two of us we oughta be able to whip your ass because he works for Jesus Christ himself!"

When the bastard opened his eyes and smiled, Tyrone stood up, making ready to kick him again. But just then the nurses' aide named Betty came in.

"What's going on here? Did he fall? Can't you help him?" Betty rolled the guy onto his back, knelt down beside him, placed her hand on his forehead, took his wrist for a pulse.

"Tyrone! Don't just stand there! Get help! Don't you know anything about procedure? My goodness, you'll be fine, Mr. Babe. You'll be fine. Get going, Tyrone!"

On his way to the nurses' station, Tyrone nearly tripped over a white dude in a leather jacket and baseball cap who seemed determined to take up the whole damn hallway with his wheelchair. The dude didn't budge, but stared at Tyrone like someone looking for a fight.

Tyrone said, "Tough guy," then sidestepped the guy's chair and ran on.

After reporting that a resident had taken a spill while he'd been checking the heating register, Tyrone left the floor. On his way down to the first floor, he figured the elevator might as well take him on down to hell because something was sure to come of this. But when he took his time changing and said goodnight to everyone and went to the supervisor's office to say goodnight and she didn't say a damn thing about the incident, he felt like he'd been given a stay of execution by the governor.

Out back in the employee parking lot, as he slid into the DeVille, he decided he would definitely have to come back tonight and put some fear into the bastard. Stroke or no stroke, Babe had tried to choke him.

A jet on takeoff boomed overhead as Tyrone started up the DeVille. He thought about his Uncle Ezra and the really old DeVille he had. He goosed the engine on his DeVille a couple times, drawing power from it. As he backed out of his parking spot, he thought of the white dude who'd run into him in the hallway and mentally slugged the dude, making his baseball cap fly and his chair go into reverse. He put the DeVille in drive, spun the wheels on the wet asphalt, and drove fast out of the parking lot toward the road around the front of Hell in the Woods, only slowing down when he saw a cop car coming in the front entrance.

CHAPTER TWENTY-ONE

KNIT CAPS OFF, HEATED INSIDE OF THE VAN SMELLING OF RAIN, sweat, mud, and leather jackets. Tape smell, too, especially when she tries to move her mouth. Nose running because she has been slapped and because she cannot breathe through her mouth. Wrists aching where they are taped. Arms numbed because they are pulled tightly behind her. Raincoat furrowing into her armpit where the shoulder belt is fastened beneath her left arm instead of over her shoulder.

At first they had taped only her hands, apparently expecting her to tell them what they wanted to know. They put her in the rear seat of the van, one man holding her while the one with the deep voice asked repeatedly, "Where do we go next?" It was dark in the van and she could not see who was talking. Then, when the man holding her left the van and she sat alone in the back seat and they began driving and streetlights flashed by, she saw that the hood from Marjorie Gianetti's funeral named Dino, the same hood who had shouted to her through the closed window of her car, sat on the floor of the van facing backward, facing her.

When they'd been driving for a time, Dino got up from the floor of the van and sat on the rear bench seat beside her. He ripped tape from a roll and taped her mouth quickly and brutally, the way someone might slap a sticker on the bumper of a car. After taping her mouth he reached across and belted her into the seat, pulling the combined shoulder and lap belt beneath her arm, buckling it and cinching it up tight. At one point she tried kicking him, but this only made him angry and he had slapped her hard across the face.

Although the van had only front bucket seats and a rear bench seat, it was quite long. The center part of the van was taken up by the wheelchair lift she'd been held down on after they took her from her car. The handicapped man sat up front in the driver's seat. She could see a partially folded wheelchair at an angle in the space between the front seats. Except for the sliding door through which the lift extended when in operation, the van had windows all around. However, by contrasting the street lighting coming in the front windshield with that of the lighting coming in the side and back windows, she judged all but the windshield were darkly tinted. Up front, beneath the dashboard, she saw red and green lights, and realized, when she heard the muted chatter of police calls, the van was equipped with a scanner.

When she heard a male voice say, "Code-seven," she recalled Steve teaching her the basic codes when she was learning to use his scanner. Code-seven meant out of service for a meal break. She recalled it vividly because that day Steve had taken her to a restaurant to have lunch with the pair of cops who'd just gone code-seven. She recalled one of the cops complaining that he hoped he was able to retire before he was ten-fifty-five, which had nothing to do with his age. Ten-fifty-five was one of the "ten" codes. It meant dead body.

She wasn't sure how long they'd been driving, perhaps a half hour. The amount of light visible through the front windshield beyond the knit cap on the driver's head had brightened. At first, when lights sparkled from within beads of raindrops swept by the windshield wipers, she'd thought the sparkles were in her head and she was on the verge of passing out. But now she saw that the flashes of color were gas stations and restaurants and traffic signals. When she turned her head she could see Dino sitting in the rear seat beside her. Because of the darkly tinted side windows, his face was profiled against near-darkness, the face changing color with traffic signals and streetlights and shopping center lighting coming in through the distant windshield.

Knit cap off, eyebrow ridges prominent. Sitting back, legs crossed, arms folded. Saying nothing and not looking at her, as if his job is finished and someone else will take over.

Only the two of them with her in the van. Front passenger seat empty. The other cars that had chased her gone, or perhaps following because she has not seen them up front. Her car taken because she heard the rasp of its exhaust as they fought to free it from the mud after she was put into the van, one man holding her down from the front, popping the top buttons on her blouse, while the other—Dino—kept asking her where they should go next.

Just as she began to wonder how much longer they would continue driving, the van turned, bumping up into a yellow-lit parking lot. The driver parked behind a brightly lit building. She caught a glimpse of windows and people sitting inside as they pulled into the lot, but now all she could see was a windowless wall of the building. When the driver shut off the engine, the windshield wipers stopped mid-stroke, hands about to clasp in prayer.

The driver reached between the front seats, pushing the wheelchair back and somehow unfolding it behind the seats. In one quick motion like a huge ball bounced from the front seat, the driver spun himself around and propelled himself back between the seats into the wheelchair facing the back of the van. During the transfer the wheelchair clattered and the man grunted. It was obvious the driver had no legs at all. She recalled the warning someone had given back at the end of the road where they'd captured her. *"I wouldn't recommend it, Legless. You'll get those skinny wheels stuck in the mud and end up on your stumps."*

Because of the light through the windshield behind the driver she could not see his face. But now that he was closer, she realized his head was larger than she'd thought, the knit cap resembling a small appendage. His breathing was heavy and labored, yet slow. Then the motor that operated the lift exploded into life, opening the sliding door while at the same time moving the legless man in his wheelchair outward. Once outside, the lift lowered him, then came back inside empty as the door slid closed.

She could smell meat being grilled, and the heavy odor of deep frying. Now that the engine was off and the whirring of the lift motor and its components had stopped, the only sound in the van was the intermittent patter of rain on the roof.

Dino said nothing. Because of the bright yellow light through the windshield from what was apparently a fast-food restaurant, she saw that he sat with his legs crossed and his arms folded, staring straight ahead. His lips moved slightly as if he were cleaning his teeth with his tongue. His face was expressionless. He did not react when she tried to call out and succeeded only in making a kind of high-pitched hum. The pull of the tape tugged at her skin and made her nostrils feel as if they'd been torn.

When the driver returned, the lift conveyed him into the van as if he were a component on an assembly line. He had a bag on his lap. She could smell greasy cooked food and coffee. The driver opened the bag noisily, brought out a covered paper cup he handed to Dino. Then the driver turned to the front, placed his bag on the passenger seat, and with more heavy breathing and another grunt, propelled himself back into the driver's seat.

The driver sat in the front and ate, retrieving his meal from the passenger seat. When he turned, she could see him in profile alternately munching on a huge burger and lifting a container of fries to his face. The sounds of chewing and swallowing and the rustling of the packaging filled the van. While the driver ate, Dino sat staring straight ahead, not saying a word, not reacting in any way except to clean his teeth with his tongue. Then, after the driver took a swig from a drink in a large paper cup with the straw, she saw Dino hold up the cup he'd been given.

Dino carefully lifted the cup's plastic cover. She could see steam rising from the cup as Dino held the cup to the light for a moment, as if he were admiring the steam. Then he reached toward her with the cup, held it above her lap, and slowly tipped it.

She spread her legs and tried to push farther back into the seat, but the coffee caught her on the insides of her thighs. She felt the tape tearing at her chin and nostrils as she tried to scream. It was as if her slacks had been set ablaze. She moved her legs rapidly up and down as the coffee-soaked material of her slacks licked at her thighs. Then, when the coffee finally cooled, and she began to feel relief, he held the cup out again and this time emptied it.

After the second dose of coffee had cooled and she was able to rest, relieved that the coffee was gone, but still in pain and not sure what was next, Dino went forward, gave the empty cup to the driver, then came back and once again sat beside her. The driver noisily crammed all the wrappers and cups into the bag on the passenger seat. Then he methodically propelled himself into the wheelchair, activated the lift and was out the door, this time leaving it open. The bright lights from the parking lot shown in through the open door as she watched the driver wheel himself in the rain to a garbage receptacle at the front corner of the van. When the driver returned to the van and was being lifted inside, he turned to her and smiled. It was an insane smile full of creases darkened by beard stubble.

The driver was much older than Dino, perhaps in his early fifties. He had a thick nose and wide-set eyes. A series of scars like meandering streams ran between one eye and his chin, distorting his mouth and misshaping his head. He reminded Jan of drunks from the distant past when she was a dancer and they would sometimes reach out for her. He stared at her as if he had suddenly discovered a way to get even with every woman who had ever rejected him. He seemed to read her mind while he paused there, licking raindrops from his lips before he wiped his mouth with his sleeve. Then he turned to the front of the van as the side door whirred shut.

Once back in his seat, the driver started the van and let it idle. The driver's scarred face reminded her of Lydia's scar, and of Lydia's pain, and of the fact that she could have been with Lydia tonight if she had left this whole thing alone like Steve had wanted. Her pain and fear was heightened by the driver's relaxed movements. She could hear the driver belch several times as the windshield wipers swept back and forth. She tried to hear if any other engines started after the driver started the van, but could hear none. Then the driver backed out of the parking spot, drove out of the lighted parking lot, and they were on the move again.

The pain was nothing. Burns would heal, given time. But right now time seemed to have run out. No time left and nothing left except this van, Dino sitting beside her, and the driver belching up front. The most frightening part was that the world she'd known was already beginning to fade. And with it, Steve was fading, trapped in another world she was no longer part of. Would Steve remember her? Or would a therapist, in order to help Steve survive in yet another changed world, slowly begin to erase all memory of her for his own good?

When she glanced toward Dino through eyes blurred by tears, she saw him watching her. He had turned slightly in his seat to face her. She could see the glint of street lighting in his eyes, and his cheeks had an oily sheen. He leaned toward her and smiled.

"We've been to the bank, Mrs. Babe. We've gotten what we needed from the safe deposit box at the bank. You should know because you were there. So where do we go next?"

It seemed so long ago. Sitting in the bank watching Tony Gianetti Junior and his attorney come from the safe deposit box vault carrying their briefcases. Following the Prius south and seeing the truck move into the Prius's lane to engulf it. Watching as the men in leather jackets and knit caps went to the wreckage. The men in leather jackets and knit caps had not been there to help. They had been there to retrieve something from the two briefcases.

Dino tilted his head and looked puzzled. "Should I take off the tape so you can speak? Don't nod unless you're prepared to tell me, Mrs. Babe. If you nod and I take off the tape and you don't tell me where we should go next, we'll have to get more coffee. Only this time we'll get a large, and we won't let it cool."

Everything was going too fast. The bank, the wreck, the men in knit caps, her being chased and caught. What she had to do now—what she must do now—was think of a reason. And so, despite the pain in her thighs, she concentrated. And when she concentrated, Marjorie Gianetti's litany of U.S. Routes played back in her head—*U.S. 6 and 45, U.S. 30 and 50, U.S. 20 and 41, U.S. 14 and 94...* Although she could not remember all of it, she knew that the place to go next must be to the next intersection. The litany is what got her to the bank where she had seen Tony Junior and his attorney. The list of routes was written down in her notebook and the notebook must still be on the passenger seat of the Audi beneath the last stack of magazines she pulled from the back seat in order to throw them out the window and leave a trail. If they found the notebook and opened it to the litany, would this be what they wanted?

Again, despite the pain, she was able to think of something besides it. She traveled back in time in order to be out of this place for a few seconds. In order to be with Steve once more. But there seemed to be another reason for the brief interlude. Steve was there, sitting with her in the living room sipping wine. She had just taken a sip of wine, had put her wine glass down, and had clasped her hands behind her back to appear coy. Steve would come to her, tell her he loved her, and she would unclasp her hands in order to hold him. But this is not what happened in the moment recalled from the past. Instead of telling her he would always love her and would always remember her, Steve seemed to know about this particular night in the future. Staring at her with his dark eyes, a sad look on his face, his hand reaching forward through time and touching her cheek, Steve recalled a then recent case in which a client with a secret had disappeared and was later found dead. She asked if it would have been better if the client had simply given in to those who had threatened him. She asked if it would have been better if the client had told the secret. Steve was serious when he spoke.

"When desperate people threaten to hurt you, and you know something they want to know, and they know that you know, never tell them. Because when you do tell them, you'll no longer have something they need. That's what I told my client, but he apparently didn't listen. That's why he's dead."

Rather than nod that she wanted the tape off so she could speak, she stared at Dino. Lights flashed on his face. Then they drove through a darker area where intermittent streetlights brought his greasy face out of darkness for only seconds at a time. While they drove, the driver turned on the scanner mounted below the dash and she could hear the muted sounds of police calls. The driver turned off the scanner when something beeped next to her. Dino took a phone from his inside pocket and unfolded it. When he put the phone to his ear and turned away, she leaned close to listen to his side of the conversation.

"Yeah, they split."

"Back at the place."

"In the parking lot."

"Yeah."

"Next to me."

"Legless."

"No other name but mine."

"At the funeral."

"Yeah, I've got 'em."

"If not, it's back to the place, I guess."

"Why you?"

"I was just asking."

"Later."

After putting away the phone, Dino sat back in the seat, staring straight ahead. For a moment she was reminded of Steve. The way Steve sometimes looked away from her shortly after his stroke as if preoccupied. He'd been in the hospital back then, unable to move his right side, unable to talk. At the time she wondered if his turning away had been a sign he was aware of flickers of memory from the past. Like the summer he was a kid and that other kid named Dwayne Matusak threatened him. Was Dino thinking about when he was a kid? Yes, a kid bullied by another kid, that's what it sounded like on the phone.

Steve was right. Once these men got what they wanted, they would kill her. She knew it. And if they didn't get what they wanted, they'd kill her. It was only a matter of when. And when they did kill her, Steve would be alone with nothing more to remember her by except perhaps the diary she kept for him. When she was dead, he could forget about the uphill battle to recall the past, because then it wouldn't matter.

The van slowed and turned into another well-lighted area. Beyond the sweep of the windshield wipers was a strange tunnel. The tunnel was lit from within by bright ceiling lights and steam rose from its floor. Because of another in a series of eruptions of tears that blurred her vision, it took several seconds to determine what was ahead of the van. It wasn't until the driver pulled into the brightly lit steaming tunnel that she realized they had driven into a car wash.

The driver turned off the windshield wipers, shut off the engine, and once again left the van. The mechanical whir and clattering of the lift echoed within the self-serve car wash until the empty lift was back inside and the door slid closed. In the silence that followed she assumed that the "Legless" she'd heard Dino mention while on the phone referred to the driver. Now she knew two names. Dino and Legless. After a few seconds she heard a muted clatter of coins, then a loud pump came on and the van was being sprayed. The spray was powerful and noisy against the metal sides.

During all of this Dino had been silent and unmoving. But now, as the sweep of the powerful spray buffeted the van, she glanced toward Dino and saw him reach to her face. When he ripped the tape from her mouth, she screamed.

CHAPTER TWENTY-TWO

Two hours after visiting hours had ended at Hell in the Woods, the outside main double doors were locked, leaving only the single side door leading into the lobby vestibule open for emergencies and for employees coming and going during shift change. This door could be locked by the guards at the front desk if need be. As stated in the chapter on security in the building policy manual, "In rare instances involving acts of nature or social unrest, the building may need to be secured for the continued safety of residents, whether they be located in rehabilitation facilities or in dining facilities or in private rooms or lavatory facilities, and for the ongoing safety of employees, whether they be attending to their tasks or making use of employee recreational or dining facilities or using lavatory facilities."

One of the two guards at the main desk read from the building policy manual, mostly to pass the time, but also because he was new at Saint Mel in the Woods Rehabilitation Facility.

"This here book's real interesting," said the new guard. "Especially these parts about residents and employees having the right to be safe while they're sitting on the crapper."

"Yeah," said the other guard, who stared at the closed-circuit monitors. "The book got a lot thicker for homeland security. Someone from up on three told me that nurse named Betty probably wrote it. She'll talk your head off if she gets a chance. I figure they put her on three because it's all strokers up there and it's good for them to hear a lot of jawboning."

"She must've written the policy manual they had back at the hospital, too. Of course that one's about two inches thicker than this one, being they got all those highly-paid docs and all that expensive medical equipment and locked-up drugs to talk about."

"They got drugs here, too."

"I suppose they do. But not so much of that IV stuff they got back at the hospital. There, they want you out for the night, they put you out for the night. If it weren't for IV drugs there'd be all kinds of screaming and commotion and relatives staying all night long bitchin' about staff not giving a damn about all the pain in that place. Not as much pain in this place."

"I suppose not," said the veteran guard, staring at the empty hallways shown on the monitors. "Maybe that's why most visitors go on home when they're supposed to."

"Makes it nice and quiet," said the new guard, turning a page in the policy manual. "I think I'll like it here."

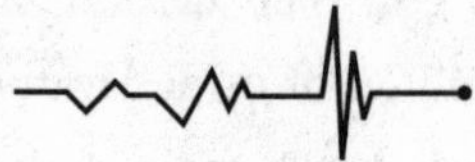

Although Steve had not remembered his mother when she visited with his sister, he did know about mothers. And now, as he dressed in the dark, a voice from a commercial recently on television came to him. A voice telling him to dress warmly so he would not catch cold. But instead of the generic mom's voice of the commercial, he imagined his own mother telling him to dress warmly. Not simply because it was a cold wet March night, but because he had work to do. And, considering his obvious physical weaknesses, he needed all the help he could get.

From foot to head he wore black high-tops and jeans and two sweatshirts, the black hooded one on the outside. He'd put on his right leg brace beneath his jeans and tightened it so his leg wouldn't collapse in case he was under stress and had to be on his feet and forgot to will the muscles in the leg to hang tight. On his head he wore his White Sox baseball cap, which was also black except for the Sox insignia above the brim.

He had his wallet and the two-hundred dollars in cash Jan had taped to the bottom of one of his dresser drawers about two-hundred years ago shortly after they transferred him here from the hospital. He knew Jan had done it as a test back then to see if he would remember the money. And when he remembered the money, she'd left it there. She said he'd need it to take her out to dinner when he graduated from Hell in the Woods. While he was thinking about his wallet, he took it out and checked his credit cards and his driver's license to make sure they hadn't expired. After he put the wallet away, he reached around with his left hand and patted his right pocket, knowing he should have something there, but not sure what it was. Then, when he was about to close the dresser drawer to which the money had been taped, he saw the keys to his and Jan's apartment and felt a wave of inadequacy come over him. He stood there for a minute grasping the drawer, actually thinking the words *drawer* and *key* and *inadequacy*. He wondered for a moment why there were two keys and decided one must be for the building entrance. Finally he took a deep breath and put the set of keys in his left pocket.

He considered taking his portable computer along, stood staring at it atop the dresser for a minute, imagining it spitting out explanations to people he might encounter. But finally he decided the computer would only be good for taking notes or maybe sending a FAX or getting on the Internet if he hooked up to a phone line.

Crazy bastard. Things like that, especially waiting for someone to read a damn FAX or mailbox entry, or getting on the Web and trying to do research about Max Lamberti. . . All of it was much too slow for what he'd be doing tonight. But before he turned from the dresser, he reached out and pocketed his portable thesaurus. Maybe he'd need it, maybe not. If he couldn't come up with a word to call the bastards who . . .

No, couldn't afford to think of that. Jan was fine, and all this preparation most likely for nothing. They'd have a great laugh tomorrow because Jan would chalk up tonight's excursion into the cold rainy world as simply more good therapy, mind over matter and mind over muscles, getting the damn right side to do what *he* wants it to do for a change.

Not only had he followed Mom's advice about dressing warmly, but he'd also eaten well. After the struggle with the aide named Tyrone, and after convincing the nurse on duty that he must have dozed off in his wheelchair and fallen forward out of it, he'd gone down to dinner with the others. Before returning to his room, he'd snuck behind the counter in the nurses' station to see if he could grab his nighttime medications, but of course the tray wasn't there. Medications were always locked up until they were needed.

Too bad. He'd be gone by the time his nighttime medications were doled out. Yes, he'd be long gone. So much for Tegretol, Coumadin, Heparin, Amitriptyline, and Dilantin. Although, just in case, he had managed to squirrel away a couple of Valiums during his stay at Hell in the Woods and he'd taken these along. While he was out in the world, the Valium might come in handy if his muscles got spastic. He knew he risked having another seizure without Dilantin, but he also knew it would make him sluggish. Going out in the world without his medication was a chance he had to take.

On the way down to dinner Steve had seen the man in the baseball cap again. This time the man was loitering near the elevators, his baseball cap and jacket on as if he were a wheelchair-bound relative or friend heading home. On the way back from dinner he had not seen the man. Although it was possible the man had been there, he had not wanted to reveal to the man he knew he was being watched. Let the man in the baseball cap relax this evening.

On the way down to dinner, when the man in the baseball cap was obviously watching, Steve had made a point of acting tired and depressed and confused. He even muttered the word *sleep* loud enough for the guy to hear before the elevator door closed. Some of Steve's fellow residents seemed surprised at this setback. At dinner he sat across from Linda and Frank, the two right-brainers, and instead of talking incessantly to one another as they usually did, they both seemed concerned about Steve, Linda asking several times why he wasn't smiling tonight the way he usually did. His only reaction to this was to say again that he was tired, "Really, really tired."

Although Steve had been unable to speak when he'd gotten the news from Tamara about Max Lamberti's connection to Phil Hogan, and about Antonio Gianetti Junior's death, he had been able to think. Thinking without having to converse allowed him to think more clearly. He'd noticed this in bed at night when he was unable to sleep. Although he'd never quite been able to explain it to Jan, at night in bed was when the things they went over during the day really began to coalesce and make sense.

Yes, when given the opportunity, Steve knew he was able to think things through. But he also realized this ability to think clearly, when he was not forced to converse, could be a double-edged sword. He knew that too much thinking had to be held in abeyance in order for him to be able to both think and communicate at the same time. Gwen, his occupational therapist, had taught him that. For this reason he decided that tonight he would communicate with others as little as possible. He'd go into the night a nocturnal creature, avoiding human contact. He'd be able to think more clearly and act upon his thoughts and not have to explain anything. Later, when this was over and Jan was safely back, there'd time for speech therapy. And if he couldn't get Jan back safely, then there'd be no reason to ever communicate again.

Steve's final act before leaving his room was the old trick of stuffing extra blankets under the top sheet on his bed and arranging his pillow to make it appear he was there sleeping. He knew he'd probably be discovered missing eventually this evening, especially when the nurses began their medication rounds. But at least he'd buy himself some time in case he was looked in on before that by an aide or by the guy in the baseball cap. Before dinner, after closing his door, he'd unscrewed the cover over the night light low on the wall near the door. He'd loosened the bulb so the light would not go on. This way, if the guy in the baseball cap tried to sneak into his room in the dark, the lump on the bed would look all the more real.

Sitting in his wheelchair just inside the door to his room with the lights off, dressed in black, his hands gripping the wheelchair's chrome push rims, he felt suddenly quite bizarre. As if, once he rolled through the doorway he would be leaving the only world he knew. His brain had been damaged by a stroke, things he had done and the person he had been had walked over a cliff up there in his noggin. And because of this, all critical moments in his existence—as this surely was—had become akin to standing at a precipice.

He recalled having tried to express this to Marjorie and Georgiana one afternoon in speech therapy. He recalled them agreeing that this was a good way to put it. The things up in his noggin had simply walked over a cliff. But maybe those things were still there, like cartoon characters walking out into space and not falling until they look down and realize what they've done, or like a character in a Hitchcock film grabbing onto a ledge at the last second.

As he sat just inside the door in his darkened room, he wondered if the lump of blankets he'd made on his bed to look like he was sleeping there might have more going for it. Maybe when he rolled himself through the doorway, the lump of blankets would become Steve Babe.

He shuddered at this thought not so much because of the insanity of it, but because of the reason for having the thought in the first place. There was a chance he might never see Jan again. Yes, that was the fear. Goddamn anyone to hell who would hurt Jan!

And so, when he was aware of an absence of footsteps or any other sounds in the hallway, he eased the push rims forward, his left hand doing the work while his right hand went along for the ride, peeked out in both directions, saw an aide, waited, peeked out again, saw a resident, waited, peeked out again, and finally, flew beyond the edge of the cliff.

As he rolled down the hallway toward the elevators, he could hear the sound of the large screen television in the lounge behind him. He kept turning to look, but saw no one at the rear of the television lounge where the man in the baseball cap would have had a view of the hallway, saw no one coming out of a doorway, saw no one at the nurses' station.

After he turned into the short entry hall leading to the service elevator hallway, Steve spun the wheelchair around and peeked back, his breath coming in gasps while he waited. In a little while he saw what he wanted to see. Amid the stroboscopic flashes of the television, changing scenes rapidly as a commercial played in the background, he saw the man who was obviously there to watch him. The man did not have on his baseball cap, nor his leather jacket, and he was too far away to recognize, but Steve knew it was the man just the same.

The man backed his wheelchair slowly away from the flash of the commercial so he could have a good look down the hallway. Yes, it was him, down to shirtsleeves for the long night ahead because the heat was up due to the change of weather. As he watched the man in the television lounge, obviously looking down the hall toward the room where the clump of blankets slept, a jet on takeoff passed overhead, rumbling the hallways of Hell in the Woods and vibrating the wall against Steve's cheek. When the man rolled back forward and was out of sight, Steve turned and pushed his way through the door to the service elevator hall.

After wheeling up to push the button for the elevator, he backed up quickly to get beneath the range of the ceiling-mounted closed-circuit camera. When the elevator arrived he sped onto it so fast he bounced off the back wall. As the elevator dropped, he felt a surge of strength, and anger. Nothing to lose if Jan was hurt. Right, nothing to lose. He'd even go to hell if he had to.

The second floor rehab center was quiet, as he knew it would be. Running the rats through their mazes had ended for the day and the staff had gone home. Unfortunately, they had also locked the double doors to the center.

He checked the ceiling behind him for a camera. Although there was none in the short entry hall, he knew there was one in the long hall that ran perpendicular, the hall he had just come down. Maybe one of the guards from the front desk on the first floor was already on his way. But then again, maybe not. He had rushed down the hall and probably been on the screen only a few seconds. Later, after he and his wheelchair are found in the trunk of a Lincoln, both of them shot to death, they'd replay the tape and see he had escaped alone.

A joker. Envisioning his wheelchair folded into the trunk of a Lincoln, shot to death. If there were a mirror handy he'd probably see an idiot smile on his idiot face. But maybe thinking this way was something he'd always done. Self-preservation. Envisioning himself shot to death so he'd be careful. At least careful enough to do everything he could to find Jan. And if there was some shooting, maybe he'd be the one doing it. Especially if they've done something to Jan.

Janitors' closets were handy things to have around. Especially if one needed to spill water on a floor to make it appear an elderly stroke victim out on an adventure slipped in a puddle and died. Or especially if one needed a place to rendezvous with a cohort for some illegal activity. Or especially if one needed something with which to pry open a locked double door.

The right double door was securely locked in at floor and ceiling. But the left door, which was locked to the right door, had enough play in it so he could just get one edge of a window squeegee between the two doors. Once this was done, he backed up and used the full length of the long wooden handle on the squeegee as a lever. The squeegee bent and he thought the handle would break. But the separation between the two doors widened slightly and he was able to spring open the loose door by kicking out at it with his left foot.

Although he saw no wires at the entrance, he could not be certain it was not alarmed. No alarm sounded when he broke through, but again, one of those guards might be coming, and so he raced into the rehab center and hid himself in Georgiana's speech therapy room.

He sat in Georgiana's room for a minute or so, his wheelchair rolled back into a dark corner. As he waited for his breathing to settle down, he became aware of pain throughout his right side from neck to toe. The only part of his right side that didn't hurt was his head. Yes, up there where the ambushed brain cells on the left side lay dead or injured or screaming for help.

Idiot. He's had a stroke and here he is thinking he can do this. Easy to say mind over matter when your entire right side isn't on fire. Oh so easy for a therapist to tell you it's all nothing but circuitry and that all you have to do is recreate neural pathways by eliminating learned non-use. Right, nothing but signals passed from neuron to neuron.

He closed his eyes. He envisioned Jan before him, laughing at the situation and the explaining he'd have to do for being down here. Then he envisioned Jan not smiling, Jan somewhere else and not smiling at all. Like when he first had the stroke and she came to him. When she was there he felt comforted, but when she was gone . . . when she was gone, the circuitry remaining tricked him into wondering if she'd really been there at all.

Within the world of circuitry that was his brain, he spoke to his right side, telling the muscles they were no longer flaccid, telling the muscles they could perform if given the opportunity. He envisioned right side nerve endings like skinny octopi wriggling their tentacles, mocking him while they send an overload of pain signals back to the brain. So why couldn't he send signals back to the little fuckers? Maybe he could, if he concentrated hard enough. Concentrate. Concentrate!

He rolled forward to Georgiana's desk, turned on the small desk lamp, and set up the tape recorder. His plan was to douse the light if he heard someone coming, then slide out of his chair and hide beneath the center opening of the desk.

With a fresh cassette in the recorder, and the microphone pulled close so he would not have to talk loudly, he leaned in to the desk, rested his elbows, turned out the light, closed his eyes, and relaxed the way Georgiana had taught him to relax before trying to do a speech exercise she had prepared. He imagined Georgiana sitting here, smiling at him, her short brown hair like that of a little boy. He imagined Georgiana sitting here because he needed to relax to do this. And if he made it seem like simply another speech therapy session, perhaps he could do it.

After he felt relaxed enough he opened his eyes and turned on the lamp. He pulled a notepad to him and wrote down the words he wanted to say. Since he'd been at Hell in the Woods, his left-handed writing had improved greatly. At least that's what Georgiana said.

He read the words over and over, not out loud, but imagining Georgiana saying them. Some of what he'd written didn't sound quite right, so he changed a few words. These were sentences, he knew, but the only way to get through this was to treat each word separately. It was the only way he could get his message across without a face-to-face meeting. The only way to avoid complications that would waste time.

And so, when he finally got down what he wanted to say, he set the tape recorder to Record-Pause so he could simply push the microphone button to start recording and release the button to stop recording. Then he closed his eyes and tried to relax again, this time working at it very hard in an attempt to forget what the message said, because he knew if he could forget what the message said and concentrate on one word at a time, he might be able to do this.

When he opened his eyes, he began meticulously recording one word at a time. He did this by pointing to the word with his finger, staring at it and concentrating only on the sound of that word. Then he would push the button, say the word, release the button, and go on to the next word and do the same.

The names were the hardest. Staring at them brought faces into view, and faces brought recognition, and recognition brought people, and people in the real world brought complication. But he clenched the microphone in his left hand and, instead of thinking of the people who went with the names, he thought of Jan in danger and, finally, was able to utter the names that went with the faces that, momentarily, seemed to float disembodied in his head.

It took nearly an hour to make the recording. He played it back several times, then fixed a couple of the words he felt he had done badly. When he was finally ready, he pulled the telephone from the other side of Georgiana's desk, rewound the recorder, set it on Play-Pause and made the phone call.

He almost panicked when Tamara's direct number was not answered after four rings. But when her voice mail came on saying cheerfully that he should leave a message, he decided this was the only thing he could do. After all, there would be no discussion about the matter. Either his message would work and Tamara would do what he asked, or she would refuse. Or, worse yet, she wouldn't retrieve the message and it would remain in the circuitry, useless.

It was unfair. Yeah, unfair like a stroke that shoots up the place. His entire plan hinged on whether or not Tamara retrieved a phone message. He'd counted on Tamara listening to his recording and doing what he asked. Now he had to count on her getting the message in time.

He and Tamara had been lovers once, long ago before he met Jan. Now, as he recalled Tamara visiting at the hospital before he came here to Hell in the Woods, as he recalled her reminding him they'd once been lovers, he remembered she had not been upset or angry when he did not immediately respond. Because of this, he knew she would do what he asked. She would do it because she had to do it for his and Jan's sake. Taking a chance that she would retrieve the message in time was the only way.

At the tone, he said, "Tam. Steve. Very important do. Please."

Then, when he pushed the Pause button, the recorder played the message he had prepared.

"Tam. I recorded because I cannot say directly. Need help right away. Need help finding Jan. Please access motor vehicles on computer. Get year and make and license on all vehicles registered to following: Tyrone Washington, Chicago address. Max Lamberti, Chicago or suburb. Antonio Gianetti, Chicago or suburb. Dino Justice, alias Dino Deveno, Chicago or suburb. Phil Hogan. When you get information, call my home number and leave it on voice mail. I will call it up. Please, Tam."

Because Tamara was not there, he quickly rewound the tape and played it once more. Then he hung up the phone, took the tape from the recorder and put it in his pocket, shut off the lamp, and turned his wheelchair toward the exit.

CHAPTER TWENTY-THREE

As the Learjet 45XR broke through the clouds hovering over central Florida, the seatbelt lights went out and both Valdez and Hanley left their seats to go to the plane's refreshment center. Hanley selected iced tea from the refrigerator. But Valdez, anticipating the cold Chicago weather, heated water for his tea in the microwave. Both men had removed their jackets and golf caps for the flight.

Back in his seat, Valdez put his teacup on the fold-down writing table and finished stirring in sugar. When he finished stirring he stared for a moment at the bull's-eye turbulence in the teacup. Valdez looked up from his cup, across to Hanley. If he were flying with anyone else he might have commented about the bull's-eye as an imagined scene from a disaster flick. The tea in the cup bull's-eyed by a defect in one of the engines. But he knew Hanley was much too serious a person for such a comment.

They sat in the middle two swivel chairs. The other four swivel chairs and the aft fixed seat were empty. The only others on the plane were the pilot and copilot behind the closed partition. Valdez looked out the starboard window while sipping his tea, trying in vain to spot lights from cities along the east coast. When he turned his chair toward the port side of the plane, he saw that Hanley had finished his iced tea and had put the tall glass on his writing table.

Valdez did not have to speak loudly to be heard above the gentle whine of the engines. "You're going to have to use the facilities with that much tea in you."

Hanley swiveled his chair. "I've never been in this model. Where are the facilities?"

Valdez pointed aft. "You lift up that seat in back. There's a divider that slides across."

"At our age we need to plan these things in advance," said Hanley. "If I drink up early in the flight I'll have time to empty it out a little at a time past my swollen prostate during the remainder of the flight."

"Good thinking," said Valdez, toasting Hanley with his teacup.

"How is security on this plane?" asked Hanley.

"Security?"

"You know what I mean. Word was they recorded these flights."

"That was long ago," said Valdez. "A couple administrations back they were that worried about special prosecutors. As far as I know none of the recordings were ever used and the new director had them destroyed."

"Good," said Hanley. "I don't know how they expected anyone to get any work done."

"I took a couple flights back then," said Valdez. "It was very quiet on board."

"I can imagine."

Valdez took a gulp of tea and put his cup down on his writing table. He reclined his chair slightly and leaned back. "So, are we going to go over things before we both doze off?"

Hanley reclined his chair and looked up at the ceiling. "Yes."

"And?" asked Valdez.

"I feel like I'm sitting in a dentist's chair," said Hanley.

"I'm the dentist, ready to pull your teeth, is that it?"

Hanley turned and smiled. "Unfortunately, I have no teeth to pull. Full dentures."

"I've got all my teeth," said Valdez. "A lot of caps, but I've still got the roots."

"Any root canals?"

"A couple."

They both sat in silence for a time, listening to the whine of the jets. Hanley continued looking toward Valdez. Valdez looked out the starboard window again, saw only darkness, turned back to Hanley.

"Kindly tell me something," said Valdez. "Have you had a stroke or is there another reason for the delay?"

Hanley smiled. "I'm savoring it for a while. It's been nice being one of a handful to know what went on in Chicago in 1980."

"I thought you said this had to do with Presidential politics," said Valdez.

"It does," said Hanley, turning toward the port window for a moment, then turning back. "Carter was President. Do you remember the high interest rates and the oil crisis?"

Valdez did not answer.

"Of course you do. We're both old enough to remember. The speech Carter gave in 1977 was about sacrifice. He wanted all of us to use less oil. He wanted the nation to become energy independent. But if that had happened, energy prices would have plummeted. Businessmen, a lot of them from Texas, stood to lose billions during the following decades if Americans became conservers of energy. Ironic, isn't it? Conservatives threatened by conservation. Anyway, a group of influential business leaders determined that the best thing for business, and, in their minds, for the country, would be for Carter to be defeated by Reagan."

When Hanley paused, Valdez said, "And he was."

"Right," said Hanley. "But there was a plan set in motion to guarantee it. Early in the campaign, Reagan's victory was not assured. The plan was to make sure it happened."

"How?" asked Valdez.

"Illinois."

"They were going to steal votes in Illinois?"

"Not exactly," said Hanley. "If Illinois went to Reagan, then he would win for sure."

"As I recall, Illinois did go to Reagan, along with most other states."

"Correct," said Hanley. "However, there was a plan in place to send the Illinois results to the courts if need be. If Illinois had gone to Carter, massive corruption would have been uncovered in the Chicago area counties."

"So that's where the Gianetti family comes in?"

"That's where Antonio Gianetti Senior came in," said Hanley. "Back then he was still powerful enough to influence highly placed Democrats. Over the years, Gianetti corrupted them. If, after the 1980 results were in, they had been needed, Gianetti was in a position to leverage a win for Reagan in the state."

"How would he have done it?" asked Valdez.

"The highly placed Democrats, in order to save their own hides, would have uncovered so-called corruption in the ranks below them. So much so it would have opened up a court case that was positioned to go Republican."

"Why would Gianetti have gotten involved? I know he was a fan of Reagan, but a mobster's got to have more reason than that."

"You're right," said Hanley. "Even adding in the fact that Carter called for an assault on organized crime, there had to be more reason for Gianetti to put the Chicago mob on the line. As has been said so many times in the past, what you have to do in this case is follow the money."

Hanley leaned forward, picked up his glass and drank down the water from melted ice cubes. He put the glass down, glanced back toward the aft of the plane at the fixed seat beneath which the hidden toilet waited, turned back to Valdez, smiled, and continued.

"If you recall, there was a huge drug bust in Chicago about that time. An equivalent street value in excess of a quarter billion dollars was confiscated. But the money that needs to be followed in order to find out what really happened was never recovered."

"And the money is still out there?" asked Valdez.

"It is," said Hanley.

"So what you're saying is someone supplied drugs and money to set up a phony drug deal so the mob could walk away with the funds to guarantee Illinois to Reagan."

"Not exactly," said Hanley. "The original arrangement was that the mob would walk away with the drugs. But when the drugs were confiscated, they took the money instead. And, because he had the most leverage, Gianetti kept the bulk of it. On the whole he did pretty well for himself, managing to keep most of it out of the hands of his cronies, both in the mob and in law enforcement, and hiding it away for his heirs."

"I see," said Valdez. "And now, with remnants of the Chicago mob trying to get their hands on the money, some very important people, who stand to lose their shirts if this ever came out, are becoming nervous."

"You've got it," said Hanley. "Very important people. Most of them spending a good portion of their year in Washington."

"There's one more thing," said Valdez.

"What's that?"

"Exactly who funneled the money and the drugs to the Gianetti family?"

Hanley smiled more broadly, then turned toward the dark window. After a moment, he turned back to Valdez, nodded, stood with a grimace, and walked slowly toward the back of the plane.

"Time for a pit stop," said Hanley, before sliding the divider shut.

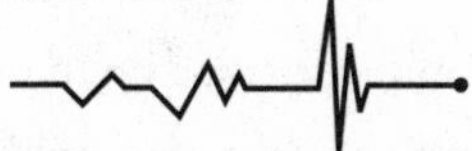

When Hanley came back from his "pit stop" he settled into his chair and continued where he had left off.

"The money," said Hanley, "had been set aside over a period of years. It came from special investigation budgets that somehow managed to go under budget at the agency."

"What about the drugs?" asked Valdez. "Where did that come from?"

"During the seventies, the drugs had been confiscated from flights originating in South America and the Far East. Coincidently, and conveniently, the drugs in question were warehoused for many years outside Chicago. Officially, the confiscated shipments were recorded as having been destroyed."

Hanley took his glass and downed the remainder of the melted cubes. After putting the glass down he reclined his chair.

"That's all there is to it?" asked Valdez.

"Pretty much so," said Hanley. "In short, you and I have been assigned to close down the search for the money and to make sure no one else knows how any of this originated. The hoods are in it now.

They've taken out our first contact and our second contact is floundering. The agency needs to be certain that, in the process of going after the money, the hoods don't, as they used to say in mob parlance, upset the apple cart."

"So they send in two old men," said Valdez.

"Yep," said Hanley. "It's better not to involve more people who might begin to wonder how this thing originated."

Valdez smiled. "Two old farts with not much to lose."

"You've got a point there," said Hanley. "But look at it this way. Who better to be seen at a rehabilitation facility than two old farts?"

"What makes you think the hoods will go back there?"

"They have to because the detective holds the key to what they're after. Or at least they think he holds the key."

"Should we see about our number one contact when we get to Chicago?" asked Valdez.

"No," said Hanley. "I'm told he won't be able to help. But we might run into the young and lovely Maria. She's been told to return to the rehabilitation facility to watch the detective. A babe watching a Babe."

Hanley's smile irritated Valdez. Hanley continued.

"By the way, did someone from Langley send you the photographs of the hoods?"

"They did," said Valdez.

"And you committed them to memory so we'll know who's who?"

"I did."

"Good. So did I."

Valdez turned back to the starboard window beside his chair. The cloud cover had cleared somewhat and in the distance, at the horizon beyond the wing, he saw the lights of a city. Depending on the route the Learjet had taken, it could be Knoxville or Winston-Salem.

As he stared out at the lights on the horizon, Valdez recalled the photographs of Max Lamberti and his cronies, but he also recalled the photograph he'd seen at the Miami office of the contact named Maria. A slender young woman with dark hair and eyes. A young woman who could pass for a college student or a nurse or the daughter of a stroke patient. A young Hispanic woman who could have been his daughter if he and his wife had had children.

He glanced away from the window and saw across the aisle that Hanley had closed his eyes. Judging from the smile on Hanley's face, Valdez assumed he, too, was envisioning the young woman. A girl, really. A girl whose photograph reminded Valdez so much of his wife years earlier when they first met.

With memories of his wife at various ages playing back in his mind, Valdez turned back to his window and looked out. Only now he envisioned another woman. A more mature Maria, whom he had met several times at Hanley's house in Naples. Maria, the woman who had made her way into his dreams of late, pushing the image of his late wife aside.

Valdez felt his eyes grow moist. He took out his handkerchief, wiped at his eyes, then leaned back in his chair, closed his eyes, and rested.

CHAPTER TWENTY-FOUR

The brightly lit 24-hour convenience store located at one end of a newly-constructed strip mall in the far southwestern suburbs was busy because housing developments in the area had spread as fast as the corn once grown in these wet fields. Some customers had left their engines running and the wagging fingers of windshield wipers swept back and forth. The customers came out of the convenience store carrying lottery tickets, soft drinks, cigarettes, candy, and evening editions of Chicago newspapers.

The strip mall was new enough that most of its promised "Prime Business Locations" were dark and vacant. In fact, the only business being transacted seemed to be at the far ends of the mall. The convenience store doing its brisk business at one end, while at the other end, a self-serve car wash not doing such a brisk business because of the weather. Only one vehicle was inside the car wash, a full-size van being sprayed by what appeared to be a legless man in a wheelchair. Some patrons of the convenience store commented on this strange sight as they drove out of the parking lot toward their split levels and multi-story homes.

From the back seat: "Daddy, that guy's got no legs."

From the front seat: "Yeah, no brain either."

Also from the front seat: "Honey."

"How come he's got no brain, Daddy?"

"Mom's right. I didn't mean he doesn't have a brain. It's just that it's raining and when he's done washing his van it'll simply get dirty again. But if it makes him happy . . ."

"He's kind of roly-poly, isn't he?"

Laughter from the front seat. "Yes, dear. But I think your father would agree we wouldn't say that to him if we met him."

From the back seat, head twisting to look out the back window. "No, I guess we wouldn't, 'cause that would be mean."

Her thighs stung where they had been burned, the dampness of her slacks chilled her, her mouth felt raw where the tape had been, and she smelled like coffee gone stale.

Dino leaned forward in the seat beside her, his elbows resting on his knees. He stared at her with narrowed eyes, never letting a slight grin leave his face. His voice was matter-of-fact but loud enough so he could be heard above the sound of the pump and the blast of the high-pressure spray against the side of the van.

"We know all about you, Mrs. Babe. We know your husband was a private detective and before that a member of the Chicago Police Department. Both you and your husband were close to Marjorie Gianetti. Although she had a stroke, she and your husband spoke of things, and your husband told you about these things."

He paused, letting this sink in while he cleaned his teeth with his tongue. He did not glance toward the front of the van when the spray began on the windshield.

"We have a golden opportunity for you, Mrs. Babe. The opportunity to go home and, eventually, go back to visiting your husband and helping him on his road to recovery. It's an opportunity that gives both of you a chance to have a normal life.

"You went to see Tony Gianetti today. After leaving, you didn't follow him, yet you showed up at the bank. There's no reason why you shouldn't tell us everything you know. Who could it hurt? Marjorie Gianetti's dead, so no matter what you say, she won't be hurt. Her son was just killed in that terrible accident, so he can't be hurt. It's a win-win situation, Mrs. Babe. You know where we should go next because you were at the first location. Marjorie Gianetti revealed something that led you to that bank."

He paused again, this time glancing toward the front where the driver was still spraying the windshield. When she glanced there, she could see only the distorted shape of the driver's knit cap through the spray pounding the windshield. The driver was down low, and the imagined image of the legless man circling the van was bizarre.

"Mrs. Babe, whatever opinion you might have had of Marjorie Gianetti and her son, it must be obvious to you by now that they've been hiding something. Before his death some time ago, the senior Tony Gianetti misappropriated a large sum of money which did not belong to him."

Dino gestured toward his chest with both hands. "It was our money, Mrs. Babe. Everybody has family. We're a big family. All we're doing is trying to get our money back."

He reached down to the floor between him and the side of the van. He showed her a bulky manila envelope. He held the envelope by the top between two fingers and shook it. She could hear the jangle of metal. If there were coins inside, they were large coins.

"Do you know what's in here, Mrs. Babe?"

Keys. Steve had said Marjorie was obsessed with some kind of keys kept secret within the Gianetti family. Jan could only assume the keys had been in the safe deposit box at the bank, and that the men in knit caps—perhaps one of them had been Dino—had retrieved the keys from the wreckage of Tony Gianetti's Prius. Perhaps the keys belonged to other safe deposit boxes at other locations, locations pointed to by the litany of U.S. routes. She did not answer.

Dino's pushed the envelope closer to her face. "I asked you a question."

"I . . . I don't know what's in there."

He pulled the envelope back, held it in his lap, and carefully emptied the contents into one hand. He held his hand out for her to see. "Keys, Mrs. Babe. You knew that. Your husband told you."

"No. He never said anything. Marjorie and I talked about things sometimes, but I could never make sense of it. The only thing she did say once was that I should go to this bank."

"She told you to go to the bank?"

"Yes."

He returned the keys to the envelope and placed the envelope back on the floor. "Why did she tell you to go to that particular bank?"

"She said it was a good place to do business and that I . . ."

He slapped her hard, jolting her head to the side. The sound of the car wash sprayer went away for a moment, and when she heard it again she felt Dino's hot breath on her face.

"You were at that bank today while Gianetti was there! Without following him, you knew he would be there! We want to know how you knew! If we don't get it out of you, we'll get it out of your husband!"

He held her blouse, twisting it and shouting into her face. "Don't fuck with this! It's a family matter and if you fuck with it, there's no way you or your husband will survive!"

When he let go of her blouse, he made a show of straightening it and smiling. She stared at Dino, her face stinging where he'd hit her.

"You have to understand, Mrs. Babe, we're in business. Like any business that's going to survive these days, we've become a little leaner and meaner. I've got a boss to answer to. That's the down side of the business, but here's the up side. When you tell us everything you know, which, as I said, does nothing to hurt you or your husband or anyone else, you'll not only go back to your husband, but you'll never have to worry about money again for the rest of your lives. Think about it, Mrs. Babe. Never worrying about money for the rest of your lives no matter how many specialists your husband needs. You'll be able to hire private nurses. You'll be able to bring him home. And if you're worried about this business ever coming back and biting you, don't. We know you have friends in the Chicago Police Department who sometimes do favors for you. But we also have friends in the Department. No matter what you tell us, we can guarantee it will never come back on you."

He reached out and touched her cheek. "It's a tough world. Sometimes we do things we'd rather not do. We have the keys. We own the keys. All we need from you is where we should go with those keys."

He held up the envelope again and shook it. "These are all keys to safe deposit boxes, Mrs. Babe. All we need now is to figure out where to go with them. What's in those boxes belongs to us. If you help us, we'll help you. If you don't help us . . ."

He shrugged his shoulders, stared at her and waited some time before continuing.

"Perhaps I can offer some encouragement," he said, leaning forward a little as he stared at her. "You don't know the details, but you do know things we'd like to know. Perhaps if you simply start talking about your visits with Marjorie Gianetti something will come out that will help. So why not try? It won't hurt anyone to try, will it?"

She recalled her visit to the library that might just as well have been years ago instead of earlier the same day. She recalled the newspaper articles about the Gianetti family. Tony Gianetti, the behind-the-times mobster who ended up in the trunk of his Lincoln in 1986, allegedly killed for giving organized crime a bad name. Tony Gianetti, who valued his private life with Marjorie and Tony Junior and maintained a low profile in the years prior to his death.

Then there was Max Lamberti, who had demonstrated at Marjorie's funeral he was the boss Dino referred to. Had this been Max's plan all along? To grab her because she knew something that could help him settle a drug-bust feud he had with Gianetti? Max Lamberti, the "fly in the ointment." Max Lamberti, the "black sheep" of the family. Max Lamberti, admitting in the video at the library that his Uncle Tony was in the mob.

And now there was Dino, the man sitting beside her, the man staring at her. The same man as the younger Dino in the video cruising out of Burnham Harbor on Lamberti's motor yacht. Dino Justice, who had changed his name from Deveno after his encounter years earlier with Steve at the produce market. Dino Justice, whose father dropped out of organized crime after the 280-million-dollar drug bust in 1980. Were these men related to the rise in deaths Steve had told her about? An increase in deaths among Chicago detectives that took place following the drug bust?

Then she recalled another piece of information she'd come across at the library, something that just might get Dino off the track, something to make him think she'd been searching for information that had nothing at all to do with Max Lamberti.

"I . . . I'll try to help," she said, doing her best to look defeated. "Before his stroke, Steve was working on a case that had to do with health care brokers. Something about people who put pressure on big companies to make deals with their own insurance companies. I never knew much about the case except that families and friends of the ones running the scam were sometimes put on the insurance rolls of the companies for nothing. Steve was looking into it for a client when he had his stroke and I was trying to help jog his memory."

Dino continued staring at her, no sign of anger on his face, simply mild interest. So she continued.

"When I discovered who Marjorie's husband was, I asked her a few questions. But she never seemed to know what I was talking about. The only thing she mentioned was that she didn't like to talk about her husband's business. Once, she mentioned her nephew Max, saying he was in the kind of business her husband had been in, but that was the extent of it."

When she finished her speech, Dino stared at her a few more seconds, reached down to the floor and came up with the wide roll of tape. He tore off a fresh piece of tape and slapped it across her mouth, pressing so hard the tape pushed between her lips and against her teeth.

The car wash pump shut off and the spray on the van stopped. Beyond the windshield outside the forward exit door of the car wash it was still raining, the drops slanting through the lights shining down on the puddled asphalt.

The next stop was somewhere dark. They had driven only a few minutes from the car wash before the lights faded and the road became bumpy. At first she thought they might be back in the field at the end of the road where they had caught her. But then she heard something scrape along the side of the van and caught a glimpse of wet leaves.

When the van stopped and the lights went out, Dino made his way forward, going between the front seats. Although she could barely see him, she could tell from shadowed movements and sounds that he was in the front passenger seat. As she stared toward the front of the van, she saw the shadows of both the driver's and Dino's heads against the scarcely perceptible light coming in through the windshield. The sky was overcast, and below the sky she could see the outline of bare treetops that looked like thin arms appealing to God for help.

Dino spoke softly to the driver in his deep voice.

"You still hungry?"

"I'm always hungry," said the driver, his voice phlegmy.

"Eating all that fatty food's not good. You should have more fiber."

"I get enough of that at home."

"Vegetables and grains?"

"Yeah."

"Well, then, I guess you'll live a long and healthy life."

"Yeah. I only eat junk food when we're out like this. Instant energy, I guess."

"You don't need that much energy to drive."

"I know, but I might need it for something else."

"Could be. But if you don't, be sure to go to the gym in the morning and burn off some of that cholesterol. You don't want to have a stroke and screw up your retirement. That's what happens to lots of guys. They work like dogs all their lives, and when they finally get into position for that golden parachute, wham, blood clot in the brain."

"You're right. Can't be too careful. Especially guys. Why is it women live longer?"

"Less stress. Not out there hunting for food all day for the clan back in the cave. I gotta take a piss. You mind?"

"Be my guest."

After Dino left the van and the door slammed shut, the only sound was the thud of drops on the roof of the van, large drops apparently blown from trees by the wind. But then she heard another sound, a phlegmy breathing sound, and realized the driver had turned toward the back of the van. She could see the shadow of his head against the dull light of the sky. He was moving himself slowly into the narrow space between the front seats. At first she thought he would catapult himself into his wheelchair like he'd done before. But instead of catapulting into his chair, she heard the chair bump the side of the van and saw the driver had lowered himself to the floor and was making his way into the back of the van.

A terrible chill ran through her. At first she thought the rear door of the van had been opened. But then she realized it had not been opened, the van was simply becoming cooler because the engine was off and the heater had stopped. Perhaps she was chilled because she *wanted* the rear door of the van to open, she wanted the door to open and someone to take her out the back because the driver was obviously on the floor, coming in her direction.

His breathing became louder as he moved closer. He was making his way slowly over the apparatus for the wheelchair lift. She saw a vague shadowy movement before her, heard the sound of the driver dragging himself closer and closer until he was at her feet.

She pressed her knees together tightly and thought she could feel his warm breath just below her knees through her slacks. There was more movement and something jarred the seat. When he vaulted onto the seat beside her, she tried to scream, felt the tape tear at her lips, and tasted her own blood.

The smell of onions on his breath washed over her as he came close and whispered in her ear. "Be my guest, sweetie."

She tried to twist away when his bearded face rubbed against the side of her face.

"Be my guest, sweetie."

When she felt his hands caressing her breasts she pushed herself forward against the shoulder belt fastened beneath her arm. There was no way to get away from him. He worked on the buttons of her blouse patiently, not stopping until he had pulled the blouse out from the waistband of her slacks and unbuttoned the last button.

"Be my guest, sweetie."

Then he waited. Not touching her, not saying anything, simply breathing in her ear. She knew this was part of the plan. She knew this deliberateness was meant to terrorize her. For some reason they thought the location of all the safe deposit boxes would be revealed when Tony Gianetti and his attorney opened that first box. And, thinking that, they had done away with them.

"Wanna see my scanner, sweetie?" he whispered. "It's better than etchings, one of the latest eight-hundred megahertz trunked systems with decriptor. Paid a bundle for it."

He continued breathing in her ear, then whispered, "Wanna know what happened to my legs? Eggplants, that's what happened. Wooden crates full of 'em fell on me and I was turned into one of them eggplants."

He laughed a raspy, guttural laugh.

"Naw, that's just a line I use with the ladies. Actually, I was injured in 'Nam when I was a kid. In a way it's good I was injured. Got me this job because the boss likes to help us folks. I wish more of you gals felt sorry for us old 'Nam vets."

Without taking the tape from her mouth, he kissed her, his nose fleshy and oily against her nose. He kept his face close to hers while he continued.

"Sorry Dino had to tape your mouth. Usually he's not such a bad guy. But this is real important. I can help you get through this. It's all about money. Isn't everything? How do you think we can afford an eight-hundred megahertz trunked system with decriptor? We've got all the technical stuff just like the cops. Well, maybe not everything. Like fingerprints, for instance. We don't have access to those files. Anyway, look at it this way. You tell Dino what you know, we get our money, and everyone's happy, especially you and your husband when we let you go."

He was talking too much, telling her things he shouldn't. The captor identifying with the captive because he knows they plan to kill her no matter what she says or does.

When she felt him reach across to her opposite shoulder and turn her toward him, she wished she could work the tape off her mouth so she could bite him. Maybe if she rubbed the tape against his sleeve the edge would come up. Maybe then she could . . .

She stopped rubbing the tape against his sleeve when she felt cool steel between her breasts. She held perfectly still and did not breathe as he used an unseen blade to cut the facing between the cups of her bra.

"Be my guest, sweetie."

CHAPTER TWENTY-FIVE

Going through the main exit was out of the question because the guards at the front desk would know he was a resident. There'd be calls upstairs and counseling and delay after delay. But worst of all, if the guards stopped him, the man watching his room from the television lounge would discover his attempt to leave because news about the patient who'd gone nuts and tried to bust out would travel fast.

So, instead of going out through the lobby, Steve went back to where it all started, back to the first floor nursing home wing. It was a little late for visitors to the nursing home wing to be about, but it wasn't that late. And if someone on staff questioned where he was going, he'd try to act as if he was on his way back to his room on the third floor.

He took off his White Sox cap and tucked it in next to him on the chair. Then, when the elevator doors opened and one of the guards glanced his way, he smiled and slowly rolled across the lobby toward the double doors that led to the nursing home wing. He hoped the guard did not notice he was a bit overdressed. He knew it didn't matter to the guards that it was a little late as long as he didn't try to go out the front door.

Two residents, both women he didn't know, sat half asleep in their wheelchairs near the nurses' station. The aides were apparently busy in residents' rooms, putting residents to bed, the pair at the nurses' station waiting their turns. Even if an aide did see him, he'd figure out a way to stall the aide until he could get away. He took his time, passing the two women near the nurses' station who looked up as he slowly made his way toward the end of the wing.

As he headed down the hallway, he wasn't sure what caused it, perhaps the forlorn looks he got from the two women at the nurses' station, but a great wave of fear came over him. The smells in the nursing home wing—smells he was certainly familiar with—became the smells of death. He began sweating like a horse and felt he would pass out. Somehow he kept going, but the squeak of the rubber wheels of his chair on the polished floors became rhythmic, and that rhythm, combined with the beating of his heart and the heat in the place, had a strange effect on him. He wasn't so concerned that the squeak of his wheels would give him away. What concerned him was that Jan was in serious trouble and he was as helpless as the two women waiting at the nurses' station to be put to bed.

Despite his confusion and doubt he kept going. He had to do what he had to do, and if confusion and doubt came, tough.

When he finally got down to the end of the wing and ducked around the corner, he wiped his forehead with the sleeve of his sweatshirt. Then he gave the chair a shove with his good hand and headed for the door to the loading dock. If a nurse or aide had come out of a resident's room in time to see him duck around the corner, it didn't matter now, because when he opened the door the alarm sounded, beeping away inside its box on the wall above the door.

The door opened inward so he had to back up and wedge his chair into the opening. He pushed through quickly, the door banging closed behind him, and though the door was closed, the alarm continued its sickening peal. Even though the short hall parallel to the kitchen was noisy with the sounds of blowers and what sounded like a huge dishwasher that vibrated the walls, he could still hear the alarm.

The outside door was ahead at the end of the short and noisy hallway. He was going fast when a side door to the kitchen opened and a fat kid holding a dishrag and wearing soiled kitchen whites stepped in front of him. The kid couldn't have been more than nineteen, face pasty, head sides shaved but hair long on top. The kid held out a chubby palm for him to stop.

"Where you goin'?" shouted the kid above the noise in the hallway.

No use trying to explain, but he didn't want to hurt the kid.

"To hell!" he shouted back, catching the kid off guard.

The kid apparently saw something in Steve's face that frightened him because the kid stepped aside as he flew past.

At the outside loading dock door, struggling to get it open, he glanced back and saw the kid standing like a sad lump of flesh, like the kid who's always made fun of in school, the kid who always gets beat up, the kid who has power nowhere but at his lousy noisy night job in the Hell in the Woods nursing wing kitchen. And now this guy in a wheelchair has even denied him that. This made tears come to Steve's eyes as the loading dock door slammed behind him and he sailed down the concrete ramp into the cold wet night.

Compared to the hallway where he'd confronted the kid, the night was dead quiet. Even with warm air blowing out a couple of vents in the side of the building it seemed quiet. After turning to make sure no one had followed, he felt the cold rain on his scalp and put on his

White Sox cap.

He was in the back parking lot. Darker here than the front lot overlooked by the windows of the television lounges on each floor. But he had to get to the front lot in order to leave this place. He knew the grounds of Hell in the Woods were completely fenced in except for the main entrance road. He also knew the main lot was lit brightly and that a guard outside the main entrance having a smoke, or an aide sent out to look for whoever had set off the alarm, might see him. Even the man in the third floor television lounge might look outside and wonder why a guy in a wheelchair was wheeling his way across the lot from the direction of the access road that went around to the back of the complex.

And so he stayed close to the building and found a sidewalk that wound its way through bushes along the side of the nursing home wing. As he rounded the corner of the wing, the lights of the main lot shown brightly through the thin leafless branches of the bushes. Several times his wheels were stopped by something in the path and, before he could continue, he had to back up and reach down to clear dead branches that had fallen during the winter. When he did this, rain chilled the back of his neck.

The sidewalk came out of the bushes near a set of benches at the side of the main entrance. A young couple stood huddled together near one of the benches smoking. Both boy and girl wore jackets but no hats. Their hair was dark and long and wet and wind-whipped as they made the tips of their cigarettes glow. First the boy, then the girl saw him. They stared at him and he stared at them as he wheeled from the bushes past them. They were in their late teens and the girl had on dark lipstick and eye shadow. They looked like death. As he approached the main entrance from the side, the smoke from the two followed him in the wind. The smoke was stale as if it had been inside them a long time before being exhaled.

He paused beneath the shelter of the lighted portico at the entrance, but behind one of the portico supports so the guards would not see him. He could see the exit road and the main road beyond. Traffic rolled past out there, where he must go. A lighted city bus came along the main road and stopped at the entrance road. As the bus drove off he could see through the lighted windows that someone was walking down the aisle.

When a door to the side of the main doors opened, he felt the heat from the place. Two women walked past and out to the parking lot. He felt weak and insignificant as he watched the two get into a car and drive off. He knew that when he went out into the parking lot he would be visible from the entrance if one of the guards should look outside.

Just then, the two teenagers who had been smoking walked in front of him. Lit up by the lights in the portico they looked like vampires, their skin white and wet, their hair in vein-like rivulets on their foreheads as if their brains were being nourished from the outside.

For a moment this made him think of his brain, how part of it had been deprived of nourishment. But he fought against this thought, realized this was his chance, and wheeled away into the parking lot as the teenaged ghouls went inside. There, the guards, or anyone else who happened to be in the lobby so late at night, would glance at the ghouls, perhaps curious, or perhaps jealous of their youth and willful indifference.

Once away from the building, the parking lot and entrance road were downhill and he had some trouble steering. Downhill left turns were okay because he could grip the push rim with his left hand. But to turn right he was unable to use his hand and had to lean to his right and drop his elbow onto the right wheel, which made for a jerky turn.

After negotiating the parking lot, it began raining harder, and during the ride down the dark entrance road he put up the hood on his outer sweatshirt.

At the bus stop where the entrance road met the main road, a large woman made room for him in the small Plexiglas-walled kiosk so he could get out of the wind and rain. She wore a black overcoat and a black brimmed hat. In one hand she held a satchel, in the other she held a long umbrella with a dangerous-looking pointed tip. She looked somewhat familiar. At first he thought she might be an occupational therapist he once had. How appropriate because she could help him relearn how to take a bus. But if she had been one of his many therapists, would she remember him and question his being here? Then he realized he had seen her in the first-floor cafeteria when the strokers occasionally went down there for dinner on weekends. She worked behind the counter, dressed in white instead of the black she now wore.

The way she glanced at him, he knew she was thinking he was probably a resident. It was a look of appraisal, and when she turned away to look down the street he knew she wondered whether she should take time on this cold rainy night to push this guy on back to Hell in the Woods where he belonged. He decided not to take any chances. If he said something intelligible, maybe he'd set her mind at ease.

He concentrated, had to get subject and verb in the right order or it could be all over. He put down the hood on his sweatshirt. Then he clenched his fists, imagined he was in Georgiana's rehab room on an ordinary day of rehab, and managed to say, "Bus coming soon?"

She lifted the umbrella tip toward him as if to skewer him with it. But then she let her overcoat sleeve slide back and looked at her watch. She said, "Fifty-fifth Street bus should be here any minute."

"That's mine," he barely managed to say, realizing her motherly look of concern had almost made him stumble.

As they waited in silence, he wondered if he should say something more. But he decided against it and instead practiced the sentences he knew he would have to say after the bus dropped him off on Cicero Avenue just north of Midway Airport.

He thanked God and his Honor the mayor and all the aldermen and women for buses equipped with handicapped lifts. The inside of the bus was warm and dry and he didn't have to speak with anyone else during the ride east on Fifty-Fifth Street, not even the driver who came back to get his fare and make sure his chair was locked in place. And when it was time to get off near Midway Airport, he simply held his hand up toward the reflection of the driver in the large rearview mirror as if he were a child raising his hand in school.

But when he wheeled his chair off the bus he had a setback. He was alone on the sidewalk, yet the street was busy with traffic. He had taken the bus to the area around Midway Airport, but the reason for having done this eluded him. An airport? Where would he fly? The sound of a jet taking off reminded him of overhead jets at Hell in the Woods. He looked up at the jet as its lights disappeared into the overcast. Jets on takeoff passed over Hell in the Woods during weather like this. If he closed his eyes would he be back there in his room staring out his window? No, the jets that passed over Hell in the Woods were from O'Hare Airport to the north. He was at Midway Airport and the reason . . .

After the bus was gone, traffic flowed past steadily like blood flowing through arteries. The mist from tires settled on his face. Here and there a face in a vehicle stared at him as they drove past, wondering if this man in a wheelchair has any idea where he is going.

A battered Chevy Blazer drove slowly past. A ragged bumper sticker contained part of a name. The left half of the old red, white, and blue political sticker was gone. But the right half said, "Edwards."

A Vice Presidential candidate from some time back. He recalled seeing the guy's smiling face in one of Jan's magazines but did not recall the year of the election. And as he sat there in his chair within the spray of vehicles he could not even recall what year it was now.

Wait. That's not why he was out here. Even though Marjorie had said things in rehab about votes, things about waiting for all the Illinois votes to be counted, his main reason for being out here was to find Jan. His job now was to keep his mind from wandering.

Waiting for votes. Politicians in business suits. Won't see them waiting at bus stops. Won't see them worrying about their wives. Their wives are safe at home while his wife . . .

"Jan!"

His shout into the night startled him. But it also forced him to concentrate. He needed a car. He had taken a bus to Midway Airport and gotten off at this stop for a reason. He'd known there would be plenty of places to rent a car on Cicero Avenue near the airport. After getting off the bus, his right leg began to burn with pain. But he didn't have time for pain. And so, finally, he wheeled himself to the car rental agency nearest the bus stop.

The windows were lit brightly, inviting him inside. As he made his way through the door, he felt a sense of accomplishment, having made it this far. He had practiced his dialogue during the bus ride, but as soon as he got inside the small warm office and saw the woman standing behind the counter, everything he'd practiced floated away.

She wore a blue blazer with the agency insignia on the left breast pocket. Her white blouse was open at the neck. She had sandy brown hair and smiled at him as he paused across the small waiting area from the counter. There was no one else in the office and the only word he could think to say was . . . Jan.

But he said nothing. Although he knew this was not Jan, the

woman reminded him of Jan. True, this woman was only in her twenties and Jan was in her forties. But something Jan had said recently made this woman into Jan in a way he could not explain. It was the last time he'd seen Jan, just before she said goodnight to him the day of the funeral, just after they had returned to Hell in the Woods from Szabo's Restaurant. Jan had said she wanted to confess something. She said she had paid too much attention to the relatively recent past. She said she had avoided telling him about her life before they met. She'd been a stripper while in college to pay her tuition. She'd been drawn into the life of having and spending money. She'd worked at massage parlors when massage parlors were allowed in Chicago. She came close to becoming a prostitute and had some scrapes with drugs and wanted him to know all this. She said the only reason she married her first husband was because he was the first guy who treated her like a normal woman. Then she cried when she told him that he had been the second.

He recalled it vividly. It was the first time he could remember recalling something so vividly. The warmth of her, the touch of her wet cheek, the smell of Szabo's Restaurant in her clothes mixed with the smell of her hair. He had wept, too. He could feel it, the two of them holding onto one another as if they were the last two souls on earth. Holding onto one another in the television lounge on the third floor of Hell in the Woods.

The young woman in the blue blazer was a guardian angel. She sprouted wings and flew around the counter, landing beside his chair, stooping down, one hand on his shoulder. She wore a blue skirt to match her blazer, her knees like Jan's knees, so close he could touch them.

A box of tissues appeared. He wiped his eyes and blew his nose. She stared at him with a look of great concern on her face. He wanted to say,

"I don't care about your past. All I care about is that I have you."

But to have any chance of Jan being part of his life again, he'd have to say other things. He'd have to say things to save time and get him out of here driving a car. And so, even though the young women's hair was sandy brown like Jan's hair, he imagined her hair brunette and closely cropped. He made the young woman in the blazer into Georgiana. Georgiana understanding these brief outbursts of weeping because it was common in speech therapy with strokers. Georgiana waiting for his response to the drill.

"I'm sorry," he said. "You remind me of . . . you remind me . . . my wife. Just landed and need a car. She . . . she's in . . . having surgery at . . . at Saint Mel's."

And then another drill from Georgiana. This time explaining to someone that you want to rent a car. "A big car," he said. He pointed to the wheelchair. "Easier with this."

The guardian angel in the blue blazer suggested a Lincoln Town Car because it had a huge front seat with a center armrest that lifted up for three-across seating and it would easily accommodate his wheelchair.

The Town Car was white. Steve watched through the office window as it zigzagged its way from the back of the lot toward the building. When it approached the brighter lights of the rental agency portico, the car seemed as if it should have the remnants of wedding decorations hanging from it. The boy who delivered the Lincoln to the portico looked too young to drive. But when the boy opened the door his legs swung out long as telephone poles. Young face, but well over six-feet-six and he wore a Chicago Bulls jacket. The future Michael Jordan jumped out and held the door for him, but Steve wheeled around to the passenger side. As he rounded the back end of the Lincoln, he recalled having imagined him and his wheelchair found shot full of holes in the trunk of a Lincoln.

After the future Michael Jordan followed and opened the passenger door for him, he watched as Steve did a quick transfer in. Then Steve lifted the Lincoln's center armrest, folded the wheelchair, and slid over to the driver's side as he pulled the chair in onto the floor. Steve pulled his right leg up out of the way, put his left foot alternately on the brake and gas, waved to the guardian angel in the blue blazer who stood watching at the office window—the guardian angel who determined that one of his credit cards had not expired and who had been patient as he signed the forms with his left hand trying his best to match the signature on his driver's license—and drove slowly and carefully out of the lot, feeling an intense rush of adrenaline and freedom along with the weird sensation of driving with his left foot on the pedals. Because he had not fastened his seatbelt, the warning sounded for a time, but then it finally stopped.

He wished he had a steering wheel spinner like he'd seen in an equipment catalog at the rehab center. To drive using only his left hand he had to keep shifting the position of his hand on the wheel and, therefore, had to take corners slowly. Using his left foot on the gas and brake felt much more awkward than steering with his left hand, but he got used to it. Although it was slow going on city streets, because of his awkward steering, he was able to drive faster once he got on the expressway and only had to make minor steering adjustments. The rain had let up, changing to a light mist, and somehow this seemed a positive sign. As he drove, he recalled the words of Tadashi, his occupational therapist when he was still in the hospital.

"You will be able do many things, Mr. Babe. After you get out of hospital and go to rehab place, you will learn more than dressing and eating and taking shower. Some day you will even learn to drive again."

Tadashi had been right. He was driving. He was driving.

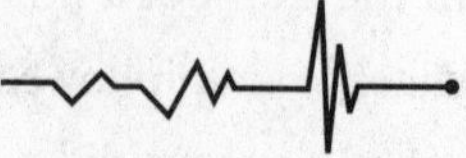

Although he hadn't remembered having owned a gun or a portable police scanner radio during the days following his stroke, Jan had used both to help him recall who he was. She had insisted that back in their apartment under lock and key was a semi-automatic pistol nicknamed Attila. The nicknamed pistol made him question what kind of nut he had been before his stroke. The radio she had brought into the hospital to demonstrate its use. During those early days after his stroke, remembering he owned a gun and a police scanner, and for that matter recalling he had been a detective, remained vague and distant.

What he recalled immediately after the stroke was nothing. The initial memories that dug themselves out during the first few days had to do with Jan. And as time went on, more and more things dropped by for a visit. Of course most of this had been Jan's doing, Jan helping him relearn the things he should recall. Jan did everything she could to bring him back, to love him, to nurture him, including sneaking Attila, unloaded, into his hospital room one day so he could feel the heft of it in his left hand.

Once he got his left hand on his pistol again, he knew he wouldn't be a very good shot. But he was convinced it wouldn't matter. He'd get close to whoever was responsible for taking Jan away. He'd get very close and do what he had to do.

It felt strange driving back into the neighborhood in Brookfield. When he saw the signs for the zoo he felt he could almost recall having seen them before. Maybe he did recall having seen them before. Maybe he recalled all of it. Or maybe, because of the details Jan always used when describing anything, he had simply relearned it. He did recall the apartment, however, because one afternoon last winter, just after the New Year, Jan received permission from his doctor to bring him home for a visit. They spent the afternoon sitting in the living room, just sitting. No television or radio, not even much talking. Jan understood that this was what he needed back then. To see where they lived, to absorb it into his skull. The visit to the apartment had been before Jan got the landlord to move them to the ground floor apartment when the downstairs people moved out. During the visit to the old apartment he'd been carried up to it and back down again by two hospital volunteers. According to Jan the new downstairs apartment was identical to the one upstairs.

"Same layout exactly," she had said. "And I placed the furniture and filled the cupboards the exact same way. I even had it painted the same color so you won't know the difference. The cabinet where you keep your gun and other stuff is in the spare bedroom exactly where it belongs. And I hid the key in the same place in the bathroom."

"Key?"

"Yes, don't you remember? You keep the key hidden in the bottom of the band-aide box in the medicine cabinet."

Something about keys. Marjorie's keys. The keys to the kingdom.

"And what kingdom would that be?" Georgiana had asked Marjorie one day in speech rehab.

"Bridal suite," Marjorie had said, then correcting herself, "I mean, Presidential suite."

"Like for the President of the United States?" asked Georgiana.

"Yes," said Marjorie. "The Carter smarter suite. No. Not him. Highway robbery. Oh, never you mind. Never you mind your own dirty laundry."

"Keep talking, Marjorie. It's interesting."

"Not interesting. Not anything. Bridge under the water. Oh, fuck the Pope."

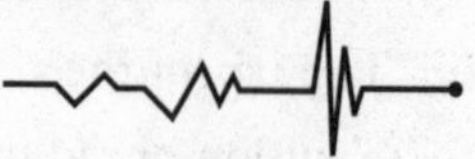

The small parking lot for the apartment building had a single overhead light near the sidewalk to the front entrance. He parked directly beneath the overhead light in one of the handicapped spots. When he shut off the Lincoln he slid over as far as he could so he could open the passenger door with his good left hand. It was quite a struggle to lift the wheelchair from the floor, shove it outside, drag his feet toward the door, and, at the same time, unfold the wheelchair. As he attempted the transfer from the Lincoln to the chair, his right leg caught the edge of the chair and the chair traveled backward. He almost fell to the pavement and caught the wheelchair before it rolled out of reach. On the next try he put both wheel brakes on before doing the transfer.

After he slammed the Lincoln's door, and finished swearing at the wheelchair, it was very quiet and still in the parking lot. He could see one car parked in a dark corner of the lot and wondered why someone would park so far away. Yes, he was certainly feeling his limitations now, the few hundred feet across a parking lot looking like the length of a football field.

In the distance, coming from the darkness beyond the parking lot, he heard an elephant shriek. Although he wasn't sure if he had ever heard the sound before, the elephant's shriek brought back memories of Jan telling him about being able to hear the elephant house from the parking lot. He sat there for a moment, wondering what an elephant might be thinking on a cold and drizzly night like this, and also wondering if elephants ever had strokes. If elephants did have strokes, what kinds of memories would they lose? Would they forget that elephants are never supposed to forget?

Another memory of Marjorie in rehab assaulted him. Something about pinning the tail on the donkey, only Marjorie wanted to pin the tail on an elephant. They were in group rehab and the blond recreational therapist everyone called Charming Charmaine was up front and Marjorie was going on about elephants until Charmaine said maybe Marjorie was referring to the two major political parties and that because they had a donkey up front maybe Marjorie wanted to give equal time and they should get an elephant. This upset Marjorie, so much so she did not utter another word, not even her usual "Fuck the Pope" for the rest of the day.

As Steve wheeled up the sidewalk toward the apartment building entrance, he tried to concentrate on the job at hand. Memories of Marjorie in rehab would do him no good now. Right now he had to concentrate on finding Jan.

At the entrance door he used the key to the outside lock and made his way through the entryway toward the door to his and Jan's first floor apartment. He had a vague feeling of having been here before. But then he again reminded himself that their apartment had been upstairs and Jan had moved down to an identical apartment on the ground floor, the apartment to which he now had a key. He stared at the number on the door. Twelve. One less than thirteen. That's how he had tucked it into his botched up memory. How lucky.

He unlocked the apartment and bumped his wheelchair over the threshold. Even though he knew the visit with Jan after his stroke had been upstairs, this apartment did seem familiar. It looked, felt, even smelled like home. But to make it a home he would need to have Jan here.

Thinking of Jan. Trying to see her here. He closed his eyes, but insane thoughts came into his head. Dwayne Matusak waiting here for him, hiding behind a door, or in a closet. Like at home once. Yes, Dwayne Matusak had chased him right into the house one time and . . .

He could not remember what happened after that. All he remembered at the moment was Joe Friday on the old black and white television. Joe Friday. Dragnet. Like the hairnet Marjorie spoke of. Yes, a net to catch important things and let other things go. Let go of these memories of elephants and donkeys and Presidential suites and the fact Marjorie became upset about strange things like her husband bad-mouthing Jimmy Carter. What he needed to do now was capture important memories and let everything else go on through so as not to muddle up what he needed to think about and organize in order to make something happen!

He was home, and the reason was to do what he could to find Jan. He put the keys to the apartment in his pocket. He needed another key, the key that was in the band-aide box.

After wheeling into the bathroom and reaching up to the medicine cabinet, he found the key where Jan said it would be. And now, holding the key in his hand as he rolled slowly to the spare bedroom where the cabinet would be, he thought of Marjorie's keys and wondered if Jan had found a key, and if she had, what had been behind the door unlocked by the key.

Going past his and Jan's bedroom and seeing the bed made him want to weep again, but he rushed past it to the other room to open the cabinet.

The cabinet was not locked. He tried to recall if this was ever the case when he was still at home but could not. No, it had to be locked. Jan had stressed its always being locked when she told him about the key being hidden in the same place he always hid it. He studied the cabinet door and, after a few seconds, found what he was looking for.

There was an indentation about a half-inch wide on the corner of the wood near the latch. He could feel it more than see it as he ran his finger along the edge of the door. A careful, professional job had been done. And he was certain that if it were possible to slam the door to lock it, whoever had broken into the cabinet would have locked it. But to lock this door would have meant making another, perhaps deeper, indentation in the edge of the door. Someone other than Jan had recently been inside the apartment. He was sure of it.

Inside the cabinet, the shoulder holster hung from a hanger, empty, but the forty-five was on the side shelf with the police scanner. Just the way he always left it. Someone had broken into the cabinet but had left the forty-five and the ammunition.

He took the pistol, several boxes of cartridges and the extra magazine, the scanner, and a flashlight. The only other things in the cabinet were several beat-up sport coats and a couple of suits, and he wouldn't need those.

In the living room he looked for other signs of a break-in but could find none. There were no locking drawers on the desk, and everything looked neat and tidy. If Jan were here, she might know if anything was missing or out of place, but Jan was not here.

Before doing what he had come to do, he locked the main lock and the chain lock on the door. Then he rolled back to the desk. He moved the desk chair aside and pulled his wheelchair up to the desk, got out a note pad and pencils, placed the scanner, pistol, ammunition, and flashlight on the desk, and picked up the phone. He called the voice mail number, put in the code and waited. "One message," said the voice mail lady. And as he played the message from Tamara back, Steve Babe, the detective, began writing it down.

There were three Tyrone Washingtons in Chicago with vehicles registered. A Buick was registered to one of the Tyrone Washingtons, a DeVille to another, a Ford pickup and a Honda to the third. Phil Hogan had a three-year-old Chevy, but he also had a one-year-old Mercedes registered to his name, making Steve wonder if anyone on the force knew about the Mercedes or if Phil used it only for out-of-town trips. Dean "Dino" Justice owned a Lexus. Antonio Gianetti Junior, deceased, owned a Toyota Prius, a Chevy Tahoe, and an old Packard, not really as heavily invested in vehicles as Steve would have thought. But the mother load was Maximo "Max" Lamberti. Not only had Tamara come through with the vehicles owned personally by Max, but she had done her homework and found a fleet of vehicles registered to Lamberti Produce.

A Land Cruiser and a Fleetwood were registered to Max himself. The produce company owned a Ferrari, two Harley Davidson motorcycles, a Lincoln stretch limo, three Ford Crown Vics, two Ford vans, and a large Ford panel truck. The two vans and the larger truck might be used to haul produce, but he wasn't so sure about the rest of the vehicles. The three Crown Vics were the most telling, all two years old and registered at the same time. To Steve this seemed like the fleet for "the boys" who were so attentive to Max's needs and safety at Marjorie's funeral.

Tamara spoke quite rapidly on the recording, saying she wasn't sure how long of a message the voice mail recorder would take. Steve played it back six times in order to get all the makes, years, models, license numbers, names, and addresses written down.

No time to lose. He loaded Attila and the extra magazine and put both in the deep left pocket of his hooded sweatshirt. The notepad with the registration information he put in the pocket of his jeans. Then he rolled his wheelchair into the kitchen, got a paper sack out of a lower drawer, and put the scanner, cartridges, and flashlight into it.

After he rolled back into the center of the kitchen he sat there for a while. Then, suddenly, something edged its way in from the past. He stared at the kitchen sink, trying to figure out what it was. The saying "Everything but the kitchen sink" went through his mind for a while until he recalled what bothered him.

When he'd been trying to tell Jan about the glass he had taken from the janitors' closet on the first floor, Jan had said something about the kitchen sink at home. He closed his eyes and imagined Jan with him in his room at Hell in the Woods. She sat close to him. She was warm and fragrant.

"Oh," she'd said. "You mean the way we always keep a glass on the kitchen sink at home?"

After he opened his eyes and saw there was no glass at the back of the sink where it should have been, he began searching through cupboards. The lower cupboards were easy, but to get to the upper cupboards he had to grasp the edge of the counter to lift himself up from his chair and brace himself against the counter while opening each door.

There were no glasses in the cupboards. Not one. And immediately next to the coffee cups in the cupboard to the left of the sink, there was an obvious empty space that took up an entire half shelf. And empty space where drinking glasses would be stored.

With Attila and the extra magazine in his sweatshirt pockets, and with the sack containing extra cartridges, scanner, and flashlight on his lap, he wheeled out of the apartment, and out of the building. Finally, back in the Lincoln, he turned on the scanner and adjusted the squelch control. He was not surprised at remembering how to do this. That was the way it was with his stroke. Physical things like eating and dressing and even driving and adjusting his scanner seemed automatic. Right, automatic like it would be if he had to shoot his semi-automatic.

He started the Lincoln, then sat there for some time, waiting for the seatbelt warning to stop, not quite sure where he should go next. He felt suddenly helpless and vulnerable like he was horizontal on a hospital bed with tubes running into him and not knowing why.

The terrifying feeling came over him that there was someone in the back seat. Someone from the past. A man. He thought again of who this man from the past could be. His father? Joe Friday? Jimmy Carter? Sandor Lakatos? Or perhaps the man was from the future. The man there to warn him about something.

But when he turned to look, the back seat was empty.

CHAPTER TWENTY-SIX

What to do when your hands are behind your back and you can't move. Where before the beast had called her *sweetie* as his stubble rasped her cheek, now he called her *gook bitch* as he pushed the wire brush of his face down across her neck and onto her breasts. He had grasped the seat back on either side of her and pulled himself onto her. Despite the absence of legs he was heavy, causing her feet to splay out on the floor of the van. When she tried to turn sideways to tip him off balance so he might roll off her, he growled at her. His lower torso was hard in two places, apparently what remained of leg bones. Or perhaps the protrusions were his lower hip sockets. If he had a penis, she was not aware of it.

Because of the tape on her mouth she was unable to scream when he slid his knobbed torso down the length of her legs and put his face at the coffee-soaked waistband of her slacks, pulling at her waistband with his teeth. Though she tried to remain in control, she choked saliva up her nose when he did this, not because of where his face was, but because of his weight on her left leg. The leg had gotten wedged beneath part of the wheelchair lift and she felt the sharp stab of pain and heard the sound that traveled through her body, making her certain he had broken her ankle. When he bounced on her outstretched legs, apparently having some kind of unfulfilled orgasm that made him angrier and angrier, the pain shot through her left ankle again and again.

She tried to think of Steve while the beast was at her. But when her ankle broke, survival instincts took over and she was able to think only of her efforts to push the beast away. When the pain in her ankle became so severe she thought she would pass out, the beast must have sensed it, because he shifted his torso to the side, and finally she no longer bore his full weight. After this he turned her toward him and began cooing, his foul breath spreading over her skin, which crawled with the coolness of his saliva.

Now, all that was left was to try to think of Steve.

Steve! What about our life together! Answer me! What about us? Don't you remember? We had a good life, something to be thankful for when we're old and lying on our deathbeds. But not now, not here, not like this!

When he finished with her, the beast dropped down off the seat and pulled himself along the floor, across the wheelchair lift and back into the driver's seat. Against the dull glow of the night sky through the windshield, she saw him pull his wheelchair back within reach between the seats where it had been.

The front door opened and Dino returned, making his way back to sit beside her. Although she could not see his face, she recognized the outline of Dino's head and assumed he would now expect her to talk. Surely he would rip the tape from her mouth and expect her to talk. But instead, the van started up and someone else was talking. It was an authoritative male voice, and for an instant she glanced toward the front of the van expecting to see her rescuer. But all she saw in the front of the van from the direction the voice had come were the red and green lights of the police scanner. And now the authoritative male voice was replaced by a female voice, then another male, then voice after voice as if in litany as the scanner scanned.

They were moving again, the van backing up, branches scraping its sides before they sped forward. As the van bounced on the rough road, Dino leaned toward her and pulled her blouse and raincoat closed, buttoning one button on the raincoat. She tried to cry out that her ankle was broken, but the tape would not allow it.

After several minutes, she could see they were heading into the city. The expressway was familiar. The white-on-green lettering of overhead signs telling her they must be inbound on the Stevenson Expressway. Then, just after the sign for Harlem Avenue, the van slowed and they exited.

They headed north for several minutes, then west away from the city. Soon she knew where they were going, and knowing this created a pain in her heart. When the van slowed she could see the sign for the entrance road and the bus stop kiosk. The van turned into the entrance road and drove the short winding road toward the lights of the building the way she had driven it so many times. So many times.

And so they were back where it began, back at Hell in the Woods where Steve first told her about his suspicions concerning Marjorie's death, about Marjorie's paranoia concerning the staff at Hell in the Woods, about Marjorie's mysterious stories of a family and keys and her litany of U.S. Routes.

U.S. 6 and 45, U.S. 30 and 50, U.S. 20 and 41, U.S. 14 and 94, U.S. 14 and 45, U.S. 20 and 83, U.S. 30 and 34, U.S. 7 and 30, U.S. 30 and 45 . . . U.S. 6 and 45, U.S. 30 and 50 . . .

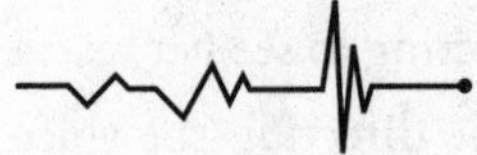

Driving fast made him think of a speeding bullet, and this made him recall what he sometimes called his stroke. Brain bullet. He'd told Jan about it. He also told Marjorie about it and Marjorie responded by reciting Presidents' names. JFK and Lyndon Johnson and Jimmy Carter and Ronald Reagan and George Bush. "Brain bullet" most likely triggering a recall of the Kennedy assassination, and that recall bringing forth the names of other Presidents.

He sped southwest down the Stevenson Expressway—Stevenson who ran for President against Eisenhower but was defeated. He had passed Harlem a ways back and was already out of the city. Instead of the heavy rain of earlier, there was a light drizzle and the spray from other cars and trucks. To avoid being stopped for speeding, he tucked in behind a couple of speeders playing the lane change game. By doing this and letting them run interference for him, he was able to keep the Lincoln at seventy-five.

It seemed so stupidly simple when he finally remembered the plan. He had been sitting there beneath the overhead light in the apartment parking lot staring at the broad expanse of the Lincoln's hood and listening to the police scanner when it hit him. The rhythm of a back-and-forth dialogue on the scanner had resurrected the rhythm of Marjorie's litany of U.S. Routes.

U.S. 6 and 45, U.S. 30 and 50, U.S. 20 and 41, U.S. 14 and 94, U.S. 14 and 45, U.S. 20 and 83, U.S. 30 and 34, U.S. 7 and 30, U.S. 30 and 45. And after that it repeated over and over starting with U.S. 6 and 45.

He had heard Marjorie recite it many times, both in rehab and outside rehab. He had memorized it. But then, sitting there in the parking lot, his brain betrayed him, tucking the litany away somewhere until the rhythm of police calls brought it out.

U.S. 6 and 45. The same area Antonio Gianetti Junior and his attorney had been killed in a supposed accident only hours earlier. It was too much to be a coincidence. Of course, with the vehicle registration information from Tamara, he could go to Max Lamberti's home, or to the address of Lamberti Produce, or to Dino Justice's address, but he had a feeling this would be like treading water. Men like Max Lamberti and Dino Justice made a career of denial, and he of all people would have a hell of a time trying to grill them with questions. Or he could go to one after another of the addresses for Tyrone Washington, but he had a feeling Tyrone had nothing at all to do with Jan being missing. There was something much bigger going on. Something having to do with the Chicago mob and corruption in high places.

And something else, another reason for going to the accident scene. If Jan didn't go to Wisconsin with Lydia, he was fairly certain she'd decided to poke around using the information they'd gotten so far concerning Marjorie's death. If Jan were here in the car with him now, he'd really show how upset he was with her for doing this. But of course she wasn't here. Next to him, resting on the floor and leaning against the seat was his folded wheelchair. As he glanced at it, he momentarily transformed the movement of the car to the movement of the chair with him on board and Jan behind, pushing him down the hall, maybe back from the television lounge to his room on one of those nights she propped a side chair against the door and they made love.

Yes, there was something else, another reason for going to the accident scene. He knew Jan. Despite his stroke, he knew Jan better than anyone in the world. She'd done all she could for him in her efforts to help him rediscover who he'd been. And because of this, he was convinced Jan must have taken Marjorie's death more seriously than he thought. Even keeping the incident in the janitors' closet with Tyrone and his flat-nosed friend from her made no difference. She was a strong woman with a mind of her own and he should have known she would do something like this. He should have known, once he started the ball rolling by going to the funeral and examining everything he could remember Marjorie saying, that Jan would do something. It was his fault. Either he should have kept his mouth shut, or he should have gone to the police. And if the whole thing had gotten buried the way things sometimes do when the police come in and stir the pot, then so be it. Son of a bitch! It was his fault!

Another reason for driving to Orland Park was the alleged accident Tamara had mentioned. Because of who Jan was and what he knew she would do, he was certain that sometime today, Jan would have been there. She would have looked things up. Probably at the library where they used to spend time together. She'd find out about the Gianetti family. Maybe there had been a key tidbit of information in a newspaper article. Maybe there was an event or something in Orland Park today and it had been clear to her that Antonio Gianetti Junior would go to this event. The Orland Park Shopping Center was there. Maybe something was going on there and Jan had somehow found out Antonio Junior would be there and . . .

Would she have approached Antonio Junior? Would she have simply walked up to him and told him there might be more to his mother's death than an accidental slip in the hallway? And if she approached Gianetti and cousin Max had been around and had reason to want to leave well enough alone and not let some woman stir things up . . .

Of course Jan had gone to Orland. She was missing. Someone she would have wanted to question was dead, along with his attorney, in a questionable accident, and Jan had been seen at Marjorie's funeral by the hoods. Max Lamberti, Dino Justice, and all the other hoods who might be in their Crown Vics right now. And why? What were they after? Marjorie had said it all. The keys. The family keys. The keys and the fly in the ointment. The fly in the ointment who could be none other than Max the Fly. And another thing he recalled Marjorie saying. The keys to the Presidential suite. Perhaps that was an indication of just how much someone had to gain or lose because of what Jan might be stirring up.

And so, he drove to Orland Park where he might or might not see Jan's Audi or the vehicles on the list he got from Tamara. If he saw any of the vehicles out there, then he'd know for sure. And if he found that his suspicions were correct without finding Jan, he could always make his way back to the addresses in the dead of night and become death. Because if something happened to Jan, he wouldn't care what happened to him as long as he got to the one responsible and put a bullet through a brain.

Although the vehicles involved in the so-called accident had been towed away, it was not hard to find the scene. A Chicago television crew had decided to do coverage for the morning news, and their van was in the left lane with its microwave dish aimed and its lights on the commentator. Traffic wasn't heavy, but everyone slowed down to see what was going on. Some even parked on the right shoulder, including a man in a white Lincoln who watched from his car.

The commentator walked on the left shoulder of Route 45 as he spoke. The cameraman followed and so did the news van at walking speed with its high beams on and its emergency blinkers flashing. An Illinois State Police car moved slowly behind the van with its strobe lights going, and another was parked on the same shoulder a hundred yards back, just ahead of a bridge where there was a slight hill and the shoulders on both sides narrowed.

The commentator pointed out the skid marks coming across the road from the right lane on the downslope of the hill. He said that at this point the Prius driven by Antonio Gianetti Junior was apparently being dragged beneath the semi-trailer of the truck. The commentator pointed out where the skid marks stopped on the left shoulder. He said that at this point the rear wheels of the fully-loaded double-axle trailer apparently rolled over the Prius. The commentator pointed to the side to a deep rut lit by the van's spotlight a hundred feet or so down in the median. He said when the Prius emerged from beneath the truck's wheels it became airborne and hit where the first rut was visible. Farther down the road the commentator pointed out a series of water-filled ruts in the mud down in the center of the wide medium where he said the Prius flipped end over end until it came to rest.

Steve watched the commentator from the Lincoln. After the commentator and cameraman went inside the van and the dish tilted back down to its closed position and the van moved ahead, he watched the State Police taking photographs and re-measuring the length of skid marks. Several officers searched the muddy area down in the median with flashlights, but other than that, there was nothing else to see. None of the vehicles on the list were there, and the only thing that had come in on the scanner relating to the accident was a call to State Police Headquarters that they'd soon be wrapped up at the scene and would have all the flashing lights out of the area in a couple minutes.

Because he had driven down Route 45 to the scene of the accident without stopping, Steve decided to go back north toward the shopping center and the intersection from Marjorie's litany, U.S. 6 and 45. He drove through the parking lots of various businesses at and near the intersection. Most of the parking lots were nearly empty because it was late and the banks and stores were closed. A couple of eat-in restaurants and a few fast-food places near the intersection had crowded lots, but none of the vehicles on the list were there.

A mile north of the intersection, the Orland Park Shopping Center parking lot was also almost empty, the stores having been closed for a while, and this frustrated him. If there had been a lot full of cars he could have driven up and down aisles and felt like he was doing something. But it didn't take long in the shopping center. So he started going through the parking lots of restaurants and fast-food places along Route 45 in the vicinity of the center, working his way from north to south until he was back at the intersection of U.S. 6 and 45.

While going through the parking lot of a fish and chips place, he saw the yellow flashing lights of a tow truck heading north on 45 and drove in behind it. It was a flatbed, and on it was a Mercedes with the Illinois license BBROWN. He followed the flatbed with the Mercedes on board because the plate BBROWN meant something. He could not think of what it was, but he was certain the plate meant something.

While he followed the flatbed, he tried to recall everything he learned before leaving Hell in the Woods. He remembered being in his room, getting ready to leave, putting on warm clothes, putting the pocket thesaurus in his pocket. He felt for the thesaurus, took it out and put it on the seat. Back at Hell in the Woods he sometimes used the thesaurus to recall a concept. But that was before he began using his computer. And what would he look up? The color brown?

Brown. It had to mean something. BBROWN. B. Brown. The boy. The shoe. The dog. Buster Brown! Tamara had said that Antonio Gianetti Junior had been killed with another man. With his attorney whose name was William Brown, but who was known as Buster Brown.

But what now? Of course Buster Brown's car is being towed. He's dead and can't drive. He and Tony Junior probably met at one of these restaurants earlier and now his car's been found. So what could he possibly gain by following the tow back to Chicago? Maybe he'd find out where Brown lived, or maybe he'd find out where Brown had his car serviced. And those things didn't seem useful at all, not at all.

As he slowed the Lincoln and pulled into yet another parking lot to look for vehicles he might have reason to follow, Steve reached over and turned up the volume on the scanner resting on the seat beside him. It was already set up to stop at broadcasts on suburban and State Police and Sheriff's Police and Chicago Police channels. While he slowly cruised through parking lots listening to the endless babble, he imagined God listening in, becoming angrier and angrier and tearing the entire goddamn thing called civilization down because of this babble and because of all the lights of commercialism and because of global warming and because of war and terrorism and because of the absence of anything that would help find Jan. But then, as he turned south on 45 and headed back toward the scene of the accident to have another look, he picked up a call from Frankfort headquarters to one of its cars. It was a brief back-and-forth dialogue between a female base station operator and a male officer.

She mentioned the traffic jam caused by the accident earlier that evening. He said he was glad it happened before he came on duty. She mentioned something about all the "crazies" out there this night and wondered if there was a full moon hidden by all the clouds. He asked what kind of "crazies" and she mentioned a report about cars and a van traveling at high-speed on a back road just before he came on duty. Something about a red car and a van and a couple other cars with people throwing garbage out the windows. She said a farmer called it in and called back a while ago wanting to know if it was all right to go down a certain road.

When the scanner jumped ahead to the next frequency in its sequence, Steve cradled the steering wheel as best he could with his rotten right arm and reached across with his left hand and picked up the scanner. He held the scanner against the steering wheel, trying to push the correct button. But he was unable to do it and quickly pulled to the side of the road and stopped. Then he punched the button to go backward in the sequence until he was back at the Frankfort frequency, and froze the scanner there.

The frequency was silent. He sat there, staring at the scanner. He had pulled into a right-turn lane and knew he could not stay there long, so he drove ahead and turned right into the parking lot of a bank. The frequency was still silent. He adjusted the squelch until he got the hiss of FM static. Still nothing.

Then, suddenly, the male voice boomed out. "Frankfort. Where'd you say the farmer saw the speeding litterbugs?"

Then the female voice, even louder. "North to south on Parker Road just north of Thirty. Says they were throwing trash out when they turned eastbound on One-hundred-eightieth. Pavement ends there for railroad tracks. Farmer says they parked for a time, then took off, but he's not sure if they all left. Happened a couple hours ago so could be he's on edge."

"Roger, Frankfort. Guess I'll make sure. If anybody needs sleep, it's farmers."

After having a hell of a time finding the location because the rental agency map wasn't detailed enough, Steve sped south on Parker road staring out into the darkness. He had the Lincoln's brights on and could see a sign for a T a quarter mile ahead. Then he saw a squad car cross the road at the T and slowed the Lincoln to forty. There were farms spaced out in the area, a few of the houses with lights on, but nothing else. It was after eleven-thirty.

He slowed the Lincoln to a crawl well ahead of the intersection where the squad had crossed. He paused at the T, waiting at the stop sign until the taillights of the squad were out of sight to his right. He was about to turn left when he noticed something lying in the middle of the road. It looked like a jumble of paper. The call on the scanner had said someone had been throwing trash out. As he stared at what he now could see was a magazine on the road, he remembered that before he spotted the squad, and while he was driving slowly after that, there had been an abundance of paper, perhaps other magazines.

He put on the Lincoln's brights and turned down the road the squad had come out of, already making up an excuse should the squad come back. Something about looking for U.S. 6 and 45. The Frankfort frequency on the scanner was silent, but he figured he'd probably hear another call to the squad if the farmer who called in was still watching.

As he drove down the road he saw more magazines and thought, kids. A stash of dirty magazines that can't be left in mom and dad's car or can't be brought into the house. Right, a stash of dirty magazines thrown out by kids in vehicles borrowed for a night of joy riding.

But as he drove more slowly, a shiny magazine cover blew up in the wind and he saw the familiar yellow bordered cover of a *National Geographic Magazine*, then he saw another cover, its title *Time*. As if he were in therapy trying to solve a complex puzzle, he had a sudden feeling of success, but it was followed instantaneously by a feeling of dread.

He pulled far to the right on the shoulder and stopped next to a magazine. He opened the door and reached down, bracing his good leg beneath the steering wheel so he wouldn't fall out onto the road. The magazine was cold and wet. This one was *U.S. News and World*

Report. The cover had something about The Iraq War. He looked at the date. 2003.

He threw the magazine on the passenger seat, kept the door ajar while he drove and pulled to the right again. Another *U.S. News and World Report.* The magazine had flipped open to a page showing photographs of George W. Bush and Al Gore in debate. He remembered relearning about the 2000 election from Jan. Going over and over news from magazines just like this that Jan brought in to Hell in the Woods whenever she visited. Magazines she'd gotten from the librarian who said they were online and would be thrown away. Magazines that filled the back seat of Jan's Audi.

He threw this wet magazine on top of the other on the seat beside him and drove ahead. He did not stop at other magazines on the road but sped toward the dead end. Now there were no more magazines and he passed a sign that said, "Pavement Ends." The dead end was marked not by a dead end sign, but by a sign with double arrows pointing left and right.

It was dark at the end of the paved road. Rather than an actual dead end, there was a narrow gravel road to the left and a muddy two-track to the right. He shut off the Lincoln's lights and engine. He threw the wet magazines into the back seat and got his flashlight out of the bag on the floor. He slid to the right, reaching over to open the passenger door. The transfer to the wheelchair took only a couple minutes.

The rain had stopped completely and the only sound was the drone of traffic in the distance. He wheeled along the edge of the pavement scanning the ground with the flashlight. There wasn't much to be seen except some broken glass and smashed beer cans. But along the edge of the pavement where the mud two-track went south, he saw what looked like fresh tire tracks. The tires had sunken deep into the mud. Where there were puddles the tracks were simply trenches without pattern. But between the puddles, where the ground had drained, he could see the patterns of tire treads.

He found a spot along one side of the tracks where he could roll his chair on the weed bed without sinking in. He examined the tracks, determining that at least two vehicles had recently turned in and backed out. He also saw footprints, most of them large, one set medium size. He knew someone had been here recently because the heavy rain from earlier in the day would certainly have washed the detail away. It had not rained for long on these tire tracks and on these footprints. But unless he were able to study the tires on Jan's Audi and unless he knew exactly what kind of shoes she was wearing . . .

In the dark, at a dead end, sitting in his wheelchair in the weeds, he wept. Back in the car with the heat on high to take off the chill, he wept. He swore aloud at himself. "Goddamn fucking stroke! Crying no fucking good now!"

The only thing of significance he was able to gather, without the aid of forensic equipment and records and expertise and time, was that one of the vehicles which had turned into the muddy two-track had rain tires. He recognized the tread design with the deep center groove, recalled seeing commercials for rain tires on television. Unless Jan bought rain tires without telling him, he did not think her Audi had them. If she had bought rain tires, she would have told him because she told him everything. Everything.

A call blasted out of the scanner, the female base station operator again. "Car ten. Frankfort."

"Go, Frankfort."

"Farmer called again. Insists someone's at the dead end."

"Roger, Frankfort. I was there a while ago. Probably saw me."

"Farmer's on the phone now. Says someone's there."

"Okay. I'm ten minutes away, but I'll check."

He turned on the Lincoln's lights, turned the Lincoln around being careful not to drop a wheel in the mud, and drove back down the road. For a moment he wondered if he should pick up more magazines, but decided it would be pointless. He turned the scanner back on automatic full scan and drove away, heading west, then north, then back east to Route 45. The babble on the scanner was back.

Heading north back on 45, he decided to try the parking lots one more time. The pain in his right side had increased substantially. He reached into his left pocket, took out one of the Valiums he'd brought along and spit-swallowed it. Then everything changed, but not from the Valium. It was like another stroke. A stroke that turned back the clock and made the present time into a time that hadn't happened at all. Maybe he had brainwashed himself into believing it could happen. Maybe he *was* having a stroke, neurons wagging in pain as they died. Maybe this time the bullet in his brain was out to give him a brand new fantasy world. Maybe the light would go on in his room at Hell in the Woods and he'd wake up in bed and Jan would be there all smiles, face cool and smelling of outside night air.

The call came in from one of the Chicago channels. He skidded to the side of the road and hit the scanner's freeze button as soon as he heard the first part of the call.

He was making it up. He had to be making it up. But then the call continued.

". . . located in parking lot, Saint Mel in the Woods. Red Audi, Illinois license J-B-A-B-E. Registration matches missing person Janet Kowalski-Babe. Car unlocked. No keys. Driver's door window smashed in."

CHAPTER TWENTY-SEVEN

Dino had Legless park in the front lot at Hell in the Woods. The van backed into a spot far out in the lot in the last row that bordered the woods along the entrance road. Her ankle throbbed, tears came from her eyes, and the tape on her mouth tore at her face. Although Dino sat beside her and turned to stare at her from time to time, she was not sure if he was aware of the pain she was in, or if he did know and did not care.

Dino told Legless to turn up the police scanner and they sat there listening to the litany of police calls. When the announcement came that her Audi was in the parking lot at Hell in the Woods, she looked ahead through the windshield. There it was, her Audi parked here at Hell in the Woods. Although a police car was parked next to it, she could not help imagining that her Audi was here because she has come to visit Steve and has gone inside to be with him.

The Audi and the police car were up closer to the building. One policeman stood outside the squad car having a smoke while another shined a flashlight into her Audi. The van was parked too far out in the lot to draw the attention of the policemen. And as she stared at the Audi and the policemen who were so close, yet so far away, she realized her captors had parked here because they wanted her to see the Audi. It had been brought back here to make an impression on her, to let her know they could do anything.

Beyond the Audi she could see the front entrance of the building. As she stared at the entrance, she felt at any moment she would see a man in knit cap and leather jacket wheeling Steve out in his wheelchair. Steve would be strapped into the chair so he could not move. And when they wheeled him calmly out into the parking lot, past the policemen and to the van . . .

No! She'd have to do something. Tell them something to delay whatever it was they had planned. But even if she could think of something to say that might delay them, how could she with the tape on her mouth?

She glanced to Dino and saw him watching her. When she looked back out at the Audi and back to Dino, he turned toward the front and said, "Okay, let's go."

As the van began driving off, she struggled. Despite the pain, she struggled, knowing it was pointless, but wishing nonetheless she could do something to attract the attention of the policemen.

Tyrone wished the rain hadn't stopped because the streets were still wet and the spray from other cars coated the DeVille with road slime. He hated having the DeVille get dirty almost as much as he hated coming back to Hell in the Woods. Especially when he wasn't scheduled to work. That was the shit of it, having to come back to this place at night when he should be banging Latoya back at her apartment.

Because he was just visiting, Tyrone stayed in the front lot instead of driving around back to the employee lot. After parking the DeVille in one of the empty handicapped spots near the entrance, he rummaged around in the glove compartment for the handicapped permit. He'd found the permit some time back. An old fart with memory half gone had left it lying on the reception counter. He'd never used it here at Hell in the Woods where someone he knew might see him coming in to work. But the late shift had started a while ago, no one coming on or going off for a few hours at least, and he felt somewhat reckless tonight. Feeling reckless was part of the act, part of preparing himself for what he had to do. When he finally found the permit, he hung it from the rearview mirror and got out of the car.

Farther out in the parking lot, as he walked toward the entrance, Tyrone saw a cop standing next to a squad car and almost turned back to the DeVille to move it. But the cop seemed to be attending to another car in the lot. Tyrone couldn't see the car the cop was messing with because it was behind the squad, but he saw the cop shining a flashlight around and figured the cop was busy hassling someone else and so he kept walking.

Fool, he thought. Come to scare a cripple, got help coming even, and you're scared of a goddamn bluecoat doing his traffic thing.

After Tyrone went through the front entrance he veered off to the side, directly toward the office where the time clock was. This made the guard at the counter ignore him. Dumb shit guards makin' just above minimum wage didn't give a shit, and who could blame them?

In the hallway outside the time-clock room, Tyrone checked his watch. Flat Nose wasn't due for a half hour. That would give him time to clear the way at the loading dock entrance. As he headed down the office hall that led to the exit, which would take him to the nursing home wing, Tyrone imagined how big that Babe guy's eyes would get when he was awakened by both him and Flat Nose. No messing around this time. In the morning he'd probably think he'd had a nightmare. Yeah, a nightmare from Hell in the Woods he'd never forget. A nightmare that just might shut his fucking mouth forever. So much for therapy, fuckhead.

But once he was in the main hall to the nursing home wing, Tyrone had second thoughts. Not that he wouldn't go through with it. His second thoughts were about him calling Flat Nose. He must have really wanted the fucker's help because he had to call several times, getting the same message at Flat Nose's apartment, then finally getting through to the fucker on his cell and having to listen to the fucker's lip.

As he stood in the dark hall, the thought of going down to the end of the wing to let Flat Nose in depressed him. He knew Flat Nose would jive him about being a pussy. Or maybe Flat Nose would even say something to DeJesus about Tyrone not being able to handle it.

Tyrone looked at his watch again. Still at least twenty-five minutes before Flat Nose was due. And in twenty-five minutes . . . yeah, maybe there was time. Maybe if he went up to three and the fuckhead was asleep and he took care of things himself and *that* got back to DeJesus, then Flat Nose wouldn't be the only tough motherfucker. Maybe that was the only way to move on up the ladder, get a flashier set of wheels than a DeVille, impress the hell out of the chicks.

He knew he could be smarter, much smarter than Flat Nose. He'd go on up to four first, in case he met up with anyone he knew on the elevator, then take the stairs back down to three. He'd take care of everything himself. And when it was over, he'd just ease on out to the loading dock and tell Flat Nose a thing or two about who's got the balls for this business. Yeah, he'd get tight with DeJesus, even make like he's a woman-hater just like DeJesus if he has to. Exaggerate the old gang-bang days, make off it was like being in the military, maybe even hint he'd iced a couple assholes while he was gang-bangin'. And when he and DeJesus had meetings, he'd talk about his ma a lot, because DeJesus lives for his ma.

Tyrone could almost smell the inside of the brand new Benz as he headed for the elevator.

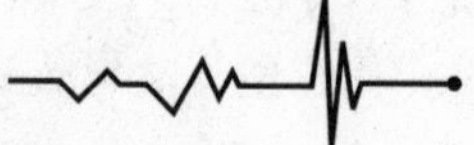

Instead of driving away from Hell in the Woods after seeing the police at her car, they drove around to the back of the complex, far out toward the dark woods surrounding the nursing home wing where she knew employees parked. Before the van pulled into a spot, she could see there were two newer large cars parked amongst the older, more battered employee cars. The van pulled in next to one of the newer cars. She was not certain, but she thought these were the cars that, along with the van, had chased her. Because they were parked in a darkened area between overhead lights spaced far apart in this remote part of the lot, she was unable to see into the cars, but assumed there must be men inside, perhaps the men in knit caps and leather jackets, waiting to be called on their cell phones and told what to do. Just like the driver of the semi that had driven over Tony Gianetti's Prius had probably been told what to do.

After the van parked and the engine was shut off, Dino spoke to the driver.

"Tell the others we'll stay put here for a while. Get in with them and stay low. No smoking and no one out walking around in case a cop cruises by. Turn on the scanner in the car and let me know if you hear anything."

Because there was some light in the van from distant overhead lights, she was able to watch as the driver made his way into his wheelchair and backed it onto the lift. As he sat on the lift and the door was sliding open, more light came in the open doorway and she watched as he glanced in her direction. He had his knit cap back on, and pulled it down more tightly on his head as he stared at her. After the lift moved the driver outside and down to the ground and the lift returned empty and the door closed, she heard a car door slam.

Dino turned. "I'm going to take off the tape in a little while, Mrs. Babe. Before I do, you'll need to know the situation. We know all about your husband. We know where his room is. We know that right now he's in bed after having had a trying day. When things get back to normal you'll be able to go to him. He needs you, Mrs. Babe. Our man on the inside said he was distraught today. Perhaps you don't realize just how much he needs you.

"We've done our research. We know, for instance, that at times you and your husband have closed the door to his room in order to have privacy. Since the police found your car in the lot with its window broken, I'm sure they'll want to find you to let you know it's been broken into. I think you can see we have very little time to chat.

"What will happen now, Mrs. Babe, is that I will take off the tape and you will tell me where we should go with our keys. When you tell me, we will take you to your husband, and sometime later this evening, after being unable to reach you at your home number, the police will eventually make some connections and go to your husband's room and discover you decided to spend the night with him. They'll tell you that your car has been broken into, you'll go out with them to see, and that will be the end of it. Very simple, very clean, no more trouble.

"However, if you do not tell me where we should go with our keys, I'm afraid the police will find something entirely different in your husband's room. They'll probably call it a mercy killing—slash—suicide.

"So, that's it. I'll even take the tape off more gently this time."

When the tape was off, she cleared her throat, coughed, swallowed the phlegm that had accumulated, and said, "My ankle. That bastard broke my ankle."

Dino did not respond, but she could tell by the shadowed shape of his head that he still faced her. She knew he was considering the difficulty of her being found with a broken ankle. Dino had given her a scenario to think about. Years earlier Steve had told her of the method. Describe a scene in which everything comes out all right. Just like good-cop-bad-cop. One harangues the prisoner, while the other paints pictures in which the prisoner sees a light at the end of the tunnel. In this case Dino was playing both the good cop and the bad cop. Except he was no cop, and she was no ordinary prisoner. No ordinary prisoner because she knew there was no light at the end of the tunnel if she cooperated. And she had a strong feeling Dino knew that she knew.

Dino's phone beeped and he took it out of his inside pocket. Instead of turning away from her as he had last time he was on the phone, he continued facing her when he spoke. She kept her mouth shut and listened.

"Nothing except some story."

"Health care, insurance brokers, all that."

"Nothing's out of hand. What makes you say that?"

"Okay, okay. But for someone who wants the old days back, you sure don't talk like it."

"Well, fuck you, too."

After folding the phone and putting it back inside his coat, Dino turned from her and stared out the side window.

From Dino's side of the conversation it seemed they might be getting desperate. Of course, what good did that do her? Desperate was something she'd been as soon as one of those cars came up alongside and rammed her, forcing her off the road. So desperate she had taken to throwing magazines out the window. And now here she was out in the dark employee lot between shift changes where no one would hear her even if she did scream.

Dino turned toward her again.

"I think you might want to talk to me, Mrs. Babe. You'll have to talk eventually. I guarantee it."

"Put it in writing."

"Don't fuck with me."

He had not changed his tone when he said this, and it frightened her more than if he had shouted it.

He drew in a breath, as if about to say something more. But before he spoke, a car pulled up very close and a door slammed. As she watched him, Dino turned slowly to look toward the front of the van. Now she could see his profile against a light coming through the side window. Where before, when she saw his profile, his mouth had been active, either talking or cleaning his teeth with his tongue, now his mouth was tightly closed. Perhaps he was wondering, like her, if this arrival would put an end to it. A quick and violent end.

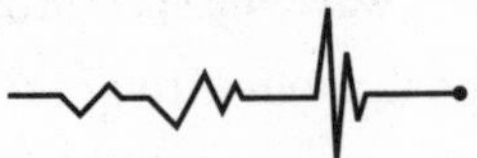

When he exited the Stevenson Expressway and the car ahead slammed on its brakes—skidding to a stop on the wet pavement instead of going through a yellow like any normal Chicago driver—Steve's brain tried to send the emergency signal to his right leg instead of his left leg. But his left foot was on the brake and before he had a chance to compensate for the error, before he had a chance to press down hard on the brake pedal with his left foot, the signal got through, somehow bypassing the blown circuits, and the big thigh muscle lifted his right leg and swung it over, knocking his left foot off the pedal. Suddenly his feet were in a tangle and the uncontrolled pressure on the brake pedal applied by good foot and bad foot fighting it out was not enough to keep him from hitting the car in front.

Two teenaged boys with haircuts from another planet jumped out of a Honda Accord. There would be an argument. His inability to converse normally would be mistaken for drunkenness. Even if he were able to get through to the two boys that he had an emergency to deal with, they might overpower him, make him stay in order to justify the damage to a parent's car borrowed for the night. He could see the terror of teenaged boys in their body language, the driver of the car actually holding his hands to his face because of the horror caused by seeing the smashed taillights.

There was no choice in the matter. They'd live. It might be hard for them when they got home, but they'd live.

He put the Lincoln in reverse and backed off to the side of the ramp, motioning them to do the same. And when the driver got back into the Honda and pulled to the side, Steve shut off the lights so the license plate light would go out making it more difficult to read the plate. Then, looking both ways, he sped around the Honda, saw his opening and fishtailed the Lincoln through the red light and into traffic northbound on Harlem.

Cars honked and tires screeched, but when he turned the lights back on and floored the Lincoln, other drivers seemed to sense his desperation and moved out of his way.

The boys did not follow. In his mirror he could see them standing outside the car jumping into the air and shouting. No guns came out. They did not chase him. They would wait for the police. Good kids. Thinking of these poor boys he had encountered so briefly conjured up elusive boyhood memories, memories the stroke had somehow left him with, thoughts of times when he'd been treated unfairly, and he was momentarily brought to tears.

But there was no time for tears. Jan was in trouble. According to the police radio her car was at Hell in the Woods. He wiped his eyes with his sleeve and drove on, honking when a cab got in his way.

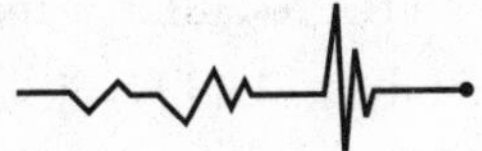

After they landed at Chicago's O'Hare Airport, Valdez drove the rental car while Hanley fiddled with the GPS. It was wet and windy, the reflections off the pavement and the buffeting of the wind making it necessary that Valdez concentrate on his driving.

Valdez drove out of the rental car agency and onto the southbound expressway. He exited within a mile to a warehouse district near the airport. It was a familiar drive Valdez had taken many times during visits to Chicago.

Both Valdez and Hanley went inside a small office attached to one of the warehouses and showed their credentials to a young man. The man photocopied their credentials, compared their fingerprints to those on file, had them each sign a form, then opened a locked cabinet and brought out two briefcases. The young man handed a briefcase to each and they left. The only words spoken were the greetings. Back in the car, they put their briefcases in the back seat, Valdez drove toward the expressway, and Hanley went back to the GPS.

"I can never figure these things out," said Hanley. "First it asks me for a street address, then it asks for a city. You'd think it would be the other way around."

"Did you try points of interest?" asked Valdez.

"Points of interest? We're not on a tour. Maybe we should be, though. A motor coach tour like you see old folks on. One of those reclining seats wouldn't feel so bad right now. I hear that on some of those tours the seats are heated. Good for the arthritis."

"Not tourist points of interest. I mean on this GPS system if you select points of interest it gives you category choices." Valdez glanced toward the GPS. "You'll be given categories like hospitals or health care facilities along with all the restaurants and things."

"Give me back the old days," said Hanley.

After a bit more fiddling, Hanley said, "Ah, here it is."

The smooth sexy voice of the GPS lady came through the car's speakers. Valdez had gotten back on the expressway southbound and now the woman said to stay on the current road and that the exit would be on the left in seven miles.

"Can we get back to our plan now?" asked Valdez.

"First I'd better try our contact again," said Hanley, taking out his phone.

Hanley punched in a number and spoke quietly on the phone. With the road noise and the hiss of tires on wet pavement, Valdez could hear only a couple words. The conversation was short. Hanley closed his phone and looked out the windshield.

"Well?" asked Valdez.

"I think they'd better upgrade their recruiting tactics," said Hanley. "She's not back to the rehab facility yet. I told her she might as well take her time and we'll meet her. She said when we get there we should look for a side road that goes around back. There's an entrance at the loading dock. She'll probably get there first and she can watch to see if anyone else is around. I told her to stay on the side road and watch for us from there."

"Does her voice sound like hers?" asked Valdez.

"Who?" asked Hanley.

"The GPS lady."

"Oh, yes, young and sexy with a slight Hispanic accent."

"So the plan," said Valdez, "is that the three of us go into the place and find the detective?"

"Right," said Hanley. "Assuming no one else has gotten to him."

"You think Lamberti and his men might have grabbed him?"

"It's possible," said Hanley. "If they think he knows something, they'll probably question him there. I doubt if they'll take him anywhere because there'd be no need. They'll figure they have the upper hand being the guy's had a stroke."

"Why are you so sure they'll go to the rehab facility?" asked Valdez.

"It's where our contact thinks they'll go. Before she lost them they were after the guy's wife. Whether or not they've got her, whether or not they get something out of her, they'll want to verify their findings at the source."

"So we're trusting the instincts of a rookie?"

"Not totally," said Hanley. "She's made calls to other Chicago contacts. We've got word that Lamberti is on the move, and the direction he's moving will put him at the rehab facility a short time from now."

Valdez glanced in his mirror at a tailgating semi and moved over one lane to let it pass before speaking. "Finally, I've got to ask this."

"What is it?" asked Hanley.

"If there's an indication that this whole thing is going to blow up, what then?"

"No choice," said Hanley. "If so, we'll have to open our briefcases."

"It could be messy," said Valdez.

"I know. But look at it this way. When it's finished we'll simply be two old farts in a panic with all the other old farts."

"I didn't mean we'd have trouble getting away," said Valdez. "I meant it could be messy eliminating everyone involved."

Hanley leaned to the side and stared at the GPS map where the little arrow made its way along the expressway. "Yes, I'm sure it will be messy."

"And all because back then some other old farts wanted to guarantee an election victory."

"All because of that," said Hanley. "Even though half of them are dead now, they've passed down the legacy. Not only that, this thing was carried on after the election."

"How so?" asked Valdez.

"They needed to make sure that neither Carter, nor anyone like him, ever tried to run for President again. And that, my friend, leaves a hell of a lot of worry in DC about this thing ever blowing up."

"How far up the ladder does it go?" asked Valdez.

"Between you and me?" said Hanley.

"Between you and me," said Valdez.

Hanley turned from the glow of the GPS screen and stared at Valdez. "All the way to the top."

"I wondered if it did," said Valdez.

"That's why we can't bring anyone else in," said Hanley. "That's why it's up to you and me. It's got to be closed for the sake of future generations."

The GPS lady chimed in, "In two miles, prepare to exit on the left."

Valdez put on his signal to start moving over. In his side mirror the spray from the car lifted into the headlights of cars and trucks bearing down. Although the speed limit was fifty-five, everyone was going seventy.

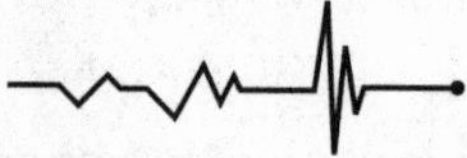

Dino held his hand over her mouth so she could not scream while the door was open. Even if she could have screamed it would not have mattered because, while the door was open, a jet was taking off overhead, its deep rumble accompanying the visitor inside.

The visitor was Max Lamberti. She recognized him when he opened the front door and climbed into the passenger seat. Although the interior lights in the van were disabled, enough light filtered in for her to recognize Max's mustached face, despite the fact he wasn't wearing the hairpiece he'd worn at the funeral. Max glanced into the back seat before closing the door, rubbing his bald head with one hand.

After Dino took his hand from her mouth, Max said, "What? No screams?"

"It's taken care of," said Dino. "I laid it out for her."

"Laid what out?"

Max was turned, facing her and Dino. Dino did not answer.

"Mrs. Babe, Mrs. Babe," said Max, obviously faking solicitude. "We meet again like old friends. That's the best thing there is in this world. Old friends. I'll get right to the point, Mrs. Babe. My old friend by the name of Tony Gianetti, God rest his soul, gave a lot of responsibility to me when he passed. Unfortunately, when he went kind of sudden-like, he was unable to tell me some things he was supposed to. And now we find out his wife knew these things all along. But unfortunately, as you know, she had a stroke.

"Mrs. Babe. We know Tony Senior opened safe deposit boxes before he died, quite a long time before he died. We also know that you and your husband know where these safe deposit boxes are located. We have the keys, the contents of the boxes belong to us. We're a family, and families like to keep what belongs to them in the family.

"And so, Mrs. Babe, here it is. You tell us where the boxes are, and we'll be off to O'Hare Airport booking flights. We'll be too busy to worry ourselves about you or your husband because we'll be on our way to getting what's rightfully ours.

"We're more like a business these days, Mrs. Babe. No, better than a business. We're like the military, lean and mean. Every business has to be lean and mean to survive financially these days. Even the church has to be lean and mean despite its call for mercy.

"Did I tell you I was in the military? Served in the all American 82nd Airborne. And I'm also a regular member of the church. The diocese counts on my weekly offering, I can tell you that. So anyway, what will it be, Mrs. Babe? Make an offering to the church?"

"I don't know what you're talking about."

Max turned back to the front of the van and his voice went hard. "Fuck it. We got to do this fast, Dino. No fuckin' slip-ups. Jimmy told me about the cops findin' her car."

"We'll do it fast," said Dino.

"Let's go."

"Where?"

The van rocked as Max made his way quickly to the back seat, stooping down in front of her, his face close so he could spit the words at her.

"We fuckin' bring him out here! That way time's on our side. And it won't hurt to let them fuckin' see one another fuckin' die if we don't find out what we need to find out! I saw the two of them at the funeral, the way they fuckin' looked at us! And now she tries some bullshit about insurance brokers! That was on the east coast. I fuckin' watch television, too!"

Max reached out and grasped her hair, pulling her head violently against the side window, then he spoke harshly into her ear. "That's right! I saw you and you saw me! We met at a funeral, of all things! How fuckin' appropriate!"

He pulled her hair harder. "Appropriate because a bitch like you always talks in the end! Unless she wants to attend a quick and dirty double funeral!"

She cleared her throat. "I . . . I'll talk now."

"Go ahead," said Dino, moving in closer to her side.

But Max pulled even harder on her hair. "Yeah, you'll talk all right! You'll talk enough to get us out of here! No way, bitch! No more bullshit! We get him and you together and we go somewhere else and you'll talk all right! Only then it won't be bullshit!"

She shouted, "I'll tell you! Just take me somewhere and I'll tell you!"

Max put his hand over her mouth until Dino got the tape back on. She tried to get a scream out while the tape was going on, but Max's other hand clasped her neck.

"What now?" asked Dino.

"Same," said Max. "No fuckin' stall, no fuckin' time wasted. We bring him the fuck out here, we take them somewhere, and she'll talk all right."

"But if someone sees us . . ."

"Shut the fuck up! I'm handlin' this now! I already called Patty and he'll make sure the third floor hallway is clear. We do it like the old days. Quick and quiet and private. Then we get the hell back to our business!"

Max let go of her and moved back to the front of the van. "Speaking of business," he said, "I got business in this hell-hole because they fuckin' killed my Aunt Marjorie, didn't they? Bring that tape."

"The tape?"

"Don't fuckin' ask questions! Just bring the fuckin' roll of tape!"

After they left, the driver was back. The lift bringing him and his greasy oniony smell back inside. Instead of sitting up front, he turned his chair toward the back, vaulted to the seat and sat where Dino had been.

It was over. Speaking openly in front of her proved that. They'd bring Steve. They'd take them to a place where screaming did no good. She'd eventually tell them what they wanted to know as a last resort, as the only way to give her and Steve a few more seconds of life. Then they'd kill them and no one would ever find their bodies.

As if to stress the truth and the hopelessness of this, the beast beside her—the same beast who had broken her ankle—reached out, put his hand between her legs before she could clamp them shut, and kneaded her gently through the fabric of her slacks.

"There-there, sweetie," he said. "I always feel sorry for a date who spills her beer on herself. 'Course, who can blame you? That boss, he's a scary sum-bitch. Took weight training in the army, and still does so he can stay scary. I did mine after. Part of the therapy they give us at the VA hospital. Did therapy to music. At night someone pulled a few strings, because at night these volunteer ladies brought in beer. Can you picture it? Music and ladies dancing us around in our chairs right there in the VA hospital dining room."

Then, as he continued rubbing her through her damp slacks, the beast began humming what sounded like "The Beer Barrel Polka."

CHAPTER TWENTY-EIGHT

HE'D SHOW FLAT NOSE AND DEJESUS A THING OR TWO. HE'D take care of Babe and by the time Flat Nose showed up he'd have everything under control. No need to worry about Babe bein' a flap-jaw, he'd be able to say. Yeah, he'd show them who was a piss-cutter.

But after Tyrone eased down the hall, being careful not to let anyone see him, and after he ducked into the room, just in time because there'd been the shadow of someone down at the end of the hall in the TV lounge, and after he snuck up to the bed in the dark, glad the night light was blown and maintenance had fucked up as usual, and after thinking he'd lucked out—after all this, he discovered Babe was not there.

Instead of Babe in bed there was a pillow and a couple of bunched-up blankets. When he failed to find Babe he made his way back to the door, carefully pulled it all the way closed so the latch wouldn't make any noise, and turned on the light. Nothing. Not a Babe to be found anywhere. No Babe in the chair in the corner, no Babe under the bed, no Babe in the can. And no wheelchair, meaning that his job would be a little harder than he thought. Either he'd have to look around the place and find Babe, or he'd have to come back another night.

Another night at Hell in the Woods trying to talk a Babe in the woods into not talking. Or maybe it wasn't as bad as all that. Maybe the shadow he'd seen down at the TV lounge was Babe and all he'd have to do is wheel his ass back here and give him hell.

Voices in the hall, men's voices. He shut off the light and moved closer to the door. He pulled the door open enough so he could look out through the crack. Two guys in jackets were standing at the far end of the hall near the TV lounge with their backs to him. One guy was bald and both guys were big. The backs of their necks were thick, pale like concrete slabs, white guys. They were talking to someone in a wheelchair, and when the bald guy stepped a little to the side, Tyrone recognized the black leather jacket guy he'd seen hanging around the floor, the smart-assed tough guy who'd hogged the hallway and put a tough shit look on his face.

After a while it looked like the meeting in the hallway was over, the leather jacket guy turning his chair back to the TV lounge while the two big guys spun around and started walking his way down the hall. As the two guys got closer, Tyrone thought, No way, they can't be comin' here. A jet began its pass overhead as the two guys came closer, and Tyrone thought, Yeah, they'll just pass on by and head straight for the elevators. But the two guys seemed to slow down as they came closer. The jet overhead was making its presence known now, its roar coming into the building muted, but enough of a rumble to maybe help him get the hell out without these guys or anyone else hearing him or seeing him.

Tyrone eased the door closed, lifting the handicapped handle carefully. He stood for a while with his back to the door not feeling like much of a piss-cutter after all and wishing he'd waited for Flat Nose.

When the jet was gone he heard voices again. He turned and put his ear to the door to listen. The two guys argued in harsh whispers right outside the door, and he knew they were definitely not doctors or patients or relatives of patients because of what they said.

"How do we get him out?"

"You fuckin' carry him. You're the one lifts weights."

"Shouldn't we just wheel him out like we're visitors?"

"Not this fuckin' time of night. Besides, he's not comin' easy."

"And if someone tries to stop us?"

"That's why we got silencers. Quit fuckin' worrying. Patty's cleared the way and nothin's gonna happen."

"Right, nothing'll happen. So who was that guy Patty threw down the stairs?"

"Fuck the guy on the stairs. He probably worked for an ambulance chaser."

Tyrone could see shadows moving where light from the hall came in beneath the door. He reached out, felt his way along the wall, turned the corner, and followed the wall until he found the threshold for the doorway into the can. He made his way around the open door and once inside, being as quiet as a mouse, carefully pulled the door shut behind him. As he stood in the dark he could hear his heart pounding. Every breath he took sounded like the rattling breath of an emphysema guy from the VA hospital. Somewhere else in the building a toilet flushed. He could hear the faint whine of the plumbing. Then the whine ended and it was dead silent, not even a jet on takeoff.

Damn Hell in the Woods. Doors to the cans opening out so the dumb-fuck patients won't block the door if they fall. But for him it meant he couldn't hide behind the door if it opened. And then there wasn't even a fuckin' lock on the door.

Because there was no window in the can, he was in complete

darkness. He heard the muted sound of the latch on the door to the room, silence for a while, some whispering, then silence again until the latch on the door to the can made a slight squeak. He backed up in the darkness until the backs of his legs touched the crapper. He imagined the light going on and two silenced guns pointing at him. He pulled down his pants and sat on the crapper. He formulated a scene in which he claims he was simply ambling down the hallway minding his own business when all of a sudden he had to take a shit. Stomach flu or something. In the scene he puts on a step-and-fetch-it smile and says something dumb-ass like, "And when a guy's gotta go, a guy's gotta go." Maybe he could fake a barf. Maybe he wouldn't have to fake the barf.

When the door opened he could see the dim light filtering in from the window in the room. And framed against this dim light he could see one of them, probably the biggest one by the look of the shoulders. He was about to start his story with a line about a guy not being able to have privacy in this place, let them know he wasn't Babe, if Babe was the one they were after, when he saw what looked like the shadow of a giant bird with outstretched wings loom up and cause the man in the doorway to step aside. The shadow came toward him, blocking what little light there was, and all he could think of was a fuckin' black hole from outer space come down to swallow his ass.

A blanket was thrown over him and he was slugged in the head before he could open his mouth. Although he was dizzy and felt like he would barf, he tried to say something. Tell them he's not their man. Tell them they made a mistake. Politely ask if he could pull up his pants. But all that came out of his mouth was a bunch of moaning that didn't even sound like him.

His wrists were taped behind his back, tape was put over his mouth, and he was being carried. He could feel the movement and a brush of air where the blanket separated at the backs of his legs. When he kicked out, there was another slug, this one even harder, and he lost consciousness until he felt cooler air on his legs.

He was dropped to the ground. Cold cement ground because they were no longer in the building. The blanket was off and he was pushed face down so he could feel the cold grittiness of the concrete trying to push up his nose. If it wasn't for the tape on his mouth, he would've eaten some grit, and maybe chipped a couple teeth. As it was, he could taste blood.

He turned to the side, his cheek on the cold concrete better than his nose smashed into it. When he lifted his head to look around he saw that he was on the loading dock and wondered how they had gotten through the door without the alarm going off. His legs were trapped and he knew that before he could run, he had to stand up and try to pull up his pants.

They were behind him. One of them said, "Who's this fucker with the black ass?"

The other said, "How the fuck should I know! Maybe Patty knows."

"Well, it ain't who we wanted so we'll have to fuckin' tell Patty he fuckin' blew it!"

Although it was difficult with his hands taped behind him, Tyrone managed to get up onto his knees and grab hold of the elastic on his shorts with one hand while getting the thumb of the other hand through one of the belt loops on the back of his pants. As another jet on takeoff passed overhead, he conjured up images of being able to fly away home. He rocked back and forth from one knee to the other, trying to pull up his pants, not wanting to look behind him and piss these guys off any more than they seemed to be pissed off already. While he rocked back and forth trying to pull up his pants he stared out into the parking lot looking for his DeVille in its regular spot out at the far end of the lot where no one would ding the doors, then realized the DeVille wouldn't be there because he'd parked out front in handicapped. Then he wondered if he was now eligible for a handicapped sticker because of the way he'd been pounded.

Before he could get his shorts and pants part way up, an arm came around his neck and his arms were shoved halfway up his back. The upward pressure on his arms continued until he realized they wanted him to stand. When he stood the pressure eased off, but he sure did wish he'd been able to pull up his pants. The jet was gone, a faint rumble in the distance.

"Who the fuck are you? What the fuck you doin' in Babe's room? Tell us where Babe is or we'll shoot off that thing makes fuckin' spooks like you so fuckin' cocky!"

If it wasn't for the tape on his mouth he would have told the guy he wasn't cocky at all.

The guy who wasn't holding Tyrone circled around to the front. Big white guy in a jacket and black sweatshirt holding a gun with a silencer, the overhead light on the loading dock making the guy's eyes flash and scaring the shit out of him because all he could think about, besides the pain in his arms and neck and face, was the flash from the gun and the time it would take for the bullet to cross the space between it and his dick.

The guy holding him from behind ripped the tape from his mouth, taking some skin from his lips, then pushed up harder on his arm. The pain made Tyrone's words come out like the squealing of a pig.

"Shit, man! I don't know nothin'! I's jus' takin' a shit!"

The guy in front moved closer, lifting Tyrone's cock aside with the barrel of his gun and shoving the nose of the barrel up into the soft tissue between his balls. "He fuckin' knows somethin' or he wouldn't've been in Babe's room!" He pushed the barrel up and in. "So where the fuck is he?"

Tyrone tried to think of a good lie. Had to be a lie because he didn't know where the hell Babe had gone. Had to be a good lie so they'd feel confident enough to check it out and maybe let him pull up his pants. He was about to say he thought Babe had been picked up by his wife earlier that evening when an engine gunned loudly at the far end of the parking lot and the guy with flashing eyes holding the gun to his balls looked toward the sound of the engine.

When the engine gunned again and headlights from the road into the back lot swept across the guy's face, the barrel eased out of the flesh between Tyrone's balls. The guy backed off, held the gun on him.

"Pull 'em up, and no other moves 'cause I'm a good motherfuckin' shot!"

When the guy holding him let go, Tyrone thought he would take the tape off his wrists so he could pull up his pants. But instead, the guy behind grabbed a handful of pants and yanked them up hard. Tyrone tried to wiggle into the shorts in order to make them more comfortable, but the attempt failed and the top part of the shorts ballooned out above the top of his slacks. They were the oversized shorts with hearts Latoya had given him for his birthday. He wished he were with Latoya right now, and the hell with any other women.

The light that had swept over them swept back the other way, even brighter, and when Tyrone glanced back and saw the Christ Health Care Supplies truck pull up to the loading dock, he felt a slight tingle of relief, like maybe now he wouldn't get shot in the balls after all. If there was any time for the tough little fucker to show his stuff, now was that time.

The guy with the gun spun Tyrone around, holding the gun to his back. The guy who had held Tyrone from the back stood watching as the Christ Health Care truck braked hard, skidding and banging into the edge of the loading dock with a thud and bouncing back a couple feet.

Flat Nose jumped out without shutting off the engine or lights. After leaping up onto the dock to face them, Flat Nose turned his baseball cap backward, took his fighter's stance, and stood there, glaring. Now the fucker would explode into a ball of fire. He should drop, let Flat Nose know there's a gun in his back. Flat Nose would go for the gun and take a hit and he could make a run for it. But after a couple seconds of looking meaner than hell and glancing to Tyrone, then to each of the two guys, Flat Nose said, "What the fuck you guys think you're doin'?"

Before Flat Nose could make a move, the guy without the gun took a step back, faking retreat, then made his arm into a blur and let Flat Nose have it with a vicious right. Flat Nose fell off the loading dock, landing in the narrow space between the front of the truck and the dock. The guy went down after Flat Nose, held Flat Nose's head up, his face in the glare of the headlights as he flattened Flat Nose's nose again and again with more vicious blurry rights that spit some of Flat Nose's blood onto one of the headlight lenses. Then the guy lay Flat Nose down on the ground like putting a baby to bed, whispering a warning to him, and calmly walked around to the side of the truck, opening the door and shutting off the lights and engine.

The Flat Nose who was supposed to have exploded was a lump of flesh doing all he could to breathe through his spit and blood. Flat Nose's baseball cap, which he'd turned backward moments earlier, was nowhere to be seen.

Before Tyrone could react, the guy with the gun poked the barrel hard into Tyrone's back and said, "He fuckin' knows somethin'! We'll take him to the van and get it out of him! Kills two birds because the bitch'll think it's Babe if we keep him wrapped in the blanket."

After they put the tape back on Tyrone's mouth and the blanket over his head and arms, he was lifted over a shoulder. As he was carried, the guy in charge, who wasn't the one carrying him, moved in close and said, "Go easy, man. None of that kicking like before or I'll shoot your balls off right through this thing."

Then to the other guy, he said, "I'll get Jimmy to help. Keep him this side of the van 'til we get her out. One way or another, we'll get what we fuckin' want!"

"Like in the old days?"

"Yeah, like in the old days."

CHAPTER TWENTY-NINE

UNDER NORMAL CIRCUMSTANCES SHE MIGHT HAVE FELT PITY FOR him and not thought of him as a beast. Under normal circumstances she might have thought it cruel that his cohorts had nicknamed him Legless. But these were not normal circumstances.

Legless, who had earlier roughed her up and broken her ankle, kissed her, walking his slimy lips over her cheeks and nose and forehead and eyes. If not for the tape she would have bitten him, and even though she could not bite him, he seemed to sense this and steered clear of her mouth. Perhaps he didn't want to feel the tape on his face. Perhaps that would destroy the fantasy. The button Dino had fastened on her raincoat was still fastened, and as Legless kissed her face he mumbled something about being sorry for the way he had acted earlier and that he would make it up to her.

As Legless began fiddling with the button holding her raincoat together, the tailgate behind the rear seat suddenly opened and the cold wet air of the night came inside the van. When she turned to look back she saw the outline of a bald head. Max Lamberti came in through the tailgate, stepping up into the narrow space behind the seat and cuffing Legless away from her.

"Fuck off on your own time," growled Max, a shadowy hand at his scalp as if expecting to find hair to straighten. "You and Jimmy take her in the car. We got someone else to put in the hot seat and there's not enough room in here to do what we got to do."

When her shoulder belt was off, Max leaned close to her ear and whispered.

"Who knows, Mrs. Babe. Maybe if things go right and we get what we want, you and hubby might even be able to go back into that hell-hole and finish out your fuckin' lives."

In a louder voice meant for Legless, Max said, "Take her out the side door. Keep her with you guys while we get hubby ready for therapy. And if therapy don't work, fuck it, there'll be more food in the world for those less fortunate."

Although this final statement had been meant to sound like an aside, or to sound as if it contained some kind of upside-down ethical principle, Jan knew what it meant. There was no way Max would let them go whether they told him what he wanted to know or not. And, even though he'd had a stroke, she knew Steve would feel the same way.

After Max was gone, Legless and the guy named Jimmy, also wearing a knit cap, hustled her out of the van. It was still windy but the rain had stopped. Although her ankle exploded with pain whenever she put weight on it, she felt unfettered compared to inside the van. If she dropped to the ground, maybe she could roll to one side and trip the one named Jimmy who was smaller than Max or Dino or even Legless. Maybe she could stand up and run. Ignore the pain and run like hell. Or maybe in the process of falling she could rub her face against one of them, dislodge the tape, and scream loud enough and long enough to be heard clear across to the other side of the building, or even inside the building.

As she thought about this, Max and Dino came out from behind the van. Dino carried a bundle over one shoulder. Although it was dark in the parking lot, her eyes had grown accustomed to the darkness and she saw legs dangling and realized the bundle was someone wrapped in something. When a barely audible moan came from the person being carried, she knew it must be Steve. If she was going to make a move, now was the time. But something stopped her.

It was a voice, Steve's voice. Not his voice coming from the bundle, but his voice coming to her from the distant past, back when they first met. She had been telling Steve about her past, about her life as a stripper. She remembered the way he had looked at her for a long time before saying, "Nothing in life is ever what it appears to be. When you were working in those places, you weren't at all what you seemed. Although the men watching you had thoughts about who you were, we both know those thoughts were simply illusions. Just as illusions change from moment to moment, people also change from moment to moment. Who we were a moment ago is not who we are now. When it comes to time, we're all wandering Gypsies."

Recalling Steve's words made her want to plead that she be allowed to embrace him. But recalling these words from the past also stopped time. And in that instant of stopped time, she felt as though she had absorbed into her mind some of the precious thoughts that had been lost to Steve when he had his stroke. Details not only from their lives together, but details from every case he'd ever had. Among these details was the strong impression that the bundle being carried by Dino was not Steve at all, but someone with much longer legs.

And so she did not struggle when they led her to the car and put her into the back seat. Jimmy crawled in first and dragged her in behind him, then Legless vaulted in beside her, folding his wheelchair and dragging it in so that it rested on the floor in front of him. From inside the car she watched as the bundle was loaded into the van, Dino and Max climbing in after it and activating the mechanism that brought the lift back inside. The transfer into the van had been done carefully, like transferring someone in pain from wheelchair to bed. Or like transferring someone so as little as possible could be seen of him.

As she sat between Jimmy and Legless in the back seat, watching and listening as Legless lowered the window, she was convinced the man carried into the van was not Steve. If they wanted them to talk, wouldn't they have kept them both in the van? And if they had them both, why stay here instead of driving somewhere else? But, no sooner had these thoughts consoled her for the decision not to act, and she began to have doubts. What if it was Steve in the van?

Between the headrests of the front seat of the car she could see the red and green lights of a scanner mounted high in front of the dash. But, although the scanner was on and sometimes flashed its lights indicating it was moving to a new signal, no sound came from it. Then she began to hear noises coming from the van, dull thumping noises followed by long, deep moans. As the moans that might or might not be coming from Steve drifted in through the car window with the damp cold air, Jimmy and Legless began running their hands over her body, quickly finding places to go inside beneath her clothes.

The moans from the van became louder. The cold, cold hands searching her flesh absorbed whatever warmth was left in her. She began trembling uncontrollably.

Because of the turn of events that led him to Orland Park, and the radio call that brought him back to Hell in the Woods, Steve knew Jan's investigation of Marjorie's death had touched a sensitive nerve. Jan was missing, and regardless of his condition he was determined to find her.

As he drove through the main parking lot he saw Jan's Audi, its red finish glowing wet beneath the overhead lights. A squad car was parked next to the Audi with only its parking lights lit. He drove down the aisle slowly and could see that the Audi's driver's side was dented and scratched and the driver's side window was open. No, smashed in, the radio call had said the window was smashed in. Mud was spattered on the downslope of the rear fenders, and as he continued down the aisle away from the Audi, he tried to reconstruct the damage to the side of the Audi in his screwed-up brain so he could garner what he could from the details.

The image was still there, glowing beneath the overhead lights in his brain. Not a clean sweep, not scratch marks going in one direction. Zigzag scratch marks as if someone had driven into the side of the Audi. And then there were the tires. Not rain tires with the deep center groove the way he'd expected. But wait. Jan hadn't said anything about buying rain tires. His brain had created that. But there was something about rain tires.

Suddenly he recalled a brightly lit tire store, the strong smell of rubber tires and a particular tire in a display stand as he ran his finger down its deep center groove. A discussion comparing the grooves in the tires to arteries had taken place in his room at Hell in the Woods while he and Jan looked at an illustrated magazine ad for rain tires. But it was not Jan's Audi that had rain tires. It was his old Honda.

The train of thought was moving too fast, moving away from where he wanted it to be. The rain tires were important because he had seen rain tire tracks at the dead end. The dead end was important because that's where the police calls and the trail of discarded magazines had led him. The trail of magazines was important because they must have come from inside Jan's Audi. And if they had come from inside the Audi, then Jan must have thrown them from the Audi as she was being pursued.

One of the obvious things he could do tempted him. He could turn down the next aisle in the lot and approach from the other direction. He could pull into the vacant spot facing the squad car that was parked next to Jan's Audi. He could flash his lights and one of the officers in the car would come to his window and he would struggle to tell the officer his dilemma.

But there was danger in this train of thought. Down the line, after the struggle to explain—first to one officer, then to the other, then to a detective who would be called—he could visualize his being taken back into Hell in the Woods where one of his therapists—or even one of the crack Hell in the Woods psychological interns—would have made the drive in to assist with the questioning. He could see it all, an endless night of not being able to explain, while the possibility of finding Jan becomes more remote. He was a stroke victim, the inside of his brain like a snake eating its tail, especially if it has to think of too much at one time. During the questioning, as the possibility of finding Jan faded, his attempts to logically explain the situation would become more and more futile.

Even thinking about being questioned was dangerous because he imagined a man in shadows questioning him, and this man became the one from the past, the one who could be his father, or Joe Friday, or a grown-up Dwayne Matusak, or even Sandor Lakatos who would at any moment reach behind him for his violin, put it beneath his chin, close his dark eyes, and begin playing. Or it could be Jimmy Carter. What was there about Jimmy Carter that kept dipping into the soup?

Was it Marjorie's mention of her husband's distain for Carter? Was every crazy thing ever told him by Marjorie simply adding to the jumble in his head?

He kept driving, circling the huge parking lot, pausing only to glance down at the notes he'd written and remembering to look for cars or vans that matched the descriptions and plate numbers he'd gotten from Tamara. But even though he looked for vehicles and plate numbers, he could not help thinking about the magazines he'd seen strewn on the road, and about the rain tire tracks he'd seen in the mud at the dead end, and about the Audi's dented side and broken window and the mud on the downslope of its fenders.

As he approached the section of the lot adjoining the long nursing home wing that stuck out into the woods, he saw the narrow road that led around to the back lot where staff parked and where trucks made deliveries to the loading dock, the same loading dock onto which he'd emerged when he escaped from Hell in the Woods earlier that evening. Out through the delivery entrance because there were no guards there. And if one or more of Marjorie's relatives, or whoever else might have killed her, had reason to take Jan, then they might have come back here to get him, to take him out through the delivery entrance where they would not be stopped.

That must be it. He knew something they needed kept quiet, something to do with family secrets. Or maybe he knew something they needed to know, something to do with the keys Marjorie referred to. If either of these possibilities were true, Marjorie's killer, or killers, would come after him by going into Hell in the Woods the back way, the same way they went in when they killed Marjorie in the first place.

When he turned onto the narrow road leading to the back parking lot, headlights blinded him. A tall vehicle, a truck, came at him, going fast, bouncing up and down on the uneven pavement so that the blinding caused by the headlights was complete and he had to pull the Lincoln to the side and stop.

As the truck roared past, he glanced up at the boxy shape of it and saw something that made him pause, something that brought back recent words spoken to him harshly while he lay in pain on the floor of his room. Stenciled on the white side of the truck box in huge black letters were the words, "Christ Health Care Supplies."

The truck continued past him down the narrow access road toward the main lot. Steve watched it in his side mirror. It said, "Christ Health Care Supplies" on its back doors and as he stared at the receding truck, strange thoughts went through his mind. When he was young, his mother had wanted him to become a priest. He wasn't sure if he actually remembered this or if he was simply recalling what he'd been told by Jan following the stroke. His mother had wanted him to become more Christ-like. But this also seemed strange because in his mind now was an intense feeling that Christ was evil. No, not Christ, not Jesus Christ himself. A friend of Jesus Christ. Yes, a friend of Jesus Christ would come along next time to warn him about his interest in how Marjorie slipped and fell in the hallway near the janitors' closet where he was first warned by—what was his name?—Tyrone! Yes, Tyrone had warned him in the janitors' closet, and very recently—was it last night?—Tyrone had warned him again. And within that warning had been the threat that a friend of Christ himself would come next time.

He cranked the steering wheel around and floored the Lincoln, spinning the tires on the lawn and squealing them on the access road as he chased after the Christ Health Care truck. Probably because the truck slowed down in the lot so as not to attract the attention of the cops next to Jan's car, he caught up to it on the main road just beyond the traffic signal at the Hell in the Woods entrance.

The truck had double rear wheels and he knew it was not the vehicle with the single set of rain tires. Also, it was not one of the vehicles on his list. But the fact the truck was here now, with Jan missing and someone worried about what she knew and what he knew, along with the fact the driver of the truck seemed in a hurry . . . all of this was enough to make him follow.

Maybe he'd been wrong all along in thinking Marjorie's death had something to do with her family, or with some conspiracy. Maybe the aide named Tyrone really did have something to do with her death. And if he did, then maybe Tyrone, and whoever was driving the Christ truck, knew where Jan was.

As the truck moved farther away from Hell in the Woods, the driver eased off, not seeming so much in a hurry. And in the traffic, Steve was able to tuck in close behind, out of sight of the side mirrors, and imagine that maybe Jan was in the back of the truck. Or, if not, maybe the truck had been sent after him and, having failed to find him in his room on the third floor, was returning to wherever Jan was being held. Maybe the leather jacket guy from the television lounge, having discovered that he was missing from his room, was also inside the Christ Health Care truck.

Details. A reason for everything. A reason for living. The engine of the Lincoln responding to his left foot as he tailgates the truck on which the word "Christ" is stenciled. The word "Christ" drawing him forward toward salvation.

Toward Jan.

As Valdez exited east on Interstate 290, he saw a sign announcing they were on the Eisenhower Expressway and he thought, yet another expressway named after a dead President. On the Eisenhower, traffic slowed and became sluggish, making Valdez think of sluggish economies and inflation and recessions of the past. Spray lifting from the wet pavement coated the windshield of the rental car. The wiper blades, obviously in need of changing, left phlegmy streaks that reflected red taillights and yellowish overhead lights. Beside him, Hanley cleared his throat as if about to say something, but was silent.

Their last conversation had been about Jimmy Carter's defeat at the hands of Ronald Reagan in 1980, and about an unnecessary conspiracy to guarantee the election's outcome. Valdez wondered if Jimmy Carter would ever have expressways named after him. Perhaps he already did in Georgia, but Valdez had not traveled to Atlanta in a while and was not sure. The Jimmy Carter Expressway simply sounded like something that should be on evening traffic reports in Atlanta.

Valdez thought back to his phone conversation with Skinner on the secure line as he was about to eat his dinner back in his Miami apartment. Although the phone call had been earlier in the day, it seemed like several days had gone by. He should have known when he became part of Operation Maturity that it would some day come to this. Clever name, Skinner had insisted in the beginning. OM as in Old Man, from his and Skinner's amateur radio days, but in this case it really meant Old Men because there were several still alive who knew of the various election games played in recent decades.

Although one side of the political spectrum played a little rougher, both sides had played these games. And, Valdez knew, both sides and the entire political fabric of the nation would be severely damaged if any of the games were revealed. The media and the public were excited by contests. They cheered and jeered the contestants as if they were sports figures, but in the end they would abandon the game if they knew what had gone on behind the scenes. In a way the nation would have a stroke, a final stroke in which the stroke victims forget everything handed down by the forefathers.

When traffic slowed to a crawl, Valdez was able to turn off the windshield wipers. He glanced toward the passenger seat. Although it was dark out, the overhead expressway lights allowed him to see Hanley had closed his eyes.

"Looks like it will be a while before we arrive at the rehabilitation facility," he said.

"So it does," said Hanley, opening his eyes.

"You don't seem anxious about it."

Hanley cleared his throat. "I'm not. Our contact will wait for us. Whatever happens happens."

"That's not like you," said Valdez.

"It's the weather this evening," said Hanley. "Did you ever notice that when the weather is like this, the years seem to catch up?"

"Yes," said Valdez. "I was just having nostalgic thoughts. Expressways named after Presidents who were in power when we were young men."

"I know they've got an Eisenhower and a Kennedy Expressway in Chicago," said Hanley. "What others do they have?"

"The others are named after local dead politicians," said Valdez. "Except the Stevenson. From Illinois, but a national figure. Remember Stevenson at the UN during the Cuban Missile Crisis?"

"I do," said Hanley. Then in an oratorical voice, "Mr. Ambassador, I'm prepared to wait until Hell freezes over for your answer."

Valdez chuckled, "Now we really sound like two old goats."

"But not old enough to know about those elections," said Hanley.

"What about them?" asked Valdez.

"I was simply wondering if tricks had been played during the Eisenhower-Stevenson or Kennedy-Nixon campaigns. I guess enough time has passed. By the time someone decides to look into those elections in more detail, any heads that might have rolled will be six feet under."

"I know what you mean," said Valdez, as he signaled to move into the right lane.

"Is our exit coming up?" asked Hanley. "I didn't hear the GPS lady."

"Not yet," said Valdez. "But I can see by the arrow on the display that our exit will be on the right and I don't want to be held hostage in this lane."

"That's a telling comment," said Hanley.

"What is?"

"Being held hostage," said Hanley. "You've obviously been contemplating what I said earlier."

"What's that?" asked Valdez.

"Come now," said Hanley, turning part way toward him in his seat. "You know what this is all about."

"How could I?"

"Skinner's spoken to you, too, hasn't he?"

"He has," said Valdez.

Hanley turned back to the windshield and looked ahead. "Yes, he told me you knew some of it. And I can only assume you've guessed the rest." Hanley smiled at the windshield. "Mentioning hostages like that."

"All right," said Valdez. "Maybe I guessed the hostages were purposely held until Reagan was inaugurated. But many pundits and bloggers have also pondered this."

"It's not so much the timing of the release," said Hanley. "More important are the maneuverings that took place in order to return Iran's eight billion in frozen assets. Part of the maneuvering that occurred can be linked directly to the situation we've been assigned to address. In short, if someone manages to follow the money—all of the money—they might find out that a portion of the frozen assets, albeit a tiny portion, was liquidated by a long-gone idiot who funneled funds to Illinois."

The GPS lady interrupted, saying to prepare to exit on the right in two miles. Traffic still crawled, so despite the GPS lady's forewarning, it would be a distant two miles.

Valdez turned to glance at Hanley, then looked back out at the tail-lights of the car ahead. "There can't be many who know about this."

"Let's hope not," said Hanley.

Hanley turned in his seat again, this time to reach into the back seat. He retrieved one of the briefcases they had picked up at the company warehouse, placed the briefcase on his lap, and stared back out the windshield at the traffic.

Steve pulled alongside the truck at a stoplight to take a look at the driver. Because of the height of the truck, he had to lean to the side toward the passenger window in order to look up at the driver. Normally this would not have been a problem. But he was a stroker, his brain thinking the right foot would take care of things as the left foot slipped off the brake allowing the Lincoln to roll forward into the intersection. A car speeding across the intersection swerved and sounded its horn as Steve sat back behind the wheel and slammed the brake back on.

He glanced into the mirror to make sure no one was behind him, then put the Lincoln in reverse and backed up. After he reached over with his left hand and put the transmission into Park, he leaned over again to have a look. Inside the truck, a man with dark hair held something white to his face. When the man removed the white thing, holding it in front of him and looking at it in the glow from the streetlight above, Steve saw what looked like a handkerchief.

The man's nose was bleeding. A flat nose. A flat nose and something familiar in the man's eyes when he suddenly glanced down at Steve. The man's eyes opened wide for a second before he faced forward and the truck's engine roared and the letters "C-h-r-i-s-t" flashed past as the truck sped away.

As Steve chased the truck, weaving in and out of traffic, his left foot back and forth between gas and brake, his left hand dancing on the wheel like that of a mad puppeteer, memories of where he'd seen the man with the flat nose emerged from the traffic jam in his head.

Hell in the Woods. Someone on staff. No, with someone. Tyrone. The man with the flat nose had been with Tyrone in a small dimly lit place that smells of cleaning fluids and the sweat of angry men. The janitors' closet.

The truck turned west, then north, then east, trying to lose him on dark narrow side streets. When the truck sideswiped a double-parked car, Steve knew the chase was on. When he sideswiped the same car, the jolt sent spasms of pain through his right side. He thought he heard himself shouting in pain, but his voice came to him from a distance. There was no time for pain. Not here, not now. He glanced in his mirror and realized the shouting in the distance came from a man running down the middle of the street.

Several blocks farther on, at a stop sign, the truck turned south, back on a wide street with streetlights and other traffic, back the way Steve had come earlier. If the truck continued this way they'd cross over the Stevenson Expressway. But if the truck got on the expressway . . .

No! He couldn't afford to prolong this. Jan was in danger and the man with the flat and bloody nose knew something.

In a dimly lit section where traffic eased up, Steve floored the Lincoln and managed to get up on the right side of the truck. His plan was to try to push the truck into parked cars on the other side of the street. He would push it with the Lincoln's left side because he needed the right-hand door to get out into his wheelchair.

The Lincoln tore into the truck just behind its front wheel. The cowling beneath the Lincoln's front bumper ripped back into its tire and the left front fender of the Lincoln pressed against the truck's tire, making buzz saw sounds. The Lincoln's left headlight blew.

Despite the noise and vibration, Steve continued steering into the truck. The guy with the flat nose knew something. If he died trying to stop this guy, well then, he'd just die. At least he'd die knowing he'd done what he could to find Jan. The possibility of Jan being dead made him turn the wheel even more to the left.

Parked cars coming up fast ahead. Collision soon. But the pavement was too wet and the truck too heavy for the Lincoln. Steering wheel turned full left, but the Lincoln continued straight ahead, then to the right, across the road. Parked cars there, too. No choice but to straighten the Lincoln's wheels and slam on the brakes at the last second.

The Lincoln's left front shuddered when he continued the chase. He could see by the unevenness where the hood was supposed to meet the top of the fender that he'd done a job on the Lincoln's left side. Fine, a guy crippled on the right side driving a car crippled on the left side. As he drove he realized he was sitting toward the center of the front seat, having apparently moved over while the Lincoln was doing its best to force the truck into parked cars.

Most of the businesses and stores they passed were dimmed for the night, some with security gates pulled closed. But when they passed a brightly lit drugstore, Steve had a sudden flash of memory that threatened to sidetrack him.

A drugstore in Cleveland. Arriving there after the shooting. Sue shot and not a damn thing he could do about it. Suddenly it was there before him. A night long ago paralleling this night.

Expressway coming up. No way to catch the truck if it gets on. No way for the Lincoln to keep up with its front end so badly damaged. And cops. Someone will see the two of them speeding down the expressway and call the cops, and instead of finding Jan, there'll be nothing but questions without answers.

He had to do something. And so, when the truck slowed to make its turn at the corner onto the expressway ramp, Steve maintained the Lincoln's speed, jumped the curb up onto the sidewalk, just missing a light pole, put the Lincoln into a slide that took out a trash can, and slid the tail end of the Lincoln onto the entrance ramp and into the side of the truck.

This time the Lincoln made its mark, changing the direction of the truck and forcing it off the ramp, over the narrow shoulder and down an embankment into the tall chain-link fence that kept pedestrians from wandering down the slope of the hill and onto the expressway. The Lincoln also started down the embankment backward, but Steve straightened the wheel and floored the Lincoln, barely managing to keep it up on the road.

Although traffic moved below on the expressway, the ramp was quiet and dark and no one else had turned onto it. He stopped the Lincoln on the edge of the ramp facing down at the cars speeding along the expressway just in time to see the flat-nosed man jump out of the truck's passenger door and begin running along the fence back up toward the lights on the overpass.

Despite pain in his right side that felt like the lick of flames, he had no choice. He didn't know it for certain, but there was a good chance this man could help him find Jan. It was time to do another of those automatic things he'd been able to do after his stroke. He gave the Lincoln a burst of speed in reverse, slammed on the brakes. He lowered the window all the way, reached into his side pocket, took out his forty-five, and cradled it in his impaired right hand while he released the safety with his left thumb. He carefully repositioned the barrel and held it tightly in his left hand. The flat-nosed man was on a steep part of the embankment near the fence, his figure silhouetted against the lights beneath the overpass as he climbed frantically, reaching forward to grab at the wet weeds.

Steve shouted, "Stop, motherfucker!"

When the man did not stop, but kept climbing closer to the overpass sidewalk and escape, Steve held the gun in his left hand, steadying his arm on the doorsill. Then, knowing full well he'd been a right-hand shooter, he aimed and squeezed the trigger with his left hand.

Above the sounds of traffic on the expressway, the man's scream, as he stumbled forward then slid back down the wet embankment, sounded like the chirp of a bird. He fell like a bird, scrambling on the ground, his arms flopping around like he was trying to fly off the face of a cliff. He did not fly. Instead, his arms and legs found the ground and he began crawling, regaining the ground he'd lost. As he climbed, the man looked behind as if the bullet had come from down the embankment instead of from the side. Although he crawled awkwardly because of the bullet in his foot, the man seemed oblivious to Steve, even when Steve shouted he would shoot again. The wound did not seem fatal, but the man was like an animal crawling into a corner to die. To the flat-nosed man, the only thing that seemed to matter was getting to the top of the embankment.

Steve opened the driver's door to make sure it was not damaged in either of the collisions with the truck. The door was okay and he slammed it and put the Lincoln in reverse and backed all the way up the ramp. Then he shut off the Lincoln's lights and pulled onto the overpass in reverse, backing slowly along the curb, then up onto the sidewalk to the place where the fence on the embankment joined the fence that kept kids from throwing things down onto the expressway from the overpass.

By backing the Lincoln onto the sidewalk he blocked the path of the flat-nosed man. A car going onto the overpass slowed, a man and woman inside staring at the idiot who had not only pulled onto the sidewalk, but was facing the wrong way. But the couple in the car continued on their way and he was thankful that, until now, he hadn't seen one squad car except for the one in the parking lot a couple miles back at Hell in the Woods.

When the flat-nosed man appeared at the top of the embankment he was still looking behind him. Although Steve could not hear him because of the din of traffic on the expressway below, he could see, by his rhythmic movements, that the man was panting from exhaustion and in a state of panic. If he pointed his gun at the man and told him to stop, he'd probably turn to go back down the embankment, or fall backward down the embankment.

He needed to talk to this man. And so he positioned the Lincoln, inching forward a bit to put the driver's door even with the man. Then he shoved the transmission into Park, and, just as the man reached the edge of the sidewalk and turned to see where he'd go from there, Steve pushed the heavy door open as hard as he could and caught the flat-nosed man full in the chest.

The weeds beyond the edge of the sidewalk were wet. He could feel the wetness on both hands, but mostly on his left hand. He had thrown the forty-five on the passenger seat before diving out onto the ground with the flat-nosed man. The courtesy light on the Lincoln's door shown in the flat-nosed man's eyes as he lay on his side staring at

Steve. They lay side-by-side in the weeds like kids playing hide-and-seek for just a moment before the flat-nosed man began scrambling away.

When Steve reached out and grabbed a handful of jacket, the man fought him, screaming, "You shot my fuckin' foot!"

The man was wriggling away, Steve's left hand barely hanging on as the man pulled him along. Right hand seeming to flop around uncontrollably. But then Steve managed to get his right arm around the guy's waist, and when he did this he let go with his left hand and reached for the guy's neck. But the flat-nosed man was too fast for him, and he slid down the guy's flank. It was like trying to catch a reptile. And soon the reptile would slither away.

He needed to know what this man knew! He needed to do something! He'd had a goddamn stroke and there wasn't much he could do. He needed an edge. So he reached around the man, and with his left hand, grabbed a handful of the guy's crotch and squeezed.

The guy's fists seemed relentless, so much so that Steve thought he might go unconscious. But he stayed with it, squeezing as hard and he could, and eventually the screaming and cursing and flailing subsided, the guy realizing that the squeezing was reduced only when he stopped swinging his fists. During this tirade, Steve got hit a couple good ones in the neck and jaw. As it had many times since the stroke during bouts of intense pain, his brain put on an illusory show, making him visualize his nerve endings as tentacled creatures separate from himself. Then he screamed into the face of the flat-nosed man.

"Fuck you, pain! Little worm bastards inside me tougher than you! Little bastards'll get out and eat you! Eat me from inside out, then eat you, motherfuck! Burn me up, worm fuckers! I give a fuck! Burn me up, nerve fuckers!"

The pinkish-bluish glare from the overhead expressway lights gave the flat-nosed man's face an eerie radiance and Steve could tell by the look on the guy's face that his own face also looked eerie, perhaps even more so because he probably had on his stroke grin. And now that he'd said what he'd said about his nerve endings, the guy's eyes had opened wide.

When he said, "No time for mess," the guy gave him a puzzled look, but his eyes were still open wide and he began shaking like any tough guy who's forced to cross a certain threshold.

"What, man? What?!"

"Talk!"

"Talk to who? About what? You shot my fuckin' foot and . . ."

He gave the guy's balls a good squeeze to let him know this wasn't the way he wanted the conversation to go.

He pushed his face closer, their noses touching. "Desperate! Got to know what at Hell in Woods! I'll fucking take you apart down there! If . . . if you don't tell . . ."

"Tell what?!"

"Why?"

"Why what? Jesus Christ!"

"Why Jesus Christ truck left fast?"

"I left fast 'cause I wanted the hell out of there! I'm tellin' the truth, man. Quit squeezin'! Jesus Christ!"

"What happened?"

"What happened where? Holy shit! Okay! Okay!"

"Talk!"

"I was goin' there to meet someone."

"Who?"

"Oh shit!"

"Who?!"

"I was goin' there to meet Tyrone!"

"What happened?"

"How the fuck? Oh, Ma! Geez!"

"Who and what? Exactly! Now!"

"Okay! I was goin' there to meet Tyrone. He meets me at the loading dock for deliveries. Only this time instead of him meeting me, I see spaghetti heads carrying him out the back door and he's screamin' for help! Hey! Easy! Goddamn! Okay! So I try to help, but this heavyweight spaghetti head comes over and lays a pile driver on me. Then I get the fuck out!"

"What about woman?"

"Woman?"

"With Tyrone!"

"Was no woman, just spaghetti heads."

"Where's Tyrone?"

"You mean right now?"

"No. Back there!"

"Those guys took him."

"Where?"

"Somewhere out in the parking lot. I saw a bunch of 'em by a van. They stuck Tyrone's ass in the van and got back in their cars. That's when I got the fuck out!"

When Steve let go his grip and began crawling as fast as he could toward the open door of the Lincoln, the flat-nosed man held himself with both hands and curled up in the weeds like a baby. The last thing Steve heard him say was, "Oh shit, what kinda night is this?"

Back inside the Lincoln Steve got the engine started but couldn't get his left foot to the pedals because his right leg was in the way. He reached down with his left hand, pulled at the leg and realized the leg brace had slipped, allowing the leg to go crooked and helpless. He reached down with both hands, trying to force the right hand to help, and after several tugs was able to pull the leg brace back into place, allowing him to lift his right leg back where it belonged. For all he knew it could be broken, but he didn't have time for that now.

After he put the Lincoln into drive and bounced it down the curb and across to the right side of the road, the seatbelt warning sounded and the pain in his right side threatened to take over the way it had when the flat-nosed man was pummeling him. Only this pain was even worse. More pain then he could ever remember. But he was a damn half-brainer, and half-brainers weren't supposed to be able to remember everything. So why not forget pain? He'd probably had greater pain than this. Right side muscles not on fire from pain but from exertion. Concentrate. Concentrate! Fuck the pain!

While driving back to Hell in the Woods, he felt as if he'd gone beyond a critical threshold. The pain was still there, but it didn't matter anymore. The pain didn't tell his muscles what he could or couldn't do anymore. He clenched and unclenched the fist of his right hand as he drove. Of course it was still weak, but it would come back with therapy. He'd promised Jan he would do his best, take the therapy all the way to its completion. Now maybe he'd have his chance.

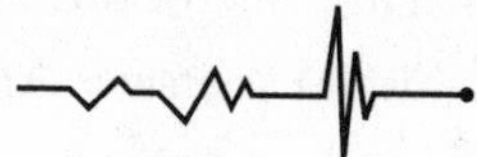

There were three worlds.

In the first world, the side door to the van was open slightly so she would be able to hear the beating taking place a few feet away. Besides the obvious sounds of blows landing on flesh, she heard guttural moaning. Random syllables, the kinds of sounds Steve was able to make when he first came to after his stroke.

In the second world, a large man without legs and a smaller man with legs groped her beneath her raincoat and slacks. Because there were two of them and they were crammed into the back seat of the car, resisting seemed pointless. Whenever she turned away from one, the other would be there.

In the third world, she inflicted great pain upon her wrist, bending it far back, then using her weight pressed upon the bent wrist to bend it back even more. She was Houdini, about to escape the locked box so she could rescue her lover from another locked box. By bending her wrist in a way it had never been meant to go, she had managed to get one finger beneath the edge of the tape and she wiggled this finger back and forth, tearing ever so slightly at the tape with her fingernail. In this world, the other two worlds might come crashing down. She could see it. The tape off. Then she strikes out, disabling her molesters long enough for her to leap from the car and tear open the van door to see if the man they are beating is really Steve. And if it is Steve?

If it is Steve, they might as well both die.

Suddenly, one beastly hand apparently touched another beastly hand in an attempt to reach deeper inside her slacks, and her molesters backed off and grunted as if an unacceptable line had been crossed.

Jimmy lit a cigarette and opened his side window to blow the smoke out. Legless lowered his window further and rolled his bulk toward the window to stick his head outside. And as she leaned forward and curled her shoulders together so that her raincoat fell back down to cover her breasts, a conversation began.

"Not like when the old man was around."

"Fuck no. None of this business when the old man was around."

"Family man."

"Yeah, fuckin' family man."

"So what's wrong with that?"

"Nothin'. Except in those days we'd be muscling each other. Today we nuke whoever the hell gets in the way."

"Money talks."

"Yeah, I can hear it. You hear it?"

"What?"

"Money. It's talkin' up there in the rain clouds."

"What the fuck you talkin' about?"

"Jets takin' off over where people are lined up in beds tryin' to get better."

"Well, as least it stopped raining."

"That's true. Weather channel said it'd rain all night. Guess they were wrong."

As another jet on takeoff rumbled above, she began to wonder if perhaps Steve had been right when he first came out of his stroke. Maybe sometimes it was better off being dead in this insane world.

CHAPTER THIRTY

A LONG TIME AGO, BACK IN THE NORMAL WORLD WHERE HE wasn't getting beat to a pulp, Tyrone recalled that Flat Nose called them spaghetti heads and said DeJesus got along real good with spaghetti heads. But if DeJesus knew these guys were going to be here, he certainly wouldn't have sent Flat Nose in because Flat Nose was probably still looking up at the front bumper of his truck wondering how the hell they got a truck up into a fight ring. One of the spaghetti heads beating on him had hair, the other one, obviously the boss, was bald.

When they let up on him, giving their fists a rest, one of them turned on a police scanner and listened for a while, saying something about hoping he'd get his money's worth out of all the expensive equipment. When the guy turned off the scanner, the two started talking like guys on a coffee break, quiet and calm like none of this was happening, or like he wasn't even there. But he was right there with them and they must have known he could hear them.

"I should go see the fuckin' doc."

"Heartburn again?"

"I fuckin' hope so."

"A guy's job'll do that, especially when he takes it serious. You need a vacation."

"I know. We're not as young as we used to be. Be nice to be a buck again, fresh out of boot camp. I still had some hair then."

"You don't believe in that Samson and Delilah shit, do you?"

"You're younger than me. When you get to be my age, things start to creep up on you."

"Anything I can do to help?"

"Yeah. Win the Powerball and give me half."

"You think our odds are bad in this thing?"

"No, we got all the numbers. Or, if we don't got all the numbers, we at least got all the folks who got all the numbers in their heads."

"Too bad about your aunt's stroke."

"Yeah. If it hadn't been for that, I think she would've told me about it a long time ago."

"So what makes you think she told him?"

"Them."

"Okay, them. He knows, so she knows. Why'd she tell them?"

"Therapy. Going at it day in and day out. One day it slipped out. Only we didn't find out about it for a while because of that fuckin' Hogan. He should've been on top of the wife every minute. By the time we found out, aunty had another seizure and was in even worse shape."

"Booze makes a guy slip up."

"I think he'll have to be fucked up when this is over. If it's ever fuckin' over."

"It will be."

"Yeah, one way or another. Let's get back to it."

"You or me?"

"I'll fuckin' do it."

And so they went at him again, this time the bald guy while the one with hair kept propping him up, while jets took off for Vegas full of folks whose pockets were full of cash and whose heads were full of dreams.

He'd promised to take Latoya to Vegas one of these days and he'd do just that if he ever got out of this van alive. There was no better woman than Latoya when it came right down to it. She's the one nursed him back after that fight he got into with those Blackstone shorties, the six of them wiry as hell and all over him like flies on shit. Yeah, he was the shit for hasslin' the dumb little shorties in the first place. Not as big of fists as this guy has, but there were six of 'em. No, not as big of fists as this guy. These fists might even be bigger than DeJesus' fists.

If only they'd've let him talk in the first place he would've told them anything they wanted to hear. But he couldn't talk in the first place because of that damn tape they put on his mouth, same sticky tape they had on his wrists. When they got him in here and sat him in the back seat and put the damn seat belt on—joking about him being a pimp in the back seat of his limo and them wanting to take good care of him—he really wanted to talk. But they proceeded to beat shit out of him. And then, after beatin' shit out of him, they rip the tape off. But he can't talk, can't make his mouth do what he wants it to do. It's like being at the dentist and having a thousand shots of Novocain. Except this Novocain doesn't take away the pain, it delivers pain.

He was thankful when the guy stopped hitting him, so thankful he wanted to reach his arms out and hug the guy like he was his long-lost uncle. But his arms were taped behind him and he couldn't hug the guy, although he wanted to in the worst way because this would show the guy how grateful he really was. He tried to thank the guy, but all that came out were moans.

The guy moved in close as if he knew about the hugging. The guy's face was at the side of his face. The guy whispered into his ear.

"Okay, shithead, we're gonna let you talk now. You don't have to talk loud. I'm right here. You're gonna help us out, and in return, I'm gonna help you out. See, we're businessmen. And as you know, businessmen are sometimes in a hurry for information. That's why there are so many computers. We businessmen live on information. And sometimes, if we don't get the information we need when we need it, whole shitloads of cash get lost. You get my meaning?"

Tyrone nodded and moaned.

"Like I said, no need to talk loud. Just whisper it to me. I'm here for you."

"Ah . . . I'll . . . I'll tawk," Tyrone managed to get out after swallowing the blood in his mouth.

"Good, that's real good," the guy whispered back.

"I'll . . . I'll talk," Tyrone repeated, realizing whispering was a lot easier than talking out loud when all he could move was his tongue.

"Okay. I'm gonna listen real good. It's better if I hear what I want to hear the first time, because if I don't hear it the first time, there probably won't be another time. That's the way this business works. Okay, where's Steve Babe?"

Tyrone wanted to tell this guy exactly what he wanted to hear. He wanted to do it in the worst way. Unfortunately, he didn't know where Steve Babe was. He knew the guy wouldn't be happy if he told the truth, if he said he'd been in Babe's room looking for him because he wanted to hassle him some, but what else could he do? Maybe if he dressed it up some, maybe then the guy would be happy.

"The business world is waiting. Companies are being bought and sold as we speak."

No, he couldn't tell the truth. The last thing this guy wanted to hear was that he didn't know where Babe was. He'd have to make something up. He'd have to dress it up good and stick to it, otherwise this guy would see through him. He swallowed some blood clots that had gotten tied in knots at the back of his throat.

"I'm listening," whispered the guy as he put his ear to Tyrone's mouth.

"He . . . he had a stroke."

"I know he had a stroke."

"No, 'nother one. Tonight. They took him to hospital. Happened 'bout seven. They sent me to his room to get somethin' they needed at the hospital."

"What?"

"They sent me to his room to get somethin' they needed . . ."

"What did they send you to get?"

"They sent me to get his . . . medication."

"Don't they have plenty at the hospital?"

"Yeah, but they needed to know what doses he's on."

"What were the names of the medications?"

"I think Citicol was one . . . somethin' like that. They didn't tell me 'xactly. Jus' said get any medication vials he had in his room."

"Don't they have that on his chart at the nurses' station? Doesn't the staff deliver medication?"

"Yeah, but they think he had a stash an' been takin' more than they handed out. They think it might have somethin' to do with this new stroke he had. I was lookin' for vials in his drawers. I couldn't find nothin' and I just turned off the light and had to take a shit. We're not supposed to use the patients' cans so I didn't turn the light on."

"You know what, shithead?"

"What?"

"I think this story of yours is gettin' a little too fuckin' long.

Nurses don't give pills to patients so they can take them whenever they feel like it!"

The guy backed off, paused a second, then hit Tyrone hard in the gut.

The world was full of shit. The fuckin' world with its fuckin' shorts with hearts and its fuckin' hospitals keepin' zombies alive and fuckin' jets takin' fuckin' losers to Vegas was full of shit. Flat Nose was full of shit, and DeJesus was full of shit, and this guy hitting him was full of shit. Medicare and Medicaid and the whole goddamn system was full of shit!

As he lay back in the seat, Tyrone tried to breathe in as much of the cool outside air coming in where the side door was cracked open. He tried to breathe all the cool night air there was in the universe into his lungs. He tried to suck something good out of the cool night air, something that would make the puke go back down, something that would make the shit in his shorts go back inside where it belonged.

The puke stayed down. The inside of the van stopped tossing and turning. For a moment he could rest because as long as they were talking, they couldn't be hitting him.

"So maybe he did have another stroke."

"No fuckin' way. Patty would've seen them take him away."

"Well, he wasn't there, and Patty didn't see him leave, so maybe Patty didn't do such a great fuckin' job."

"What about that guy Patty threw down the stairs? Maybe there's more than one nosy aide in the place."

"You think there are others who know about this?"

"I don't know what I think anymore. Anyway, you're the one brought Patty in on the job in the first place, and if something's up with Patty . . ."

"I can't know everything about everyone!"

"Fuck it! Enough!"

They had raised their voices, now they whispered again.

"She's got to think it's him in here. We got to count on that."

"What'll we do?"

"Get the fuck out before some cop decides to cruise back here."

"Where to?"

"Someplace graves are handy. Tell Jimmy and Legless to drive her in the car. You drive the van."

"Should I call up Patty?"

"No, leave him be in case Babe decides to come back."

The guy with a full head of hair turned and looked outside. "Hey, who're they?"

"You got your balls in an uproar. Didn't you hear what Patty said? According to my watch, this must be it. A few cars'll come in and they'll park and some folks'll go inside. After that, a few folks'll come out and get in their cars and drive away. It's called a shift change."

"I know what it's fuckin' called. Do we take off now or not?"

"Wait 'til the shift change is over. Shouldn't take long."

When Tyrone heard this it took him a second to realize the tape was still off his mouth before he took a deep breath and did his best to scream. What came out was more like a death rattle. And just as the death rattle began to change into a real scream, the bald guy's two big hands closed around his neck and cut him off.

Instead of simply applying a piece of tape to his mouth like last time, the guy with a full head of hair reached over the top of the bald guy doing the choking and wrapped a length of tape around Tyrone's head several times, covering his mouth *and* his nose.

He was dead. He knew it.

But then the guy who'd been doing the choking took hold of the top edge of the tape near Tyrone's eyes and yanked the tape down so it was bunched up just below his nostrils. The guy used the bunched up tape to shake Tyrone's head up and down in an exaggerated nod.

"Next time we ask for answers, we'll fuckin' get 'em, right?"

Where a moment earlier the cool night air had been somewhat of a relief, now the air was damp and smelled of tape adhesive and the wet trees and wet earth that bordered the parking lot. All Tyrone could think of was a hole in the ground with him in it, the damp earth covering him and stopping the breath of life. Suddenly he began to shiver uncontrollably.

CHAPTER THIRTY-ONE

As Valdez turned onto the exit ramp, the GPS system sounded the double bell indicating they were at their turnoff. Beside him, beneath the bright overhead lights of the exit ramp, Valdez could see that Hanley had finished loading three magazines and was sliding one of the magazines into a Sig Sauer pistol. Valdez caught a detailed glimpse of the pistol.

"Did they give us P229s?" asked Valdez.

"No," said Hanley. "It's the newer Sig Pro that the DEA and the French use. It comes with an attachment."

Hanley reached into the briefcase and pulled out a tubular object. He held up the object and Valdez could see it was a silencer. Hanley put the pistol along with its silencer and the magazines away carefully beneath his golf jacket, then he dug inside the briefcase once more and held up several pairs of latex gloves. "Extras," he said.

After putting the latex gloves away in his jacket, Hanley reached again into the back seat, returning his briefcase to the back and retrieving Valdez's briefcase. Hanley opened this briefcase and began the process of loading Valdez's Sig Sauer along with two extra magazines.

Once off the Eisenhower Expressway, Valdez headed south. He saw by the GPS display that Saint Mel in the Woods Rehabilitation Facility was five miles away. On city streets at this time on a Friday evening, Valdez figured it would take them less than a half hour to get there.

Hanley returned the second briefcase to the back seat and sat with Valdez's pistol, silencer, extra loaded magazines, and latex gloves in his lap. "I'll hang onto these until you get stopped by a light," he said, looking straight ahead.

"Do you think we'll need the Sigs?" asked Valdez.

"I don't know."

"Do they have night sights?"

"Yes."

At the next stoplight, Valdez put the magazines, silencer, and gloves into the inside pockets of his golf jacket and tucked the pistol into his waistband.

"How will we know if Lamberti or his men are straying too close to our territory?" asked Valdez, as he started off from the stoplight.

"I suppose we might ask about the condition of Mrs. Gianetti, a longtime rehab friend of our spouses," said Hanley.

"Do you think we'll have an opportunity to converse on that level?"

"From what our contacts have told us, I doubt it."

Valdez stopped the car at another stoplight and glanced at Hanley. "If we need to use our Sigs, what will the cover be?"

"An underworld dispute," said Hanley. "Langley arranged it with the New York office. East Coast bosses will have gotten upset that they lost drugs and money a long time ago and just now found out who was to blame. They will have sent in someone to represent their interests. Coincidentally, our Sigs were confiscated in New York not that long ago. And, to add to the confusion, Gianetti and his crew also use the Sig Pro. It's replaced their venerable Berettas."

Hanley stared at Valdez for a moment, then looked back out the windshield. Valdez thought he saw a slight trace of a smile from Hanley and wondered about it.

"The light is green," said Hanley

Valdez accelerated abruptly and glanced Hanley's way again. Although Hanley still stared out the windshield, Valdez thought he noticed a change in disposition in Hanley.

"If it comes down to it," said Valdez, "how will we be certain we have closure?"

"Perhaps we'll never have closure on this one," said Hanley.

"Is that because there are others out there?" asked Valdez.

Hanley was silent, so Valdez pressed him.

"If we follow the money to its end, will there be others?"

Hanley took off his golf cap, scratched his head, put his cap back on, and said, "Yes, there will be others."

Valdez looked at the GPS display and saw they were only three miles from the rehabilitation facility.

Although one guard at the front counter was new to Hell in the Woods and the other was a veteran, both of them were young.

"Must be shift change," said the new guard. "Back at the hospital you'd hardly notice shift changes."

"Why's that?" asked the veteran guard.

"Because things were more hectic at the hospital," said the new guard. "And because at the hospital there were a lot more exits."

"Were they monitored?" asked the veteran guard.

"Yeah. That's another reason I like this place better. My eyes used to get sore staring at all the monitors. Here you only got a few. And we hardly ever see anyone on them at night."

Both guards nodded toward a group of employees who were leaving, taking turns holding open the unlocked door to the side of the locked main doors.

"We should do a sociological study on the employees in this place," said the new guard.

"What do you mean?" asked the veteran guard.

"I was just noticing how many of the folks arriving and leaving by the front door are minorities. Too bad we don't have a monitor on the loading dock to see how many minorities come and go that way."

"We don't need a monitor back there," said the veteran guard. "Whoever's on kitchen duty makes sure only employees use the back door. But if we did have a monitor there, what do you think we'd see?"

"I think," said the new guard, putting a finger to his chin, "we'd see a higher proportion of minorities in and out the front door, while a higher proportion of non-minorities would be going in and out the back door. Kind of ironic when you think about it."

"You use the back door," said the veteran guard, smiling.

"That's because I've got a set of wheels," said the new guard, also smiling. "These folks without wheels use this entrance because it's closer to the bus stop, whereas folks who go out the back door, through the proverbial bowels of the building with all its noisy machinery, tend to be driving to their split levels in the suburbs."

"I live in a crumby one-bedroom apartment in the suburbs," said the veteran guard.

"I guess we're both exceptions. Me, because I've got wheels. You, because you don't own a split level. But I bet you will some day."

"On this salary?"

"Yeah, you got a point there, man."

The two guards watched as several late night shift stragglers rushed into the building, running through the door at the side of the lobby that led to the time clock.

"It's going to be a long night," said the new guard, standing and retrieving some change from his pocket.

"Yeah," said the veteran guard, staring off into space.

"How about I buy us a couple cups? You like yours black, like your women, right?"

The veteran guard turned to the new guard and grinned. "Yeah, thanks. Except you bought last time."

"I know, but these extra quarters'll wear out the pockets of my new uniform."

The veteran guard watched as his partner for the night strode to the side door that led to the vending machine room. After his partner was gone, the remaining guard turned and stared out at the dark night, his face reflected back to him from the glass of the front doors.

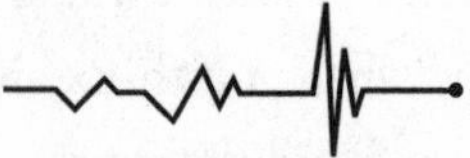

"What kinda night is this?" Steve said aloud to himself as he turned the Lincoln into the lighted entrance past the bus stop kiosk. Several people stood inside the kiosk, and several more were walking along the entrance road toward the kiosk, their heads down in the wind.

Once past the overhead lights at the entrance, he could see the darkened area resulting from the blown left front headlight of the Lincoln. Because he had slowed the Lincoln after the rush to get back here, the front end stopped rattling and shimmying and he could hear sirens in the distance. He had driven a different route back to avoid the area where the Christ Health Care truck and the Lincoln had sideswiped a double-parked car. At one intersection he had seen flashing lights a few blocks over and turned on the scanner. He heard several calls for the area go out, one of them significant. Someone had called to report seeing a truck off the road back at the expressway and a man lying in the weeds. An ambulance had already been dispatched. If Jan were here with him—if only she were here with him—he would repeat the words to her. "What kinda night is this?"

As he drove into the front parking lot, he saw the squad car was still there parked next to Jan's Audi. Inside the squad car, silhouetted against the bright lights at the main entrance in the distance, he could see the passenger hoist a large drinking mug to his lips. He looked at the tires on the squad car, then at the tires on Jan's car, then at the mud caked on the downslope of the Audi's fenders.

Tires. The word *tires* meant something. He had just said, "What kinda night is this?" and now, because of the pain in his right side, a wave of confusion and nausea came over him. It was as if all the confusion he'd had while in residence at Hell in the Woods had come flooding out the door of the main entrance and into the parking lot, the confusion spilling out like vomit, the pain throwing up a smokescreen.

He'd been here before. He'd heard the radio call about Jan's car being found and now he was back at Hell in the Woods. He was supposed to look at tires, but as the police scanner chattered beside him, other words got mixed in. And when the word *tired* emerged in his brain, he had to acknowledge that, yes, he was tired. Or was he retired? Seeing the cop drinking from a mug had stirred another memory. He was tired, and he was retired.

Confused, he drove up an aisle and came back around to drive past Jan's car once more. This time, because of the lack of reflection, he saw the driver's side window was open. No, not open, idiot! Busted out! You've been here before!

And he was here again because he'd seen tire marks south of Orland, then he'd heard the call go out about Jan's car being found. Tire marks south of Orland, and among those tire marks were the distinct tread imprints of rain tires with their deep center grooves.

He began driving slowly up and down the aisles of the parking lot looking carefully for cars with rain tires, glancing down to read the list of vehicles he'd gotten from Tamara to see if any of those vehicles, or a vehicle with rain tires, or both, might be here somewhere at Hell in the Woods. He'd seen rain tire tracks in the mud, and although it was a long shot, he felt Jan would be here at Hell in the Woods.

For a moment he speculated about the wobble in the Lincoln's front end and the unevenness he could see on top of the left front fender. Details raced around in his head and he had difficulty associating the damage to the Lincoln with his reason for being here until he recalled the run-in with the flat-nosed man on the expressway overpass. What if he'd had another seizure? Or, worse, what if his search for Jan had brought on another stroke that had already begun to plunder bits and pieces of memory trying to make connections, trying to rebuild the case?

The case! Marjorie Gianetti's case. Marjorie Gianetti dead at the far end of the nursing home wing. Marjorie Gianetti whose husband was a mob boss. Marjorie Gianetti who had kept secrets inside her for many years. Had the secrets come out in rehab? Without realizing it, did he now own those secrets? Family secrets that might have something to do with mob money or health care scams, or anything for that matter. Even Presidential elections. There was something about Presidential elections that bothered Marjorie whenever the topic came up. Something.

As he reached the end of an aisle and saw the narrow service road that led around the nursing home wing, he recalled the Christ Health Care truck coming toward him. He had turned around and chased it and confronted the flat-nosed man! The man had said, "Oh shit, what kinda night is this?"

No! The flat-nosed man had said more than that. Men had taken Tyrone out to a van in the back parking lot.

Headlights came down the narrow service road as he drove into it. Instead of driving to the side he held his ground, straddling both lanes and slowing down. The car coming toward him slowed. Then, when it was almost stopped, it veered off onto the grass and eased past him. The driver's window came down and he saw a young man shaking his fist at him and shouting something. Although he could not hear what the man said, he recognized the man. Young guy. Comes into his room after dinner to empty the wastebasket and replace the liner. New guy, no name yet because they haven't paraded him through name-recall therapy.

It was shift change. He pulled the Lincoln to the right in case other cars came out. If it was shift change, he could be an employee coming in for the late shift. An employee who had reason to drive into the back lot and look for a spot.

The back lot was dark compared to the main lot out front. There were lights at the perimeter of the lot, and lights at the loading dock, but the center of the lot was unlit, parked cars appearing as shadows flecked here and there with pinpoint reflections from windows and chrome. He recalled seeing employees use the nursing home wing for an indoor shortcut. He recalled that the door to the loading dock was alarmed, and assumed employees probably exited through the kitchen with its Employees Only sign on the door. But there were no employees to be seen and he realized the shift change must have come and gone.

Despite the blown left headlight, he did not turn on the Lincoln's brights. He drove neither too fast nor too slowly. As he drove up an aisle amongst the parked cars, he scanned the tires of the cars on both sides as soon as the single right low beam illuminated them. He also scanned the shapes he passed. Most were cars, but there were a few pickups and vans. When he reached the end of the aisle he had seen one set of rain tires with the characteristic center groove, but the tires were on an older small Nissan, not one of the vehicles on his list.

He pulled into a spot at the end of the aisle and turned off the lights, watching for any movement in the lot. He picked up his notepad from the seat beside him and held it up in the dim glow from an overhead light some distance away. He read through the vehicle registration information he'd gotten from Tamara. Things were beginning to fall back into place in his head. He hadn't had a stroke or a seizure earlier, but simply a lapse in his already feeble memory. He was tired, physically and mentally, and for a moment, when he'd first driven into the front entrance, he'd forgotten why he'd come back here.

After studying the registration information for a minute or so, he put the Lincoln in drive and allowed it to inch ahead by using the parking brake rather than the foot brake so the brake lights would not illuminate. After he had moved the Lincoln ahead two aisles, he turned on the lights and drove down this aisle neither too fast nor too slowly so he would appear to be an employee leaving after work.

Rain tires. The deep center groove. And above the tires, mud coming out from inside the rear fender wells, mud dripping from the fender wells onto the asphalt of the parking lot.

It was a Ford van. He could see the Ford insignia above and to one side of the rear plate. The plate on the van had a handicapped emblem, and it matched one of the plate registrations he'd gotten from Tamara.

Although the van had rear windows, they were very darkly tinted. But as he drove past, one of the overhead lights at the loading dock lined up just right and he could see its muted glare through the inside of the van. It was enough to make out the shadows of two people sitting at the back of the van. He was given a vague impression of heads and shoulders, that was all.

He kept moving, the Lincoln inching ahead. Next to the van was a full-size Crown Victoria. The plates on the car were on the list he had just studied. A van and a car, both registered to Lamberti Produce. Because the car was lower than the van, light from the loading dock did not shine through it. But as he passed the car, he could see that the rear window of the car on the side facing the van was partially open.

He did not stop, but kept the Lincoln moving up the aisle. Then, on the other side of the aisle, several parking spaces away from the car and van, he saw what appeared to be two men sitting in another Crown Victoria. He could see shoulders and heads, but no other features. Because of the shapes of the heads, he assumed both men were wearing close-fitting hats. The plate on this car was also on the list, also registered to Lamberti Produce.

Vehicles registered to the company owned by Marjorie's nephew were here. And from what he'd seen, he had to assume all three vehicles had passengers inside.

The nephew—Max the Fly, the fly in the ointment—was here, or at least his men were here. The son and his attorney dead in a so-called accident. Jan, obviously having been at the scene of the accident. Rain tires on the van . . .

All three vehicles faced the building, the van and one of the cars parked side by side, the other car parked across the aisle several spaces away. Steve studied their locations in the rearview mirror as he continued down the aisle. Rather than turn back up the next aisle, he kept going, driving out the way he'd come in on the narrow access road, steering the Lincoln with his left hand, but doing his best to assist in the steering by using his right hand.

Legless said, "Be my guest, sweetie."

"What the fuck you talkin' about?" asked Jimmy.

"That's what she said to call her," said Legless. "Ain't that right, sweetie?"

When a car drove slowly past behind them, Jimmy turned to look out the rear window. "How many times they change shifts in this place?"

"Who cares?" said Legless. "We don't care, do we, sweetie?"

"That's the same wreck with one headlight that came in a minute ago," said Jimmy.

"Young lovers lookin' for a place to make out," said Legless, touching her cheek.

Trying to cut the tape using her fingernail had not worked. But now, although her wrist felt like it would break, she managed to get a finger beneath the tape on her wrists. When the tape began to curl she pulled at the tape as hard as she could, not to tear it, because she knew she could not do that, but to take some of the pressure off the finger she had bent to such an excruciating angle. As she pulled at the tape, she realized it was slipping ever so slightly down her wrist. She shifted her weight to help the tape along.

"Look at this," said Legless, moving his hand along the side of her face and cupping the back of her head. "See? She wants more of what an experienced guy like me can give her. Ain't that right, sweetie? She'd say yes if it wasn't for the tape on her mouth."

Legless let go of her head and lifted himself by his arms, moving closer to her. Then he rolled over onto her the way he had in the van. His weight pressed down on her, pushing her back into the seat so she thought she would break her finger. She pushed harder at the tape, easing it farther down her wrist to relieve the pressure on her finger. When his weight pressed down on her leg, her foot was shoved forward beneath the front seat, her ankle bending sideways causing her to moan in pain.

Hearing this, Legless eased off, letting the weight of his torso slide off onto the seat, repositioning himself on his back so his head was in her lap.

"What the fuck you doin', Legless?"

"Takin' care of my sweetie. And she's takin' care of me."

"Yeah, real sweet," said Jimmy. "She probably pissed in her pants and you're layin' in it."

"It's coffee. She had an accident in the van."

"You spilled hot coffee on her?" asked Jimmy, with a touch of disgust in his voice.

"So what if I did?" said Legless.

"Yeah, I guess you would," said Jimmy.

"What's that supposed to mean?" asked Legless.

"Forget it," said Jimmy, lowering his window slightly and lighting another cigarette.

Legless rolled himself upright. "You gotta fuckin' stink it up in here again? How'd you like it if I cut a big one? I could pump out a good one after that burger and fries."

"That how you blew off your legs?"

"Oh, that's real funny. I bet the lady's impressed by your clever wit. We all got our crosses to bear. You, because you're a lousy grunt instead of in the driver's seat like you used to be. And me? Why, my cross pales by comparison."

"What the hell's the purpose of bringing that up?"

"The purpose of it was to have a conversation that would show the lady we're not complete barbarians."

"I think that would take some doing."

"You mean I have to do something more than simply talk to impress her?"

"No, I mean you'd have to spit out the Encyclopedia Britannica."

"Kinda like a saying a hundred Our Fathers and Hail Marys?"

"Yeah, something like that," said Jimmy, taking a deep drag on the cigarette, lighting his gaunt face orange, then exhaling and throwing the cigarette out before closing the window.

Keeping his face turned toward the window, Jimmy said, "Fine, I don't gotta fuckin' stink it up in here. But if I can't smoke, the least you could do is show a little respect."

"Respect for who?"

"Well, not me. But I think you owe it to her."

Legless leaned forward, whispering so he wouldn't shout, his foul breath on her face as he spoke harshly to Jimmy. "I don't owe nobody nothin'! Gook bitches who turned into Vietcong at night got my legs blown off, so as far as I'm concerned, I don't fuckin' owe nobody!"

Jimmy turned from the window. "And as far as I'm concerned," he said in an equally harsh whisper, "they fuckin' blew off the wrong fuckin' end of you!"

She thought Legless would roll over her lap and attack Jimmy. But instead, he grabbed her face and began kissing her.

"You're crazy," said Jimmy.

"I know," said Legless, smacking his lips on her neck.

"Fuck this," said Jimmy. "I don't need this shit. Why does there always have to be crazy shit? It's bad enough we do what we do, but why do we have to go crazy all the time?"

"Because that's the way God made us," said Legless.

As Legless rolled his bulk onto her lap once again, he said, "In the beginning God made Adam, and then he took one of Adam's ribs . . ."

Legless grabbed her raincoat, but instead of popping the one button that held it together, he carefully unbuttoned the button. Then he pulled at the cut apart sides of her bra that now hung down at her armpits. "Who the hell did this?" he asked, mockingly. "Who the hell would cut apart a lady's bra?" Then he was at her breasts, his face a wire brush. He held her shoulders and pulled her toward him, forcing her down into the seat, pinning her hands and wrists painfully beneath her.

She took the pressure off by turning into Legless, and by straightening her hands out behind her back in the empty space on Jimmy's side of the seat. Jimmy had moved against the door, facing the window and every now and then repeating, "I don't need this shit."

She hoped Jimmy would not turn and see what she was doing with her hands. Even though the adhesive on the tape tore at her skin with each twisting motion, she worked her arms back and forth. Now, besides the chatter of the police scanner mounted on the dash of the car, and the panting of Legless, and the occasional comment from Jimmy, all was silent.

She had gotten the tape down onto her palms, just above her thumbs. She released the trapped finger, its main joint still in pain from having done its work. She realized she had begun breathing heavily through her nose and tried to calm herself, taking long, deep breaths.

"I don't need this shit," said Jimmy again.

It was working. Her finger had loosened the tape, working her hands back and forth had lessened the grip of the adhesive. She had managed to get the tape down onto her knuckles. Only a little way to go. Yes, only a little way to go. Then what?

No time to think about that. One thing at a time. For now, get the tape off.

As Legless pushed his face into her lap and lowered her slacks and gripped her underwear with his teeth, Jan pulled her thumbs from beneath the tape. Once this was done the pressure was released and she was able to pull her hands free.

While Legless bit at her underwear and Jimmy repeated his refrain, she moved her right hand from behind her back, carefully bringing it up her side in such a way that Legless would not see her arm in profile against the dim backlighting outside the window. She gently lifted the lower portion of the tape on her mouth. Just enough to scream when it was time, not so much that they'd see the tape has been loosened.

When she had loosened the tape below and at the corners of her mouth, she moved her hand slowly back down and put it behind her back. While doing this she was tempted to grab Legless by what little hair he had and push him away. But she overcame the temptation, and was glad she had because, the moment she put her hand back behind her, the sliding door on the van opened, Legless sat up quickly, closing her raincoat, and there was a figure at the window.

"All right, we're gettin' the fuck out of here."

"Where?" asked Legless.

"Somewhere we can have a more serious business meeting without being constantly interrupted. You stay back there with her. Jimmy'll drive the car."

"Who's gonna drive my van?"

"I will. We want to keep talkin' with Babe while we drive. Don't worry. I know how to use your hand controls."

It had been Dino, not as rough-sounding as Max. When Dino was back inside the van, Jimmy got out, went around the front of the car and got into the driver's seat.

Legless reached over and buttoned the single button on her raincoat. Then he sat back and draped one arm around her shoulder as if they were old pals. After a few seconds, he said, "Start 'er up, why don't you?"

"No," said the driver. "I see headlights in the mirror. I think Dino's waiting."

"Aw, start 'er up and put on the heat at least. We need some heat back here."

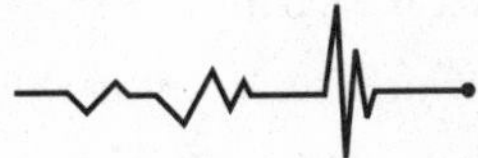

When Steve made a U-turn in the front lot, he'd seen in the reflection in the shiny back end of an SUV that not only was the Lincoln's left headlight out, but also the parking light. So he tried the Lincoln's brights and this illuminated both sides.

As he again drove neither too fast nor too slowly down the narrow access road to the back parking lot, Steve pressed his right arm to his side. He had wedged his gun between his right arm and his side so he could quickly get to it with his left hand. He was surprised his right arm was able to perform this function, acting as a kind of holster, and wondered if, of all times, he was beginning to see the next stage of his physical therapy paying off. He had lowered his window and a cool damp breeze buffeted his cheek.

The Lincoln's brights lit up the way ahead. He focused on the spot in the back lot where the van and the two Crown Vics were parked. He went over his plan again and again, trying to make it an integral part of whatever brain cells were available, just like he'd been taught in therapy.

Out in the main lot, as he drove around trying to figure out what he should do, he recalled a detail. On the surface, it might have seemed a trivial detail, but the more he thought about it, the more he became convinced he was doing the right thing. He'd once been a man of detail, a Sergeant-Joe-Friday-kind-of-guy who turns over stones one at a time until all the pieces to the puzzle are there on a table in the rehab center.

The detail was something he'd seen when he passed by the back of the van. The detail consisted of a thin line coming off the shoulder of the person in the left rear seat of the van, a thin line leading toward the side wall of the van, a thin line he concluded must be a shoulder belt. The head of the person wearing the shoulder belt had been much lower than the head of the other person on the rear seat. Although the shape of the head was vague, there did seem to be more of an outline of hair than on the person on the right of the seat, and the shoulders seemed less prominent. It could be a man slumped down in the seat, or it could be a woman. This was the only detail he had to go on. And, more than anything else, he needed something to go on.

If someone was kidnapped by men using two cars and a van, he assumed they would use the van to hold that person. Despite his awareness that holding Jan in the van meant they might be abusing her in order to get what they wanted, he had to make this assumption. Being here at Hell in the Woods further deepened his conviction. If they wanted to get information from Jan, what better place to bring her? And if Jan was inside the van, he had to do something.

Rather than drawing attention to himself by driving by twice, as he had done earlier, he headed straight for the aisle behind the car with the two men in the front seat. He recalled that the parking spots behind and across from the van had been empty, and since no one else had gone into the lot since he'd come out, he assumed this was still true. He also recalled that the parking spots ahead of the van had been empty.

Overhead, through the open side window of the Lincoln, he heard the beginning rumblings of a jet on takeoff as he drove not too fast but not too slowly to the parking spot directly behind the van. When he glanced up and back toward the sound he could see it was a big one, perhaps a 747, and that its trajectory would take it directly over Hell in the Woods. One of those takeoffs that rattled medication trays at the nurses' station.

The plan was simple. Dangerous but simple. Jan was in danger, terrible danger. The only solution was to get her away from her captors, to get her far enough away so she might be able to get into the Lincoln with him. He had to count on her being able to do that. They would not kill her during an escape attempt because they assumed she knew something they needed to know. At least they would not kill her until they either got what they needed, or until they were finished with her.

He would get her and the van as far away as possible from the two cars, both probably with men inside. He would get her away from them and, at the same time, cause enough commotion to make whoever was in the van with her get out in order to either escape or confront him. The sounds of the jet on takeoff would enhance the confusion. He knew he was taking a terrible chance, but there was nothing else to do. As Marjorie Gianetti might have said, "You just make waves, Mr. Babe. You just fuck the Pope and make waves."

He turned into the parking spot two back from the van, then rolled slowly ahead like someone deciding to move ahead to the empty spot in front in order to have a more convenient exit. But he did not stop the Lincoln there. Instead, he continued rolling ahead across the aisle. Halfway across the aisle, with about six feet to go before contact, he braced himself against the wheel with his left hand while clamping down tightly on his gun with his right forearm, and floored the Lincoln.

The Lincoln was more powerful than he expected, its tires moaning as they spun, getting more and more grip as they dried the damp asphalt. The moan of the tires and the collision with the rear bumper of the van joined in with the rumble of the jet on takeoff, creating a wonderful moment of chaos.

The van lurched forward, moving not inch-by-inch but foot-by-foot. The van's tires chattered, transmission trying to hold the van in place, but failing because the pavement was still wet and the van's tires were not molten like the Lincoln's tires.

It was like going backward in time, coming out of his stroke for the first time. The silence of night exploded, not simply into a babble of sounds, but into a chaotic din into which he and Jan might escape. The organic brain was alive, while the non-organic rubber and asphalt and plastic and metal and glass of the world protested violently at being torn apart.

He shouted, "Jan!" through his open side window and steered the sliding van ahead, keeping it in a straight line between parked cars, aiming it toward the loading dock.

He screamed, "Jan!" and saw the van's side door slide open and a man look out, lurching from side to side while hanging on precariously to the doorframe.

He wailed imploringly, "Jan!"

If he was in pain, he was not aware of it.

When she heard the crash and saw the van parked next to the car being pushed forward, Jan tore the tape from her mouth. Legless and Jimmy opened their doors, Jimmy got out, and she heard a voice amidst the commotion and noise, but did not have time to listen. She braced herself as best she could against the back of the seat and kicked out her good leg, shoving Legless out the rear door. As Legless rolled out onto the asphalt, she saw him reach into his jacket. He was still on his side on the pavement when the pistol came out.

No time to think. Just do it. Despite the pain in her ankle she jumped from the car and kicked out at the hand holding the pistol. The pistol skittered across the asphalt and she limped after it. But Legless was upright and after her, using arms and hands like legs and feet.

It was grotesque. Legless had hold of her bad ankle, but he did not look like a legless man. He looked like a man buried in the earth nearly to his waist. He looked like he had come from hell to get on with an eternity of torture.

Some distance away Jimmy ran after the car that was pushing the van. Not really running, stopping and starting like a man in a silent movie. But it was not silent. All during this the wheels of the car and the van gave off a piercing howl while overhead a jet was taking off. Behind her, she could see that another car had started up. Its lights were on and it turned and began driving down the parking lot aisle as if looking for another parking spot, as if nothing at all was unusual in this place. Yes, it was grotesque.

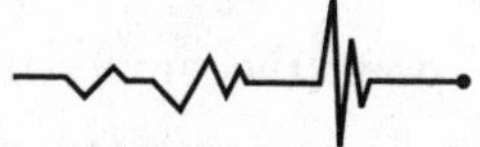

When he saw Jan in the rearview mirror he thought he'd had another stroke, the signals inside his brain bouncing off the inside of his skull the way images bounce off a mirror. Marjorie Gianetti ricocheting around inside his head with everything else. Marjorie saying something about her husband being interested in politics, so interested he'd struck a deal to rig votes during a Presidential election. And now, suddenly, Steve recalled trying to tell Jan about this confession Marjorie had made, but failing. Jan staring at him as if from a distance with a confused look on her face as he tries to reveal Marjorie's secret. Jan staring at him as they sit in the television lounge on the third floor. His confusion keeping Jan at a distance.

But they were not in the television lounge. He was not having a stroke. Jan was staring at him from a physical distance. She was in the mirror!

The Lincoln. The parking lot. One good hand and one bad hand on the steering wheel. Jan here in the parking lot. Jan behind him in the mirror. It wasn't in his head. It was real.

There was a whole man and a half man in the mirror with Jan. The whole man had a gun and was alternately pointing it toward him, then back at Jan. The half man was on the ground tilting back and forth as if bobbing in water. The half man had hold of Jan's ankle and Jan had fallen to her knees and was trying to crawl away, crying out and looking in his direction. At him!

As he became certain Jan was really there, that this was really happening, there was a rapid dip, as in an elevator. In the mirror the earth came from below and swallowed Jan, along with the whole man and the half man. When this happened he looked back through the windshield and reacted.

The ramp. The Lincoln nosing down. When he jammed on the brake, the van continued down the ramp, slamming into the concrete loading dock wall as the Lincoln skidded to a stop behind it. He reached across with his left hand and shoved the Lincoln into reverse. He turned in the seat and began backing up. Jan was there. The whole man and the half man were there. He accelerated hard. No time to trifle with whether this is real or imagined. No time to analyze.

Gun aimed at him, so he buried his head behind the seat. Then, not hearing a shot amidst the din, he looked out the rear window and saw the man with the gun running off to the side. But not fast enough. The man dove to the side and there was a muted thud and a shout as the Lincoln clipped the man's legs and sent him spinning on the asphalt.

Jan and the half man separated. She stood and limped to one side. The half man clamored along the ground like an elf. She kicked at something and the elf went in the direction she had kicked.

Steve could tell she was injured. One leg collapsing beneath her so badly she had to struggle to hold herself upright. Her raincoat was buttoned on top but flew open below and he could see the tails of her blouse and her bare midriff.

For a moment he thought he was in the midst of a stroke again, or a dream, or a seizure. He was with Jan back in his room on the third floor. They had propped the chair against the door and he was in bed and she was unbuttoning her blouse. But it was too real to be a dream.

He cranked the wheel of the Lincoln violently, bringing it to a stop with its passenger side facing Jan. In a way he had become the Lincoln and the Lincoln had become him. Jan was there, seeing him, reaching out for him, touching him.

The image of Steve, looking at her through the window, was beautiful. When she pulled open the door he was still there. His wheelchair was on the floor leaning against the seat, so she crawled in next to him, kneeling on the seat while she slammed the door shut.

The car was already moving when she turned to him. He was real. He was beautiful.

"Steve!"

"Yeah!"

She hugged him. She wanted to tell him this is all she wished for, all she ever wanted in the world. To be able to hold him and tell him she loves him.

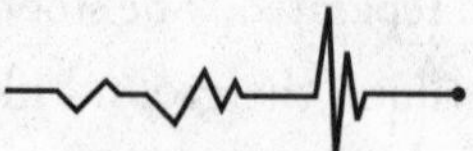

Another plane took off from O'Hare, its rumble beginning to shake things. If the 767 had been able to linger for a minute or two, hovering over Hell in the Woods instead of hurrying off toward Orlando, passengers on the starboard side with window seats would have been able to see it all.

A Lincoln trying to leave the parking lot. A Ford Crown Victoria ramming the Lincoln from the side before it could reach the entrance road. An injured man dragging himself toward another Crown Vic and, after great effort, crawling inside. A fat elf-like creature without legs crawling toward a van with a damaged front end parked nose-in against a loading dock. Two men leaping from the van, one of the men holding his head, both of the men running past the elf-like creature toward the parked Crown Vic into which the injured man had crawled. The Crown Vic with the injured man and the two men from the van pulling out of its parking space. The van with the elf-like creature inside backing away from the loading dock.

When the Crown Vic rammed the Lincoln's rear fender, they were spun around facing back the way they'd come. He did not want it to end this way. He wanted to drive out of here. He had Jan and he wanted to drive the hell out of here! But the Lincoln was turned around and the Crown Vic that had rammed them was turned around and was backing toward his door.

It was a demolition derby. Steve floored the Lincoln just in time and the Crown Vic sped past the tail of the Lincoln in reverse, then quickly did a half turn, reversing its direction and coming after them.

He wanted to tell Jan to hang on, but there was no time for that, and she was hanging onto him, he could feel her hands squeezing his bad arm. In spite of all that was happening, the pressure of her hands squeezing him felt wonderful.

He drove ahead and picked an aisle amongst the parked cars. But when he drove halfway down the aisle, headlights appeared at the other end of the aisle and the other Crown Vic sped toward them.

From above, if the 767 had lingered instead of moving off, the parking lot would have appeared like a video game, a video game played amidst the thunderous roar of the 767's engines as it climbed and turned hard south so it would not disturb the west side of the city. The game had four moving parts: a dark van, two dark Crown Vics, and a white Lincoln.

The Lincoln avoided a collision with one of the Crown Vics by turning into vacant parking spots and getting over to the next aisle of the parking lot. The other Crown Vic came down that aisle chasing the Lincoln. The van circled the perimeter of the parking lot, apparently waiting for the Crown Vics to chase the Lincoln out from amongst parked cars.

When the Lincoln made a run for the only road leading out of the parking lot, it was rammed in the rear driver's side by one of the Crown Vics. The Lincoln drove a wobbly path, turning away from the road because the van had now stationed itself there. The Lincoln drove back toward the building along the edge of the lot, ventured off the pavement when the other Crown Vic sped past in reverse on a collision course, fishtailed in the mud, almost getting stuck, then came back on the pavement and continued toward the building.

The Crown Vic that had rammed the Lincoln was still running, but its airbags had gone off and one headlight was out and instead of rejoining the pursuit of the Lincoln, it drove slowly out of the lot on the access road.

As the Lincoln neared the back end of the building, the other Crown Vic did a half-circle of the lot and was back again, turned around and driving in reverse down one of the aisles. It sprung from the aisle like a blade concealed in the handle of a knife and hit the Lincoln in the front passenger side, slowing the Lincoln's already slow progress toward the building. Then the Crown Vic pulled off, going forward back down the aisle to the far end of the lot.

The windshield of the Lincoln was fogging up from steam emerging from beneath the hood. The sweet-sour scent of antifreeze filled the inside of the car. Both front wheels were damaged, the right front tire apparently flat from the last collision.

The Lincoln was no longer useful as an extension of himself. And because of this, he was no longer useful. Jan would have been better off running into the woods instead of joining him. He had done what he had set out to do. He had made waves, injecting chaos into the situation. And Jan had done what she was supposed to do. She had run. Except she should have run away instead of running to this crippled fool! She was alive and healthy. Goddamn it! She needed to live!

Jan had reached over and was helping him steer, keeping the wheel from spinning back in the opposite direction when he had to let go of the wheel to reposition his left hand on it.

"They're coming around again!" she screamed.

But they would not hit him again. He was heading for the ramp that led up the side of the loading dock, the ramp he had sailed down in his wheelchair earlier that night.

"Is it wide enough?" shouted Jan.

He nodded and held onto the wheel, steering the Lincoln directly toward the ramp.

The railings were welded steel pipe. He wasn't sure if it was wide enough, but he felt it was their only chance. The railing on the right side did a ninety degree turn to the right and continued along the loading dock drop-off until it stopped where trucks backed in. If they made it through to the top and he put the nose of the Lincoln against the building, there would be just enough room to open the passenger door.

"Not wide enough!" shouted Jan. "But we can scrape through to the top! If the door opens we can get out and run inside before . . ."

"You out!"

"No, Steve! Both of us or neither of us!"

Ramp coming up fast. Like threading a needle. A little to the right. More to the left.

As the Lincoln climbed the ramp, the steel railing bent outward but also tore into the side of the Lincoln. Inside, it felt and sounded like huge grinding wheels had been applied to both sides. They had threaded the needle, but too fast, and he slammed on the brake.

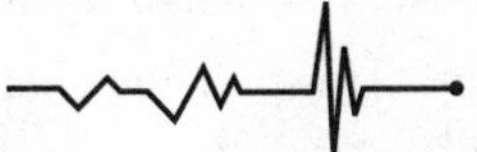

Her head throbbed and a female voice came from somewhere, a matter-of-fact female voice saying something about an accident reported at Saint Mel in the Woods. At first she thought she was still in that other world between a man with legs and a man without legs. At first she thought one of them had hit her so hard she'd been thrown into the front seat closer to the police scanner. But the voice came from beneath her and she realized she was lying on the radio. Steve's radio! He had driven up the ramp and they had crashed into the building!

The collision had thrown her at the windshield, but the wide passenger side airbag had saved her. Because she had been prone on the front seat, the impact of the bag was at her midriff, knocking the wind out of her and smashing her head sideways against . . . Steve!

"Jan! Hurry!"

Adrenalin, Steve's voice pushing her on. She reached out and tried the door handle, but it was stuck. She kicked out at the door with her good leg and it pushed out to the safety latch with a thud. She pulled at the handle and pushed as hard as she could with her good leg and the door finally lurched open with a metallic squeak.

Outside, she could still hear the sound of the climbing jet in the distance. But she could also hear a car. They were coming. Max and Dino coming so they could get her and Steve to tell what they know, then kill them.

Despite the pain in her head and ankle, she climbed from the car, pulling the wheelchair from beneath the airbag that had draped over it like a death shroud. Then she pulled at Steve.

He'd also had the wind knocked out of him, but was alert now, moving as quickly as he could to get out of the car. She barely had a chance to turn and push the wheelchair against the door opening before he landed in the seat. He spun the chair around, and when she turned to limp toward the loading dock door, Steve pulled her into his lap and they were off in his wheelchair, rolling along the loading dock to the door.

As they rolled nearer the door she wondered why the men were not already upon them. Both the van and the car had skidded to a stop near the bottom of the ramp with its bent-out railings. All they had to do was run down into the loading dock well. From there they could easily shoot up at them . . .

No, they couldn't shoot them! Despite all that had happened, she hadn't told them what they wanted to know!

But why weren't they coming after them? Why were they simply standing there?

She got her answer when she reached out to open the heavy steel door. Something reflected on the door's enameled surface. At first she thought it was the flash of the gunshots. But when she glanced back, she saw a police car driving down the entrance road to the back parking lot, and she saw Max and Dino standing at the open side door of the van, looking back at the approaching police car.

Steve shouted, "Don't stop now!"

"But the police are coming."

"Hurry! Hurry!"

As soon as they were inside and the door slammed shut, Steve pulled her back into his lap and they rolled down a short hallway, noisy with machinery, and through a door propped open with a crate. They would speed off down the long hallway through the nursing home wing. Nurses and aides and guards would be there to help. Phone calls would go out. The police coming into the back parking lot would be radioed.

But that's not what happened. The wheelchair was top heavy with her on board. One wheel of the chair caught the edge of the crate holding open the door as Steve tried to turn into the long hallway. They fell and Jan hit her head on the hard tile floor.

She was vaguely aware of Steve struggling beneath her. She could hear his voice.

"Jan! Jan! Hey, you in there! Hey, kitchen!"

It was a dream. He was calling to a kitchen. But with his stroke . . .

Kitchen! They were near the kitchen and he was calling out to whoever was in the kitchen for help. But how could anyone in there hear Steve? How could anyone in the kitchen hear anything with all the racket? First jets climbing from O'Hare, and now what sounded like the largest automatic dishwasher in the world. So loud it vibrated the floor against her cheek.

CHAPTER THIRTY-TWO

The world was full of shit. The fuckin' world with its spaghetti heads waving guns and fists around until everyone goes fuckin' nuts was full of shit. The world was also fuckin' hell. First they beat the shit out of him, then they tape his mouth *and* his nose and leave him that way a few seconds so he figures he's dead, then he gets whiplash when the van gets shoved into the loading dock and the damn shoulder belt nearly strangles him. And, sure as shit, it wasn't over.

It wasn't over because the craziness hadn't gone out of it. The craziness hadn't gone out of it because of who showed up after the two spaghetti heads blamed it all on him and jumped out. It wasn't over yet because the cracker drivin' the van had no fuckin' legs! Not even stumps! Maybe not even a dick or asshole for all he knew. He'd seen the guy roll in through the side door and roll up front and hoist himself into the driver's seat.

Even though the van's front end was smashed, the cracker with no legs had managed to get it started, had backed up the ramp, had chased around the parking lot for a while, nearly strangling Tyrone several times on the shoulder belt, and then had driven back up to the building giving Tyrone a front row seat to an accident in which a white Lincoln drives up the damn loading dock wheelchair ramp and smashes into the building. All during this a police radio is chattering away, and after the Lincoln crashes into the building he sees the fuckin' monster drivin' the van on the phone and expects him to call an ambulance. But instead of calling an ambulance, the monster just says, "Cop call just came down." Then, after a pause, "Yeah, I'll stay put."

When the side door slid open, Tyrone was trying to cough because of being choked so many times on the shoulder belt, but since his mouth was taped, he snorted out the cough through his nose and tears ran from his eyes and into the cuts on his face.

He'd seen a man and woman get out of the Lincoln and ride double on a wheelchair into the back door of the building, apparently escaping from the spaghetti heads. He couldn't see too well because of his swollen eyes, but he figured it was Babe and his wife. Now, all he could think about was that they'd lost Babe and his wife and they'd be pissed when they came inside and blow his brains out with one of those silenced guns and dump his body in a dumpster next to the loading dock and the flies would feed on his eyeballs until day after tomorrow when the garbage was picked up.

But even though the door was open, no one came inside. Instead of coming inside they stood outside the door and talked to one another and to the monster in the driver's seat.

"We gotta do this fast. Stay inside, Legless."

"Where's T.J. and Mario?"

"I sent them to get another car. Theirs was fucked up worse than ours."

The cracker named Legless turned in the direction of flashing lights coming in through the side door. "Looks like a two-man squad."

"Yeah, we gotta take care of 'em. Any other calls go out?"

"Not that I heard."

"No call-back?"

"Nope. Gizmo on the scanner would've picked up a local signal."

"Turn off the scanner." The guy giving orders came inside the van. "You got that blanket in here, Legless?"

"Yeah, under the back seat."

The guy rummaged under the back seat, shook a blanket loose and threw it over Tyrone. "Don't move, fucker. Leave the blanket on or your balls come off."

The blanket was dusty, making him sneeze through his nose and ears. He froze, waiting for the bullet in his balls. But none came, and he could hear the guy leave the van.

"I'll do the talkin'. Wave to 'em, Dino. Act like somethin's funny in the van. Friendly. Yeah, real friendly. That's it. Over here, boys."

Tyrone heard the unmistakable sounds of a squad car arriving. The squeak of overused brakes, the sounds of the police radio coming from inside the squad as the door opened, then another door opening, probably the cop on the other side, hidden behind the car, maybe with his service revolver out of its holster just in case.

"Evenin', gentlemen. Little accident here?" Sounded like an older cop, white. He'd heard plenty of them back in his gang-bangin' days.

"Yes, officer. That's why we stopped. Two of us were just comin' off the late shift. We were drivin' out when . . ."

"Is anyone in the car up there?"

"No, officer. Some nurses came out already and took the injured guy inside. Guess he was bleedin' pretty bad."

"You involved in the accident?"

"Yes, officer. I was drivin' my car here when the guy in the Lincoln sideswipes me before he plows into the building."

"The van involved?"

"No, officer. But the driver, who's handicapped, works here with us and he stopped to help. It's really kinda funny in a way, officer."

"Tell me about it."

"Well, the two of us just got in my car here and were startin' out when we see the back door to the building fly open and this woman comes running down the ramp in her birthday suit. Yeah, she didn't have no clothes on, nothing.

"Anyway, the Lincoln's driving into the lot at the same time we're driving out and I guess the guy in the Lincoln got distracted, turning around to have a look, and the next thing I know he turns right into me, sideswipes my front end. Then I guess his foot slips off the brake and onto the gas pedal or something because he ends up flyin' up the ramp there. Good thing no one was on the ramp."

"Okay, and where exactly is this naked lady?"

"She's in there. Refuses to go back into the building, so we put her in there to keep warm and put a blanket over her. We tried talkin' to her but we couldn't make no sense of it."

Tyrone could hear the cop coming inside. Was this it? Maybe the bastards planned to slam the cop inside and take off. But what about the other cop?

Despite the sounds of another jet in the distance, starting its climb away from O'Hare, Tyrone could hear the meaty thud, the unmistakable sound of something heavy and hard on someone's skull. Then the cop's body fell onto his legs and dragged him farther down the seat, the shoulder belt choking him again, the blanket pulled from his face. Through it all the guy outside kept up his chatter, louder because of the approaching jet, fast like he was in a hurry.

"See what I mean? She don't want nothin' to do with goin' back into that place. Oh shit, lady, keep the blanket on or you'll get pneumonia. What? Yeah, sure. Officer? Your partner wants you. Maybe you can talk sense into her. Geez, lady, don't do that. He's just tryin' to help."

Because of the jet overhead, he could not hear the other cop walk up to the door of the van. But now that the blanket was pulled off his face he could see the cop's shoulder and one edge of his cap. The cop just stood there, shouting to be heard over the rumbling of the jet.

"Looks like I picked the wrong night to leave the video camera back in my locker," said the cop. "Well, that's all right. Least I can do is take a reading on the situation." A black cop. He could tell by the voice. *Pull your piece, man!*

Tyrone knew they'd get him and there wasn't a damn thing he could do about it. Even if he grunted through his nose, even if he could make himself heard above the roar of the jet, the cop would figure it was his partner inside. He felt sorry for the cops. Doin' their jobs, tryin' to help out, and maybe get a look at a naked lady, and they get their heads smashed in. As soon as the cop turned and put one knee up on the floor of the van, they let him have it. The pipe, or whatever it was, looked like a blur coming in from above like a fuckin' meteor.

The next unmistakable blow to the head seemed harder than the first, the guy who did the slugging giving off a wheeze of breath with the effort. Bastard hitting the black cop harder than necessary.

When Tyrone opened his eyes again he could see flashing from the squad car's lights coming through the open door, but then the lights were shut off and all he could see in the dark were the hulks of the two bodies at his feet. Neither of the cops budged and, as he recalled the sounds of the thuds, he figured both were dead. A black cop and a white cop, pretty widows and two or three kids apiece at home.

The whole thing hadn't taken a minute. Other than the two bodies, the van was empty except for the gargoyle up front who had his head turned and was gawking back at him.

At first he thought the gargoyle was speaking, but it was the voice of one of the spaghetti heads who had leaned inside and was pulling one of the cops by the ankles. The cop's body hit the pavement with a thud. The next cop out made a moan when he hit the pavement and Tyrone heard another heavy blow. Yeah, they were dead all right. He heard car doors slam and figured they put the cops back in their squad car. The spaghetti head spoke through all this like it was something he did every day.

"Here, make sure their portable units are off. Dino, you get on their car radio. Call in a Code 4, say it's a minor parking lot fender bender and we've got it under control. Then shut off their radio and their computer and make sure there's no camera. Shut everything off and drive it back there in the corner where it's dark. We don't want more fuckin' cops back here, and if they don't see another car they'll figure they're in the wrong place and move on."

There was a pause, then the guy giving the orders continued.

"I don't see anyone in any windows up there. Patty says it's all storage rooms and shit in this part of the building. No patient rooms. Legless, you drive around to the main entrance and park in a handicapped spot. Watch the front in case they come out there. If they do, follow them, but no ruckus. We don't want to draw any more attention to this place than we have."

The squad car started up, moved off a short distance, then shut off and a car door slammed. It was quiet for a bit, with the guy outside mumbling like he was on the phone, then footsteps as the other guy who had moved the squad car came back.

"Okay, I sent the Code 4."

"Good," said the guy giving orders. "I called T.J. and Mario. Now that things are calmed down they can get their asses back here and watch this door while we're inside."

"Should we call Patty?"

"Call him on our way in. Tell him to stay by the elevators on the third floor. No way they'll be takin' any stairs. You got those stockings? Okay, let's go. We'll get what we want out of 'em inside and fuckin' leave 'em in there."

The gargoyle spoke. "The door."

"Yeah, right," said one of the spaghetti heads.

After the door slammed shut with a meat locker sound, the gargoyle started up the van and Tyrone felt the shoulder belt dig into his neck as they did a quick U-turn.

Yeah, a full-of-shit world, all right. Hospitals keepin' zombies alive inside while outside the folks who take care of their asses get beat up and the cops who protect the zombies get their heads smashed in. As far as he was concerned, the world outside Hell in the Woods needed Medicare and Medicaid a whole hell of a lot more than the zombies inside.

Now that the van was closed up, Tyrone could smell his shorts. The shorts with hearts Latoya had given him for his birthday messed up because of him. Again he wished he were with Latoya right now. The hell with all this shit, and the hell with any other women.

Tyrone got choked up thinking about Latoya. But then the van in the hands of the gargoyle up front turned violently and he got puked up instead. This time he couldn't hold the puke down and, because of the way he was slouched down and hanging by the neck from the shoulder belt, he snorted out chunks of the stuff and messed himself up good, the acid in the puke setting fire to the inside of his nose and to the cuts on his face.

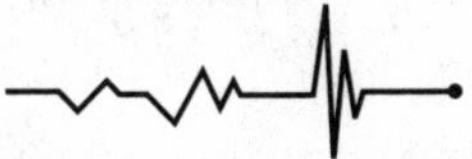

In her deep voluptuous voice, the GPS lady announced they had arrived at their destination just as Valdez turned into the Saint Mel in the Woods Rehabilitation Facility entrance road.

"I thought our contact was to meet us here," said Valdez.

"Not here," said Hanley. "She'll be at a side road that goes around back. She said to go through the parking lot toward the back of the building."

"Not much traffic in this place," said Valdez.

"That's because it's not the kind of place people are drawn to on a Friday night."

"So we'll go in through the back?"

"Yes," said Hanley. "According to our first contact, that will take us through the nursing home wing. Anyone going in or out who doesn't want to draw attention to themselves would go that way, and we can become spouses of residents, or even residents if need be. Myself, I had practice with a walker and a wheelchair while recovering from my last surgery, and I'm sure there are plenty of those about."

"Using a wheelchair might be more useful," said Valdez.

"Good point," said Hanley. "One old man pushing another old man."

"I'm a better shot standing up," said Valdez.

"That's fine by me," said Hanley.

As he rounded the perimeter of the parking lot, Valdez saw the road that went around back. The car driven by their contact, a black Honda Accord, was parked to the right side in the distance facing the back parking lot. Valdez slowed the rental car as he approached the Accord, taking his time.

"Tell me one more thing before we go inside," said Valdez.

"What is it?" asked Hanley.

"In case one of us is disabled, we should both know where the money trail could possibly lead after tonight."

"It's about time you asked," said Hanley. "I would have told you eventually for just that reason."

Hanley adjusted himself in his seat, then zipped up his golf jacket. "Do you remember Tom Christensen from Langley?"

"Of course. Wasn't he the deputy assistant for a while?"

"That's him," said Hanley. "Hell of a nice guy. Probably one of the brains behind this."

"Didn't he retire a long time ago?" asked Valdez.

"Yes, but not under his name. He and his second wife live in a retirement community south of Flagstaff in the mountains. His wife is twenty years younger than him. Almost ninety and the bastard still skis."

"I can't wait until I retire," said Valdez, pulling up to the left of the Accord.

"You can say that again," said Hanley.

The face of Maria, familiar because of the photograph he'd seen, looked out the driver's window of the Accord as Valdez pulled up.

Hanley lowered his window at the same time Maria lowered her window.

"Good evening," said Hanley.

"Good evening, yourself," said Maria.

"Has anyone come out this way?"

"A handicapped van came out a minute ago, " said Maria. "I saw only a driver. I didn't recognize him. Before that, maybe five minutes, a police car went in and didn't come out."

"Is there room to park on both sides of the loading dock?"

"Yes."

"Okay. You drive ahead first," said Hanley. "Park to the right of the loading dock and we'll park to the left. Not too close in. Simply visiting, and we're not sure where the main entrance is."

"Should I go in with you?" asked Maria.

Valdez leaned forward to speak to her. "No. Let us go in alone. We'll be less conspicuous. Watch the back and if anyone else shows up, call us. If the police are back there and haven't gone inside, keep them busy."

Hanley turned to look at Valdez, seeming to question his instructions.

Valdez quickly added, "We need you out here to guarantee all three of us get away from this place."

"Right," said Maria, raising her window.

Valdez followed the Accord at a distance as it slowly circled around to the back of the building. The wooded area behind the building was quite dark, the parking lot lit but not brightly. There were no other roads leading out of the back lot. As he drove, Valdez memorized the way out and hoped he would be on his way soon. In the distance, Valdez heard a jet overhead. The jet became louder and louder as he followed the Accord.

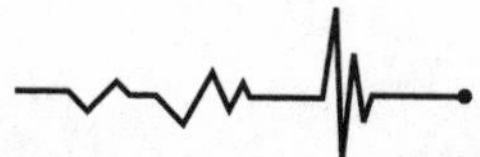

The van stopped after driving a short distance. When Tyrone lifted himself up a little in the seat so he could look out, he saw the Hell in the Woods main entrance.

Now what? he thought. Maybe they'll come out with a gurney and take him inside. Maybe the spaghetti heads have a room commandeered where they can take care of him in private. The skeleton night staff probably out on that balcony they're not supposed to use having themselves a few smokes while he sits in his own shit.

He turned to his left and saw his DeVille. There it was, sitting right there, and in his pocket he could feel his keys biting into his hip. He lay his head down against the back of the seat and stared at the DeVille. So close, but so far away.

Up front, the Gargoyle had turned up the police scanner. No calls to hurry out to Hell in the Woods. Only traffic calls and domestic disturbances.

Amid the chatter of the scanner, Tyrone could hear the Gargoyle humming a tune. Nothing Tyrone recognized, but it sounded like a tune from the forties or fifties. Something Sinatra or Como would croon. Any second the Gargoyle would burst into song. Then the insanity of the night would be complete.

CHAPTER THIRTY-THREE

The wheelchair was tipped over and he had blacked out. A stroke victim. Useless to himself or to anyone else. A stroke victim alone in his own world. A stroke victim who'd be better off . . .

No! Jan was here! He and Jan had fallen from the wheelchair. He had turned the corner too fast and caught a wheel on a crate holding open the door to the main hallway. Amid the noise of machinery from the short hallway behind them, he had heard Jan's head hit the floor.

Desperate, he banged on the locked door to the kitchen, wasting precious time trying to get the attention of whoever worked the kitchen at night. There was no answer, and when he looked back and saw Jan sprawled on the floor, he knew only he could help her.

He touched his jacket pocket and felt the reassuring weight of his gun. He glanced at the small window in the closed door to the loading dock and, seeing that the lights from the police car had gone out, decided one stroker with a gun would never be enough.

He called Jan's name and shook her shoulders. He lifted her into a sitting position. When she opened her eyes he could see she was in a daze. She slumped against the wall in the hallway, staring back at the door to the loading dock, back the way they'd come.

He pulled the wheelchair upright, sat down, positioned the chair at Jan's side, put on the wheel brakes, and, using all his strength, dragged her back into his lap. Although she'd been able to limp earlier, he could tell by the cut on the side of her head and the faraway look in her eyes that she was in no condition to limp now.

He wasn't sure whether he'd also been knocked out for a while. His head throbbed and the noise coming into the main hallway through the door held open by a crate was deafening. He had a feeling that, for a few seconds, or perhaps longer, the noise had not been there.

Too much time had gone by. He'd seen Jan's captors watching as he and Jan came in through the loading dock door. He'd seen the police car coming into the back lot. He'd seen it was only one car and knew Jan's captors were professionals, and were desperate. But maybe, just maybe, the cops had come through. Maybe they'd been lucky and there was no need to run.

He was in pain, but pain was something he'd managed to put up with this night. His leg brace was askew, digging into his flesh, but he didn't have time to mess with it. Not now. Not here. Not in this in-between place where the word *maybe* wasn't good enough.

It was insane. He had expected to see aides and residents about. He had expected a scene from Dante's *Inferno*. Heads poking from doorways, old people in the nursing home wing looking out to see what was going on. But even when he had banged at the locked door to the kitchen near the loading dock exit, there had been no response.

As he raced around a corner with Jan on board and into the long hallway through the nursing home wing, his mind also raced. He thought he heard music playing. Music as ancient and melancholy as the curious faces he'd expected to see looking out doorways. The music came from violins, but the violins were not here. The violins wept sadly in his memory making the nonexistent faces into ancestors looking back from the grave to see what humans have done with themselves and with the world.

He remembered having seen, a few moments earlier when he was not certain whether he'd been knocked out, that there had been tape on the latch of the alarmed door, the alarm not ringing even though the door was held open by a crate. He should have taken the tape off so the alarm sounded and the guards at the front desk would have been notified. But at the time, the connection between the door alarm and the tape hadn't registered. The professionals had planned ahead, clearing the way for an undetected entrance.

For a moment he considered turning back. But the word *maybe* kept him moving. He and Jan could not afford to give time to desperate men because time was the only thing on their side. Time and the distance they could keep between themselves and their pursuers until they could either hide, or figure out a way to defend themselves without shooting up the place and getting residents and aides killed or injured in the crossfire.

Yes, it was insane. People housed in the nursing home wing waiting to die, while a man and woman aboard a single wheelchair race down the hallway as if anxious to get on with their own deaths. A man and woman racing past parked wheelchairs, wheelchairs empty as if . . .

No! Don't think about death. Don't give up!

He had to lean sideways to see around Jan. On the right side of her head, behind her ear, blood oozed from the cut at her hairline. Any other time he would have wanted to forget about everything else and tend to Jan's injury. But this was not any other time. And he was thankful she was not bleeding too badly.

The nursing home wing had a long hallway and he began to think that having come this far they might get away. But just as he thought this, just as they approached the nurses' station centered in the hallway, the sounds of running footsteps echoed from behind.

The nurse at the station stared at them in disbelief. There would be no time to explain, no time to tell of the danger. But suddenly, Jan came out of her daze and, as if able to read his mind, shouted to the open-mouthed nurse.

"Hide somewhere! Men with guns! Hide anywhere!"

The word *guns* had its effect. Before they reached the nurses' station, the nurse ducked below the counter and disappeared as the sounds of footsteps grew louder, the men obviously rounding the corner at the far end of the hallway.

His gun was in his left jacket pocket; he could feel its bulk press against the armrest each time he gave the left wheel a forward shove. Jan was helping now, reaching over the side to push on the right wheel and, at the same time, managing to help steer the chair by extending her right foot to the floor ahead. She had taught Steve how to correct the steering of his chair months earlier using gentle taps of one foot on the floor left or right of center. And now, Jan was doing so well at it he stopped trying to steer with his foot and concentrated on using his left hand to propel them forward.

For a moment he considered turning into one of the resident's rooms in order to hide. But it was too late for that, the footsteps coming closer and closer, the men obviously within sight of them. He paused in his pushing of the chair to get his gun from his pocket. He thought Jan might misinterpret his intentions and steered the chair around so they could make a stand, using the nurses' station for cover. But she kept pushing forward toward the double doors at the end of the hallway. She, too, must have known that the only thing to do now was to get through both sets of double doors to the lobby where there might be some fire power to back them up.

If they made it through the first set of double doors there would be no searching through rooms, no shooting here. No bullets ricocheting down the hall, through walls and doors and into the rooms of residents. And if they made it through the second set of double doors, the confrontation would take place at the front desk where they would receive help from the guards. At least two guards on duty every time he'd looked. A plan. They had a plan. Either Jan *was* reading his mind, or he was reading her mind.

As they fled down the length of hallway between the nurses' station and the double doors that led to the lobby of the main building, thin legs and a wheelchair appeared in a doorway and a head peeked out. A familiar face. A face he'd seen before.

Sue! So-long Sue who visited the third floor to compare herself to stroke victims, proving to herself she still has spunk. And behind Sue, the music he thought he had imagined earlier was replaced by a man shouting at the top of his lungs. Sue held something up in her hand for them to see and screamed to him and to Jan in her high-pitched voice.

"I turned up the volume! That'll help! Gets their attention every time!"

A remote control! The music was not from the past. The man's voice was not from the past. Not the result of his stroke. Not an ancestor summoning him and Jan from the grave. The man's voice was that of a late night news anchor. Sue had turned the volume of her set full blast. And now he recalled Marjorie trying to explain in rehab how Sue sometimes turned up the volume on her television as a form of protest.

But despite the volume of the television, and despite the crazy smile on Sue's face, he was aware of the unmistakable heavy footfalls echoing in the hallway behind them. Sue reacted to the sound by glancing down the hallway, quickly losing her smile, and doing a backward caterpillar walk into her room.

No time to look back. Double doors ahead. His left foot out and Jan's right foot out to impact the doors. But they are automatic doors, and as the doors swing away, helped by their feet hitting them, a man's voice behind them shouts.

"Babe! I'll shoot if you don't stop! I'll shoot her!"

As they slam through the doors that aren't opening fast enough, he feels Jan's reaction. Her muscles go taut, she screams, and when he hears the scream, all he wants to do is hold her to him. In that moment, to hold her to him and die with her in his arms seems all that is left.

Because of the late hour, the hallway connecting the nursing home wing to the main building was empty. The only doorways along the hallway were staff offices, all the doors closed and, Jan knew, locked for the night. She recalled walking in this very hallway weeks earlier on one of the nights Steve was doing badly. The staff on the third floor had told her to go home, but she had not wanted to go home until Steve was better, until she knew he'd gotten enough drugs and was resting for the night instead of suffering the intense headache caused by swelling in his brain. She had walked the halls that night, coming down to the first floor and discovering this long connecting hall between the nursing home wing and the main building.

Her head throbbed from having hit the floor when the wheelchair overturned. Although her injured left foot was propped on the wheelchair footrest, each time she tapped her right foot on the floor to correct their steering, it sent a signal to her left foot that resulted in a searing stab of pain that nearly immobilized her. When they passed a drinking fountain to one side of the hallway, she was aware of the raw dryness in her mouth and throat.

But there was no time to dwell on pain and thirst. There was only time to flee from Max and Dino. There was only time to concentrate on making it to the next set of double doors, the doors that opened into the lobby and the reception island where guards were posted.

Perhaps a guard had seen them on one of the closed-circuit monitors, a man in a wheelchair with a woman in his lap speeding crazily down the hallway. Perhaps the bedlam in the nursing home wing—the men running after them, shouting—had appeared on a monitor. But she knew there were no monitors in the nursing home wing. She had walked the halls often enough to know that security cameras were limited to the main building and its approaches. Now she could only hope the guards were alert and awake, not dozing like she'd seen them doing many times during her late night walks.

When she and Steve reached the double doors that opened into the lobby, she could hear the sounds of heavy footfalls closing in. She braced herself, holding her foot out to hit against the second set of automatic doors that would open much too slowly for the speeding wheelchair, but also braced herself for the shots that would surely kill them.

No! Dino and Max would not kill them because she and Steve still held the key, Marjorie's litany of routes that would lead them to the drug money that had already destroyed the lives of Marjorie and her son and her son's attorney, and God knows how many others.

She could see one of the monitor cameras now, off to the side of the doors they were flying through, her left foot on fire as the jolt of her right foot hitting the door made its way to her injured ankle. Lobby ahead, no visitors, no one sitting in the chairs along the walls.

The only movement she saw was the large screen television playing silently to an audience of vacant chairs. And behind the counter? No movement there either, only two heads slumped over until the one nearest slowly begins to turn.

The guard, prompted by the doors banging open, and perhaps having glimpsed a wheelchair approaching at high speed, and perhaps having heard the echoes of following footfalls, ever so slowly turns his head toward them as she struggles to scream out a warning.

"Help! Help us! Guns! Coming!"

First the guard who had turned her way stands, then the other stands. Their uniforms are identical, symbols of order and harmony and safety, but they react much too slowly. They are young and have that terrible look of innocence on their faces that demands proof they are not being tricked by elders. When no guns appear she screams at them again.

"Guns! Can't you hear? Guns!"

She steers the wheelchair to circle the reception island, to put the island between them and the doorway. She can hear the doors opening. She can see, above the counter, that one guard bends slightly while looking at the doorway, and the other guard simply stands there, alternately glancing to her and to the doorway, looking like a boy who has done something wrong and is about to be caught.

She feels movement beneath her and sees Steve's left hand lift forward, his hand holding his gun. His gun!

She stabs her foot to the floor to turn the chair fully around so Steve can point the gun at their pursuers.

The counter blocks her view of the doorway. She cannot see Max and Dino but sees the guard who had bent over stand back up and look toward the footsteps and aim a pistol.

But the guard moves too slowly and a shot drives him against his partner who stumbles behind him and gives off a whimper.

Dull thud of a shot. Silencers! And now another shot that hits the other guard before the first disappears behind the counter. Both guards down and all she can see is the counter and all she can hear is a man's voice whispering harshly.

Dino's voice. "Never mind! Just get the fuck down here! Guards are out! Get the keys and lock up the front! We'll go out the back!" Then it is quiet.

Dino and Max are hidden on the far side of the reception island. They want them alive. They still want them alive! Not telling what they know has saved them. But for how long?

When she hears rustling from both sides, she realizes they are circling the reception island. They come upon them so quickly there is no time to react.

A shot from one side of the island. Steve grunts and his arm whips across her, this followed by the muted thud of another shot from the other side of the island. Steve's gun skitters across the tile floor and onto the carpeted area where the television with the volume turned down plays to empty chairs. She looks down and sees Steve's bleeding left arm. His good arm!

Max and Dino appear before them. But it is not Max and Dino. These are monsters with noses and hair and ears flattened and dark as if seared off in a terrible fire.

No, not a fire. They are wearing masks! They are wearing women's stockings for masks! The cameras! They are aware of the cameras and they are wearing masks!

They both carry silenced pistols with long barrels. One of them looks over the counter, as if looking down into hell, then carefully lifts his gun over the counter, casually takes aim and fires another shot.

The other comes toward them, kicking out violently, hitting her leg so that she screams. But she forces the scream to end despite the pain. They are wearing masks. They do not want to be seen. They do not speak. Except for whispers when they were behind the counter, they do not want to be heard. But if someone else speaks, if she speaks . . .

"I'll tell!" she manages to get out. "Listen, Max, I'll tell now because . . ."

But this is all she can get out before he hits her across the face with his gun.

Everything happens very fast then, a nightmare rushing to its conclusion. She hears the muted thud of another shot from one of their guns and opens one eye to see a man in a gray housekeeping staff uniform fall back against a Staff-Only doorway next to the elevators. She is aware of Steve struggling beneath her, trying to get up and trying to talk. She is aware that he has been hit. She can tell by the way his attempts at speech come out in moans of anger and frustration. She is aware of being lifted from Steve's lap and being put into another wheelchair. She is aware of a tearing sound and tape being put on her arms and legs. She is aware of being taped to the wheelchair, then being wheeled rapidly and seeing through one barely open eye that Steve is being wheeled ahead of her.

A voice says, "She was gonna talk. Maybe you should've let her."

They go back the way they came, back through the same double doors, this time waiting for the doors to open inward before being pushed through and into the connecting hallway. A distant voice echoes in the connecting hallway, apparently the sound of a television turned up loud. Then there is another voice. An angry horrifying voice that drowns out all the other sounds.

"Yeah, she'll fuckin' talk all right! But not here! Not in this fuckin' place! She talks here, she gives us shit 'cause she thinks we'll leave 'em! Not here in this hell hole! This is fuckin' war now!"

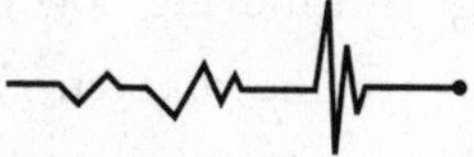

Jan was gone, removed from him. They had taken away the only part of him worth anything, the part of him necessary for life, the part of him that made life worth the struggle.

When he opened his eyes he saw a hallway moving toward him so rapidly he had a sensation of falling. The hallway was a vertical shaft and he was falling through it. As he fell, a voice shouted, then loud music came down the hallway. There was someone in the hallway now, and if someone was standing there, then this was not a dream of falling.

The woman stood perfectly still as he sped in her direction, propelled from behind. At first he thought the woman standing in the hallway might be Jan. But this woman's hair was darker than Jan's, and when he got closer he recognized her uniform.

She stood in front of a nurses' station centered in a widening of the hallway. Her arms were down and he could see her hands outstretched behind her on the vertical front of the counter surrounding the nurses' station. At first he thought she had an angry look on her face, a widening of the eyes, tenseness in the muscles of her neck. A nurse angry because one of the nursing home residents has turned up the volume on a television set. But as he got closer he could see that the look on the nurse's face was not one of anger, but one of intense fear.

As if triggered by the fear so obvious in the face of the nurse, he became aware of the pain on the left side of his face, and of the pain in his left arm. And feeling this pain, he suddenly knew the recent past.

He and Jan in the wheelchair trying to escape, entering the lobby and screaming for help, although now he could not remember if he had screamed at the guards to get their guns, or if Jan had screamed at them. And then the guards moving slowly, hesitating, one of them reaching somewhere beneath the counter. Whether the guard who had bent for something had retrieved a gun or not mattered little. The two men were upon the guards before they could react, killing both within the confines of their island in the center of the lobby. After that came the shot to his arm, then a violent blow that sent Jan tumbling off the side of the wheelchair. The violent blow just after Jan had called one of the men by name. Max . . . Max Lamberti. After that, there was the blow to the side of his face that knocked him out.

Shortly after realizing he was being wheeled rapidly down the hallway in his wheelchair, shortly after reconstructing the recent past, he saw movement, something dark and tubular to the right of his head.

There was a muffled explosion at his ear. This followed by a scream. When he opened his eyes that had shut in response to the explosion, he saw a discharge of blood on the nurse's uniform. The nurse clasped her chest, rebounding off the counter and falling forward.

The smell of gunpowder and another scream as his wheelchair swerved around the nurses' station. But this scream was not that of the nurse, and as he turned he realized Jan was in another wheelchair. Jan's face was bleeding, both he and Jan were being pushed by the two men in stockinged faces, and the men had shot the nurse without hesitation even though she posed no threat to them except that she had seen them.

When he tried to move his left arm—his good arm—to swing back and strike out at the one pushing his wheelchair, intense pain shot through his shoulder. He had been shot in his good arm! His gun was gone and he had been shot! Although he was able to grip and re-grip his left hand, try as he might, he could not raise his arm.

He was also unable to move his left leg, and when he looked down he saw that the wheelchair footrests were down and in place and that both his ankles were taped to the footrests with duct tape. When he glanced back at Jan he could see her ankles *and* her wrists were taped to her wheelchair. And now, when he looked back to his arms, he saw both his forearms taped to the arms of the wheelchair. He had been unable to lift his left arm, not because of the wound but because of the tape. And he had been unable to lift his right arm, not because of its weakness from the stroke, but because the arm was bound to the arm of the chair.

As the wheelchair rolled quickly down the hallway, he twisted back and forth, making the chair wobble, and at the same time making his forearms pivot, twisting the duct tape. As he did this, a low growl came from deep inside, an intense anger from nowhere and everywhere. And with this anger came a feeling that his past, Jan's past, all the pasts of all civilized human beings was tied up in a single knot of anger that could explode and blow all the bastards he'd ever known to hell!

All the bastards he'd ever known!

Every goddamn bastard who ever leveled a gun at him!

Every goddamn bastard who ever threatened an innocent!

Every goddamn bastard who ever walked into a store and, for a few bucks from the till, shot a young woman. A girl really. Just out of school. A degree in Pharmacy. Cleveland. A girl he was to marry. A girl named Sue. A girl with the same name as So-long Sue.

Once past the nurses' station, he saw So-long Sue halfway down the hallway. She emerged from behind one of the tall stainless steel food carts parked on the left. The television that had been turned up earlier was turned down and there was Sue caterpillar-walking out from behind the food cart, glancing quickly at him, then disappearing into a resident room.

Sue! The name dug into his soul. He had lost Sue. He had not been there years earlier when another man with a gun entered the drugstore, demanded money and . . .

He had not been there! But he *was* here! They were taking Jan! They were going to kill Jan! He was here! But he could do nothing!

He twisted more violently in the chair, causing it to rock back and forth. He stared at the tape on his right forearm, watching it twist and stretch. His bad arm since his stroke. The stroke that had taken away so much. The bastard stroke he had fought all these months. No! Not a bad arm! Not a bad arm at all, just a fucked-up signal!

He stared at his arm and at the tape twisting back and forth. He clenched and unclenched the fist of his bad hand. Yes! It was a bad hand all right. Bad to the fucking bone!

Ahead. Ahead he could see *a head*! Crazy words mixing it up in his noggin. Couple of crazies, Marjorie used to say.

Gray hair. Crazy smile. Sue. Sue standing inside the doorway she had caterpillar-walked into moments earlier, and now if he doesn't do something they'll shoot her, too.

When he lunged to the side, flinging out his right elbow and pushing the weight of his upper body against it, the tape at his wrist busted and at the same time he saw Sue casually step into the hallway, face them, close her eyes in a swoon, and faint dead away directly across their path, her outstretched arms crashing against the food cart parked there.

His wheelchair stopped so suddenly he nearly fell forward out of it. But the tape on his wounded left arm had not been broken and he was held in the chair, the arm feeling as though it had been torn in two.

The footrests on his chair pressed into Sue's prone body as the man who had been pushing the chair ran forward, tucked his pistol into his belt and bent to clear Sue out of the way. The bastard grabbed Sue by the ankles and pulled her toward the room she had come out of. But Sue's hands firmly gripped the rungs on the lower shelf of the tall food cart.

Sue's eyes were open, her mouth held in a tight grimace as she hung onto the cart with all her strength.

Now was the time, the only time, the chosen time, the time granted. Such a short time, he thought, as the food cart, with Sue hanging onto it, began to roll into the center of the hallway, opening a path.

The man's attention was on Sue and his gun was tucked into his belt. Steve knew there was another man and that one of the men was Max Lamberti. But what did it matter who these men were? What mattered was that this was the only opportunity given and he had to take it.

He concentrated, trying to send signals to his right hand. *Damn it! If you can't get anything from the left side of this fucking head, then take instructions from the right side!*

The hand moved. He could see it. Arm down. Lower. Cool touch of the wheelchair's push rim. Grip. Grip, goddamn it!

He gripped, harder than he had gripped anything in his life. He pushed, harder than he had ever pushed in his life. The chair lunged toward the man pulling Sue across the hallway, catching the bastard at the back of one knee and sending him over.

A man's voice from behind. "Max!"

A scream from Jan. "Steve!"

He turned. Arm up, swinging out, making contact with the other arm that was coming down, gun in hand.

He was turned in the chair when the blow came down. His right arm held high to meet the blow acted as a lever and he went over. But so did the man who had tried to hit him from behind. The upturned wheelchair entangled the man's legs and his follow-through had done the rest.

Something solid and thick hit the tile floor a moment before his shoulder hit the floor. The gun! The gun down and bouncing away! He tried to kick out at it, but the capsized wheelchair was still taped to him at the ankles. Then the right arm that did not seem to belong to him—had not belonged to him for months—lunged out and trapped the gun between the chair and Sue's body. In another instant he curled up, going into a fetal position that put his right hand nearer the gun. In this new position he could not see the gun, but he could feel it. He could feel it!

Metal warmed by a killer's hand. Killer's blood pumping through killer's muscles and killer's brain cells.

He had succeeded in knocking over Max Lamberti with his wheelchair, had succeeded in disarming the man who had tried to hit him. But Max recovered quickly, crawling to him and gripping his neck, pulling at him just as Steve got hold of the gun that had fallen.

The face, though covered by stocking mesh, was obviously that of Max Lamberti. Max spit "Fucker!" at him. Steve twisted his body and came around with the gun, praying to God his finger was on the trigger and praying to God he could squeeze the trigger hard enough to . . .

He shot Max in the gut. Max arched from him and fell across Sue, holding onto his gut with both hands. There were screams. Jan and Sue screaming. But Jan's screams making sense.

"The other!"

Steve twisted, the chair flopping with him, and was about to fire in the general direction of running footsteps. But he waited a fraction of a second, long enough to aim, long enough to home in on the other killer and do damage. He hit a shoulder and heard a grunt.

The injured killer continued running down the hallway, right shoulder slumped, gun transferred to his left hand. But then the killer stopped, turned, stooped, and fired three rounds.

One bullet ricocheted on the floor and hit the downed Max in the leg, making him grunt and pushing his body against Sue who had her eyes open wide and actually seemed to be smiling.

The killer running down the hallway ducked toward a doorway, about to lunge inside for cover. But something stopped him.

An old man appeared in the doorway and faced the killer. The old man wore a white shirt, but was naked from the waist down. The old man was skeletal, his skin luminescent in the bright overhead lights. The old man had dark eyebrows and his head seemed huge for his body like a concentration camp visage from a black and white film. The old man smiled at the killer and held out a hand.

For a second the killer paused, aiming his gun at the old man. Then the killer turned and looked back down the hallway where Steve aimed at him, then he looked back to the old man just in time to see the old man smiling a toothless smile as he reached out, placing his hand on the killer's shoulder.

The killer shoved the old man back into the room from which he'd emerged, turned once more to look down the hall, then ran.

Time. Short segments of time that affect the entire future. The future of one or two people, or perhaps even the future of hundreds or thousands. The ointment ruined by the fly in it. The secret coming back to kill Marjorie and her son, trying to kill Jan, killing the guards and the nurse. A secret like that better off abandoned, better off dead.

The signals to Steve's right hand crashed about for a moment, but finally the hand swung over and obeyed, using Sue's body as a firing platform.

"I'm going to shoot," he heard himself say in a quiet voice.

"Go right ahead," said Sue.

A brain bullet was out of the question. He leveled the gun at the killer's back and, just before the killer rounded the corner at the end of the hallway, a signal—squeezed from his very soul, squeezed from the moment he found out his fiancée in Cleveland had been murdered, squeezed from the moment he found out Jan had been kidnapped—made it to the hand and the hand clenched tight and the finger on the trigger squeezed and the gun fired, sending the killer into a headlong skid that crashed his skull against the far wall.

A smiling face. So-long Sue. A smiling face and a tangle of arms and legs amid upturned wheelchairs and duct tape.

Jan's wheelchair had tipped away from him and he could not see her face. He dropped the gun and pulled himself along to her up-ended chair.

"Jan?"

When he was close enough to reach her, he grabbed onto the foot-rest of her chair and slowly turned her.

"Jan!"

Her head was slumped to the side, eyes closed. She was bleeding from the right side of her head, blood oozing from her hairline behind her ear. But there seemed to be much more blood than earlier, too much blood for the cut he had seen on her head, the blood soaking the shoulder of her raincoat.

He pulled Jan's wheelchair close, then pulled himself up to the side of her chair. He reached up with his right hand and cupped her head, trying to hold in the blood that was oozing out, trying to capture what he could of her before it bled from her, trying to capture Jan before she was gone.

But the blood was not coming from Jan's head. The source was lower. When he opened her raincoat, he saw that her blouse was torn and finally discovered the source of blood at the side of Jan's neck. His right hand moved so quickly it surprised him. His right hand covering the entry wound in an attempt to hold the flow back. The hand that had been useless until tonight seeming to act independently. But he knew the hand was not acting independently. He knew he was concentrating harder than he'd ever concentrated in his life for one sole purpose. To make his hand into a dam that would hold Jan's life inside where it belonged.

As he held onto Jan, feeling her warmth escaping between his fingers, waiting for help to arrive, he saw Max open his eyes. Max had his hand on the gun Steve had dropped and now he was struggling to stand.

"It ain't over," growled Max, rocking back and forth, aiming the gun.

Sue grabbed at Max's leg and he backed away, holding his gut with his other hand. When she reached out to grab Max again, he shot her through the head.

Max came closer, stooped down beside him and Jan. He put the barrel of the pistol to Jan's chest. "It ain't over, Babe. It ain't over 'til you tell me where to go with the keys. And if you don't, well, then it'll be over."

A man's shout drew the killer's attention. "Hello there!"

Max turned and as he did so Steve let go of Jan and swung out with his right arm, knocking the gun out of Max's hand.

Two old men wearing jackets and caps approached in the hallway, a Hispanic man pushing another old man in a wheelchair. The man in the wheelchair had a blanket covering his lap and smiled broadly, a smile that made Steve think the old man was a stroke victim. Perhaps they were both stroke victims. Two old men wandering down the hallway, continuing in their direction despite the other killer shot at the end of the hallway, despite So-long Sue lying in a pool of blood, despite Max crawling over Sue's body toward the gun Steve had knocked away.

Steve returned his hand to Jan's neck, pressing down on the wound to keep it from bleeding while at the same time stretching himself atop her as best he could. He watched as the two old men continued toward them. Then, a spark of hope came down from wherever hope originates when he saw the old man in the wheelchair take a foot off the footrest and kick the gun away from Max's grasp. The gun skittered down the hallway behind the two old men.

"Is anyone here named Max Lamberti?" asked the old man in the wheelchair, smiling broadly.

"Yeah," said Max, as he continued crawling toward the gun. "I'm Max and you're dead!"

As Max crawled past the man in the wheelchair trying to reach the gun, the wheelchair turned and Steve saw that the Hispanic man pushing the wheelchair was holding his own gun. And latex gloves! He was wearing latex gloves! Obviously they were not residents of the nursing home wing. And they were not visitors or two old men who had wandered in from the street, or even mobsters like Max Lamberti. These men represented something else. Something from Marjorie's past. A secret important enough to have them come here and . . . and what?

Just as Max reached his gun and rolled over, pointing it at the old men, two shots emerged through the blanket on the lap of the man in the wheelchair. Max did not have a chance to fire, but lay his gun down gently, leaned back on the floor, groaned loudly, and lost consciousness.

The old man pushing the wheelchair went to Max, felt his throat, took the gun from his limp hand, and stood beside the man in the wheelchair. Both men turned to Steve and frowned. The man who had been pushing the wheelchair moved forward and aimed Max's gun at Steve.

The other old man in the wheelchair took his feet off the footrests and sat forward in the chair. "I'm sorry it has to be this way, Mr. Babe."

"No," said Steve. "Help her."

"It's out of our hands," said the man, throwing the blanket aside to reveal his gun and standing up from the chair. He turned toward the man at his side, the Hispanic man who had been pushing the wheelchair. "Let's not delay this."

The Hispanic man put his own gun away in his belt and continued holding Max's gun on Steve. He moved in close. He bent over and stared into Steve's eyes. The man's dark eyes reminded Steve of Marjorie's eyes. A touch of confusion, but a resolve, a deep wish to reveal something from the past.

"Hurry up," said the other old man.

"In a moment," said the Hispanic man, as he moved even closer and stared even harder.

The man moved his face to the side of Steve's face and whispered in such a way that the other old man would not hear him. "Who was the smarter politician, Mr. Babe? Was it Jimmy Carter or Ronald Reagan?"

Then the man looked at Steve dead on, watching for his reaction.

Steve recalled Marjorie saying "Carter smarter," and recalled how she once tried to tell him her husband had been involved in trying to rig votes for a Presidential election. But he was holding onto Jan and he had to do what he must for their survival. This was no time to answer questions. And, he knew from the look in the man's dark eyes, this was no time to react. So he did his best to show no reaction at all. Better to show the same reaction a stroke victim would show to any mundane words. Neither concern that he doesn't know what the man is talking about, nor confusion. Since these men were obviously not going to get help for Jan, it would be best to simply show no reaction at all. And this seemed to work because after a moment the old man sighed and stood up.

"What are you doing?" said the other old man, turning to look down the hallway.

The Hispanic man turned and, despite the fact he was holding the gun he'd taken from Max, he took his own gun out of his belt and pointed this gun at the other old man. When the other old man turned back, the Hispanic man shot him three times.

The Hispanic man reached out and guided the other old man back into the wheelchair where he slumped to one side. The Hispanic man put away the gun he had used to shoot the other old man. Then he picked up the cast-aside blanket, returned it onto the lap of the old man in the wheelchair, picked up the gun his partner had dropped and carried it to Max's body. He dropped the other old man's gun down beside the body, then he put Max's gun into Max's hand, moving it about in Max's hand. It was obvious to Steve the man was making certain Max's prints were back on his gun rather than being smeared by his latex gloves.

Finally, the Hispanic old man turned to Steve and Jan once again. He looked down at Jan for a second, then at Steve. "I hope we have an understanding, Mr. Babe. If not, you'll receive a visitor in the future. Carter was smarter, by the way. He did not allow bad memories to ruin his life or the lives of those around him. Rather than dwelling on the past he chose to spend the remainder of his life helping others. He was a modern day Don Quixote. But unlike Don Quixote he selectively dismissed elements of the past he could do nothing about, elements of the past that, if dwelled upon, would have made him a bitter old man. The historically proven greed of the Chicago mob offers closure, Mr. Babe. For your good and for hers, forget everything else."

Steve wondered if he was smiling, because now the Hispanic

man smiled. "Keep pressure on the wound, Mr. Babe. I'll call an ambulance."

The Hispanic man stared at Steve with a smile on his face a moment more before he turned. He quickly propped the other old man's feet up on the footrests, grabbed the push handles of the wheelchair, hurried with his passenger toward the end of the hallway and the loading dock, and finally disappeared around the corner.

In the opposite direction, coming through the double doors that led to the lobby, Steve could hear voices, two men shouting for someone to drop a gun. A pause, then another man saying, "Okay, okay!"

Back down at the end of the hallway, a door slammed and there was another voice.

"Hey, what gives here?"

Standing outside the door to the men's room, a pasty-faced, heavy-set young man in a soiled white kitchen uniform carrying a towel stared for a moment at the dead killer sprawled on the floor at the end of the hall. "Holy Jesus." Then he turned toward Steve and Jan and the bodies of Max Lamberti and So-long Sue. "I mean really, what gives?"

CHAPTER THIRTY-FOUR

Faces smiled at her. Voices said she'd be all right. When she tried to speak but could not, one voice said the man who shot her had no hair on his head because his hair was in his pocket. This made the others smile before they loaded her into the ambulance. All of it seemed long ago. Or perhaps it was only an hour ago. She couldn't be sure. As for the man's hair being in his pocket, it had taken her a while, but she thought she had this figured out.

The man's hair was in his pocket because when she last saw him inside the van he was bald, and since he had plenty of hair on his head at the funeral earlier in the week, she assumed he must have taken the hairpiece off in anticipation of the busy night ahead. A busy night of tears and pain and fake smiles from a man without legs.

She knew about smiles. Especially on the face she now saw. She'd seen this face often enough, and under sufficient circumstances, to know when the smile was real, or when it was caused by stroke. Steve smiled at her now, his face close. He touched her forehead with his right hand. His right hand! She turned her head slightly and saw that his left arm was in a sling and he was sitting at her bedside in his wheelchair. When she tried to ask if he was all right, the words gathered in her throat like hot coals and she flinched because of the pain.

"Don't talk. Shot in your neck, but okay. Surgery over and out. You'll be fine. You're at hospital, not in hell."

He put on the sour face he sometimes displayed when he used the wrong words. "I mean you're not at Hell in the Woods."

She was in a hospital bed, IV and monitors to her left, Steve in his wheelchair and others standing behind him to her right. The last time she recalled being conscious it had been night. She had come awake while they loaded her into the ambulance. She had glanced to the side and seen the loading dock. Crashed into the building at the top of the loading dock ramp was the car in which she and Steve had tried to escape. She remembered trying to talk to a policemen inside the ambulance and not being able to and taking a pen from the policeman and writing some things on a notepad the policeman held up for her. She'd written that the bald killer was Max Lamberti, and that Max had been after not only the keys, but the litany of routes.

Lydia appeared with Steve at her bedside, Lydia's long black hair hanging down, brushing against Jan's hand. Until then she hadn't been aware of her hands, and now she grasped some strands of Lydia's hair with her right hand and gave a tug. Lydia smiled when she spoke.

"The doctor was here a while ago, says your voice will be okay in a couple days. I'll visit again and we can talk about the reunion you missed."

Lydia glanced at Steve. "This guy here says you'd want to know the particulars about the investigation. Tamara came here to tell him about it."

After Jan nodded, Lydia backed away and Tamara pulled a chair close to the side of the bed beside Steve's wheelchair.

Tamara said a lot of what the police knew so far had been pieced together from things Steve told her. Some of the explanation seemed vague, but Jan knew this was because of the painkillers they'd given her. She listened as best she could, hearing what she needed to hear. During the explanation she reached out and took Steve's right hand in hers.

Max Lamberti and Dino Justice were dead. Others were in custody, including the handicapped driver of the van. The keys taken from the safe deposit box were found in the van along with an aide named Tyrone Washington, who was also here in the hospital because of the beating he sustained. The litany of routes Steve had memorized matched the one found in Jan's notebook shoved between the seat and center console in her car. The police obtained a judge's order to open safe deposit boxes at banks located at the intersections designated by the litany. There they found information on foreign bank accounts registered to the Gianetti family. A quick check of several accounts had already tallied over a hundred million dollars.

The Gianetti family secret, vaguely alluded to by Marjorie Gianetti in rehab with Steve, was that the money gathered in 1980 for a drug deal was put into the foreign accounts. Some time prior to his death, Tony Senior hid the information about the accounts in safe deposit boxes all over the Chicago area. The litany of routes, a jingle memorized by Marjorie before her stroke, and apparently also memorized by Tony Junior when he was a boy, specified the intersections at which the banks were located.

When Marjorie had her stroke, she took the purpose of the secret with her. The only thing Tony Junior was aware of was the litany of routes. It meant nothing to him until he came across the safe deposit box key after his mother's stroke. This key opened the first box, and inside the first box were the keys to the other boxes. But to get to the other boxes, one had to know the list of intersections, which were in the same numerical order as the order of the key numbers. Therefore, once Tony Junior got the keys, he could have gone to the next intersection and used the key with the lowest number, and so on. But he never made it to the next intersection.

Max Lamberti inherited knowledge of the phony 1980 drug deal from his father. Somewhere along the line, Max discovered that his Aunt Marjorie knew the secret. He killed his aunt—or had her killed—because he feared therapy would reveal the secret to the authorities. Max assumed once he had the keys he'd be able to retrieve the money. He knew that when his aunt died, something, somehow, would be passed on to Tony Junior, and he felt he would be able to step in at the right moment, get Tony Junior out of the way, and claim the money he felt rightly belonged to the mob, namely him.

But Max jumped the gun when he eliminated Tony Junior, along with his attorney, Buster Brown. Brown may have been paid off by Max, and could have tipped Max off about the existence of the safe deposit box key and the trip to the first bank in Orland Park. If so, Max must have decided to get rid of Tony Junior and Brown at the same time.

Several foreign bank accounts were pointed to by documents in the first box, but these amounted to a small fraction of the total. Tony Senior apparently did this on purpose. If someone eliminated his wife *and* his son, he provided pointers to a small fraction of the money as a way of getting even, letting whoever got hold of the contents of the first box know they'd come close, but no cigar.

When Jan was spotted at the scene of the "accident," Max assumed she knew where the rest of the boxes were. That's what kept her alive. She knew something Max needed, and as long as she didn't tell him . . .

Tamara paused in her explanation and looked up to the other side of the bed. When Jan looked there she saw a nurse injecting something into the IV port near her arm. The nurse glanced at Tamara and Steve, then to Jan, and said, "Sedative, so you'll rest."

It took only moments for the sedative to take effect. Although Jan wanted to hear more, she felt warm and happy and ready to sleep.

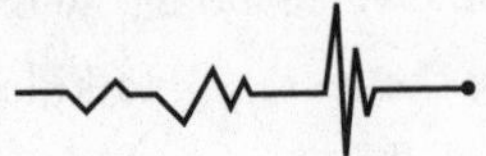

The room was dark, only a faint glow of night light through the curtains at the window. The room was also warm, as if the heat had been turned up. Or perhaps some time had gone by since the incident and it was warmer outside. Summer instead of spring, and the air conditioning was turned off or broken.

He had been dreaming about the shootout in the nursing home wing. So-long Sue lying on her side before him and he had just rested the gun on Sue's ancient child-bearing hip to steady his aim as he struggled with all his will to squeeze the trigger. He had come awake at the point he always came awake. He had come awake the moment after he fired. He had come awake the moment he turned and saw Jan lying unconscious in the overturned wheelchair, blood spurting from her neck and him trying desperately to stop the flow.

The dream always ended before Max regained consciousness and retrieved his gun. The dream always ended before the two old men came down the hallway, first killing Max, then the Hispanic old man who had pushed the wheelchair executing the old man who had been in the wheelchair. Before executing his partner, the Hispanic man had stooped down to where Steve was trying to keep Jan from losing too much blood. The Hispanic man had stared into Steve's eyes and asked the oddest of questions.

"Who was the smarter politician, Mr. Babe? Was it Jimmy Carter or Ronald Reagan?"

He could still see the look in the old man's dark eyes, the man watching for a reaction the way therapists and even Jan watched for his reactions to things they said following his stroke. Jan and the therapists looking for any sign he knew what they were talking about.

Yes, it had to be that. The old man had been looking for evidence that Marjorie had revealed to him something about Presidential elections, or something about a specific Presidential election.

"Who was the smarter politician, Mr. Babe? Was it Jimmy Carter or Ronald Reagan?"

The man had also spoken of Don Quixote and Steve wondered if the man considered himself a Don Quixote, a righter of wrongs.

As he lay with his eyes open, staring at the faint glow coming through the curtains, he heard something. A clicking like someone very far away down the hallway tapping on a counter with the tip of a pencil. He wondered why someone would tap a pencil on the counter of the nurses' station in the middle of the night, and concluded whoever it was must be listening to music with earphones on. One of the staff, bored silly at Hell in the Woods in the middle of the night, listening to a music player and tapping out a fast tempo.

But as soon as he settled on this as the cause of the sound, the rapidity of the clicking sped up and seemed to be coming closer, getting louder. It had regularity, not at all like someone tapping a pencil point, more like a machine. A cricket-like ratcheting. Click-click-click-click-click-click.

Something told him he'd heard this sound before. Something told him he'd heard this sound a long time ago before his stroke. Yes, something before he had his stroke. Was it the clicking of a semiautomatic pistol? Someone inserting a magazine and retracting and releasing the slide? But why would this be repeated again and again?

The clicking came closer, slowed a little, sped a little, paused.

He sat up. He was certain the clicking had come from the doorway, the dark doorway. The night light bulb burned out again and the door closed. But even when the door to the hall was closed, the bright hallway light always shone at the space beneath the door.

As he stared into the darkness, he could now see that this was not a closed door, but a doorway, a doorway that cast a faint glow like the glow through the curtains at the window. And someone or something was in the doorway. Although the shadow in the doorway was vague at first, he determined it was indeed a person, a person standing on one leg and curiously leaning to the side.

Was it someone who had come to get him because of what he might know? Was he still dreaming? Was this going to turn into yet another dream drummed up from childhood memories? Memories that lingered, using up precious brain cells in spite of his struggles to purge them in order to make room for more recent memories. Was this yet another recalling of the fight with Dwayne Matusak on the playground so long ago? But if he were dreaming about the fight with Dwayne, things would happen much faster, and there would be other kids. Even if he could not see the other kids, he would be aware they were there.

Suddenly, there was something else in the shadow. Thin lines down low, thin lines and two oblong circles.

That clicking, that sound. For some reason he felt he was looking at himself. *He* was the person in the doorway. Yes, *he* was in the doorway. He had no clothes on. He could feel the coolness on his skin. He definitely was not on a playground, because if he were, the kids in the dream would be laughing like crazy because he had no clothes on. No, not on a playground, but simply in a doorway. Not standing in the doorway. He was sitting. He was sitting astride something.

A few more clicks emerged and he had it. He was there. He'd been there. Right there in the doorway long ago before his stroke, but not so long ago that he'd been a kid. He'd been there in the doorway as an adult, sitting astride a bicycle, its seat feeling obscenely skinny because he was naked. He was in the doorway reaching out toward the light switch in order to surprise . . .

When the light came on, he saw Jan. She sat astride her purple ten-speed bicycle smiling at him. Her hand was still out to the light switch, but it soon came down to her side. Except for the bandage on her neck and the cast on her ankle, she was naked.

"Howdy," she said, kicking off and gliding into the room, jerking the handlebar back and forth to maintain her balance. "I thought you were asleep."

"I'm up."

"Wipe that smile off your face. I'm just learning. Re-learning."

"You need the exercise."

She frowned at him as she circled the bed, the front wheel hitting the dresser and bringing her to an abrupt stop so that she had to lean the bike sideways and put her foot on the floor. "I don't need exercise, not after last night. Or don't you remember?"

"I remember."

She swung her leg over the bike and put down the kickstand. She sat on the edge of the bed, folding her arms demurely over her breasts. She turned and stared at him. "Is that all you remember?" She smiled, but there was a seriousness to it that he understood all too well.

"No, that's not all I remember."

"Tell me about it."

"I remember magazines on the third floor. And magazines strewn across the road. Collected them in my Lincoln."

"Your rented Lincoln," said Jan. "You sure did a number on it."

"I remember the nurse . . . called 911 . . . got resident doors closed before they came back and killed her."

Jan did not comment on this, but simply lowered her eyes.

He reached out and touched her shoulder. "I remember your notebook . . . between seat and console. And on the floor . . . balled-up funeral sticker. I remember you telling me about funeral home when you snuck in to get Tony Junior's address."

Jan looked up and smiled. "The people at the funeral home thought I worked at the Sanitary District with the poor guy who'd died."

"Tonight, I remember more than at Hell in the Woods. Maybe because we're home."

"Do you remember another time I rode into the bedroom?" she asked, her smile taking on a familiar coyness.

"No. I remember me doing it. Not you telling me. I came awake to that clicking and . . ."

"Take your time."

"I remember being in the doorway. The other apartment upstairs. Me on your bike. That damn skinny seat. Me turning on the light. You in bed. Beautiful it was . . . so beautiful."

She hugged him and they lay down together, touching, recalling the softness of youth. But also recalling the not-so-distant past because of the feel of her bandages against his skin and the feel of his bandages against her skin.

"I thought I'd been shot in the head," said Jan.

"You?"

"Yes. In the hospital, when I first came awake. I remember thinking about something you came across in a rehab software program. The *Comparison* button misspelled into the *Comaprison* button. I remember wondering if I'd been shot in the head and I was in comaprison. I wondered if I would laugh at everything the way you did for a while."

"I was a cheery son-of-a-bitch. Now I'm old self, a melancholy Gypsy who plays a lousy violin. The Gypsy was there, watching over me. After the stroke it was my father, or Sergeant Joe Friday, or Sandor Lakatos, or some other old man staring me in the eyes. Which old man do you prefer?"

"I like this old man with dark eyes. Which means, I want us to grow old together. In a way I was hopeful that if I'd been shot in the head instead of the neck, the distant past before we met would be wiped out. But it was a false hope. We have to live with what we have."

"Couldn't have said it better."

"Steve?"

"Yes."

"About being a Gypsy. I never told you about the nickname. I held it back to see if at some point you'd remember being called that."

"That's me, a Gypsy wandering naked on a bicycle with a skinny seat."

She whispered into his ear. "Do you really remember that night?"

He whispered back. "Yes, I really remember."

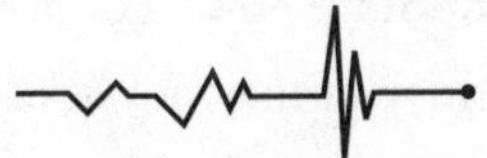

As he and Jan lay together in bed, Steve's mind bubbled with details. It was the opposite of a stroke. Instead of the brain bullet taking out memories, this brain bullet filled his head with them.

Max Lamberti and Dino Justice dead. Other men working for Max indicted by the grand jury along with Phil Hogan from the Eighth District. Another Phil at Hell in the Woods expanding his vocabulary after being told about the shootings in the nursing home wing. Phil saying, "Jesus Fuck, Steve" instead of his normal, "Jesus Fuck." Tamara wanting to know if there were things he hadn't told her, things he had left out of the "report" he typed for her on his computer.

Of course there were things he left out. Not because he wanted to leave them out, but because he had to leave them out.

A nurse, two guards, a maintenance worker, and So-long Sue murdered. The nurse calling 911 before Max returns to kill her. Steve getting the drop on Max and Dino. Jan shot in the crossfire. These details he had not left out.

But two old men arriving before the police respond to the 911? Two old men carrying Sig Sauer semi-automatics with silencers? Two old men killing Max before the Hispanic old man asks his question about Jimmy Carter and Ronald Reagan and then kills his partner? These details he had left out. The Hispanic old man who called Carter a modern day Don Quixote had offered closure. And that closure was to leave it be and let the mob take the blame. Obviously it was crucial to very powerful people that secrets told him by Marjorie be kept secret.

Not that Marjorie had spelled it out for him. All she'd been able to get out during their cryptic conversations had been that her husband hated Carter and desperately wanted Reagan to win. When Marjorie said, "Carter Smarter," Steve now knew this was her private phrase for the deeper secret she may or may not have totally recalled after her stroke. Marjorie knew something, had become talkative about it, and had been killed. She might have been killed because she knew the secret code for locating the "drug money." Or, she might have been killed because she knew a deeper political secret. Unfortunately, or perhaps fortunately, his sketchy knowledge of the political secret was limited to a few words spoken by Marjorie and by the visit of two aging assassins whom no one else had seen. At least no one alive.

Jan lay on his left arm and turned to kiss his chest.

"Thought you were asleep," he said.

"I was listening to you breathing," she said. "And thinking."

"Thinking?"

"Yes. Although your conversation has gotten better, I can still tell when you stop talking sometimes that you're trying to work things out in your head."

"What am I trying to work out?"

"Puzzles from the past."

"What puzzles?"

"Like why Max would have Tony Gianetti Junior killed."

Steve cupped Jan's head with his left hand. "Max wanted the money for himself."

"But he didn't have to kill Tony Junior," said Jan. "And he didn't have to kill his aunt. I guess mostly I see it as such a waste."

"Big money has its way," said Steve.

"I know," said Jan.

"Nothing we can do about it."

"Maybe there is," said Jan.

"What's that?"

"Tony Junior's legacy. The environment. You got interested in the environment after your stroke, didn't you?"

"I thought the world had had a stroke."

"So that's it," said Jan, putting her lips to Steve's ear.

"What?" asked Steve.

"We become environmentalist detectives. We do what we can for future generations. That is, after all, the definition of legacy."

Steve turned his face to Jan, feeling her lips slide first across his left cheek, then, although not as distinct, across his right cheek. He sent signals to his right arm and, slowly, it came across and encircled her. They kissed.

CHAPTER THIRTY-FIVE

THIS WAS NOT GOOD. INSTEAD OF BEING PART OF THE DAMN system, and maybe sometimes taking advantage of it, he was stuck in it. He'd been stuck in it for three months now, the doc saying five more surgeries yet. Two on his gut, where he'd been punched about a thousand spaghetti-head punches, and three on his face so he'll be able to breathe through his nose again. After each surgery he felt like he'd been beat up all over again. Like now, two days gone after the last bout with the surgeon's knife and he still felt like shit.

Tyrone looked up and back where his name was scrawled in fat letters on a card hooked to a clip on the wall. His full name there so some damn nurse wouldn't accidentally give him a shot meant for another Washington, or give another Washington a shot meant for him. Only good thing about this place was some of them shots in his IV port. Yeah, some of them shots did him just fine, for a little while anyway.

Most of the time this place was hell, making him think about the old days at Hell in the Woods as the good old days. He should've learned a lesson back when he had his first health care job down at

Cook County Hospital that a hospital was the last place he'd ever want to end up for three months. Sometimes he thought it would've been better to have spit in the spaghetti heads' faces and taken a deep six instead of this. But when he thought about the beating he'd gotten, he couldn't have spit in their faces because, when his mouth wasn't taped, his face and gut were so mashed in there was no way he could've spit.

So, here he was with enough internal injuries for every south side gang member, his face flattened so badly it needed to be rebuilt, his medical insurance company complaining—even though the same damn insurance company insured all the employees at this place—Medicaid just around the corner if he didn't get out of here soon, no visitors, not even Latoya, and now . . . Now!

When he saw Flat Nose walk into the room, Tyrone turned to the side and spit in the spit cup. He hadn't seen Flat Nose since that night on the loading dock at Hell in the Woods when the spaghetti heads were hauling him away and one of them flattened Flat Nose. Flat nose had grown a mustache and wore sunglasses. When Tyrone finished spitting, he turned and said, "Fuck 'ou, F'at Nose."

Flat Nose smiled, took off the White Sox cap he was wearing and smoothed back his hair with his hand. "Fuck you, too, Tyrone, my man."

Flat Nose pulled up a chair and sat next to the bed, smiling and staring and shaking his head. "You look better, man. Last time I was here you were out like a fuckin' light."

"When was 'ou here?"

"Oh, maybe a couple weeks back."

" 'onger then that."

"Okay, maybe longer. Guess it was a little while after you got here. And after the fuckin' legal eagles finally figured out they couldn't hold me for nothin'. Anyway, you look much better now. But I guess you still got some trouble talkin'."

"Trou'le? Fuck . . . my mout' need rebuildin', my sinus need rebuildin', my nose need rebuildin', ain't got no teet'. I'll say I got fuckin' trou'le."

Flat Nose held his Sox cap in his hands and leaned closer, no longer smiling. "Yeah, you got it worse than me. I just got my nose broken, and got shot in the fuckin' leg. They took care of it down at County. But you . . ."

Flat Nose leaned even closer and spoke more quietly. "Anyway, the reason I'm here is DeJesus knows that Babe guy's been here to visit and he wants to make sure you ain't said nothin'. You know how DeJesus is. I said I'd come on down and ask and you'd say, fuck no, you ain't said nothin' and that'd be the end of that."

"Wha' if I do say som'in?"

Flat Nose glanced toward the door. "Shit, man, you don't want to do that. You're just baggin' me. Right?"

Tyrone reached out and grabbed Flat Nose by the shirt. "Fuck if I'm baggin' 'ou! Tell 'eJesus he 'an go fuck hisself, 'cause I'll say anythin' I want!"

When Tyrone let go of Flat Nose's shirt, Flat Nose leaned back in the chair and put on his cap. "Okay, man, I'll tell DeJesus what you said. Is that what you want?"

"Yeah."

"That mean you said somethin' to Babe already?"

"May'e yes, may'e no."

Flat Nose stood up and looked down at Tyrone. "Man, you better not say nothin' else. Promise me you'll say nothin' else to Babe and I'll do what I can about DeJesus. You know how he is about his business and takin' care of his sick ma. And he's more powerful than ever now that his old boss is out of the picture. Promise you'll say nothin' else to Babe and I'll see what I can do about gettin' some combat pay, 'cause I figure you got some comin'."

Flat Nose pointed to his own nose. "I got a few bills for this gettin' busted again, and another few bills for gettin' shot in the leg. If I can get that much, no tellin' how much DeJesus'll give you. What say, my man? Should I tell DeJesus you're still on the team?"

When Tyrone tried to sit up in bed but couldn't, he repeated himself as loudly as he could and it came out in a gurgle of phlegm. "Tell 'eJesus he 'an go fuck hisself!"

After Flat Nose was gone, Tyrone settled back on his pillow and closed his eyes. In three months he hadn't said jack shit to Babe and now the first thing out of Flat Nose's mouth when he visits after all that time is a fuckin' tip off.

The reason he hadn't appreciated Flat Nose's visit was probably because he'd been thinking about Latoya when the bastard came in. Latoya last week saying she was leaving him because he'd gotten in trouble again. "Trouble of his own making" were the exact words when she finally decided to visit him in this place. He'd wanted to tell her they could get married and have kids when he was better. He wanted to tell her he'd always wanted to have kids because he didn't have any brothers and sisters he knew of, so he'd never even be able to be an uncle unless he got married. He'd wanted to tell her all that good stuff. But he couldn't tell any of it because of his busted up face. If only Latoya knew about his refusal to cooperate with Flat Nose and DeJesus. If only she knew it had even crossed his mind to finger DeJesus and do his part to save the nation's health care system. If only she knew that, maybe she'd come back.

As he lay with his eyes closed, he imagined Latoya visiting him again, only this time under different circumstances. This time she'd be visiting a hero. And because he was a hero, she'd treat him accordingly. Maybe lay her head on his lap. Yeah, right there so he can put his hands on her head. Her saying he has such big hands and big somethin' else when she comes up for air and looks at him and says she loves him.

As far back as Tyrone could remember he always had big hands. Not when he was a baby, but he did have big hands in his gang-bang days. Even when he was a shorty the other shorties called him "Hands." According to Flat Nose, DeJesus supposedly had even bigger hands. Not that Tyrone had ever measured his against DeJesus', but he did know DeJesus could palm a basketball. Like Tyrone, DeJesus could have been on the Chicago Bulls.

It was all a matter of circumstances. Him on the streets of Chicago so there was no chance of ever being in college ball and getting a chance in the pros, and DeJesus being in the military during his prime years so he never got his chance. According to Flat Nose, DeJesus got into the rackets he was in because of an old army buddy. Yeah, an old army buddy who was out of the picture now, based on what Flat Nose had just told him. And if the old buddy was out of the picture, then maybe DeJesus would be out of the picture pretty soon. Maybe he'd just fade away like they all do eventually.

Maybe the whole damn world would fade away the way it had during those first few days in the hospital when he was drugged-up. In some ways being drugged-up was a whole hell of a lot better than all that rehab after the first surgery. Back then, he figured rehab was a way to convince a guy to keep his nose clean. Pure torture is all it was. In fact, now that he thought about it, the occupational guy was here helping him learn how to eat one of the first times Babe paid him a visit. Babe coming into his room with a violin case under his arm and telling him he'd finally graduated from his own therapy at Hell in the Woods. Then, apparently to prove he'd graduated, Babe pulls the violin out of its case and starts playing the damn thing. Sounded like alley cats thrown over the telephone wires with their tails duct-taped together.

Babe had visited quite a few times since then. Last time he left an article he said he'd gotten at the library. The article was about the hood, Max Lamberti, who got killed that night. Babe told him to read the article and let him know if anything in it rang a bell, if anything in the article sounded like something he'd heard before. So he read the article and the only thing that sounded familiar was that Lamberti served at Fort Bragg in the 82nd Airborne. Of course the article did say something about Lamberti and another guy being questioned in the investigation of a murder of an officer and his fiancée, but that was none of his business. And so he told Babe he'd heard of Fort Bragg, but what's the big deal in that? Everyone's heard of Fort Bragg.

Tyrone hated to admit he liked Babe. He realized it the first time Babe visited and told him that So-long Sue had died in the hospital from her gunshot wound. Tyrone remembered So-long Sue and liked her and felt sad along with Babe that Sue was dead. He didn't even pull his hand away when Babe touched him after that damn tear ran down into the bandage over the latest jaw surgery and burned like hell.

During one of Babe's visits, even though he'd already told it to about twenty detectives earlier, Tyrone told Babe about the chicken-shit way the spaghetti heads killed the two cops in the van. When Babe asked how he happened to be grabbed by the spaghetti heads, Tyrone admitted he was in Babe's room on the third floor when they showed up. He told Babe he was pissed about him grabbing him and trying to choke him earlier. He told Babe he was worried that Babe was trying to finger him for the old lady's death. Of course he didn't admit to anything, nothing about Flat Nose or DeJesus or lifting stuff from Hell in the Woods.

After pretty much leveling with Babe the way he did, Babe told him what else went down at Hell in the Woods that night. How he'd gotten Mrs. Babe away from the spaghetti heads. How they crashed into the building and came inside in his chair. How the bastards chased them to the lobby. Killed McGrath and that new guard. Killed old Russell when he made the mistake of pushing his cleaning cart into the lobby. Killed that nurse who called 911. Almost killed Babe and Mrs. Babe. Shot So-long Sue.

As Tyrone lay with his eyes closed thinking about Latoya, he heard a rattling at the side of the bed, the IV clips hitting against the metering stand. Maybe it was the nurse again. Maybe she felt sorry for him and he'd get that Demerol he asked for.

Hands on this throat! Large hands pressing down! When he tried to reach out to push away the choker, one of the hands came off his throat and the choker pushed his arm down to the side, then twisted his arm up behind his back.

Even before he opened his eyes, Tyrone knew who it was. Although he'd seen him only a few times, he knew it was DeJesus with his big hands and arms as thick as telephone poles.

DeJesus' eyebrows were thick and dark, connected above his nose. And Tyrone thought, such a petite nose for such a big fucker. Thinking this despite the pain. Able to think this because after three months in the hospital and all the surgeries, he was used to pain.

But DeJesus wasn't letting up and Tyrone began to think the spic might kill him here and now. No knife, no gun, just one big hand squeezing his neck, another pressing down into his gut, the two hands threatening to undo everything the surgeons had done to put him back together.

When it was over and Tyrone could do nothing more than take one breath after another through the hole that was his mouth, DeJesus whispered harshly into his ear.

"You talk to Babe and you die, spook! With my business partner gone I ain't got no one to answer to! It feels real good, like bein' a general in boot camp!"

Before leaving, DeJesus rubbed Tyrone's head with his palm like he was rubbing a kid's head. Then he smiled and said, "We had a spook general when I was at Bragg! Bastard fucked me over a couple times. Nothin' against you personally, but it'd be my pleasure to be able to even the score."

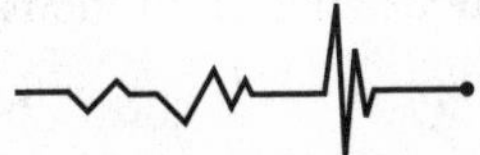

Tyrone had learned early in his health care career that all the shit started in Washington and was handed down. A congressman farts at the podium and the next thing you know there's another new rule and another new form to be filled out. Trees cut down in the boondocks to make paper they ship to Chicago where printing presses two stories tall spit out ten-part forms. The forms sent to every hospital and doctor's office and so-called rehab centers like Hell in the Woods to be filled out. The forms converted to computer data analyzed in Washington so the farting congressman will have the fuckin' data before next election to spit into reporters' eyes while he complains about government waste like he's the first to discover it.

Yeah, he learned real fast that the health care system was a thing put there to make sure most of the money funneled on up to the docs, and to the drug company executives, and to the supply company executives, and to fucks like DeJesus. All that money to fucks who could care less about poor folks hollering and screaming for God to let them live a few minutes longer.

The day after DeJesus' visit, when the doctors had finished restitching his gut and the roof of his mouth, and when the cops called by the staff had finally gone away shaking their heads—but leaving a guard at the door—one of the prettier white nurses came in and asked Tyrone if there was anything he needed.

He stared at her a moment, suppressed one of the usual thoughts he had at moments like this—Yeah, one last blowjob—and pointed to the bedside table saying, "In dra'er."

"Something in your drawer?"

He nodded.

After she held up about a hundred items—CD player, CDs, old love note from Latoya, copy of his living will, get well card from Hell in the Woods, gum he couldn't chew, mints—she finally held up the business card.

He nodded.

She stared at the card and said, "Steve Babe, that's a cute name."

He tried to draw a circle in the air with his finger. "O'er. 'Urn i' o'er."

When she turned the card over, she read the handwritten note on the reverse side, the note written by Steve Babe's pretty wife the last time they had come to see him, the last time they asked if he didn't want to unload on some of the big guns who ran scams at Hell in the Woods and who weren't doing shit for him now.

"It says, 'Give me a call when you change your mind, because after a while in this place on the other side of the fence, you just might.'"

The nurse looked up from the card with a puzzled look on her face. "You want me to call this guy for you?"

He nodded.

"You want me to say you changed your mind?"

He nodded again. But this time he struggled to speak as clearly as he could. "Tell 'im I done foun' Jesus. And I wan' help 'uture genera'ions."

"Okay," said the nurse, leaving the room. "I'll call him right away."

After the nurse was gone, Tyrone closed his eyes and tried to rest. But even though it hurt like hell, he had to laugh.

He laughed because he recalled Flat Nose telling him that DeJesus' boss was an old 82nd Airborne Division buddy, and that the big boss kept his nose out of the business but would be there in a minute if DeJesus needed protection, like if he needed to put out a hit on someone. He laughed because, now that DeJesus had mentioned Fort Bragg, he recalled Flat Nose once let it slip that while DeJesus and the big boss were stationed at Fort Bragg they came down on another soldier who crossed them, then went after the soldier's girl. He laughed because he now knew, for the first time in his life, that what goes around really does come around. Yeah, he'd have the last laugh all right. He'd get DeJesus, get him good. And when he was finished getting DeJesus and Flat Nose, he'd be sure to tell Babe how funny it was, and what a stroke of luck that he worked at Hell in the Woods so he'd end up being the one to make it happen. Not only had Lamberti gotten his, but his Fort Bragg buddy DeJesus and an asshole named Flat Nose would also get theirs.

Tyrone tried to picture Steve Babe and his wife at his bedside. He wondered if he'd been hearing things when they said they might need someone like him working for their detective agency because they'd gotten some big jobs recently working for insurance companies in the health care field. Then he recalled the theory he'd developed about white folks years earlier when he worked at the VA Hospital where it seemed most patients were white men suffering from one thing or another having to do with smoking cigarettes since they were PFCs with Betty Grable pinups thumb-tacked to their bunks. While delivering clean spit-up cups and taking away the old spit-up cups, he'd noticed the stuff in those cups made it seem like the men were slowly turning black on the inside. His theory was that just before white folks die they turn black inside and finally feel how it is to be black, but they also realize it's too late for the realization to do any good and they die screaming to the Almighty to let them live even if they have to suffer like black folks suffer. His theory was that part of the purpose of suffering was to turn everyone black so that when they went to heaven—if they did go to heaven—there'd be no racial tension.

Tyrone fell asleep deciding that, ultimately, all he had left in the world was to trust someone. And Steve Babe and his wife were damn good people to trust. Good folks just like him.

And if it all went off real nice like in a dream, maybe he'd be able to tell all about it to Latoya some day. And after that, maybe he'd be able to tell it to his kids and even his nephews and nieces. Yeah, he could have nephews and nieces because Latoya—sweet Latoya—had enough brothers and sisters to make up for his lack of them. Some day down the line, little kids would cheer when old Uncle Tyrone came to visit in his classic Cadillac DeVille. They sure would.

CHAPTER THIRTY-SIX

THERE HAD BEEN NO RETIREMENT PARTY AT THE MIAMI OFFICE when Valdez retired at the first of the year. At Langley they sometimes had retirement parties, but not at outlying offices. In lieu of a party for his old friend, Skinner had arranged a visit later in the year to Valdez's new home.

It was September, the height of the hurricane season. Although the entire city of Naples, Florida, had been ordered to evacuate for one of the hurricanes earlier in the season, and another hurricane was predicted to make landfall in a couple of days, Valdez always stayed put. He did this, not because he was especially fearless, but because his home was built to withstand even category five storms.

Though the house was on the Gulf Coast, it sat on a rise overlooking a fishing pier. The house was built like a bunker with extensive foundation, backup power and pumps, built-in storm shutters, and walls surrounding the property that were as thick as the walls of the house. During a previous storm, Valdez had sheltered several emergency workers who had been unable to move inland in time.

Skinner, having lost most of his hair, now kept it shaved. Valdez, on the other hand, had allowed his gray hair to grow, giving him the appearance of a beachcomber. The two old men sat on the porch of Valdez's home staring out at the calm before the storm. High clouds hid the sun and there was only one lone fisherman out on the pier.

"It's pretty ironic," said Skinner.

"What is?" asked Valdez.

"Your being here in Hanley's old house."

"Because of what happened in Chicago?"

"Yes," said Skinner. "And even more so because you retained the housekeeper Hanley was so obviously fond of."

"The events in Chicago were independent of what followed," said Valdez. "From my point of view I could say it's ironic that our contact in Chicago be chosen to go to Arizona."

"She was already on the case," said Skinner. "I simply felt it best to limit the numbers."

"Did she locate Christensen and his wife?"

"Yes."

"Did she . . .?"

"Yes. Both. It was obvious what needed to be done when she found they had moved to another retirement community and were living under yet another name. Christensen made the last move because he knew he had revealed too much to his wife."

"It's sad," said Valdez.

"I agree," said Skinner. "In the old days of ham radio we'd refer to him as a silent key."

"That was a long time ago," said Valdez. "Three brand new recruits pounding out Morse Code that anyone could have been listening to."

"Except we never discussed agency business over the airwaves. And as far as Christensen is concerned, he knew that if a husband *or* a wife loves their partner, they should keep things to themselves."

"Is our contact back at Langley?"

"Yes."

"I assume that means she'll carry on after we're out of the picture."

Skinner smiled. "You assume correctly. She'll be in charge."

"Besides what's left of the mob family in Chicago, will she be keeping tabs on the detective and his wife?"

"Yes. However, with the money having been located, perhaps things will begin to fade."

Valdez turned and stared at Skinner. "Do you still trust my judgment in the matter?"

"I still trust your judgment," said Skinner. "If you say the stroke distracted him adequately, I can only acquiesce."

"I hope I'm right," said Valdez, looking back out at the fishing pier. "But even if I'm not, with conspiracy theories launched at the blink of an eye these days, it would probably be a simple matter to shut it down on short notice. I assume you felt much more strongly about the danger from Christensen than you ever did from the detective."

"I did," said Skinner.

"Will the detective and his wife be under long term observation?" asked Valdez.

"They will," said Skinner. "Speaking of long term observation, what do you tell your Maria when she asks questions?"

Valdez thought for a moment, then said, "I tell her she is younger than me and, therefore, still has many years ahead of her. I tell her it would be foolish for her to know what I know. She says that everything she knew of Hanley's affairs came from vague references to visitors and phone calls he made and received. All she knows is that he called the Washington area a lot. I've told her my work revolves around concern for future generations."

"And this satisfies her?" asked Skinner.

"It does," said Valdez.

"Funny, isn't it?" said Skinner. "Your housekeeper having the same name as our young colleague?"

"Yes," said Valdez. "However, besides the age difference, there is another thing that distinguishes them."

"What's that?" asked Skinner.

"As I've said, my Maria knows nothing about our work, and will never know."

Skinner turned and stared at Valdez. "Can you guarantee that?"

"I can," said Valdez. "If it ever comes down to it, I've prepared myself . . ."

Skinner waved his hand. "No need to go into detail. I trust you. Who better to trust than an old ham buddy from simpler times?"

"I remember the old days," said Valdez. "I remember the ham radio operators in Miami serving as the communications link before, during, and after storms. I remember taking my rig into the Miami office and setting up a communications post there."

"The good old days before cell phones," said Skinner.

"You can say that again," said Valdez, just as Skinner's cell phone chirped and they both laughed.

After answering, Skinner simply said, "Okay. I'll be there," before closing the phone.

"Time to leave already?" asked Valdez.

"They want to take off a little earlier because of the approaching storm," said Skinner. "They want me at the airport in two hours."

"That will give us time for dinner," said Valdez. "You will stay, won't you? I've asked Maria to join us."

Skinner smiled. "In that case, I will stay."

Both stood slowly, stretching their aching muscles. When they went inside through the sliding door, Maria was already busy setting the table.

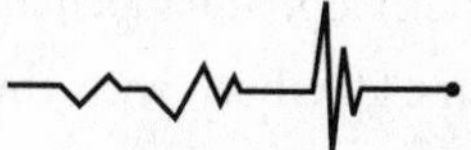

Two days later, as the slow-moving storm began coming ashore, Valdez and Maria sat together on the sofa facing the only sliding door not yet covered by a storm shutter. Despite the fact Valdez had already started the backup generator and the pumps, they sat in near darkness.

The approaching storm was named Tanya. A few weeks back, when hurricane names were coming from earlier in the alphabet, Maria had said she wished they would name one for her. Valdez had explained to her there had been a storm named Maria in 2005 and that perhaps her name would again be used some time in the future. He did not tell her his dead wife's name had been used for a hurricane in 1974. He did not tell her Hurricane Carmen had caused extensive damage to Mexico and to Louisiana and the name Carmen had been retired. No, he did not tell Maria about his wife whose name had been used for a hurricane years earlier before the cancer.

When an especially strong gust of wind drove rain against the sliding door, Maria stirred in his arms. "I understand why you are angry, Tanya."

"Why do you tell her that?" asked Valdez.

"Because of what her name has come to symbolize."

"Yes," said Valdez. "Many names have taken on symbolic meanings throughout the ages. Are you familiar with the name Barabbas?"

"Barabbas," repeated Maria. "Isn't that the name of the thief who was released instead of Jesus Christ?"

"Yes," said Valdez. "I once knew of a man whose family had been given the name Babe. It was after the turn of the century when U.S.

immigrants came from Europe. The reason the man's family had been given this name was because of the fear of being stuck with the name of the thief from the Crucifixion. It happened on Ellis Island where an official confused the name Barabbas with the family's original Hungarian name, Baberos. Trying to be helpful, the official suggested the name Babe, and for the last century, the man's family has had to live with it."

"I'm glad I do not have a name like that," said Maria as the wind flattened a palm branch against the sliding doors. She lifted her head. "We'd better close up, I think."

While waves swamped the fishing pier and winds whipped the palm trees that lined the concrete walls surrounding the fortified home, Valdez and Maria stood to attend to the last storm shutter. As the wind tore at him, Valdez braced himself just inside the door opening so he could reach up and release the weighted shutter. Maria held onto his belt with one hand while maintaining a firm grip on the sliding door handle with her other hand. After they got the last shutter closed and locked firmly to the eyebolts embedded in the patio floor, they closed the sliding door and retired into the dark house.

Outside, the storm named Tanya roared.

THE END

MICHAEL BERES

photo by KB

Michael's experiences during the Cold War and his interest in the environment have shaped his novels. With degrees in computer science, math, and literature, he worked for the government, holding a top-secret security clearance, and in the private sector, documenting analytical software. His fiction reflects our age of environmental uncertainty and political treachery.

A Canadian publisher published Michael's first novel SUNSTRIKE in the eighties when environmental and political conspiracies were considered tall tales. Today we know differently. Medallion Press published Michael's environmental novel GRAND TRAVERSE in 2005. It presents a realistic portrait of our frightening near future. His 2006 release, political thriller THE PRESIDENT'S NEMESIS, was compared to THE MANCHURIAN CANDIDATE by Library Journal and dubbed "a nail-biting thriller" by Midwest Review.

A Chicago native now living in West Michigan, Michael is a member of the Mystery Writers of America, International Thriller Writers, and the Sierra Club. He has driven a low-emissions hybrid vehicle since the beginning of the technology. His short stories have appeared in: *Amazing Stories*, *Amazon Shorts*, the *American Fiction Collection*, *Alfred Hitchcock Mystery Magazine*, *Ascent*, *Cosmopolitan*, *Ellery Queen*, *Michigan Quarterly Review*, *The Missouri Review*, *New York Stories*, *Papyrus*, *Playboy*, *Pulpsmith*, *Skylark*, and *Twilight Zone*.

www.michaelberes.com